Katie Frey has spent the better part of her adult life in pursuit of her own happily-ever-after. Said pursuit involved international travel and a few red herrings before she moved from Canada to Switzerland to marry her own mountain man. Katie is a member of the RWA and an avid writer, and *Montana Legacy* is her first novel for Mills & Boon Desire. She wrote the bulk of the book in a local coffee shop. Any excuse to stay near the fresh croissants! She is most active on Instagram, @romanceinthealps, but you can also find her on Facebook at Kate Frey Writes, on Goodreads and Bookbub or, most embarrassingly, on TikTok, @romanceinthealps. The communication she's most proud of however, is her newsletter, which you can join at bit.ly/3COLHoP

DEIA activist **LaQuette** writes bold stories featuring multicultural characters. Her writing style brings intellect to the drama. She crafts emotionally epic tales that are deeply pigmented by reality's paintbrush. This Brooklyn native's novels are a unique mix of unapologetically sexy, stylish and sensational characters who are confident in their right to appear on the page.

Also by LaQuette

Devereaux Inc.
A Very Intimate Takeover
Backstage Benefits

Discover more at millsandboon.co.uk

MONTANA LEGACY

KATIE FREY

ONE NIGHT EXPECTATIONS

LaQUETTE

MILLS & BOON

First Published in Great Britain 2022
by Mills & Boon, an imprint of HarperCollins*Publishers* Ltd
1 London Bridge Street, London, SE1 9GF

www.harpercollins.co.uk

HarperCollins*Publishers*
1st Floor, Watermarque Building,
Ringsend Road, Dublin 4, Ireland

ISBN: 978-0-263-30378-0

MONTANA LEGACY

KATIE FREY

I'd like to dedicate my first Mills & Boon novel to my mom, who never doubted for a second it would exist.

One

"Look, I'm just saying, maybe it's time you came home."

Nick Hartmann raised his voice as he adjusted the Bluetooth volume settings on the steering wheel of his Nissan Titan Platinum pickup truck. The clock on the dashboard blinked a foreboding reminder he was late, and he leaned on the gas in answer.

"I'm not coming home, Nick," Jackson snapped, his refusal ringing throughout the truck. "I'm on circuit for the season. Look, I signed the power of attorney—just make a decision and keep sending the checks." Nick's younger brother's voice was partially obscured by the roaring soundscape of a lively party. Nick tightened his grip on the steering wheel until his fingernails dug into the leather. He was tired of being the only Hartmann to know his brother's alias, which he apparently needed for riding rodeo, although it was a small price to pay for the extra vote on the board. Of course, even with Jackson's vote, Nick had held a minority voice in the face of their three siblings. Until now. Now it was two siblings against two siblings, with a swing vote no one saw coming.

The sun was rising on a new era for the Hartmanns.

"So Austin, Katherine… Alix?" Nick started, choking on the names. "It doesn't change anything?"

"No. These broncos aren't going to ride themselves. Plus, I don't see what my coming back can do for anyone at this point." It was a cavalier dismissal. *Very Jackson.*

"It'd be nice to have you back, Jacks," Nick tried again. If he stood a shot at convincing his brother to do anything, honesty was the best policy. In the four years since their father died, Jackson hadn't so much as seen the grass seed on the plot where they'd buried Dad. Sure, the deathbed argument had been a bad one. But his dad was gone, and instead of helping with the ranch, Jacks had checked out the day their dad died. Jackson's exit he could understand. Nick supposed it was easier to feel like less of a disappointment without facing the headstone of the man who'd labeled him as such.

Of course, Jackson wasn't the first Hartmann to leave. Austin had scorched the earth like an enemy trailblazer sixteen years ago, leaving with Katherine of all people. She'd been Nick's high school sweetheart, and, he grimaced with the memory, his first love. Even now, close on two decades later, he didn't know what had hurt more: Austin leaving, or the fact that he took Katherine away, too.

Yep. First Austin, then Jackson. Now, with Evie living in California, only Amelia, the bossy twin, was left to fight with him. Nick Hartmann was the only one left who wanted to keep this ranch intact.

Until now, if he played his cards right.

"You wanted to be in charge, big brother, and now you got it." Without ceremony, Jackson disconnected. *Honesty indeed.*

Nick stared ahead, wondering if it was true, the cars he followed zooming out of focus. *Had he wanted this?*

Only now, in the solitude of his new truck, was he ready to admit how he'd felt when his older brother Austin's name flashed on his cell phone at four a.m. last week. Annoyed.

The annoyance was followed by shock upon realizing it wasn't his estranged brother on the other end of the line, but a hospital administrator. Austin and his wife, Katherine, were dead on the scene of a helicopter crash. At least, per the hospital, the deaths had been quick and clean.

The feelings crescendoed; then guilt sang the loudest of them all. The guilt was still with him, a punishment for the few seconds he'd wished Austin hadn't woken him up.

The guilt deepened when Saul Kellerman, the family's lawyer, called the following day with the news that Nick had been designated guardian of Alix, his sixteen-year-old niece. A niece he had never met. Then came the silver lining—impossible to ignore and disgusting to recognize. As her guardian, Nick would vote in her stead at the family's company for two years, until she came of age. As long as Nick maintained custody of Alix, the tides would turn. And so the two votes, his and Jackson's, became three. Austin's child, the unwitting pendulum swinging favor to the coalition of siblings set on saving the ranch.

Nick was now the head of the new majority.

But his plan had one weak point. The kid. Austin naming him the guardian of his and Katherine's daughter was salt in the wound, inexplainable, but also an opportunity.

In two years, she'd vote on her own, and if she hated the ranch? Hated him? The two years could flip from a saving grace to a paltry stay of execution if he didn't manage them right. Nick swallowed his feelings, his guilt, amplified in the heat of his truck. The kid looked like Katherine. Hard to pretend she didn't. But looking like his lying ex-girlfriend was hardly an excuse for turning his back on her. She was a kid. No, he was going to do right by Alix. Nick knew exactly how it felt to be abandoned by family, and he wasn't about to do the same thing to a kid, despite her parents. In spite of Austin and whatever agenda he'd issued from beyond the grave, Nick would do the right thing for Alix and the ranch.

The best for Alix started with the best education money could buy, in the form of a world-class tutor. No one could say he was cutting corners, not even the ghost of his father. A live-in tutor was a surefire plan to help Alix fall in love with the land that ran through her blood. Commuting forty minutes to high school was not a selling point for most adolescents, and the last thing he wanted was another boarding school. No, the tutor was a key part of his plan.

Nick frowned at the signs. The tutor cleared customs in Denver, so she'd arrive at the domestic terminal. *He just might make it in time.*

Nick tilted his hat back, an action so familiar it was reflexive, and drew a hand along his jaw, rubbing the stubble as he slowed on the arrivals ramp. He didn't see her.

He stayed on the ramp, circling to take another pass, this time slowing to a crawl for the second try. There was only one woman standing at column ten and it wasn't the tutor. Couldn't be. He had hired a world-class teacher, multidisciplined and Oxford-educated. He wanted someone beyond reproach, education being a crucial element of guardianship. This woman didn't look old enough to have a teaching degree, much less bear the accolades advertised by the recruitment agency. Yet she leaned against the column, standing precisely under a clearly marked ten, and there was no one else in the vicinity. Two bags—a large canvas rucksack and a beat-up suitcase—were lined up beside her. He slowed, and rolled down the window, offering a cautious, "Mary Kelly?"

Her head shot up, and his inquiry was met with a smile. Cobalt eyes blinked at him from under a tousle of fat blond ringlets. Bedroom hair. He swallowed, dry-mouthed at the sight of her. The schoolmarm cardigan did little to disguise her figure, which was as tempting as her bee-stung lips. This was not what he'd had in mind when he'd put the wheels of homeschooling in motion. The goal was to get the kid to fall in love with Montana, not for him to fall in lust with her tutor.

"Yes?" Her curls bounced as she skipped toward him and put a tentative hand on the door handle.

Nick was out of the car in a flash, circling around to offer his help.

She was pretty, this tutor, but boy did it intensify when she flashed a smile in his direction. It had been a while since he'd been struck by an initial attraction so visceral. *It was a problem.* The last thing he needed around the ranch right now was another attractive employee temptation. He'd made poor enough decisions in that arena as it stood. If he wanted to keep custody of Alix, thus winning the vote as her proxy and reversing the family's recent vote to sell the ranch, he needed to be a suitable guardian. One who didn't just hire tempting tutors, but proper educators.

True to form, airport parking authorities passed his truck, blue lights flashing. "Mr. Hartmann, good to see you," the man said through an open window, offering a smile in their direction.

Mary paled. "Mr. Hartmann?" she asked.

His smile widened. "Yep." He paused, and lifted his hat briefly before putting it back square on his head. "And you're Mary Kelly?" He frowned and cleared his throat. "I'm surprised, that's all. You're a tutor? The Oxford-graduate tutor?"

Perhaps it was rude to lace each word with accusation, but he didn't care. Mary Kelly looked more like an Instagram influencer than a tutor, and he needed to be sure.

She bristled. "Look, it's been a long day. I'm on the other side of two red-eye flights and a bloody crap connection in Denver, and now what precisely are you saying? That I don't *look* like a tutor?" Her posh voice shook with irritation, and she eyed him narrowly.

It had been a long time since someone had talked back to Nick. And in all that time, he hadn't had any idea what he'd been missing, because the sass aimed his way was more refreshing than an aged Scotch. He stood in stunned silence, fighting back a blush of his own, a feeling as unfamiliar as it was arousing.

"Did you ever think, *sir*, perhaps *you* don't look like a rancher?" she fired back. The way her voice settled on the *sir* made him think the designation wasn't meant as a compliment, but rather an insult.

He closed the gap between them, seizing the top handle of her cracked Samsonite, swinging it beside his truck as he bit his tongue. "Look like a rancher? What does a rancher even look like?" He muttered it under his breath, but loud enough for her to hear.

In all honesty, he figured he did in fact look exactly as one would imagine a rancher to look. Skin kissed by the sun in a perma-tan, hair worn long and the same uniform sported by all the men on his ranch—worn jeans and a flannel shirt topped with an oiled Stetson.

"I wouldn't dare to presume. And neither should you. Talk about judging a book by its cover—you're a proper chav, I'd say." She narrowed her eyes at him, the final pronouncement sounding more like a threat than an observation.

"You'll forgive my audacity," he replied. Her indignation was reassuring and he did his best to sound affable.

"Right. So it's sorted, then. I'm the tutor." Her cheeks colored as she added, "The *Oxford-educated* tutor, if you must."

"Yep, I must."

She tightened her lips again. "You're not allowed to park here. I've seen them yelling at people, even if it's only for a few minutes. We shouldn't dawdle." Mary hurried toward her bags, smiling politely. "I'll just grab the rest of my things."

He waved in the direction of the squat man doing a second drive-by in the parking enforcement vehicle. "Gus, nice to see you." Mary's smile froze in place as Gus waved back with a smile.

Better she learn sooner as opposed to later that he could park wherever he wanted in Bozeman. There was a different set of rules for a Hartmann.

She felt sucker punched. What had the director of the recruitment agency said? *This family is Montana royalty.* So, fancy, she expected. The spanking-new truck? *No surprise.* But things certainly were bigger in America, hot cowboy included. One look at Nick Hartmann and all the oxygen in her body escaped her. Yep, sucker punched. Tutoring was now the last thing on her mind.

He was tall and broad, living up to every girlhood fantasy of an American cowboy she'd ever had, which, given the worn paperback romance collection she treasured, was quite a lot.

Longish dark hair was tied back and he wore a plaid shirt, the pattern at odds with the tailored fit. The way it stretched, snug across his chest, screamed expensive. Bespoke. High-end. The shirt tucked into a pair of jeans, blue-black in color, held in place with a wide leather belt. When his brown eyes made contact with hers, she wished for a brief moment she'd worn her own clothes instead of her sister's.

By any definition the man was breathtaking. *Word*-taking, really. She swallowed. He was the best-looking man she'd ever seen in real life. And he was also her new employer. *Perfect.*

The beep from his key fob opened the flatbed and Nick heaved her second bag up into the back with ease. He hadn't struggled in the least, swinging the hefty luggage as though it were a bag of crisps and not a twenty-three-kilo rucksack. He turned, bumping into her.

"Oof," she let out as her body pressed into him. "I p-packed all my books in my carry-on so they wouldn't charge me an overweight fee," she stammered. She blushed at his proximity and felt a wave of heat rush to her cheeks.

He smiled. "I've gotta admit, I'm not sure what the going rate is for a checked bag these days." Nick straightened but didn't step away. His eyes studied her and she got the distinct impression he hadn't quite made up his mind about her yet.

She was standing close to him. Closer than she'd intended, and with the realization she had crossed some sort of invisible line, she stepped back and looked up. Fingers nervously tucked a loose wisp of hair behind her ear, and she backed away a few more paces before spinning and opening up the passenger door, stepping up into the truck.

Her buckle clicked into place, the safety belt fastened securely by the time he assumed the driver's seat. Her finger tapped a staccato beat on her thigh and she stared wide-eyed at the inside of the truck. This would all be easier if he was less attractive. A little less like every cowboy fantasy she'd dreamed up and a little more like a man she could shrug away. Because men like him were dangerous, and she was not in a position to let anyone in. More importantly, she was not in a position to fail.

Nick seemed to drive the forty miles to the ranch on autopilot, replacing one hand on the steering wheel with a knee. Opening his shoulder in her direction he turned and asked, "How was your flight?"

"Which one?" She smiled, but then added, "The trip was lovely. Long, bloody tiring, but lovely." Great. If there were to be more questions, she hoped they were all this surface level.

"Yep. That transatlantic will get you."

"I guess now I know." With his eyes now on the road, she could study him, overt in her curiosity. His jaw was square and strong, the shadow of a full beard on his chin. She felt a chill despite the strong sun and wondered if perhaps she was feeling the side effects of what she'd done sinking in. Or maybe she was feeling anxiety. Her cousin might have been right about this plan being a terrible idea. She bit her lip, savoring the quick jolt of ensuing pain.

"Alix has been here a few days. She's having quite the time settling in." The muscle along his jaw tightened as he swallowed, the marvelous Adam's apple bobbing with the action.

"Sure. Well, it's all been rather fast, hasn't it?" She twisted her fingers in her lap, pulling at a knuckle until it clicked with a satisfying pop.

"Fast is one way to put it."

Looking out the window at the vast expanse of fields, she squinted at the cattle spread far into the distance. Cattle, horses and a chance to heal. For her and for Alix. She needed to focus on the girl and her own new role as Mary "Poppins" Kelly. Alix was the reason she'd come. Alix, and the letter in her purse. The promise she hadn't made to her sister, but one she intended to keep. This contract was her chance to make it up to the universe and add a much-needed deposit in her karmic bank. Not that she believed in karma. It hardly seemed a good idea to believe in something that could serve her an epic bill.

"Sure. Yes. It's been a tough week." Nick broke the quiet with his observation. She looked at the thin watch on her wrist, also formerly her sister's. Within a quarter of an hour, they should arrive at the ranch, if her research was at all accurate. Research had never been a strong suit.

So what if she was impersonating her sister, taking this tutoring gig in her stead? If she did a bad thing for a good reason, she was fairly sure it was okay.

For now, Rose Kelly stared out the window, forcing her stomach to stop twisting with every ounce of willpower she possessed as they drove toward the Yellowstone River. Toward the Beartooth Mountains. Toward a plan to make it better. Or at least to make it okay.

Rose swallowed and fought back the tears that had threatened to fall ever since her sister had died. It wasn't fair. Mary was the good girl, and Rose the wild child.

Now, Rose had one chance to make a difference, to fulfill her sister's dream and pay an appropriate tribute to the person who had raised her. Perhaps accepting a private tutoring gig only to donate the lion's share of the proceeds to blind kids in India might not have been the way she'd thought she'd spend the next six months, but to Mary? The charity was everything. And with Mary gone? Rose was going to make sure every kid Mary had promised surgery would get it. And helping a newly orphaned sixteen-year-old? Rose might not be an Oxford-educated tutor, but she was uniquely experienced and qualified to help an orphaned girl like Alix. No one could know better what it felt like to be alone at sixteen, and Rose was still rocking her own brand of grief, fresh and smarting at the mere thought of her sister.

If she could do something, anything, to make Mary's life goals happen, she was going to give it her honest best effort. Even if it meant signing her sister's name on a tutoring contract, and flying across the ocean in her stead to homeschool the closest thing to ranching royalty America had. If karma had a bill to settle, it would have to find Rose in Montana.

Two

Ben was waiting for him on Pax, the dark bay gelding he'd purchased earlier in the season, at 11:55 a.m., as agreed. Rowen, Nick's stallion, was saddled and stamping by his side. His best friend didn't say anything; instead, he tilted a cold bottle of beer in Nick's direction from atop his horse. "You're late," he accused.

Ben's dark hair was tucked behind his ears, and his beard had grown in. His bachelor status? Incorrigible. He was good-looking enough to require no effort to meet women, and the less he tried, the more he succeeded. It was an enviable quality.

"I asked Gary to saddle him up," Ben called down from Pax, nodding toward Rowen.

"Presumptuous of you. Forgive my tardiness, I've had quite the day." Nick smiled, ducking his head so the brim of his hat shielded his face. Ben had been a friend long enough to read a tight lip and, as a fellow rancher, could likely deduce precisely the distress it kept at bay.

"It's not even noon," was all Nick could think to say to the proffered beer as he slipped the toe of a boot into the stirrup.

"It's noon somewhere," Ben assured, and Nick accepted the drink with a matching grin. "Yer mom called," he added.

Nick assumed as much. Josephine Hartmann was a formidable force of nature, and, as the lawyer had informed him, executor of Austin's estate. Frankly, he was surprised she hadn't been nominated with the guardianship as well, although he hadn't ruled out the possibility she'd nominate herself in the aftermath. "Yep, I imagine she did."

Nick's phone blinked with six missed calls from Jo, but he wasn't ready to return them just yet. He exhaled and took a deep swig from the cold bottle. He needed more than a pilsner to face his mother. He needed time.

The two men cantered through an open field without the crushing pressure to fill each static moment with chatter, the hard-earned product of their thirty-year friendship.

"So Josephine told me about Alix. Hilarious. You're saddled with a kid, after all you've done to avoid 'em."

Nick turned a slanted brown eye in Ben's direction, and offered a dry, "Hilarious," in answer.

"Jo said she's at boarding school at least?"

"*Was* at boarding school. She was expelled. She's here now."

Ben let out a low whistle. "Sounds like this Alix sure is your niece, after all. Looks like you've got yourself a hell-raiser."

"Perfect, it should make running the ranch loads easier." Nick rolled his eyes.

"Didn't realize you and Austin were talking?"

Nick kept his eyes on the horizon and clucked at Rowen. "We weren't," he answered simply.

"But you're his daughter's guardian? That doesn't make sense."

"Yeah, well, that's Austin for you. Smarter than all of us, just ask him." Nick immediately regretted the sharp retort. He couldn't ask him. Austin was dead.

"You're still mad, then?"

"Why would I be mad? He and Katherine are—were—perfect for each other. I should have thanked him for chewing my leg outta that bear trap."

"Hardly the way to refer to your ex-girlfriend."

"I think the statute of limitations on ex-girlfriends expires after fifteen years."

"I didn't realize you were the forgiving type."

"I'm not. Neither was he. This…this…" Nick sputtered, turning in the saddle to face his friend. "This is exactly like Austin. Make me guardian after I swore never to have kids. He finds a way to stick it to me even from beyond the grave. Well, fine. Bet he didn't think I'd use his daughter as the vote to change the tides on this ranch."

Ben said nothing; a rancher himself, he knew the weight of responsibility Nick shouldered. In Montana, the Kingsman plot was second only to the Hartmanns' in terms of size, and while Ben's family focused more on horses than cattle, their outfit dated back generations. The Kingsman family were the only ranch in riding distance, which meant the friendship between the two men spanned decades. They rode a few more minutes in easy silence as Nick veered toward the stream, sliding off moments later to water Rowen.

"So if you're her guardian, what does that mean about the sale?" Ben slid down from the bay, voice low, and he spoke without making eye contact. It was a tough scab to pick at, but the ranch was on both their minds. How could it not be? The fight had been looming for years, ever since Nick's mother ceded early access to his inheritance.

Nick didn't answer; instead, he drew the stub of his fingernail across the label of the now empty beer bottle. The sweating bottle had dampened the paper, and it peeled away easily. Now? As guardian to Alix, the sixteen-year-old sole heir to Austin's interest, all decisions relating to her share of the estate were *his* to make. Nick peeled back another chunk of label. He wasn't ready to admit, even to his best friend, that the first call he had made, moments after learning his brother had died in a helicopter accident, had been to their real estate broker to suspend the ranch listing.

"There are two years until she comes of age. For those two years, I'm not selling. Evie and Amelia can sit tight."

Ben nodded, unflappable in his support, despite having fostered a deep affection for the twins, one of Nick's sisters in particular. "Two years can go by awful fast, Nick," he warned.

Nick flexed the muscle in his jaw. He knew the race of the clock all too well. First and foremost in his mind? He didn't have long to make the kid fall in love with Montana, with their legacy. If he could get her to fall in love with the land, she'd never sell it. He grimaced as he thought of the facility with which the twins and Austin had insisted on that very action, but that was his father's fault, not the land's.

"She's going to love it here." He repeated the mantra he'd been uttering as a prayer all week.

"You're gonna do fine, buddy, don't sweat it." Ben winked at him.

"Might help if I knew anything about teenage girls?" Nick scratched again at his label, balling up the bits he'd removed and wadding them into a small ball, which he rolled between his fingers.

"I seem to remember you were popular back in the day?"

Taking careful aim, Nick flicked the damp wad in Ben's direction, making contact with his friend's Adam's apple. "I doubt it's going to be the same."

Ben rubbed his neck and eyed his friend. "Something tells me you're gonna do just fine, buddy. Come on." He hiked himself back up onto the horse, and Nick followed suit.

They rode in silence most of the way. Until Ben interrupted, voicing another concern.

"You given any thought as to how you're going to manage to make her love it here?" Ben finally offered. "I'm not sure you're going to sell this place to a sixteen-year-old based on a forty-minute commute to the nearest high school."

"I'm not going to." Nick smiled, thanking the stars his plan didn't include a commute.

"Pretty sure school is compulsory, buddy." Ben raised an eyebrow and took another swig of beer as they trotted toward the horizon.

"Oh, she's going to do school. I hired Mary Poppins, or rather, I commissioned the lawyer to hire Mary Poppins. She goes by Mary Kelly."

"You're hiring your sixteen-year-old niece a governess? Can I be there when you tell your mom?"

Nick frowned. His friend had a point. His mother wasn't likely to be on board with the homeschooling idea. Thing was, Nick could barely remember a time he'd been doing what his mom approved of. But it was too late to turn back now. "Not a governess—well, sorta, I guess, but more of a private tutor. The tutor I hired is the recent valedictorian of the year, an Oxford grad."

"Oxford? As in England? Oh my." Ben lifted a hand to his forehead with dramatic flair.

"Alix's been kicked outta three boarding schools. According to Saul, I need the best." Nick shrugged. If the kid wanted to come home so bad, he'd see to it she never left.

"Is she hot?" Ben asked.

"I hope you're asking about the tutor, and I'll remind you she's now on my staff, but you're gonna find out soon enough to decide for yourself. She's already here, getting a rundown from Samantha." He slipped his empty into the saddlebag trailing from the rear horn of his saddle, grateful to have sidestepped the question of her appearance.

Yes. She was hot. More than hot. She was a tamale of trouble.

"Samantha? The assistant you kissed, then brushed off? Is that wise?" Ben asked. It was easy to forget his confidant knew about his past, but Ben never let him forget long.

"Samantha's capable, and there's nothing going on between us. Plus, she was the one who went over the contract with the lawyer. She's going over the Montana curricula and associated homeschooling expectations from the state. I'll meet with Mary when we get back. Her bags are still in the truck."

Ben said nothing and just raised his eyebrows. Any higher and they risked running into his hairline.

Riding with his best friend was cathartic. Ben didn't ask about Austin or Jackson. Heck, he didn't even ask about how Nick was feeling about all this. He didn't need to. They'd spent enough nights drinking and scheming together to know better.

Perhaps it was rash. Hiring a tutor, sight unseen and at top dollar nonetheless. But Alix Hartmann was home. The ranch he'd thought lost was saved, if only temporarily. Nick could suffer whatever consequences he needed to endure to keep Hartmann Estates and the ranch running. Even if it meant raising Austin and Katherine's love child as his own.

At least, for now, he had his horse, his friend and a second beer. "Cheers, buddy," he said. "And thanks."

Nick motioned for the chair in front of him. "Take a seat, won't you, Mary." He smiled at her. "Scotch?"

She arrived at the office moments after he'd stepped out of his quarters, freshly showered and ready for business. Mary closed the few feet between them and sank into the chair he motioned her toward, nodding.

"I suppose it's past midnight in London," he said. He rose, making his way to the discreet wet bar his father had installed. Four years since his dad died and it still felt like he was trespassing when he was in this office. The feeling caught him unawares when he least expected it. Nick kept the bar stocked, and as his fingers brushed the assorted bottles, they paused on the Johnnie Walker Black. Best get this conversation on the right track. Without turning to face her, he asked, "Ice?"

From the warmth in her scoff, he guessed at the smile accompanying her refusal. He determined perhaps she was more suited for Montana than he'd initially feared. Maybe Oxford, or the recruitment firm, did a good job with their screening process, after all.

"So why Montana?" he asked, handing her a glass. She studied the amber liquid, surprising him by dipping a finger into the Scotch and raising it to her lips. He stared as a small pink tongue flicked to lick an errant drip of whiskey before it dripped down her finger. He cleared his throat in an effort to clear his mind. It was not the time to be thinking about her tongue, as delectable as it might be.

"Why not Montana?" There was a flippancy to her tone, incongruent with his vision of a British nanny-turned-tutor. But that avenue of thought had proved difficult to defend earlier, so he pushed it back.

Roberta, his housekeeper, had set a fire, and it crackled satisfactorily in the wide fireplace behind them. He was struck with the realization that Mary still wore her coat. "Shall I take that for you?"

"Right, yes, sorry. After meeting with Samantha, I was exploring with Alix, and we lost track of the time." She blushed. Shifting in her chair, she shrugged off her coat, fishing one hand free at a time in an effort to avoid relinquishing her drink. He suppressed a smile.

Under her coat, poorly disguised by the cardigan, was the lush body, there for the admiring.

"She's lovely—Alix, I mean." Mary blushed.

Relieved of her outerwear, she fastened the loose button at the neck of her sweater and sat on her free hand. "I am sorry about your brother."

He grunted. It was the same song he'd heard all week. Strangers offering condolences as though they would offer a reprieve to the pain he'd shouldered every waking moment since the cursed phone call last week. Austin's death stirred up everything. The betrayal. The loss. The certainty he'd never be able to yell at him again, no matter how much he deserved it. There was one way to forget the pain, and another deep look at her lush body offered him every confidence it would be effective. Suddenly it was hard to think of anything else. He cleared his throat and answered on autopilot. "Yep, it was a surprise."

"The agency told me it was a helicopter accident." She took a sip of her drink and looked up at him.

Her eyes were pools of light blue fire. It was like looking at the center of a lit match. Similarly, he was sure if he held the gaze too long, he'd burn. She looked away first, suddenly deeply interested in the faceted glass he had poured for her.

"Yes, well, Austin always did like his helicopters." It was easier brushing off the mention of his brother rather than bringing them both down with the harsh realities of the recent deaths.

Her fingers tightened around the etched glass of her rock glass. "Private jet or nothing, that's what I say." She smiled in sarcasm and he surprised himself with a laugh in response.

"So Alix. She's in year eleven?" She raised an eyebrow…

He knew she had this information. He'd submitted answers to a barrage of questions prior to signing a contract with the agency that sent her, outlining all he knew, and highlighting a lot he didn't know about his niece. So why was she asking now? He studied her, eyes wide and open, and decided he didn't care why. Small talk had never been his forte, but so long as he wasn't doing the heavy lifting, it was fine.

"Yep. Pulled her from the boarding school. Well—" he rubbed at his chin "—I pulled her to avoid expulsion. She was caught drinking on campus, a serious no-no in the boarding school world." He took another sip, draining his glass. Hesitating only a moment, he uncorked the bottle to pour a refill. He motioned in her direction and she held her glass forward, though the bottom third of her drink was still there.

"I mean, who hasn't had a drink at boarding school, right?" she joked.

"I wouldn't have pegged you for the type, Oxford." He smiled as she reddened.

"I meant, given the circumstances." Her eyes flashed, and she pushed her shoulders back.

His desk was orderly, not a page out of place. All the files relating to his brother's estate, including his will and last wishes, were in the same stack. The Alix files were next. Three pens were spaced evenly beside the stacked files, and he picked up his favorite: a Mont Blanc fountain pen. Picking up the gift from his dad, he wiggled it on his fingers. "I don't want her to hate it here." *Sometimes when you don't know what to say you should start with the truth.*

"Well, I'll have to see how I can help with that, shall I?" She smiled and took another sip of Scotch.

He shook his head. Anything to break their gaze. He was staring again. "She's a good student, or at least it seems so." He pushed the file the headmistress had sent him across the table and Mary leaned forward. The lean offered a new angle to the view down her top and he felt his body tighten in appreciation.

"Right. Should make things easier. Of course, academics is just part of the high school experience, hardly the brilliant bit." She fidgeted on her chair, mouth screwed up in an adorable bow.

"What?" he asked because he had to know.

She pulled at a loose curl, straightening the hair to her shoulder before letting it spring back. "Homeschooling seems a bit much, don't you think? I mean, wouldn't you be miffed to go from an upstate New York boarding school to a private tutor in the Montana wilderness?" She blushed again. "Not that I'm trying to talk myself out of a job—it can just help to have a little insight."

"I didn't think you were here to interview me?" He stood, placing his cup on the desk. Beads of sweat from the glass made their way down the side of the tumbler in protest to the heat. It was unseasonably hot for May, and the cozy fire wasn't helping. Neither was the fiery tutor.

"I didn't mean—" she started.

Nick bit the inside of his cheek. *He* hadn't meant to put her on guard. "Sorry. I, ah, haven't had a lot of time to process. I think what she needs now is family. To rediscover where she came from. It's complicated."

She shifted in her seat, nodding.

"Rather a long day, I'll show you to your quarters." He moved toward the door, and she stood and followed. The last thing he wanted to do was talk about the reasons he needed Alix to love the ranch, or the drama around all things Katherine.

What began as a *how do you do* had disintegrated quickly. She followed the cowboy, as she referred to him mentally since accepting the position, out of his office.

He didn't speak as he led them through the home. *Home* felt an inadequate description for the ranch palace he—rather they—lived in. Soaring high ceilings met walls of windows offering incredible views of the Beartooth Mountain range. Polished logs paired with brass light fixtures created a rustic-chic ambience and she was overwhelmed, not for the first time since her arrival, with the feeling of being small. Everything in this ranch was oversize. The polished leather couches spanned seven feet, and were overstuffed, draped in skins and furs.

"Is that real?" She wished her voice was louder.

Nick, not pausing his stride, spoke over his shoulder. "What? The antelope?" He nodded toward a mounted head. In another setting, it would look rough, but here, surrounded by opulence, it was wild. "Yeah, we've got big-game hunting on the ranch—got that one when I was fifteen. My first buck. Dad had it mounted."

She took two paces to match each one of his long strides, and she hopped to keep up with him, not wanting to miss the tail end of his anecdotes. *A hunter?* A primal desire sparked in her stomach, but she squeezed her fingers into her palm, allowing the nails to dig into the flesh of her hand. She wasn't here for that.

He led her up a wide staircase to a second-floor hallway, lit with several skylights. The third door on the left opened into a large bedroom with windows overlooking a field of waist-high grasses. In the distance, she saw cattle grazing. In juxtaposition to the wildness of the setting, her room was the picture of opulence. A four-poster bed, with four extralarge pillows and a fluffy duvet covered in a stitched quilt. The room also had its own fireplace, which housed another cheery, blazing fire. Muslin drapes framed the picture windows, which overlooked an expanse of the most beautiful rugged countryside she'd ever seen.

"Your room," he said.

She sucked in a breath. It was a far cry from her tiny flat in London. Her cousin had been delighted to sublease it from her, even on a moment's notice, qualifying her flat as a "huge space." She doubted she'd refer to any part of England as huge ever again after this experience.

"Thanks, it's lovely. The room. The… Everything." She stumbled on the words. A small part of her felt a pang of niggling guilt for her ruse. It was harder than she expected, pretending to be her sister, but a quick, deep breath renewed her confidence in her decision. She would help Alix, and this family. There was nothing wrong about bloody well enjoying herself in the process. She believed with all her soul there was no one better suited to help a sixteen-year-old orphan than herself.

Her luggage was waiting in the far corner of her room. Nick paused in the doorway, shoulder propped against the frame, studying her.

"Quite the view," she said softly, and she heard the invitation in her own voice. *Maybe he'll stay awhile.* Although the thought was nerve-racking.

"Yep."

His one-word answers were infuriating. She cast a glance back in his direction, wondering, not for the first time, if he was biting back what he really thought.

She turned to face him, and sat on the edge of the large bed, sinking into a duvet of soft feathers. A smile spread across her face. "This is the most comfortable bed I've ever had."

"Yep. I, ah… I'll see you for dinner? Down the stairs to the left of the entrance. The cook made up a spread for us. We tend to eat at six. You'll join us?"

Us was likely him and Alix, but she was still stumbling on the first bit of his pronouncement. "Cook?"

"We have an independent staff to tend to the home. I'll introduce you tomorrow. The estate is parceled into different acreages—a hospitality and hotel branch on the east end of the lot, a fishing retreat closer to Billings. We're in the cattle end here, with our offices for the Hartmann Corp headquartered in the east wing of the home." He gestured toward a cluster of buildings set at a distance near a clearing. She nodded.

"It's a working ranch here, see?" He entered her room and walked toward the window, setting both large hands on the sill, nodding toward the fields to the west. "Hartmann Homestead is just shy of two hundred thousand acres. We also have a few fields planted and thirty thousand acres of waterfront to the Yellowstone."

His shoulders relaxed, and she stared at his shirt, tucked into another pair of dark jeans, hugging his thighs just enough to make her sweat a little.

"I could take you girls out tomorrow? On an expedition to see the grounds? Get you both on horses." He turned and smiled. A welcome change from his ever-present tight-lipped frown.

She found herself at a loss for words, nodding dumbly. How would she keep up the ruse of being her proper sister if she saw this man on a horse? It was hard to imagine her attraction could burn any brighter, but an adolescent chaperone seemed a good idea. She leaned back, the wall by her door serving as adequate support for her weak-kneed reaction to the proposal.

"Right, then. See you shortly." He turned and headed toward the door. His arm brushed against her as he shimmied past, lighting her blood on fire.

The good thing about his departure was the opportunity it presented to watch him walk away. The man was delicious. Mary would have had a heart attack. Rose choked back the thought. The levity offered through her attraction was an effective reprieve from the constant guilt she carried around, but with him gone, the guilt was back. Mary couldn't have had a heart attack. Not after Rose had been responsible for her death.

Her hand slipped to her pocket and her fingers traced across the cool comfort of the phone. Clunky, serviceable and not hers.

It was past five thirty, so not yet midnight. She dialed her cousin.

Tapping the back of Mary's phone, her finger became a staccato metronome.

"Jeez, Rose, it's nearly midnight," Ellen answered, adding mumbled curses to the greeting.

Rose fell back onto the feather bed and pressed the phone to her ear. "Right. Sorry to wake you, then." She fought a wave of exhaustion threatening to overpower her.

"Are you coming home?" The question echoed through the phone, and Rose felt a surge of annoyance.

"Home? I thought you got it, Ellen. This is home for me now. I'm finishing this. I accepted the contract, the post, for Mary, and I'll not quit."

"You're impersonating your dead sister for your dead sister?" Ellen's tone was imbued with disapproval.

"You know why I'm doing this." Rose sighed.

"Tell me you're not doing this because of *them*?"

"Mary pledged to help, and I'll be damned if I have to write the organization and say the money isn't coming, after all."

"I'm sure they'd understand." The exasperation was gone from her tone, and Ellen sounded small and very far away.

"No. I can't say it. I can't tell them."

"Tell them…?"

"That she's gone." Rose swallowed. *Gone* was a nice word for dead, but she doubted it would provide any relief for the association her sister had volunteered with over the past decade. Mary had been so excited when she was crowned valedictorian. She knew then she'd get a contract like this, and had been so confident she'd pledged to pay for the children's surgeries before signing with a family. Twenty-seven kids she'd agreed to sponsor. *Overachiever.*

Rose scratched the nail polish chipping off her thumb. Funny thing was, a contract like this *was* enough money.

She could correct the vision for twenty-seven nearly blind kids in India. Rose wasn't about to call them and say, *Sorry, the wrong sister died so you kids are plumb outta luck.* When the contract fell in her lap, she'd accepted without thinking. Now? She could fund her sister's legacy. And the best part? The job was also helping a kid.

"She's an orphan, Ellen. A sixteen-year-old orphan. No one is gonna understand this kid better than I can." Tap, tap, tap…the finger's speed increased against the phone, a thriving pulse to her temper.

"The idea wasn't to uphold the pledge at any cost. Mary trained for years for her teaching degree."

"I know," Rose snapped back. "I shared a room with her the whole time. Who do you think helped with the cue cards for her to study? Who helped prep for the exams—"

"Who never missed a student party?"

A lump formed in her throat, and she knew from her grieving in the past month that the lump wouldn't dislodge without a good cry. It was something she was ill-prepared to do on the phone, let alone twenty minutes before dinner with Cowboy and Alix. She sighed. "What's this really about, Ellen? You think I can't do it or I won't do it well enough? Or is it that you're jealous?" Perhaps the last was a low blow but she was too tired to care.

"I don't know what would give you the impression I'm jealous—"

"Alix only has a few months left of the school year and if I manage to help her through it *everybody wins.* Even the SightSavers. I might not be tutor of the year, but it's year eleven, not neurosurgery. Plus, if I pull this off, no one has to call and cancel anything. I can be there for Alix, pay for those poor kids to have surgery and make a difference. I can finish what Mary started. I owe her that."

She heard her cousin's exhale through the phone. "Right."

"Look, you're not going to change my mind. You

couldn't in England and you won't now. Anyway, I doubt there's a soul on earth more qualified to mentor a newly orphaned sixteen-year-old girl." Rose swore under her breath. She didn't need a teaching degree to help. And she didn't need a designer dress to sleep with the god of ranchers. Girl's gotta take the edge off somehow, and it was important that in pretending to be her sister she didn't lose herself. With Mary gone, she was her own conscience now.

She blushed. Sleeping with the rancher? The thought had come from nowhere, unbidden, or had it come from the stubborn spark lit in the airport? She supposed it didn't matter. Spark or not, she was not going to lean into the fire. She was here for her sister's legacy. She was here to help Alix. She was *not* going to fall for a cowboy, no matter how much she wanted to.

Three

"It's good to see you, kid." Nick stood in the doorframe of the room designated for Alix, wondering at the truth in his statement. The girl was on her bed, earphones in, back turned to him, and it was good to see her.

No answer. *Okay, not unusual for a teenager, right?* He wasn't going to express his sympathies. He knew from the past week that it was more irritating than comforting.

"I hope it's not weird. Being here, I mean." He stepped into the room and made his way over to the bed, the setting sun casting his dark shadow on her quilt. The girl looked up and Nick shuddered. She had been crying. Not his forte.

"Why would it be weird? 'Cause I don't know you? Literally, never met you in my life, and now you're my guardian or whatever?" Her eyes sparkled as she spat her answer at him. She was right, but still… He glanced at his hands, wondering what he had done to wave red at this adolescent. He had angered the bull. No clean way around this arena.

"I meant due to the fact that I wasn't here when you met Mary, er, Ms. Kelly." He shifted his weight from foot to foot. *Yep, I shoulda handled the introduction myself. Rookie mistake.*

"Whatever. I'm too old for Mary *bloody* Poppins, anyway." She laced the superlative with a mock accent and he stiffened at her tone.

"She's not a governess, if that's what you're thinking. I just figured you wouldn't want to take the bus to school." His weight faced back onto his left leg, and his hip cocked forward, nervous stance in place.

"Bus? What makes you think I'd take the bus? Isn't the one silver lining in all this that I can now afford a car for myself?" Her voice caught on the last word and Nick fought the impulse to give her a hug.

"Let's start with a good report card, shall we? I tend not to issue car keys following an expulsion, which I'm sure you can agree is reasonable." He shifted his weight from foot to foot. *Do it, Nick. Sit on the bed.* He gave in to his inner voice and sat on the edge of the bed.

"Whatever. Fine. It's fine. I'll be fine. It's all fine." She picked up her phone and jabbed at the screen, a rude dismissal, but forgivable.

"Really, kid. It's a tough hand. But I'm your uncle. This place is as much yours as mine, and I'm hoping you can find a way to make it your home." He spoke in a measured pace, calm and quiet, the way he would talk to a horse he needed to break. "When things got bad for me, the mountains, this land—" He pinked. "I mean, the land can heal you."

"Didn't think it could get too bad for the golden boy," she sniffed.

Austin had called him golden boy. Just the one time, but it had been enough. Maybe she didn't know. What her mom had done? Well, it wasn't his place to say. Not now, anyway. He cleared his throat. “Golden boy, am I now? I guess I can understand how your dad might have thought that.” He swallowed, not sure how he could unpack the fight that had led to Austin’s departure, and the slur that had followed. “You can just call me uncle. Or Nick.”

“Whatever.”

“I guess the land means something different to everyone. Maybe just find out what it means to you?”

“Sure. Not like I have a choice now, do I?” Her chin jutted forward and, for a moment, she looked twelve and not sixteen, large eyes wide and fringed with heavy lashes. The picture of Katherine.

“Dinner’s at six. Dining room is the last door on the left.” He turned. Best not to force things too fast.

“I’m not hungry.” Despite the show of turning up the volume, she answered immediately.

“We eat as a family.” Again, like a horse, he needed to show who held the reins.

He interpreted the eye roll as tacit agreement.

“So we’re family now?”

“You can’t choose your kin, Alix.” He kept his tone consistent.

“You’re telling me,” she sighed.

He stiffened and, in a fluent movement, stood up from the bed.

“I didn’t mean you,” she added, her quiet voice stopping him in his tracks. “I mean, it’s alright being here, I guess.”

“Don’t worry about it.” He turned and looked at her. “It can only get easier from here.”

He turned and left, pausing only a moment to cast a glance over his shoulder. Kid was nodding her head to the beat of whatever she was listening to. Angry, sure.

Hell, he deserved it.

Rose applied a fresh coat of lipstick and whipped a brush through her curls, jutting a quick glance at her reflection. The brush did little to tame her curls, although her look was much improved after a quick smear of hair defrizzer serum from a bottle whose packaging she quickly concluded oversold the effects but smelled good. She had on a fresh top—a simple white button-up that hugged her figure—and a new pair of blue jeans. Retrieving her heeled ankle boots, she slipped them on. She would now be three inches closer to the mouth that had driven her to distraction. Yes, it was quite a problem. She was looking for a distraction.

Without the anchor of the good angel on her shoulder, the older sister who kept her conscience, Rose felt a spell of indecision about whether or not she should pursue that distraction.

Poking her head out of her bedroom, she retraced the path to her new room, pausing at the head of the double-wide staircase. The creaking plank flooring throughout the home was double-glazed with a varnish so shiny she could make out her reflection in the polished woodwork. She smiled at it.

The dining room was easy to find. She followed her nose, and arrived at a Norman Rockwell painting. The table was heavily set with all the trimmings of what could have been an American Thanksgiving dinner, even though it was only May. Nick sat at the head of the table, with a sullen Alix to his right.

"This is quite something." Rose breezed into the dining room and took the vacant seat to Nick's left. The smells of roast turkey were mouthwatering, and the bird before them boasted a crackling brown glaze, triggering a roil of anticipation in her stomach.

"Some might say people were trying too hard." Alix did her best to sound disinterested, but Rose noticed a surreptitious swallow. It would be tough not to be affected by such a lovely dinner and the effort spent preparing it.

"Some others might find their manners and be grateful to have such a delicious meal waiting for them," Nick answered. He'd slid into the parental role with a facility that provoked the question of why such a handsome man as he didn't have kids and family of his own. *A man of mystery indeed.*

Classic teenage eye rolls answered, and Nick distributed a thick slab of turkey breast to Alix's plate, suggesting, "Try the cranberry sauce—they're from our own patch."

Rose, not to be put off by adolescent tension, helped herself to a turkey leg and all the fixings. She hadn't eaten since morning and was famished. Nick passed her the bowl of gravy, and his fingers brushed against hers. She bit her lip and looked away.

"This is lovely." She smiled, nodding at the offered wine bottle tipping toward her glass.

"Yep," the cowboy answered.

"So, Alix, I was thinking we could get a start tomorrow?" Rose busied herself slicing the meat off her turkey leg into even pieces on her plate, hoping her casual question would provoke some enthusiasm. The plan she'd conceived on the plane was to treat the adolescent the way she treated men she wanted to seduce—using nonchalance to draw them in. Be hard to get. Sitting in front of Alix now, Rose worried the idea was half-baked, but in for a penny, in for a pound. Plus, nonchalance was pretty much the only tool in her arsenal.

"If I have to." Alix shrugged.

"You have to," Nick confirmed. His tone gave no room for negotiation.

"Fine, then." She pushed her plate away from her. "I'm not hungry." She sulked as she moved away from the table.

"Alix?" Nick called. The girl didn't stop.

"That's teenagers for you, sangfroid the moment you suggest an early start," Rose remarked, before popping another slice of turkey onto her plate. The food was spectacular.

Nick tightened his mouth.

A toque blanche poked around the corner of the entrance and a small French chef arrived, balancing a plate of asparagus swimming in a yellow dressing.

"Mr. Hartmann, *voilà le plat du jour.*" He presented the platter with a flourish.

"Thanks, Pierre," Nick said. "Did you take a plate to Amelia?"

Her stomach tightened. *Who was Amelia?*

"No, sir, she's at the Stateman house this evening. It's just *vous trois*…er, *vous deux.*" The chef reddened.

"Sure, thanks."

"Enjoy your meal, mademoiselle." Pierre smiled and touched his hat in farewell. "The asparagus is perfection." He raised his fingers to his lips for a classic chef's kiss and left.

Nick refilled his wineglass, slamming the bottle back on the table without offering to refill hers. Just as well, it was still half-full. She took another sip and placed the glass back down loud enough to provoke his interest.

"Sorry, Oxford." He smiled at her, but his eyes were not focused. With his right hand, he spaced the cutlery before him evenly, three forks lined up from smallest to largest where they met his plate. He pushed his water glass out to align at a right angle.

"You have something against scalene triangles?" She laughed, pleased with herself. She'd been reading an idiot's guide to geometry on the plane and was pleased to work in some tutoring terminology. The opportunity to tease the cowboy was an unexpected bonus.

Nick swept the three forks together with the back of his hand and shook his head. "Sometimes I like to organize things so they have a place."

She pushed her wineglass to a ninety-degree angle

to her plate. "If I play by your rules, will you be nice to me?" She tilted her wineglass toward the bottle and smiled again.

His eyes flickered from her glass to her mouth, precisely the reaction she'd hoped for. Day one was coming to a close—it had to be well past two a.m. her time now—and she was tired. Too tired to keep up the charade of being her sister, of being good, and just tired enough to be deliciously herself.

He filled her glass and pushed his shoulders back into his chair. "To geometry."

"I've always preferred chemistry." The words escaped before she could stop them.

The line of muscle along his jaw flexed and he lifted his glass toward her. The dining room was so quiet she could hear her own pulse as she touched her glass to his with an exaggerated, "Cheers."

Chemistry indeed.

Four

One good thing about traveling from England to Montana was the time difference. It worked in her favor, and for once in her life, Rose was up before the sun. She was dressed before the snooze button, hit by habit, had shrieked.

Force of routine had her leaning toward a mirror putting on a quick coat of makeup and running a brush through her curls before she gave up trying to be fancy. She wanted to explore her surroundings and find a calm spot to think before her teaching duties began.

She'd stared at the ceiling for nearly an hour last night, eyes wide despite a heavy fatigue. Rose didn't want to be thinking about him. Blue jeans and cowboy boots, paired with a strong jaw and dimpled chin? Any woman in her right mind would be a little distracted, but she was going to be more like Mary. Behave in a way that would keep her sister close. It was the thoughts of her sister that stung, and finally sleep became a welcome escape from grief, sexy cowboy notwithstanding.

The front door to the ranch was eight feet across, but surprisingly light. She pulled it open and was grateful to see the hinges were recently greased. The door opened without a sound and two steps later she was in the great Montana outdoors.

From the window of her bedroom, she could spot the beginnings of a river, which was where she was headed. Her first step was to circle the home, so she turned left and rounded the manor.

The walls of the ranch were cut from large boulders of fieldstone in varying shades of gray. The stone foundation gave way to huge logs, hewn together with masterful carpentry. Never in her life had she seen such a sumptuous private residence, and the five minutes she'd allotted to round the home quickly turned into twenty. As she turned the corner of the front of the house, she discovered a second wing. This one featured floor-to-ceiling windows on the back side. She scurried past, grateful none of the main floor windows were lit at such an early hour.

The grass was wet with dew and the leather of her boots darkened at the damp licks of weeds and wildflowers. She didn't know what she was looking for per se, but was reasonably sure she'd know it when she found it. A wooden fence blocked the path, but it was made up of two logs, more to keep in cattle and horses than deter human passersby. She hiked a leg up and swung herself over. The fence had been visible from her window and she judged herself to be roughly halfway to her destination. Having cleared the fence, she pulled the phone from her pocket and dialed the voice mail.

"You've reached the voice mail of Mary Kelly. I'm terribly sorry but I seemed to have missed your call. Leave me your details and I will call you back as soon as I'm able. Cheerio." Her sister's voice was vibrant. The mix of proper and prim in her inflection firmly designated her as the good sister, as it had since childhood. Rose disconnected and redialed, listening again to her sister's voice. The words became the tone she marched to. You've reached, *two steps*, the voice mail, *three more steps*, of Mary Kelly, *three steps*. A step for each syllable, and by the third chorus she had arrived at the edge of a wood.

The gray moment before the sun rose had arrived and was breathtaking. Rose parked herself on the large rock, larger still than she had imagined from her window. Amazing how perspective could change so much. She sat on the rock and listened for the rushing of water, audible over the faint hum of her phone.

She was alone. It was breathtaking, beautiful and a massive challenge. She finally had a moment to cry. A moment to fall apart. She set an alarm on her phone. Five minutes. She was allowing herself five minutes to let go.

Putting the voice mail on speaker, she allowed her head to sink into her hands as she heard the ring of her sister's voice without having to hold the phone. It was the opposite of a selfie.

"You said you'd never leave me," she whispered. Her voice echoed with a hollow quality, reverberating off the damp air. Hearing it, she cried harder.

"You said you'd always be there for me!" she shouted this time, but fought the urge to hurl the phone away. Kicking the base of a tree, she fell back onto the ground, rubbing her toe.

Her phone alarm sounded. The five minutes felt both impossibly long and terribly short. No matter. The falling apart had to end now. She stood. The stream was nearby and splashing some cold water on her face seemed a good idea.

The creek proved easier to find than she anticipated, though it was another twenty minutes by foot from her rock. The rushing water was cold, but it wasn't the temperature that stilled her. Someone had proved an earlier riser than she, arriving before her.

He was a merman. Lithe and athletic, with not a spare ounce on him. "My word," she muttered under her breath. He looked precisely as she'd imagined. *Maybe better.*

Like a deer, frozen, she stood still. Nick was swimming in the punishingly cold creek. He got out of the water and she inhaled sharply. The man had the body of a marble statue. Even from her distance, she could count the ridges of muscle in his six—no, eight—pack. She swallowed. His arms. They had looked good in the plaid shirts she quickly discovered to be his uniform, but naked before her? She blushed. His swimsuit left not much to the imagination. The few gaps she needed to fill in herself she did with relish.

She backed up, stepping on a twig in the process. Because that's what happens to city slickers with leaden feet. They humiliate themselves in front of glorious mountain men.

"Mary? Is that you?" He was slipping on his clothes with depressing efficiency, and she quickened her pace.

"I'm just... I was just walking." Her voice carried a trace of her earlier lamenting, and she tried not to regret the crying.

Nick's agility allowed him to reclothe faster than Rose would have liked, and moments later he pulled on a shirt, fastening it as he walked toward her. "You found my swimming hole," he said as he walked, breath still short from the cold of the creek.

"I did. Not that it was hiding much. I can just see it from my window."

"I guess so." A worn towel was slung over his shoulder. Hardly the tool of such a wealthy man, but he proved down to earth, at least in private.

"You're up early." She'd mastered small talk from her

stint working at a bar. A good way to avoid personal questions was to launch your own barrage of inquiry.

"Yep." His wet swimsuit radiated cold. The hair on her arms stood on end, from the cold. *Right.*

"I'm still juggling jet lag." It seemed as reasonable an excuse as any to be wandering the estate at five a.m.

Nick grunted, then turned his head in her direction. "Did you want to try a swim? I've been starting my day in this creek since I was just a kid."

Now that he had left the creek, a frigid swim held less appeal. "Maybe tomorrow?"

At first, he'd thought he was seeing a ghost. Suddenly he was fifteen, sneaking to meet his sweetheart for a predawn swim. He choked back surprise and swam toward the creek's edge, seeking comfort in the apparition.

He stopped a few feet from shore. He was sick of talking to ghosts. They were everywhere now. His dad. His brother. Katherine. The haunted face of his niece. Even the new tutor had an ache to her aura—not that he believed in auras.

The figure backed up, and a blond curl bounced with the momentum of her retreat. *Mary? Have you come to haunt me now, too?*

He paused in the water and rubbed his eyes. It *was* her. He smiled, relieved. She looked nothing like Katherine; maybe it was one of the things he liked about her. She looked sad, and Katherine hadn't wasted a moment of her life on that emotion.

Her second day on the ranch and she'd found him first thing. Temptation followed him, and he was feeling weaker by the instant. He wanted to forget all those ghosts, and the surefire way to do so was the only thing he could think about. She was dressed in a white T-shirt. Simple. Tight. A red bra visible through thin cotton. His brain, totally occupied with the fantasy of her dressed in only said red bra, was capable of only one-word answers in response to her chatter. It was the grief, he reasoned, that fueled his one-track mind.

He did have the presence of mind to suggest a predawn swim. He'd issued the invitation before he could stop the words. It was a terrible idea to see her in a swimsuit. Terrible and wonderful, an excruciating test of will.

"Maybe tomorrow," she said.

They walked the next few minutes in silence. Her face had a puffy quality to it, and her eyes had the telltale "too bright" sheen of having just poured buckets of tears.

He wasn't going to ask. It wasn't his business.

"Did you still want to go on that horse ride today?" Her voice was tentative as she focused on the trail before them, dancing around the larger rocks in the path.

Their ride over the property was the first step in his plan to get Alix to fall in love with the ranch. Show her the land. Getting to spend time with the perky tutor was just a bonus.

"We could. Sure."

She looked up at him, and in the momentary lapse of concentration, she stumbled on the rock with an anguished, "Ow, bollocks!"

He reared like a stallion. Mary was clutching her ankle. Not crying, a good sign as there were few things as frightening to Nick Hartmann as the sight of a weeping woman. "Are you okay?" The question felt redundant given her exclamation, but he couldn't stop himself.

"I've just twisted my ankle, but I'm sure it's fine." She reached her hand up toward his searchingly.

The small hand was cold and miniature in his own, and he gripped it as he pulled her to her feet. Mary leaned into his frame as they walked toward the ranch together. Her hip pressed into his side and all he could feel was her body against his. It was electric.

For a long while now, Nick had drawn a line around

himself. A wall made of several unmovable bricks. Boss. Rancher. Son. He was the responsible one. It was a line no one crossed without asking. But here she was, pressed against him, in his space, crashing through his wall.

It felt good.

"Is this okay?" His arm snaked around her, pulling her against him, his body the support for each alternating step.

"Yes," she said through gritted teeth. Her face was drawn and white, freckles more visible against her blanched skin. He hadn't noticed the freckles until just then and was utterly charmed by them.

"We're not far," were the only words of comfort he could think of. She shifted, and he felt an arm twist around his waist, gripping his hip.

"I think I can make it if you help me."

"Sure. It's what I'm here for." And they sauntered forward. It was slow going, picking the way around ruts in the path. To her credit, she didn't complain, but following a lurch to cross a fallen log, she cursed.

"They teach you how to talk like that at Oxford?"

She paled. "No, but I moonlit as a barmaid. I've heard a lot worse, as I'm sure you have."

He smiled at the pinch he received to his side. "Indeed. Careful, Oxford, I'm playing nice." He swallowed. It was too soon to joke. Regardless of her starring role in his dreams last night, pleasantries were still in order. She was his employee. He wasn't about to start anything with the hired help. Not again.

Blushing vermilion, her eyes stood out a shocking blue, two cobalt gems flashing at him. "Ever think I've been playing nice, too?"

"Nice or not, I don't see how you're going to limp back to the house. We've got a half mile ahead of us." That was valid. What he didn't say was just as true—namely, he wanted to hold her.

She grimaced. "I'm doing okay."

"I wasn't saying otherwise, just that we'll be an hour getting back at this rate."

"I'm not sure what you're suggesting? Not likely I'll finish the sprint if that's what you had in mind?"

"Not exactly. I was thinking I could carry you. It'd be faster, and I need to meet the men at six thirty."

"Carry me? A half mile? No. You just go ahead. I'll find a stick or something and limp at my own pace. I don't want to keep you." She was blabbering, perhaps due to her own susceptibility to their chemistry, and it was charming.

"If you think I'm leaving you to struggle with a stick, you've got another think coming." He bent and, before she could object, scooped an arm behind her knees, pulling them out from under her. She fell back in the shallow of his arms. "Much better," he confirmed, picking up the pace with a dogged saunter back to the house.

She didn't say anything, but after a few strides her head settled into the nook of his shoulder. Maybe he shouldn't admit that the fit of her, against his chest, was validating. Her hair, the wild curls soft against the hollow of his neck, smelled like lavender and soap, a clean, fresh smell tempting him to close his eyes and lose himself in her femininity.

Mary was hot against his chilled skin, and he was aware of every inch of her pressed against his. Nick swallowed, renewing a concerted effort not to notice the feel of her body in his arms. How easily he'd lifted her, the slack in her neck as she fell against him. The weight of a woman relaxed in his grasp.

Too soon, they arrived. He hesitated only a moment before nudging the side door open with his shoulder and continuing inside.

"I'm sure I can make it the last few steps."

"I'm your employer, and I'm insisting on a safe delivery." A weak argument, sure, but he wasn't ready to put her down.

Her answer was to settle back, soft in his arms.

Making quick work of the stairs, he brought her up to her room where he hesitated.

"Thanks," she sighed. She slid down his body like a liquid hug, and he let her wash over him. His shirt was thin, and the warmth of her radiated over him. She didn't move; instead, she pushed her shoulders back into a prim posture. Her breasts pushed forward in answer, and he stepped back, instantly regretting it.

He cleared his throat. "Yes, well, here we are."

"Thanks again," she repeated.

This is when you leave, the irritating voice in his head advised.

"I'm going to go check in on the kitchens. Smelled some biscuits. Do you need me to come back and help you down the stairs?" He wasn't sure why it was important to him that she did in fact want his help.

Her attention focused instead on her ankle. A nice swell had set in. "I think it's just a sprain, likely not even that, just a little twist. Really, I'll be fine. But maybe we could do the tour tomorrow?"

He exhaled, unaware he had been holding his breath for her answer. "Right, then, yes. For breakfast… I'll get you in twenty?"

"I thought you were meeting your team?" She was biting her lip and it awakened a hunger in him to do the same. *Right. The men.*

"I'll shoot Roger a text, it's fine."

It was amazing, the facility with which he lied. He wasn't at all sure it would be fine. At the moment, he just didn't care. He wanted to carry her down the stairs. Watch her eat breakfast. Watch as she tried to joke with his niece.

Mary smiled at him, shyly. "Twenty minutes, then."

"Twenty minutes." He nodded and left.

Five

Twenty minutes seemed more than enough time at the onset of his mission. Now? Nick stiffened in front of the door to her office.

Amelia Hartmann ran the hospitality division of Hartmann Enterprises. She was clever, Harvard-educated and his younger sister. She was also the current head of the family coalition poised to break up the Hartmann Homestead into smaller parcels to sever and sell, although, for the life of him, he struggled to understand why.

Hartmann Ranch, while palatial in size, proved time and time again too small to house all the strong personalities in their family tree. But it was big enough for him and Amelia. *Just.* Or so he'd thought.

He looked down at the two coffees he held, second-guessing his instinct to mend fences with his younger sister. She was the more difficult of the twins, but Evie was in California and Nick was unprepared to grovel over video chat. The second step—after winning over Alix—in turning the tides on his sister's current plans was mending fences, a chore he'd hated since adolescence but had learned was a necessary evil once he'd unwillingly assumed the leadership of the Hartmann family.

"I'm working on it, just give me time."

A quick glance down the hallway confirmed he was alone, and despite himself, he pressed an ear to the door. He recognized the voice to be Amelia's. She must be on the phone.

"I know… Yes, but there's nothing we can do about it. It's a waiting game. The girl's here now… Yes, with a tutor."

He grimaced. *Amelia.* She always seemed to find out his secrets.

"Give me some time… Don't worry, we're on track with our deal."

Deal? He waited two minutes, then knocked.

"Come in." This invitation was cool. Her persona reverted to the calculated calm she effused into her everyday activities. The sister from his childhood was but a faint memory as he entered the office to face her now.

"Thought you might want one of Pierre's lattes. We just got the new beans in from Ecuador." He offered the cup in her direction, swallowing his pride at the obvious peace offering it represented.

"I'm already caffeinated, thanks." She dismissed him without eye contact, but he lingered.

Amelia sat behind an oversize notary desk, large horn-framed glasses low on her nose. Lush brown hair fell around her shoulders, and in the early-morning light, it occurred to Nick his sister was young for the responsibility she shouldered.

She shuffled a stack of papers. "Can I help you with something else, Nick? I've got a seven thirty with Sebastian to go over our fall bookings. We've got the Saudi prince in again for a month this summer, complete with his entourage, and there are some issues boarding horses."

"They're bringing their horses?" Nick drew a hand to his chin, scratching it. The nice thing about Amelia's take-charge attitude was he hadn't the faintest idea about the minutia of the hospitality arm of their business. He only saw the overview, the numbers, a net positive. The guest-house, a second palace in its own right, was on the other side of the estate, over an hour's ride away, and that was assuming a steady canter. Amelia split her time between the properties, but whenever an entourage would rent out the entire space she came back to the main house, preferring the privacy. He shifted his weight from foot to foot.

"I'm headed off, then. Alix is settled in." He added it as an afterthought.

"I know. I met her last week. In New York." Hazel eyes flashed at him, and he swallowed back the guilt he felt rising up his neck.

So what if he'd avoided the funeral? He wasn't going to pretend things were okay between him and Austin, much less between him and Katherine. "I'll not apologize for that."

"No one's expecting you to," Amelia fired back, the words hitting him like an insult.

Fine. He'd tried being nice. It didn't matter. With Alix here, he didn't need to make things right with Amelia and Evie. He held the majority vote now and the sale of the ranch was canceled. End of story.

"Nick, the lawyer's on the phone." It was Samantha, his executive assistant.

His office, recently renovated, was the perfect place for him to work. Tucked in the eastern wing of the ranch was a small suite of eighteen offices, where his heads of imports, domestic sales, export strategy, marketing and finance met weekly. The main offices were also on Hartmann land, about thirty minutes' drive from the ranch, and ten minutes from Bozeman, but Nick preferred to work from home as often as responsibilities permitted. With Alix's arrival, he would spend more time here.

"Nick here." He picked up the phone, anxious to hear what the lawyer had planned.

"It's all in order with the visa request," Saul Kellerman promised. In thirty-two years, Nick had never met a lawyer he liked. Saul Kellerman offered no exception to the rule, but he was a necessary evil.

From the corner of his eye, Nick caught Samantha's stare and swallowed. He managed to mumble agreement at the appropriate pauses in his lawyer's diatribe and wrestled himself from the conversation. Samantha shifted, waiting.

"Samantha, I'm glad you stayed."

She took another step toward him, beaming. She was attractive, sure, except for the ever-present element of trying too hard. Maybe it was the heavily lined cat eyes batting a few times too many in his direction in a given minute. They left him with the impression she was trying to remove debris from her eye. Or perhaps it was the red lipstick, a shade too bright for her pale complexion. A flash of red that should have triggered a warning, through the haze of a whiskey-inspired bad decision. It was a mistake he regretted, and one he'd never repeat.

"Of course," she simpered.

He drained his latte, setting the cup back on his desk. He cleared his throat. "I wanted to talk about last week."

Samantha took a few more steps toward him before sinking into a chair. The pleather pencil skirt she sported screeched against the leather of the wingback and he stiffened. She blinked in quick succession as was her habit and parted her lips.

"I am sorry. About the kiss. I know it's not an excuse, but

I'd been drinking." He met her gaze and withheld a smile. He didn't want to leave any room for misinterpretation.

Her expression froze, the only movement a twitching nostril. He could see her jaw jut out, then pull back with a hard swallow. She didn't say anything.

This was awkward, but necessary. With Alix's arrival, he hadn't had a chance to speak with Samantha privately since that night.

"You'd been drinking." She repeated his excuse in a flat cadence.

"As I'm sure you noticed." He met her flat tone with his own.

Samatha stood, and made her way to his minibar, pulling at the recessed fridge. She served herself a sparkling Perrier. "Want one?"

Nick picked up his hat and twirled the rim around his index finger before setting the oiled Stetsen back on his desk. He wasn't convinced his message had landed. "Samantha, I want you to know how much I value our relationship—"

"Me, too." She doubled her pace and stood far too close to his desk moments later with a second Perrier.

"Our *business* relationship." He clenched his teeth as he accepted the water bottle.

"I know you have to say that," she said softly, voice pinched. "I'm your secretary, the optics are terrible."

He cleared his throat, swallowing the memory of the kiss they shared a week ago. As drunk as he'd been, he hadn't let it go further, but he couldn't help but wonder—if it had been Mary, would he have pulled back?

He swallowed the thought; the slipup with Samantha was explainable. He'd been struck with grief, drowning sorrows in a bottle of JD. He'd made a mistake, but he wouldn't repeat it. Not even with the tempting tutor. "It's more than optics," he corrected. "The last thing I want is a relationship right now."

She smiled, winking at him. "Who said anything about a relationship?" And she left the office, brushing past the newcomer at the door to meet with him.

Mary Kelly was there, face drained of color. *How much had she overheard?*

"I was just coming to bring you this, er…a proper lesson plan." Her voice was bubbly but thin.

She entered his office and offered a thin stack of white paper embellished with notes and stickers. New information: Mary had a penchant for gel pens.

"Thanks." He accepted the stack and debated for a moment whether he should explain Samantha. "She's… Things are…" He paused.

"You don't need to explain anything to me." Mary shrugged. Her smile was easier than Samantha's. There was, however, something in her expression that left him with the definite impression he did indeed have explaining to do.

Rose willed herself to maintain her smile, mentally chastising herself for walking past the secretary's empty desk to knock on Nick's office door. To be fair, he'd asked her to drop off her notes after breakfast. She'd nodded, temporarily bolstered by the confidence she'd felt since applying her apricot lipstick. Pursing her lips, she'd stalled upon hearing the voices muted by the door. It wasn't closed, and she heard the succinct apology clear as a bell.

"I'm sorry about the kiss."

Her heart beat so quickly at the admission she felt it in her throat. It was Nick's voice.

She shook, wondering about the identity of the woman.

She wasn't left to wonder long, although the time stretched with punishingly slow seconds. She pressed her thumb against her wrist in an effort to pace the time with her own pulse, but it raced too fast.

Then an overpowering smell of Dior perfume hit her

as Samantha walked past. Rose's eyes smarted at the perfume and the cold-shouldered departure of Nick's right-hand woman.

He sat at his desk, cowboy hat casually on the front corner. Funny the things she noticed now, in her distracted half focus, in her determination not to feel anything about that apology. There were a lot of horses in the room. Lithographs of stallions, a bronze cast of a galloping yearling, a copper bookend of a rearing stallion.

Nick was hot, as usual. Dressed in a white V-neck shirt and fitted blazer, she could see the ridged outlines of his muscled body. It was hard not to begrudge a smidgen of sympathy to the poor woman who'd just left. It was impossible not to want him. But Rose? She swallowed her disappointment. Hotshot CEO and his executive assistant? She willed herself not to roll her eyes.

Instead, she pushed aside the tumult of emotions she hadn't expected and got to the point. "I was hoping we could maybe chart out your family? The next unit in Biology is genetics and I was thinking we could make a family tree, dominant versus nondominant traits." Despite her resolve of just seconds ago, she swallowed back the blush heating her cheeks at the word *dominant. Was he?* His bottom lip widened into a half smile, betraying a dimple. *Definitely.*

"Sure. I'll dig around for some stuff. Maybe we could sort through it tonight?"

"Tonight." She nodded and reached out to pet the back of the bronze yearling on his desk, a quick rub for luck.

"Excellent." He smiled again. His phone rang but he made no move to answer it.

"You can answer."

"Sometimes saying nothing *is* an answer." He nodded, still making no move to pick up the phone.

Swallowing her retort, she turned and left. His muffled voice still ringing in her ears.

"The last thing I want is a relationship right now."

The admission was not surprising, but she was surprised at her reaction. Just as well she left the room without so much as a "see you later." *Sometimes saying nothing is an answer.*

Six

"You know, I forgot how crap year eleven was," Rose said with no filter, and the teenager next to her snorted in surprise.

"Aren't you a tutor? Are you supposed to say things like that?" Alix Hartmann was trying very hard to give the impression she didn't care one whit about school, but Rose read the underlying urge to please that she herself had suppressed at the same age.

"No, I suppose not." She twirled a pencil around between her pointer finger and thumb as she spoke. "I'm meant to pretend Hemingway is clever and superfun to read. Thing is, I never did like these books. Give me a Mills and Boon romance any day. These old classics are boring sometimes, aren't they?" She smiled conspiratorially. "I was thinking, we could give this a quick look?"

Rose had dithered about whether to admit to the SparksNotes she'd brought along, but after five minutes of trying to dissect *The Old Man and the Sea*, she was ready for the crutch.

The two women sat on the oversize sofas in the second sitting room. The sullen teenager brightened at the suggestion they work from the couch instead of the "guest office" her uncle suggested.

"SparksNotes? Couldn't we just look it up online?" Alix raised an eyebrow, and Rose bit back a snort of her own. She was starting to feel old. The fact that her charge's main objection was the *method* in which she suggested taking the easy way out versus the general rule-breaking stung.

"At least this way we're still reading a book. I was thinking a little cross and compare might be a good idea?"

Alix accepted the well-worn copy of the summary. She cracked the cover and frowned at the inscription on the first page. "Rose Kelly?"

Rose inhaled. She should have scratched out her name. Very unstealthy of her.

"Who's Rose Kelly?" Alix followed up, interest piqued by Rose's stalling.

Clearing her throat, Rose set the glass of water she'd been holding down on the table in front of her. "Rose Kelly is my sister." She grimaced at the lie and added in another qualifier for good measure. "*Was* my sister."

"Was your sister?" The teen studied the inscription.

What a tangled web. Rose's head spun. "Yes. She died. About a month ago."

Alix was quiet. She bent her head forward, as though a nearness to the scratched name would give her a better sense of the woman behind the words.

Not likely.

"She was my big sister. My only family, really." Rose wondered why she added the last bit of explanation. It was both hard and easy to talk about her sister. A confounding twist of opposing feelings, but the overriding taste in her mouth was comfort.

"I lost my parents, too. I guess you know." The girl didn't raise her eyes from the page.

Yes, I know. It's why I came. Rose didn't move. She didn't want to scare away the moment. Instead, she just answered, simple yet honest, "I knew. I know."

Alix flipped the pages of the notes like they were a flip book, checking for further inscriptions among the pages like a child on a treasure hunt.

"I figured," the girl added, putting the book down.

"I'm sorry." Rose didn't add any flowery sympathies. She hated hearing them herself and figured Alix would, too.

Alix pulled a sheet of lined paper from an open binder and started sketching a flower in the absent way a person doodles to pass time. She outlined the twisting vine of a climbing clematis, shading in a leaf. Rose sat beside her, allowing the gift of a few minutes of silence.

"Aren't you going to ask me about it, then? How I feel?" Alix's voice was small, and Rose couldn't tell whether she hoped for or against that outcome.

Rose picked up the hardcover copy of *The Old Man and the Sea*. "Do you know what it's about? This book?"

Alix didn't look up from her clematis, just shook her head.

"It's the struggle between an old man and a fish. He spends eighty-four days trying to catch the fish."

"Does he get it?"

"Did you ever think, sometimes getting what you want is the worst punishment of all?" Rose whispered the thought, as much to herself as her adolescent charge. That was the crux of her problem. She couldn't get Nick, no matter how much she wanted him. Being with Nick meant risking Alix. It meant risking the kids in India, and her chance to make her sister's memory mean something.

Getting him would be the worst punishment of all, an exquisite torture worthy of its own SparksNotes.

Alix put her pen down. Her eyebrows knit together as she scratched her head. Then the girl frowned.

"Well, I guess it's good I don't want anything, then." She recommenced her sketching.

"Sure. That's one way to look at it." Rose nodded.

Alix frowned, looking at the summary again. "Isn't this cheating?"

"Not cheating." Rose reached for a thick manila folder, filled with hundreds of printouts, guidelines and teacher's tips. "It doesn't say anything in here about not using teacher's aids." Rose waved the thick file folder in Alix's direction, a gesture that provoked a quick wave of protest.

"I'll take your word for it."

"Right, so what I was thinking is we give the first three chapter summaries a quick little review, then we chat about it over a London Fog?"

"London Fog?" Against her better instincts, the girl was curious. *Excellent.*

"This drink is a game changer, trust me." Rose thrust the copy of *The Old Man and the Sea* back into Alix's hand. "I've already read it, clearly, so brush up, then read the SparksNotes while I whip us up a treat." She reached for the cane Nick offered her after breakfast, and hobbled her way to the kitchen, leaving a happy-ish teenager in her wake.

She didn't hear him. As the kettle hummed, she focused on the internet iteration of SparksNotes. The student becomes the teacher indeed. She *felt* his presence before she saw any sign of him. He entered the kitchen quietly and stood behind her.

"SparksNotes?" His voice was low and the deep rumble of a laugh spurred one of her own to match.

Blushing, she slammed the phone to her side and stammered, “No, well, yes, I suppose, I just…”

Nick waved her excuses away as he took another step toward her. “It’s fine. That old faithful basically got me through high school, why should it be any different for the teachers? I guess keeping abreast of the cheating aids helps you to spot prepackaged answers from students?”

She swore there was a twinkle in his eye that hadn’t been there a moment earlier. “Yes, precisely. I read through them to better spot plagiarism.” She blushed, fairly sure she would struggle to spell plagiarism let alone spot it in someone’s work.

The shrieking kettle allowed her a moment’s reprieve from the embarrassment, and she offered, “London Fog?”

Nick was already at the coffee machine, punching buttons and sliding an old mug with cow-horn handles under the dripping espresso machine. “I prefer coffee, keeps the hair on my chest.”

She pivoted on her spot, not wanting her thoughts to be easily readable on her face. If the coffee was responsible for the work of wonder that was this man’s chest, she would prepare him coffee until the end of days. Or until the end of term, whatever.

“How’s it going?” he asked.

“I’m feeling much better. The cane has been a great help.” Focusing all her charm into a smile, she beamed at him.

“Good to hear.” Coffee in hand, he leaned into the doorframe and watched her froth milk with a whisk on the stove.

“Looks pretty labor intensive, this… ‘London Fog,’ was it?” He raised an eyebrow at her efforts to aerate the milk. She turned her attention back to the task at hand, but he was not to be deterred. “Here, let me help with that.” He stepped toward her and covered the hand on the whisk with his. She could feel him behind her.

Close. If she leaned back a hair, she'd be pressed into his chest. Pressed against his hips… Her mouth watered at the thought and she swallowed. Focus on the latte. *Focus on the girl.* Twenty-seven impoverished kids. Yes, eye surgery was the least sexy thing she could think of. Perfect.

"You've got to whisk in tiny circles," she breathed. He nodded, chin brushing against her hair.

"It's taking quite a long time."

It felt good. Standing trapped between him and the stove. Too good. She wriggled away and huffed, "Didn't your mother ever tell you, all good things are worth working for?"

Mary had said it to her often enough; she just hadn't paid any heed to the advice. Until now.

Nick chuckled. "You might have a point there."

Satisfied the milk was sufficiently frothed, she poured the contents of the now screaming kettle into a waiting teapot, eyeing the clock on the oven to track the steep time. Nick stood still, taking in the methodical process. "You take your tea seriously."

She flushed. "I just thought, taking some time to make a nice drink, show I care. I can't teach the girl anything if she doesn't like me."

"Can I help with that?"

"Maybe. I was thinking, your offer to see the ranch would be nice. We could make a day of it?" The three-minute mark on the oven passed and she poured the tea into the bottom third of the mug, topping the cup with maple syrup, steamed milk and foam. Trouble was, she couldn't manage both mugs and her cane, a conundrum Nick assessed rapidly.

"I'll take these for you." He leaned toward her to relieve her of the cups.

Rose sported a smile of her own when she crossed into the living room. Nick had pulled Alix's laptop onto his knees and was squinting into the computer screen. "A book about fishing? Maybe school isn't so bad." She overheard his commentary on the book choice and couldn't bite back the widening of her grin.

Nick quizzed Alix on the first few chapters, coaxing out questions, and comparing the old man to different rappers he felt were outdated in their own way. His grip on pop culture was impressive. He rattled off the names of several different artists, eventually luring a reluctant smile from the teen.

"You're making me feel old," Rose said, the statement announcing her arrival. "Even though I'm heaps younger than your uncle," she added.

"Heaps younger?" Nick tried out a mocking accent.

"You don't sound British. I hope you can do better than that." She laughed, sinking onto the couch beside him. Her leg pressed against his. She didn't look over at him, but pressed her eyes shut a moment and let herself feel the strength in the limb next to her. It was as close as she was going to allow herself to get to the cowboy, so she wanted to commit the feeling to memory. If this was all she'd ever get of Nick, it might be enough. It had to be. It felt so good to be needed, but even better to belong.

"Not one bit?" He tried again, mouth pursed before his lips broke into a smile. Rose was pleased to see the mirth spread to Alix. She mirrored the teen's smile, then felt her face freeze as she realized she hadn't issued a genuine smile, hadn't felt so close to anyone, since Mary had passed.

Not a bad day, all things considered.

Seven

The horse was a lot bigger than she'd thought it would be, and not as docile as she'd assumed from the movies. Rose took a cautious step backward, bumping into Alix.

"You ever been on one of these?" she asked her charge.

Alix, wide-eyed, shook her head. The bangs of her brown hair fell into her eyes.

Nick walked toward them, chatting with a wrangler. "Thanks for saddling Betsy," he yelled over his shoulder, and the wrangler dipped his hat and lifted his chin before walking away.

"Don't you have a…*shorter* horse?" Rose sputtered.

"Shorter?" Nick spun and looked at her. "You mean like a pony?"

Rose reached a tentative hand toward the muscled animal, patting the gleaming coat, hot and hard under her palm.

"Don't worry, Mary, this horse wouldn't hurt a fly,"

Nick assured her as he checked over the straps and tightened the harness.

"I'm not sure this is a good idea," Alix spoke up. Her eyes were glued to her feet.

Nick grunted. "Yep, it is. Thing is, you've been all over New York State, but never Montana, much less Hartmann Estates. You need to see our land. Feel our roots. Plus, I heard about a botany chapter you and Ms. Kelly are gonna review?" He shifted his gaze from his niece to her tutor.

Alix cleared her throat. "I don't think I can..."

"Us girls can do anything." Rose walked toward Alix, crossing behind Betsy.

"Careful." Nick moved like lightning, pulling her away from the rear legs of the horse and hard against him. Seconds later, the horse kicked up, pillows of dust forming clouds where they had been standing. Betsy, a congenial horse by nature, was still a horse.

"You *never* walk behind a horse, especially one you don't know." He spoke the reprimand into her hair and pulled her close enough for her to feel the movement of his lips against the back of her head.

He smelled like pine. Like woods. Sharp and sweet, wild and pure. For a moment, she pressed her eyes shut, and leaned back into his chest. He didn't smell like a frat boy, or worse, a Paternoster Square banker, drunk on petty day-traded success. Nick didn't seem to need or want any validating, but as she stood with her eyes pressed closed, she couldn't help but wonder how it might have been had he wandered into her bar once upon a Wednesday. He tightened his grip on her, the quick burst of pressure bringing her to the present, before releasing her in an abrupt jolt.

"Thanks." She spun around the moment she was free of his grip. *Why did she wish he'd held her a bit longer? A bit tighter?*

"Nope. I'm not getting on that thing." Alix turned and was making her way back to the barn.

"Alix," Rose called after her, "let's give it a try, shall we?"

Alix spun. "I've never been on a horse. Like, never." Her voice was thin and quiet, and a tentative gaze looked up from under her shaggy bangs.

"Why don't you come give the girls some treats." Nick's voice carried as he lifted the flap of his saddle-bag, revealing a half dozen apples.

The bribery worked and within thirty minutes both women were on their respective saddles. The horses followed Nick, sauntering down a well-worn path toward the edge of the woods. The first hour of the ride was mostly silent, the horses falling into single file, and the distance proving an apt deterrent to chatting.

Perhaps Alix's fear had given way to awe at the raw beauty of the landscape. Rose focused intensely on the scenery to avoid reliving the hot pressure of Nick's hands on her, holding her close. Landscape. She was going to appreciate the landscape.

Soon, the silence gave way to a quiet background of forest noise. It was easy to lose time in the forest and her stomach reminded her lunch was approaching with a growl she feared could scare the horse.

Nick pulled up, turning his horse with practiced ease. He jumped off, and put a hand in front of Betsy, halting her with a mere hand sign. Alix's horse followed suit, and the two women sat stiffly in the saddle.

"I'm getting hungry. Shall we make camp here? I brought lunch."

He approached Betsy as he spoke. Rose stared, fascinated by the strong hand running down the neck of the horse, who had turned her head for the caress. The hand stopped on Rose's saddle, and he looked up at her and smiled from under his cowboy hat.

"M'lady?" he mocked, in another faux accent.

She accepted his hand, the warm grip all too familiar, and, somewhat ungracefully, whipped her leg over the saddle. Unpracticed as she was at disembarking, she hurled forward only to find herself for a second time since breakfast clutched against the cowboy's expansive chest. All too familiar indeed. Precisely the kind of familiar that would have her staring for hours at her ceiling again. Heat flooded to her face at the thought.

Nick, braced for the launch, balanced in a counterstep to her momentum and pushed her to an upright posture on her own two feet.

"Mademoiselle Alix." Nick then presented himself with a small bow in front of his niece, keeping his mock accent in play.

Alix made no pretense at grace and held both arms out.

The sun was hot against the backs of their necks, birch trees offering little shade but a beautiful silver shimmer to the leafed canopy. Nick's vest was tossed aside, and his plaid shirt opened a few buttons at the yoke, revealing a white undershirt, still crisp and clean.

Focus. On Alix. And the twenty-seven kids she could save.

With that renewed reminder, lunch was an easy repartee. Having prepped a few points on botany, she interjected a few tidbits and was quickly rewarded with a raised eyebrow and smile from Nick, and unwilling curiosity from Alix. Lunch, a mess of hearty sandwiches French style, was easy.

The day passed as they left the birch forest to explore a new creek bed and then a hidden meadow, and twice more, Nick helped the women dismount and explore different surroundings. Was it just her, or had he held her a second longer each time?

The evening fell fast, the air heavy and damp. The horses were on autopilot. Betsy, while certainly amiable, was not bred for speed. She followed Nick and soon Rose saw the ranch. A wrangler was waiting, and after Nick helped her dismount a final time, the wrangler took the leads from all three horses and walked them away without so much as a nod to the group.

"That was all right." Alix kicked at the ground. Rose could see the quick flash of teeth as the girl swallowed her smile.

"Good. Glad you liked it." Nick's answer was warm, and he leaned against the white fence, gleaming with fresh paint in the pink hue of the setting sun.

Alix walked away, rushing toward the house, kicking at any rock large enough to find purchase against her shoe.

Rose smiled. Today had been a good day.

"Did you want to have a drink after dinner?" His question came out of nowhere.

"With you?" she clarified.

"With me." He pressed against the fence and propelled his weight forward, turning to face her. "I thought we could talk about how you girls are settling in."

"As long as you're not going to grill me about my qualifications?" She smiled. *Best defense is a good offense.*

Nick smiled, too, then whistled and walked toward the house, leaving Rose to scramble behind him, two paces making up each of his long strides. *A good offense might be exactly what she needed.*

He didn't know what had provoked him to issue the invitation. He'd regretted his kiss with Samantha, finding little comfort in his offered excuse of the drunken haze, yet here he was, proposing an invitation to blur the lines of yet another working relationship, this time with not a drop of whiskey to be held responsible. Nick swallowed, but couldn't find even an ounce of regret at having asked her, propriety be damned.

Mary had begged for a few minutes to "wash off

the dust," and had taken dinner in her room, but when she resurfaced for the promised drinks, pacing in front of the door to the sitting room, she looked like a new woman. Her hair fell softly on her shoulders, a gold halo of curls, and her eyes sparkled under a modest application of makeup. Barely there, but there nonetheless. *So she cared to look nice.* He couldn't decide if he should embrace the warmth that it made him feel, or push it away.

With his left hand, he held forward her Scotch, amber and sparkling in the firelight.

"Thanks," she answered as her fingers brushed against his in the transfer. The brief touch sent a shock through his system, just as it had every time he'd touched her all day. She was dangerous, because in this moment, he wanted her more than he wanted to save the ranch. Which was a lot.

She circled the room like a cat, elegant but wary, until she sat on the love seat, her cream shirt a sharp contrast to the darkness of her jeans.

She took a sip of her drink. "You work in here?"

He took a deep drag of Scotch before confirming with a succinct, "Yep."

"With your…secretary." She chewed on the last word as though it tasted sour, pulling her lips tight.

"We have an office in town, but a few key people work here at the house with me." The fire lit the room in a warm glow, and he walked over to the love seat, sinking beside her. The down filling of the couch sank under his weight, and their bodies slipped closer together. It was a subtle difference, but it did not pass unnoticed.

"You've been working from home a lot these days," she observed, swishing her drink and watching the Scotch swirl in centrifugal motion.

"Alix has been expelled from three schools. I figure it's best I'm around. As much as I can be, anyway." He looked up at her, meeting her gaze for the first time that evening. “It has occurred to me that I don’t know much about you?”

“Who’s asking? Nick? Or hotshot CEO of this ranch?” She tilted her head back and let out a short laugh.

“Does it matter?”

“I guess it matters or I wouldn’t have asked.” She straightened and drained her glass.

“Careful, the lady bites.” Nick reached for the bottle of Scotch, tilting it toward her in invitation.

She inclined her glass in his direction. “Careful or you won’t find out.”

Did he want to find out? One look at her plump lower lip and he swallowed. Yep. Despite the promise of a heap of trouble. Despite knowing it was a bad idea. He wanted to find out.

After filling her glass, he topped off his own. “So if I were to ask, then, what would I discover?”

She took another sip, then looked at him squarely. “I’m a good listener.” The pronouncement was laced with suggestion.

“Is that so?”

“It is.” She nodded.

“Heard anything interesting lately?” He focused on keeping his face impassive, in an effort to appear disinterested.

She shrugged. “I heard about the kiss.”

He choked on his Scotch. “Damn it.” He stood, figuring it might be easier to focus without her thigh pressing into his on the damned couch.

Mary looked at him, eyes wide. The knowing tone was gone, and she once again seemed younger. He wasn’t sure why it was important to him to correct her misconception. Maybe because of her role in Alix’s life now? Because he didn’t want to fall into the same profile his father had shouldered, womanizer and liar? He took another sip of Scotch before deciding the "why" didn't matter much. At least, not right now. He sat back down beside her.

"Yeah. We kissed. Once." To his own ears, his voice sounded hollow. Beside him, Mary leaned back into the pillows of the couch.

"Once," she repeated, rolling the word around in her mouth.

"Ignited by grief. Fueled by alcohol. It never went further and it won't ever go further. I'll admit it was never about her. I don't feel that way about Samantha. It was a mistake."

"A mistake," she repeated again. She leaned away from him. The strip of leg that had been pressed against his only moments earlier was now primly pressed to her other leg. Away from him.

He wished he could read her mind. Or know his own. He cleared his throat. "To be honest, when you're sad—"

"A mistake might be enough." She set her glass down on the side table, artfully landing it in the center of a cork coaster, and clasped her hands in her lap. "I know what you mean." Her legs angled back toward his.

"Together is better than alone." He spoke the words softly, for his own benefit.

"Until it's not." She nodded, then shifted her posture to mirror his, her leg once more an unwitting distraction.

He finished his Scotch and stood again. It felt as though she was looking through him. Another glass of Scotch might lead to more, and he needed to keep all his faculties intact. He wanted her enough to recognize the danger. "I better call it a night." He clenched his jaw and tilted an imaginary hat in her direction.

She stayed seated, smiling at him. "Thanks for the drink, and the company."

"Yep." He turned and left. The walk to his bedroom

was endless. Their words echoed through his head. *A mistake might be enough. Together is better than alone.*

In five minutes, she'd sliced through his bravado, and he wasn't sure he liked the naked vulnerability she'd uncovered.

Eight

"You think you're pretty smart, don't ya, Nick?"

The woman on the other end of the phone was angry, her voice abrupt and oddly high-pitched. Nick didn't need the caller ID to identify her. He'd known Katherine's sister as long as he'd known Katherine.

"Franny, nice to hear from you." He eyed the clock and waved away his assistant. Samantha rolled her eyes and gesticulated wildly toward her calendar, but then left, shutting the door behind her.

"Don't you *nice to hear from you* me," Franny threatened, her voice carrying a faint metallic quality as he shifted her to speaker. He struggled to find focus this morning, his head clouded with thoughts of Mary. *A mistake might be enough.* With her, it might be a mistake, but if he could lose himself in her, he was willing to bet it would be transcendent. Question was, would he bet the ranch to find out?

"I'm sorry I haven't called," he started. At least that much was true. He owed Franny his sympathies.

"Obviously, you wouldn't call after what you've done."

"What's this I've done?"

Franny, expounding on her earlier accusations, continued, "If you think you're going to get away with this, you won't. I've got a lawyer."

"Is this about the will?" He jabbed at the phone and took her off speaker, pulling the phone to his ear.

"The will? You mean the unwitnessed document they both *allegedly* signed? Not likely I'm upset about that now, is it?"

"Sounds like an easy enough matter to clear up. Let's not get too upset about it now." Congeniality was not his strong suit, but his mother had instilled in him the ideology that if it was possible to avoid court, you should.

"If you think I'm going to stand by, while my flesh and blood, my own niece, mind you, is used for your advancement—"

"Listen, Franny, just say what you want to say. I don't have time for this."

"What I'm saying? I want custody of *my niece*. You're a bachelor, no better than your father. The courts are more likely to side with a woman than a workaholic control freak of a man."

"Easy there, Franny. I have everything needed to care for Alix, and there's no need for name-calling."

"Everything? Before or after you take care of your precious ranch?"

"I hardly think employment is a barrier to fatherhood."

"*Employment?* Manic obsession with governing your empire more like it."

"Sure, Franny."

"Let's see what the court thinks," she shrieked before disconnecting.

He put the phone back in its cradle and brought both

hands to his temples. Pressing a knuckle into the space on his cheek beside his ear, he rubbed in circles to ease the muscle swollen from the clenched jaw he'd sported for the past two weeks. She wanted to petition for custody? Not good. Desperate people made for dangerous opponents.

Between getting to know Alix, wrestling with his desire for Mary and now this…

He needed a break. A boys' night.

Picking up the phone, he dialed the only number he knew by heart, relieved when it was answered on the second ring. "Buddy, can I interest you in a beer?"

"Always," was Ben's quick answer.

"Want to head over? Crack a cold one?" Nick eyed the setting sun, the sky violent pinks and reds. It was late enough to justify drinking, and today felt like a string of Mondays all boiled into one.

His friend didn't answer. "If you're nodding through the phone, I can't hear you…" Nick called out his best friend's habit with a smirk.

"Yeah, why not. I'll come over—can't wait to meet this British tutor. So what's the verdict, then? Is she hot?"

Is she hot? Hot didn't even begin to cover it. "She's out of bounds, buddy, don't even think about it."

"Excellent, so she *is* hot."

His friend disconnected, and for a moment, Nick felt a wave of jealousy. It was unfamiliar. He wasn't the jealous type. *Or was he?* If Ben so much as held Mary's hand a moment too long, he would not be happy about it.

"What's got you peeling labels today?" Ben, his affable self, gestured toward the two empty beer bottles, both naked of their branding. They'd escaped to the gin deck outside, a flagstone patio Nick put in himself after his mother moved out. He'd worried initially about how he'd transform his childhood home into an adult bachelor pad. There were entire wings of the home he never entered, a ballroom for one, that did nothing but collect dust. Step one in his bachelor update? Make an area to drink with the boys. Well, with Ben.

The contractors had finished a few months ago, and a rough granite patio spread to the edge of the infinity pool. An oversize barbecue was far enough from the firepit the chef could prepare dinner, now treating them to the tantalizing aromas of dry ribs, while affording some privacy for their conversations. He grinned. Yes, the patio was a huge *Nick* upgrade.

"Francesca called."

Ben let out a low whistle. "You coulda led with that."

Nick wrinkled his nose in distaste. "I guess burying the lead is more my flavor. Didn't want to sour your impression of our newest houseguest." He nodded toward Mary, who'd turned on like a light when Ben arrived, shining and bright. Or had she lit up upon seeing *him*?

Mary was quick to accept the invitation, agreeing to join them with a smile. She was nursing her own beer in an outfit of a relaxed plaid shirt tied in a knot above the top of her jeans. After one look at the bombshell, Ben insisted she join them. Mary hesitated only a moment. When Nick smiled back at her, she nodded. *She was a barmaid before. A professional flirt. The glances mean nothing. This woman is your employee, and more importantly, Alix's tutor.* She was the one person in Alix's life to invest consistent time in the kid, and he was not going to undermine that relationship. He couldn't.

"Who's Francesca?" He felt the low vibration of her accented speech in his gut. Or was it somewhere lower than his gut?

Heat pulsed between them, a static awareness that crackled in the air. Her voice, low and warm, cut across the night air like a hot knife through butter. One of the things he loved about Hartmann Homestead was the quiet in the early evenings, and the space it now left for her. No suffering through perpetual traffic and onerous city sounds, here they had a backdrop of babbling brooks and singing birds. Now, the quiet served only to amplify his desire.

"His prom date's sister," Ben answered.

"My late sister-in-law's sister," Nick corrected. He watched her face carefully for a reaction, but her expression was a mask hiding her reaction.

"*Your* prom date married your…brother?" she clarified. Ben started a fire in their firepit, and the flames warmed her features. She looked stunning in her relaxed interpretation of Western casual.

"The way we tell it, his brother impregnated his high school sweetheart," Ben joked in a vain attempt to lighten the mood. Nick glowered at him.

"That's a lot to unpack," she answered quietly.

"That's how Alix came to be," Nick added. "Also how I ended up the uncle to a sixteen-year-old. Everyone was young then. Too young to make good choices, I guess."

It was nice she knew about the history between him and Alix's parents. True, the gory details were still his alone, but at least she knew the picture-perfect ranch wasn't quite so picture-perfect. Maybe she'd guessed it from his family's absence.

"What did Francesca want, then?" Mary asked.

"Alix." He recognized he was back to his one-word answers. A regression, sure, but given the circumstances, he was doing pretty darn well.

"Can she do that?" Ben cut in.

"No." He answered too fast. "I'm not sure. I don't think so?" His attention was focused on Mary. She blanched at the news.

"What did she say exactly?" Ben pressed.

"I don't know…she was going on about how I wouldn't get away with it." Nick cleared his throat and moved his chair back under the guise of getting away from the smoke. Really, it was to be closer to Mary. He'd always liked playing with fire.

"I doubt it will be that easy," Ben mused.

Nick nodded. "Not much I can do about it tonight, anyway."

"I'm starting to get hungry," Mary quipped.

It was a blatant effort to change the subject, and Nick was grateful for it. He grinned at her. "Me, too." He was hungry for more than dinner.

The sound of metal dragging on granite caused him to jerk his head up. She was dragging her chair nearer. Closing the last few inches, she parked her seat beside him. She feigned a cough, then smiled. "You look nice tonight."

Ben whistled. Pierre, the resident chef, interrupted the opportunity for further teasing. "How would Monsieur like his ribs?"

"Dry and spicy," Nick answered, breaking eye contact with the tutor as he offered instructions to the chef.

"Madame?"

She blushed with an answer she seemed to choke on. "Wet, please."

Suddenly his own mouth was dry. "You heard the lady." He dismissed the chef. "She likes hers wet."

The barbecue area was several feet away; however, the scent of glorious ribs soon assailed their senses, offering a mouthwatering backdrop to Ben's narration. Bless him for having the presence of mind to supply a stream of small talk. He was a good friend, because at the moment, all Nick could hear was *"wet, please"* on loop. At least Francesca and Alix were now officially the last thing on his mind.

The ribs were excellent. Better than excellent. He was famished, and the ribs, while filling, did little to quell the true source of his hunger. She ate primly, wiping her fingers between each rib, hesitating before licking the bones, then rapidly licking her fingers as she watched Ben do the same.

He felt each lick in his gut, sharp and torturous. "Pass the butter," he asked, voice hoarse. His fingers brushed against hers as she obliged, and his guts twisted again.

"This is sinful," she stated. He loved the way she spoke, the way she held on to a word a moment too long. He reckoned she could make any word sound *sinful*.

"Best ribs—your cook is awesome," Ben agreed, oblivious to the tension. Hopefully, it wasn't solely in his head.

"Yep," was all Nick could muster.

Ben rose to leave, professing an inability to eat one more morsel.

"Are you sure? They haven't brought out dessert," Nick asked feebly, not wanting to deter his buddy's departure.

"Looks like you'll be on your own to enjoy dessert tonight," Ben answered in a hushed tone, and nodded toward Mary, who had risen from the table to pace the perimeter of the pool.

"Benjamin," Nick hissed. "She's an employee."

"Right. I'm talking about what happens off the clock, buddy. You like her."

For lack of a better answer, Nick shoved his friend, hard.

Ben stumbled from the momentum and laughed. "Easy, tiger, I wasn't saying anything you hadn't already thought. I'd wager my front teeth on it."

Nick grinned. "Keep your teeth. I'm not going there. Not with the tutor."

His friend reached for his hat and grabbed his jacket. "In all seriousness, maybe you should. She's a nice girl. A stunner. And let's face it, she only had eyes for you tonight." Ben let out the few bars of a jovial whistle as he sauntered off.

Nick turned and made his way back to the pool. Just to talk. He stopped a few feet from her back, and watched the glimmer of the underlit pool dance on her blue jeans, highlighting a serious asset.

He couldn't. Not with her.

He should leave with Ben, find a bar. Find another woman. Because Mary? If he lost her, he'd lose Alix. And the ranch. Everything he'd ever wanted.

"Your friend is nice." She spoke with her back still to him. All the better to admire her, he supposed.

"Yep, he's a riot," Nick agreed. He closed the distance between them with a few steps, and stood at her side, hands trailing inches from hers. *He could look, he just couldn't touch.*

"Are you worried? About this aunt?"

He paused for a moment in consideration. "Fran? No. Regardless of her argument, and I'm not sure she even has one, I have a better legal team. Well, I will have." It was the benefit of being a Hartmann, and the assets at his disposal as CEO of Hartmann Homestead were prolific.

"That's terrific." She paced forward a few feet, then paused, cocking her head in inquiry. "Did you want to go for a swim?"

He was surprised by the offer. "That's quite the jump—I'd love to get inside your head." Then bit back the rest of his sentence. Truth was, he'd love to get inside a lot more than her head. There was a duality about her. A guarded vulnerability married with a brash confidence he found enigmatic and alluring.

"I meant the water. It's enchanting." She faced him, eyes wide and inviting.

"I'm enchanted all right. Why not?" He smiled. "It's been ages since I've been in the pool."

She didn't answer, but kept looking at him in the same unnerving way she had during dinner. She reached for the collar of her shirt and began unbuttoning. "I thought maybe we'd end up in the pool, and wore my swimsuit just in case."

"Uh, great," he answered, throat dry as he watched her fingers nimbly unbutton the rest of her shirt, moving to the waistband of her jeans before she shrugged the shirt off.

She wiggled out of her jeans as he watched. "You wearing a suit under all that?" she asked.

He swallowed again in an effort to shake his stunned feeling. It was hardly the first time he'd seen a woman in a bikini. "No, just give me a minute. I keep a suit in the cabin." He nodded toward the cabana a few feet away from the patio. He was stuck between wanting to move as quickly as possible and not wanting to miss even a moment of her undressing.

When he returned, she was already in the pool. Opting against a cannonball, he dived into the deep end, both figuratively and literally, surfacing a few feet from the bathing beauty.

"So, Oxford, how are you liking Montana?" The question was trite, sure, but in the close quarters of the pool, he wasn't ready to voice what was really on his mind.

"It's nice to get away." She dipped her head underwater and turned a clean spin, coming up for air closer to him.

"Anything in particular? To get away from?"

Her eyes were the same color as the water, a clear blue, bright as a night sky.

"Yes. For me there is, anyway." She disappeared back underwater, an elusive mermaid. So she was fleeing something. Someone, maybe. His gut tightened as a flash of white leg swam by, circling him underwater, the best kind of shark. He dipped under and gave chase, grabbing at an ankle.

"Gotcha, mermaid." He laughed as she surfaced. But she wasn't laughing.

"My sister died. Just a month ago. I don't talk about it. Not sure why I'm talking about it now." She was quiet, but her stream of consciousness hit him hard. Her sister. His brother. The unfairness of it all.

He didn't know what to say, so he took a step toward her, then in quick decision, another, closing the gap between them and pulling her against him in a hug. To be fair, it felt like he didn't have a choice. His body decided for him.

She was stiff but melted into him the moment she seemed to realize the hug was given without expectation.

He wasn't sure who pulled away, but when he looked down, her wide eyes stared back at him. "Thanks," she offered.

"I didn't know. About your sister. I'm real sorry."

The pool was underlit, with recessed pot lights offering an otherworldly glow.

"I'm okay. Nothing being sad will fix. I suppose it's normal not to be feeling aces at the moment." She sniffed and lowered her shoulders into the water.

"Sure. I get it." He nodded, and followed suit as she sank farther into the deep end of the pool. "So what made you want to be a tutor?"

She stilled, then spun to face him. "I basically raised my sister. You know, helped her through school, helped with all the details of her life. Rose, uh, she was a good kid." Her voice broke at the mention of her sister's name, and he fought the urge to pull her into another hug. Her voice was low, and detached, as though she were narrating someone else's life story, but it was a story he desperately wanted to hear. His stillness prompted her to continue.

"Well, Rose wasn't really a good kid, I guess. I mean, I always thought so, but boy was she often in trouble. Hanging with a fast crowd—that's how they put it in the movies, isn't it? Drinking a fair bit, not just on weekends." She was talking in a full stream now, and he hung on her every word.

“Bit of a wild child, then?” He took a few strokes back, and kicked himself into a hanging float.

“Right. She *was*.” Mary sank below the surface, and popped back up a moment later, curls now slick against her head.

It was a clear end to the conversation. Fair enough.

“Montana sure is different,” she added moments later.

“Different how?” he wondered aloud.

“It’s just so big. Everything here is huge.” She bit back a smile and gestured to him, surprising him with her boldness. He laughed, enjoying the sudden levity between them.

“Guilty as charged,” he said.

“I’m really pleased to be here. Working with Alix.” The water was cool, and Nick felt a chill set in, but not even a small part of him was ready to get out of the pool.

“Have you done any other one-on-one?” he asked, truly curious.

“No. Maybe it’s why I left. I didn’t feel like I had a real purpose.” She looked away.

Well, that was deep. He swam back to the shallow end in a few quick strokes, and let his legs touch bottom.

“Must be nice. Feeling like you have a choice,” he started, unsure where the sentiment had come from.

“What do you mean?”

“I’ve just always known…this ranch, this place? I would run it.”

She didn’t answer straightaway, just deepened her regard, tilting her head forward in marked interest. Finally, she spoke. “Quite the privilege, wouldn’t you say?”

“I’m not surprised that’s how you’d see it, because, yeah, it is. But isn’t it worse to get everything you’ve always wanted, only to risk losing it?” Somewhere the conversation had pivoted, and here he was, spilling his guts to the beautiful Brit in the impossibly small swimsuit.

The ranch was more than a birthright. It was the thing

that made him a Hartmann. His dad had made him promise. Maybe he couldn't voice why that promise was important to him. Why he cared. His brothers shrugged off the responsibility so easily, but Nick was shackled by it. His legacy couldn't be losing the thing that had made him. No. He couldn't fail at this. Not even to be with her, the mermaid incarnate.

She smiled her odd half smile and splashed some water at him again. "I don't think you even know all you want, cowboy." She bit her lip, drawing his attention instantly to the one thing he'd wanted since meeting her at the airport. He followed her in a second lap of the pool, catching up to her in the deep end.

"So your brother married your prom date?" She widened her eyes as she issued her question and changed the subject.

"It was a long time ago." He cleared his throat.

"Yes, you're practically ancient, aren't you?" She swatted another bit of water in his direction, which he managed to sidestep.

"Careful, Oxford." He smiled, unable to help himself. It felt good to smile, even more so when faced with the crushing sadness he'd been shouldering for the past three weeks.

"Can you not call me that?" She paused. "My sister went to Oxford. And I don't want to think about her right now." She turned away, and her cold shoulder rocked him. He took a step toward her, and with a hand on her shoulder, spun her around.

Mary's eyes shone and in them he saw a sadness he mirrored. A sadness that broke down his walls and made him feel as raw as she looked. Since they'd met, she'd been a dichotomy of strength and vulnerability, the latter overpowering him now. For a moment, the opportunity to be strong enough for both of them was inebriating, and he reached for her, allowing his hand to rest on her shoulder, her skin hot despite the tepid water. In a flash, the weight of his legacy, the responsibility of his lineage, faded with the prospect of comforting her. At the thought of being more, even just for one night.

Her bottom lip jutted forward and quivered, and she reached for him, putting a hand flat on his chest. He wondered if she could feel his heart thudding against her palm. She took a step closer, the mini wave of water hitting his waist with the movement. It provoked a response that he was unprepared for. The lapping water serving only to whet his desire.

And so he comforted her with a kiss so thorough it rocked him.

Everything he wanted to say he said with the kiss. *I'm sorry. I want you. I'm hurting. Let's forget this.* Her body, hot against his, was a welcome heat to balance the chill of the pool. It was soft and deliciously curved. The perfect answer to his desperate questions.

His tongue parried with hers and she opened to him with an earnestness that rocked him. A soft mew of submission and he lifted her legs around his, his arousal pressed plainly against her. She wrapped her legs around him, the thin bathing suit a poor barrier, and bit gently at his lip.

"I'm sorry," he started.

"Let's not be sorry, not now." Gone was the sorrow; instead, she looked at him with a burning fire that matched his own.

He groaned, hot in need of her. Maybe, for once, it was okay. To need someone as much as they needed you? And he needed her now, more than he could ever remember needing anything in his entire life.

And then he remembered.

It wasn't right.

"Mary, I'm sorry. I shouldn't have." He pulled away,

voice ragged, hating himself for the effort it took to separate from her.

"You're right." Her nose scrunched up. "I don't know what came over me. I'm terribly sorry. I shouldn't have, you must think me—"

She was out of the pool before he could stop her, but he called after her, anyway.

"Mary." The cry went unanswered, as did his need for her.

Nine

"I mucked it up. Badly." Rose sat on the rock, savoring the wet damp of early-morning dew on stone. "He'll think I was pissed—drunk—liquid courage or something of the sort. Damn..." The curse escaped as a sigh. The phone was cool against her cheek, and for a moment it was easy to imagine her sister listening to her message later, and calling her back with sage advice.

Something like, *Just pluck up, Rose. New day, new opportunity to embarrass yourself, let's not waste it, aye? Try and keep your wits, love. Take the chance to be your best self, and act accordingly, blah blah*. Mary always encouraged her to try again. Embrace the day. Gone were the days of rash decisions and living without consequence, she was here to turn a new leaf. Dream a new dream. Mary's dream.

"Worst tutor ever. Two weeks and I'm next to naked in a pool with my employer—" Just like that, the machine cut her off. One message a day. That was what she was allowed. Five minutes to lose it.

She stood and brushed her jeans. Back to the task at hand: tutoring Alix, finding a way to help the lost teenager find a center, finding a way for Rose to make everything up to her sister. She was finishing this contract. Sponsoring those blind kids… She had to succeed. This job was bigger than her. Bigger than how much she wanted the cowboy. It might not *feel* that way but it had to *be* that way.

Rose fought the temptation to sprint the last few meters to the creek, to try her hand at a profuse apology. *No.* She was here to help the girl. Make a difference. Have meaning. Her libido had gotten her in enough trouble, and while this felt different, she knew it wasn't.

A niggling voice persisted. *Well, couldn't I just do both? Help the girl and myself at the same time?*

Doggedly, she turned away from the creek, set one foot ahead of the next and marched back to the ranch.

"Let's try it another way." Rose chewed the end of her pencil. *How can I explain algebra when I barely understand it myself?* "Or maybe, we just hit pause on math for the moment? Shift to a little, um—" she thumbed through her notebook, landing on a highlighted page before brightening to suggest "—social studies?"

Her charge groaned, which provoked a smile. "Not your favorite? What were you hoping I'd say?"

"Music, maybe? No, definitely free period. We had those at school." Alix looked up from her doodling, eyes wide. *There it was, a brief smile. Yes.*

Rose bit down on the pencil, then withdrew it abruptly from her mouth. "I think you'll have to show me about these 'free periods.' I can't seem to remember any in England. We did have physical education class, though. What say we take a little walk about this fancy estate? Try our hand at some botany? That's science-y, isn't it? And if we double-time our pace for a few minutes, we can count the time as PE, right?"

Alix laughed. A full-out laugh. Rose aimed a pillow at her, but it did little to shut her up. Just as well; it was brilliant seeing the girl doubled over in a belly chuckle.

"Come on, then." Alix jumped to her feet.

"Do you think we should bug your uncle to come? He does know the place." The question escaped before Rose had a chance to second-guess herself, and to her surprise, Alix didn't frown. Another step in the right direction.

"Whatever. If you want to, it's fine."

Excellent. "Maybe you can trade in your flats for some trainers, er, sneakers? It's a bit rocky in some places. I was thinking we could walk to the creek?" Despite herself, Rose was excited. In just two weeks she'd fallen irrevocably in love with the terrain of the ranch and she was sure Alix would, too, given the chance. There was something healing about nature.

"Yeah, lemme go get some *trainers*. Meet you in ten?" Alix dashed off. Rose, unsure if the change in demeanor stemmed from actual excitement about getting outside or the fact her algebra lesson had been deferred, smiled, too. And Rose? She made her way to Nick's office, glad to have a legitimate excuse to see him, not that she needed one.

"Where do you think you're going?" Samantha blocked Nick's door, arms crossed firmly at the waist, an impassable, frowning female.

"I was just going to invite Nick, er, Mr. Hartmann, on a little escapade with Alix." Somehow, the executive assistant had a way of making Rose feel she was naughty.

"Mr. Hartmann is in a meeting. He's an extremely busy man."

"Of course, sure. Yes, that makes perfect sense. Right. Well, perhaps I can just let him know we're headed on a break, then?" Rose had no intention of leaving the premises without Nick's blessing, and this was as good a chance as any to finally chat with the man who had been steadily avoiding her all week. Avoiding her since—she reddened—their swim. Their *kiss*.

"I'm afraid I'm going to have to insist you leave. As I've explained, Mr. Hartmann is occupied—"

"I am employed by Mr. Hartmann, and I'll have his permission before leaving with his niece." Rose eyed the woman, then pushed past her.

"Ms. Kelly," Samantha called, but it was too late. Rose stood in the office, in front of his desk, only a few meters from the cowboy magnate himself.

"Mary, I wasn't expecting you." Nick replaced his phone on the receiver.

"Sorry, I was just… I haven't seen you in a bit." Against her better judgment, a hand pulled at a loose curl. It was a nervous tick of sorts, and she fought against it, forcing her hand back to her waist.

Nick's face, lined from fatigue, tightened. "Yes, I'm sorry about that. I've been quite busy with the ranch. We've been branding the calves all week. They're sixty days old now, so we need to mark them—standard practice, really."

"Sounds terrible," she murmured.

"Part of the business. Smell takes some getting used to, but it's not that bad." He pushed away from his desk and stood, putting his hands behind him, looking devastating. She closed her eyes a moment and flashed back to the musky heat she'd smelled on him the week prior. Delicious. *And inappropriate.*

"I'm thinking Alix needs a break. Thought maybe we'd take a walk around the grounds?"

"A walk? With Alix?" His eyes flickered to his glowing computer screen, and then looked beyond her to the desk in the hallway, where the SWAT leader of a secretary glowered at them both.

"That was the general idea." She assessed his posture and smiled. A winning smile couldn't hurt. It was hard, pretending she didn't want him. That she didn't care. A lie, on top of a lie, on top of a lie. Who could keep track?

"Mind if I join you?" he asked quietly.

"Do I mind?" She repeated the question as though the echo was easier to digest. "No, I don't mind."

He straightened and grabbed his hat from beside the armchair near the fireplace on his way out of the room. Did he have to wear that hat? Somehow it made him look impossibly hotter.

"Those are your best outdoor shoes?" Despite his goal of being as positive as possible around his niece, he couldn't help keep the skepticism from his voice as he watched Mary and Alix file out of the house down the slate steps to join him at the edge of the yard. The *awesome trainers*, as Mary had lovingly proclaimed them, were crisp white. Nick doubted they'd ever seen the wet side of a field, and as he cast a quick glance up at the sky, he frowned. The clouds were heavy. "Looks like it might rain," he voiced his observation.

"Skies are clear, man, don't try and talk me back into an algebra lesson." Alix's tone, normally flippant, was smug.

"I wouldn't dare." He smiled. It was the right call. Joining them. He was coming to spend more time with Alix. It fit well with his plan to get her to love the land, so she wouldn't sell. He didn't come to spend time with *her*.

Or so he told himself.

The trio made good time crossing the field, and inside thirty minutes, they were at the edge of the creek.

"This is awesome," Alix said. The girl knelt and unpicked her now muddy laces. Moments later, she was barefoot and wading in the water. "It's not even as cold as I was expecting!"

"Quite," Mary answered.

"I don't think I ever did get that swim?" Nick ventured. He was kicking off his boots, and rolling up the bottom of his jeans, intent on joining Alix.

"I'd have thought the last swim was memorable enough?" She took the spot next to him on a large log.

Nick picked up his shoes and put them on the log next to hers. "Yeah, I was meaning to talk about that with you."

"I'm so sorry," they said in unison.

He sucked in his breath. "What could you possibly be sorry about?"

She was pulling at the bark of the log, small fingers digging into the deep crevices of the waterlogged trunk. "I just was…" Her voice was small and he placed a hand over her scratching fingers.

"I was the one who couldn't restrain himself. I'm sorry." He tightened his grip on her fingers, and she met his gaze, large eyes beguiling as they widened in understanding. Suddenly he wasn't sure why he had been avoiding her. It wasn't that bad, this truth between them.

"Guys, you're being weird." Alix's pronouncement was accompanied by a splash as the teen chucked a stone in their direction.

He picked up the round rock at his foot and lobbed it back. "You don't know the half of it, kid."

They waded in the creek until their feet were pruned. Then a crack of thunder interrupted.

"How can there be thunder without any rain?" Alix was curious.

This was a great opportunity for a lesson on high-pressure weather systems, and Nick waited for Mary to jump on the chance to turn this excursion into a lesson. He'd seen the notes on weather in her lesson planning. To his surprise, Mary turned toward him and added, "Yes, why, Nick?"

"Guys, if we don't leg it back, we're gonna be soaked. That's a promise."

Alix shrieked and made a beeline for the creek's edge, her pants now wet to the knee, an ombre effect of light blue jean to dark damp indigo. "Come on, I don't want to get struck by lightning."

Mary, back on the creek-side log, was pulling on socks and sliding into her shoes. "Careful," she called after her charge, "I rolled my ankle about two hundred meters from here."

"Meters? Welcome to *America*, Mary," Alix shot back.

"Play nice, girls," Nick reminded, offering a hand to Mary. "Let's head back—no rush, really, a little rain never hurt anyone."

As they crossed the large field behind the ranch house, the rain fell. It was a warm rain, and after the initial shock of the wet shower, Mary spread her arms as wide as she could and spun with her head rolled back, face staring into the weeping sky.

Alix watched, stunned to silence. "What are you doing?" she asked, adding a private, "She's nuts," as a sidebar to Nick. *Awesome to be on the receiving end of an inside joke.*

"I can hear you," Mary called, still twirling with abandon. "Don't hate it till you try it."

Alix watched Mary, and Nick watched Alix until the young girl shocked him. She spread her arms wide and looked up into the sky, then started spinning as fast as she could.

"Try saying weeeeeeee," encouraged Mary as she turned faster and faster.

"Weeeeeeeeee," called out the girl.

Then Nick did something that surprised even himself. He spread his arms, tilted his head back and spun, howling weeeeeeeee into the sky.

Ten

Nick had started his day with a thick stack of papers and he was ready to call it quits, having made little progress on the pile. Budgets, forecasts, new employee contracts and marketing plans all melded together in an ominous to-do list. Heavy was the head that wore the Stetson today. He needed perspective.

Nick spun in his chair and took in the great expanse of field out the window. The land was beautiful. Wild. Contrary.

Like her.

He picked up the employee contract Saul had emailed over.

The paperwork was in order. Mary Kelly, of London, had signed with a loopy John Hancock in all the right places. Lettered in a neat script was her address and birthday. A Gemini, sure, but he never would have pegged her for thirty-four. Before he could stop himself, he typed her address into Google street view and was zooming in on a townhome in lieu of attending to paperwork.

The door to his office swung open and Samantha entered, swishing her hips and smacking her red lips with invitation. "I got the tickets you asked for." She held out an envelope. "I know we'd just discussed it in passing, but with everything that's happened, I thought you might be too preoccupied to remember how much I like a good rodeo." Her tone was hopeful and eyes shining. *Damn it.*

"I was going to take Alix. Jackson is riding this weekend. I figured we'd take the jet."

And he'd meant to invite Mary.

He'd been wanting to get Mary on the jet ever since her snarky remark in his office about private jets.

"We'd take the jet? Sure, I've got all three tickets." Samantha smiled again and took another step toward him.

In an abrupt swipe of his hand, Nick slapped his laptop shut. No sense making this more painful than it had to be. He'd told Samantha the kiss was a mistake and there would be nothing more between them. Looked like she hadn't believed him. "I'm taking Mary, figured we could add a little statistics homeschooling to the trip."

Her face fell. "Homeschooling, yes, I see. A rodeo seems—" she paused and bit her lip "—very educational."

"Can you get a suite at the Hilton? We'll stay the night, catch up with Jacks."

Samantha nodded.

The night away for Alix had been Ben's idea. "Might as well show her the good bits, if you want her to like it here," he had said. Nick was sure he'd been referring to Alix.

Mary had jumped at the idea of a "real rodeo," and her sheer excitement was contagious.

"Samantha?" he pressed, feeling the need to be crystal clear with her before leaving on this trip.

"Yes, Nick." She smiled at him.

He scratched his chin, then tore off the Band-Aid. "I

just wanted to apologize again. About the whole situation. I will never cross that line with you, or with any employee." He said the words, only half meaning them.

She stiffened at the statement, flush fading from her face and her eyes narrowing. "Right. Of course, I understand. No employees, that sounds fair."

He nodded. "Thanks for your understanding, Samantha. I really appreciate it." Nick didn't address the sinking feeling roiling in his stomach at the way she spat the words "no employees." It felt like a threat. Or worse, a dashed dream.

Tonight they were headed out for a surprise. Somewhere "Western," he'd promised last night during dinner.

Rose waited outside Alix's room, but when her knock went unanswered, she pushed the door open. Alix was lying on her bed, staring at the ceiling. Her face was drawn and pale. The kid had been crying. Again.

She stood in the doorway, waiting. She was channeling Nick, and his response to Alix. There was something about his calm patience that she—and Alix—appreciated. It was new to her, just sitting with someone else's big feelings, and in an effort to replicate it, she leaned into the frame. If Nick could convey quiet support that made the listener feel better, she could try, too.

"We're not leaving yet," Alix murmured.

"No," Rose agreed.

"So? What do you want, then?"

"You're not making things easy," Rose noted in response.

"Whatever gave you the idea life was meant to be easy?" Alix shot back.

"Aren't you a bit young for such pessimism?"

"Says you," Alix snarked.

"You know, my parents died when I was sixteen?"

Rose bit her lip. She hadn't intended to admit that. Certainly not while sober.

Alix sat up on her bed, pupils wide and staring from under her bangs.

"It's why I took this job. I was gonna say no. But I got the brief, read about you." Rose took a step into the bedroom and put a hand on her hip.

"Isn't this a great job for a tutor?" Alix asked. "I'm guessing it pays better than a lot of others." Alix rolled her eyes and fell back against the pillow.

Rose made her way toward the bed. "I'm not for sale, Alix. I came here because I wanted the job. I wanted to work with you. I'm not even keeping most of the money." She reddened. The admission was another slip.

"What do you mean, you're not keeping the money?" Alix pulled herself into a seated position on the bed, and eyed Rose curiously from slanted eyes.

"It's not very—" Rose bit her lip, searching for the word "—couth. To talk about money. Let's talk about this rodeo." She was desperate to change the subject.

"What are you gonna do with it?" Alix persisted.

Rose pulled up her phone. She'd been down this rabbit hole with Alix before. When the girl got curious, she was like a dog with a bone. Rose found the pic. The one that had kept her sister up at night. Handing her phone over, she studied her charge.

"Why are you showing me this?" Alix demanded, shoving the phone away. "You could've given me a disclaimer or something."

"Sorry. I know it's graphic."

"What happened to her eyes?" Alix's voice was soft.

"Cataracts. Treated by the local doctor, although the 'doctor' label might be putting it generously." She allowed herself another look. It was a difficult photo. Botching an eye surgery on someone so young was heartbreaking.

"I didn't know you were really into…eyes?"

Rose laughed. "No. My sister had cataracts. When she was a kid. She had the operation, was totally fine." She paused. "My sister who died."

"So you carry the picture on your phone of someone else's botched eye surgery?"

Rose swallowed. The lump in her throat was hard. "Yes. I mean, my sister had childhood cataracts. They were removed and she was fine. But because of the experience, my mom was really involved in a charity that helped kids like these, before she died. And my sister really wanted to help, too. Before she died. So when I got this contract—"

"Saw the paycheck, you mean?" Alix grinned.

"That's a whole lot of eye surgeries, if you know where to go." Rose chucked a pillow at Alix, then cleared her throat.

"So let's do this, okay? Try and have a nice night?"

"A Western night?" Alix cracked a smile. It was as close to a peace offering as Rose could hope for.

"We're bringing a cowboy, aren't we?" Rose smiled back.

"If you'd call my uncle a cowboy..." Alix rolled her eyes.

Oh, yes, she'd definitely call Nick a cowboy. In the best way.

"Just get your stuff. He's waiting."

Alix swung her feet off the bed, and followed Rose out of the home, clutching her knapsack against her as she walked toward the jet. Twenty-seven surgeries. Twenty-seven lives she could change forever. It was a heck of a tribute to her sister, and she wasn't going to mess it up. Not even for a cowboy like Nick.

It wasn't fancy. It was a rodeo. Loud and dirty, with people spilling everywhere. To her surprise, there were as many women as men. Fitted shirts and tight jeans tapered into cowboy boots of assorted colors. Rose felt out of place in her stilettos, wishing she'd pulled on the trainers she'd worn on the jet.

She stood out, and she didn't like it.

Oddly, Nick looked comfortable. He held a Molson and drank from the can.

Giant floodlights lit the outdoor pens, and Nick disappeared in a throng of cowboys, leaving her and Alix sitting on the first row of a metal bleacher.

"I won't be long," he promised.

Alix's eyes were as wide as her own, and she sipped at a Coke, elbows on her knees as she took in her surroundings.

Nick was talking to the cowboy beside the bullpen, clapping him on the back, then turning toward them as the cowboy climbed into the staging pen.

The bronco rushed from the shoot with a ferocity Rose had not expected. Nick, now seated next to her, pushed forward on the bench, knuckles white.

"Something eating you, cowboy?" Before she could stop herself, she put a hand over his.

He stiffened at her touch, then relaxed. "It's my brother." He nodded toward the cowboy in the run.

The run opened and, twelve seconds later, Jackson Hartmann won the buckle.

It was a bad idea, maybe, but he asked her, anyway.

"Do you want to come and see a rodeo after-party?"

Mary nodded. "Give me ten minutes."

Alix, safely deposited on one of the hotel's queen-size beds, was bingeing a streaming teen series. "I'm not moving from this bed again," Alix announced.

So it would just be him and Mary.

Jackson had texted the location, walking distance from the hotel. The bar was packed, with a live five-piece band strumming and beating rhythms Nick recognized. It was too loud to talk much, which he supposed suited his brother just fine. Nick reached for Mary's hand, to pull her through the crowd. Jackson was in the VIP lounge, and the Hartmann name was all it took to join him.

"Nick, good to see ya." Jackson pushed a beer in his direction, which he accepted. The bottle cold and the drink crisp as Nick sampled the local brewery's ale.

"Who's this?" Jackson turned his attention toward Mary, extending a hand. "I'm Brad."

"Brad?" Mary shot a quick glance toward Nick, confusion plain on her face.

"I ride as Brad." His brother shrugged.

"I'm Mary." She smiled, then added, "I tutor, as Mary." Her face spread in a wide grin.

He felt that smile, and judging from his brother's grin, so did Jackson.

They fell into an easy banter, Mary poking fun at *Brad*, Nick nodding along. Buckle bunnies threw themselves at Jacks, who remained aloof despite the ever-present stream of attention. It was odd. Nick hadn't known Jackson to be one to say no to the ladies, but he was aloof nonetheless. Surprisingly, it didn't bother him to see Jacks flirting with Mary. He trusted her.

"You gonna talk about the ranch?" Jacks asked when the waitress arrived with a bottle of Scotch. Following the second glass, Nick felt ready.

"Not much to say. Amelia's working up a storm. I've got some ideas in the fire. With Alix, we've got the votes, so things are all right at the moment."

Jackson took another sip of Scotch. "Don't underestimate Amelia, she's just like Dad." His voice dropped, leaving no mystery as to the intention of his comment. It was an insult.

Beside him, he felt Mary push to her feet. "I need the loo."

He stood, offering an arm, which she shook off. "I am

a grown woman. I'll take myself, thanks." With that, she turned and made her way.

"Grown woman indeed. They didn't make them like that when we were in school." Jackson grinned, face relaxing with the joke.

"I'd say," Nick agreed.

Jackson nodded, then tipped his hat off, spinning it around in idle hands.

"So she's tutoring Austin's kid?"

"Alix, you can call her Alix, man. She's your niece, too."

"I know. I've been sending birthday cards." Jackson shrugged. "I just meant, isn't Alix a big part of your plan, with the vote and the ranch…" Jackson reached for his Scotch, eyeing Nick as he tilted the glass back for a deep drag.

"Thanks, Captain Obvious. I mean, sure, Alix is a big part of the plan, you know that." Nick frowned with a deep dislike of where the pointed interrogation was headed.

Jackson's lips drew into a thin line and he frowned. "Right. So be careful. The tutor is gonna have huge influence on the kid. Don't mess this up."

Mercifully, Jackson changed the subject before Nick could answer, and continued to enlighten Nick with his insights into Amelia. They were colored by a deep dislike of Amelia's husband, Scott.

"I better go see where the tutor's got to," he interrupted his brother after twenty minutes had passed.

A blonde slipped against Jackson and looked up at him with insipid eyes. "You do you, buddy," his brother said with a smile, before turning his attention to the blonde.

The band had stopped playing, and his feet crunched against peanut shells discarded by the patrons as Nick made his way to the ladies' room. He heard her before he saw her, the British accent unmistakable through the din of American chatter.

"No, I don't want to dance," she insisted to a large brute of a man dressed in denim.

"I don't care if you've got a mandate for hospitality, I'm here with someone," she insisted again, louder this time. The man—Nick could only see the back of him—was drunk, but his intoxication offered no excuse for his behavior.

I'm here with someone. Damn right she was.

He didn't think. First, a hand on the shoulder, the grip provoking a turn from the assailant.

"What do you think you're—" The man spun and cocked his fist, but Nick was faster. Blinded with anger and surprised by the force of his feelings, his fist connected with the man's jaw. One punch and the man was on the floor.

Mary hurled herself at Nick, forehead hitting the fleshy muscle under his collarbone.

"Hush now, it's fine," he whispered into her hair. He felt her shake. "Let's get a breath, all right?"

He led them from the bar. Outside, the moon was bright and cast a blue glow on them both.

"Your brother's lovely."

It was clear from her tone that she didn't want to talk about the man who'd grabbed her. That punch still stung his knuckles, but he was willing to let it go if she was. "Sure. Feels like I barely know *Brad* anymore." Despite himself, he rolled his eyes.

"He's just sad." She nodded, and in the blue light of the night, she looked sad, too.

"Shall we?" He gestured toward the hotel, visible from the bar, but about a ten-minute walk away.

"Why don't you tell me about the last time he wasn't sad? Or…maybe about your favorite childhood memory?" She was a little unsteady on her feet, whether due to the Scotch or the aftereffects from that encounter he didn't know. He offered an arm, which she took.

"My favorite childhood memory?" He scratched his chin and set the pace. Normally, he didn't indulge in those kinds of conversations, especially with a woman, but he, too, was feeling the warm buzz of Scotch. "My favorite childhood memory is my back not hurting." He didn't know what else to say.

She was quiet.

"What about you?" he asked.

"My favorite childhood memory is not hurting, either."

He stilled. Putting his second hand over hers, he squeezed. They walked in silence for a few minutes, and Nick allowed his thumb to brush over the back of her hand.

Then her voice was clear through the night air. "Why didn't you do distance learning for Alix? Why hire a tutor?"

So she wanted to change the subject again. "You regretting your contract?"

Her shoulder pulled away from him fractionally. "No, I'm not regretting *that*."

Perhaps it was the way she paused on the qualifier. Perhaps it was the way her eyes widened a fraction as she sucked in a breath to answer. But he knew in that moment he didn't want any regrets, either.

"I'm glad you're here. Real glad." He squared his shoulders and faced her.

"Do you think it's helping? With Alix, I mean." Her eyes were wide, and for a moment, he read the hope naked on her face.

"I didn't know her before. I'm not proud of that, but it's true. But I can tell you, the kid is doing better. And it's gotta be due to you."

She smiled then, wide and optimistic. "Did you ever think, cowboy, this change in her is kinda due to you, too?"

He liked the idea, even if she was saying it just to

please him. Then a drop of rain fell, followed by another until the flash storms so frequent in spring left them both wet to the skin and running for the hotel, sheltering in the three-foot overhang of the soffit.

Two minutes later he was bidding her good night in front of her room.

"Good night, cowboy." She smiled. Her eyes sparkled and he stepped closer to her, to make space for a passing room-service trolley.

Her chest heaved with a heavy breath, and in the close quarters, her breasts pressed against him. He'd never been so glad of the service staff in this, or any, hotel. Curiously, she didn't move away. Didn't turn toward the door, just looked back at him, punctuating her heavy breaths with a deliberate bite on her lower lip. She tilted her chin toward him, closing the space between them and parting her lips.

He paused, they'd said this wasn't on the table. No kissing, but how could he not? She breathed, then he pressed a kiss, hot and firm, on her mouth. She tasted of Scotch and strawberries, tentative at first, then ardently returning his fervor. But before she could brush him off, he straightened and nodded. "Good night, then." He had to leave if there was any chance of salvaging the propriety they'd both promised to adhere to. He'd been weak enough as it stood.

She hesitated for only a moment and closed the door.

He stood, staring at her door a moment too long, wishing he had said how he felt. Problem was, he wasn't entirely sure he knew.

The knock came twenty minutes later, so quiet he'd thought for a moment he was imagining it. "It's open," he answered. He was lying on his bed, staring out the window as the cars flashed by, miniature from his penthouse view.

He heard her enter. Smelled her hair, still wet from the rain. Knew her lips to be hot from the kiss he had pressed on her in a moment of weakness. "You were supposed to go to bed."

"I'm sad." Her voice was evidence of that, wavering and thick with emotion.

He swung his feet off the bed and stood. She closed the distance between them, and there she was, in his space again.

It was a marvel, the way someone could break down your barriers, just by getting under your skin. Getting into *his* skin.

His windows were naked of drapery and the moon lit the room with blue shadows. She was beautiful.

"I'm sad, too," he admitted. It was easier being honest in the dark.

"You kissed me." She stated it as fact, and it was. But what she wasn't saying was more important.

"I kissed you because I wanted to, not because I'm sad. I'd apologize, but I'm not sorry."

She sat on his bed and started unbuttoning her cardigan. He watched, arousal building with each pearl button she released. The last button freed and the thin wool garment fell to the floor. Underneath she wore a thin-strapped camisole, and with a shrug, the straps fell off her shoulders and the camisole pooled around her waist. She shimmied it down over her tights and stepped out of it. She stood, in skirt and bra, and faced him, hooking her thumbs into her waistband. Her eyes, pools of dark blue desire, made contact with his and she deepened her gaze as she unzipped her skirt.

He sucked in a breath. "Are these for my benefit?" He reached for the matching lingerie, a cherry-red, simple cotton bra and thong. *Very Mary*, he thought. *Simple, and dead sexy.*

"So what if they are?"

"The woman makes a fine point."

"I'm more interested in what kind of point you can

make. Naked." Her hands were at his neck, pulling apart the snaps of his shirt, and permitting themselves free-range access over his torso.

"What do you think, Nick? Can you make me feel better?" Her head was pressed into the nook in the top of his chest, and she spoke into his neck.

As though the question awakened him, his hands came alive with a purpose of their own and gripped her against him. He looked at her, and pressed his mouth against hers. It didn't matter that she worked for him. Didn't matter that she was the closest thing he had to a lifeline with Alix, and moreover, his plan to keep the ranch. He wanted to kiss her again. He wanted to make his point, naked.

"I'm ready to try," he promised, refusing to hear the small voice inside reminding him this was a bad idea. She was his employee. Critical for his plan.

And right now, he didn't care.

She sucked in a breath as he kissed the spot on her neck just under her jaw. She was fresh and kind, clever and hurting. An intoxicating combination—he prayed he could handle the hangover.

He didn't know why she was sad. It could be a million reasons. Maybe a better man would have waited. Asked. But he was tired of trying to be a better man.

Her hands, insistent, pulled off his shirt, tracing the lines of hard muscle earned roping and riding. He had never been vain, but in this moment, he was glad of his physique and the confidence it earned him. He caught her wrist before it dipped into his jeans.

"It's a bad idea." His words hung in the air between them. There. He'd said it.

She laughed, a throaty chuckle he felt in his gut. "Is that meant to be some sort of disclaimer?"

She pressed herself against him, her breasts against his chest. The heat a siren call to his libido. "Disclaimer?" he managed to ask. His mind was not working. All he could think of was where she was going to press next.

She didn't answer, just raised a hand to his neck, pulling his head toward hers. Miraculously he paused. Pressing his forehead to hers, he left enough space between their mouths to breathe a thought. "The kiss. Before. It was a bad idea. But kissing you now?" He swallowed, unsure he could stop himself even if he wanted to.

"Are you going to, then?"

"Not kissing you would take more strength than I have." He delivered on his confession. Her mouth yielded, her lips parting at his slightest insistence. She let out a soft whimper.

She pulled him toward her. "I want this. I need this."

He knew then that tonight was outside his own experience. Her admission provoked one of his own. He needed this, too, but true as it was, he couldn't say it aloud. So he answered the only way he could. Tracing a finger over her jawline, he paused at the clenched muscle, pressing a kiss there before assuring her. "You're beautiful."

Her jaw relaxed and he was rewarded with a smile. Just like that, he came undone. His hands gripped her hips, fingers digging into the soft expanse of her thigh. He flexed his hands against her, into her, and she leaned into him.

If there was a woman alive sexier than Mary Kelly, he didn't want to meet her. She was a symphony of curves; but more than that, she was pliable and lithe beneath him, rising to his touch and the chorus of desire it provoked.

He dropped to his knees before her. "Tights off," he ordered. Too impatient, he pulled them down past her knees, following the curve of her calf with a hot hand.

"Yes, sir," she breathed, her voice gasoline to the fire. Her inflection, the daring lilt of the *sir*, powered him forward.

"I think I want your shoes on," he decided aloud. Wordlessly, she stepped back into her heels, legs now freed of the tights. He clicked his tongue in reproach and she kicked her feet apart, forming a triangle with a heavenly apex.

"Yes, sir," she repeated.

He caught her leg and pressed a kiss into the curve of her knee. Then followed with another a few inches higher. "You are mesmerizing," he breathed into her thigh. He ached with his need of her. "I can't remember ever being this hard." Her hands busy in his hair, he felt the tug urging him to his feet. With palatable reluctance, he stood, head filled with the alluring scent of her.

"Hard, are you?" she murmured, free hand now headed in search of plainer evidence.

"See for yourself."

She did, making quick work of his belt, then relieving him of his jeans.

Nick stood naked, watching her take in the sight of him. Her gaze lingered, but she didn't blush. Her eyes, low-lidded, flicked up at him. "So, cowboy, you were saying you might make me feel better?"

Her tone was playful, but Nick read her statement for what it was. False bravado. "Yeah, I reckon I can."

He traced a finger up her thigh and across her slick center. Her readiness as plain as his, he slid a finger into her. She was smooth and wet, velvet heat coating his finger and calling for another. Fingers coated, he raised them in search of a button he intended to make his. She arched into him, nipples hard against his chest.

"I want you so bad I'm gonna burst," he admitted between kisses. His thumb, pressing with what he hoped was delicious pressure, now matched the rhythm of her grinding hips. Her hand reached for him but he pushed it away. In two backward steps he pinned her against the wall of the hotel room.

"If you want me, then take me," she ordered.

"Not so fast," he cautioned, dipping a hungry mouth

to her chest. "You're not exactly in a position to boss me around."

"So you like to be the boss, then, do you?" To his surprise, she nipped at his bottom lip.

"I am the boss, and yes, I do like it." He bit her back.

She twisted but he covered her body with his own. Then, in a move that surprised him again, she hooked her legs around his waist.

"Easy, girl." He brought an arm under her and readjusted. Keeping her high on his chest he carried her to the bed. Depositing her, he sprung off the bed, reaching for his jeans.

"You're not getting dressed," she threatened, propping herself up on her elbows.

"No." He grinned, retrieving a condom from his back pocket.

She opened the condom and had it on him quickly. Then she swung a leg over him, poised and paused. Face-to-face, she looked at him, her eyes an astonishing blue. In the dark of the hotel room, they were near-black, but he read the desire. Then with an excruciating slowness, she lowered herself until they were one.

He didn't breathe. Couldn't breathe. Her tightness enveloped him, but it wasn't that exquisite sensation that paralyzed him.

There was a vulnerability about her he could see. He could feel. One he mirrored.

In the blue-gray light of the room, he traced the curve of her chest, fingers light yet insistent. She curled at his touch, but didn't stop her agonizing tempo.

The kisses followed. Hot now, unyielding. Her palms against him, pressing him away and drawing him closer in a contradiction of pressure. He swallowed, determined not to let go. He wanted her writhing on him, and with newfound determination, he gripped her hips and flipped them, covering her body with his own.

"Nick," she said quietly, biting her lip. They had a teenager on the other side of the shared wall.

He kissed her then, covering the next moan with his mouth, his efforts redoubled. He was relentless now. Driving in and out of her as she bucked against him.

"Nick," she breathed again the moment her mouth was free. "Oh God, please soon."

Her spasms were the final nail to his pleasure, hammering a thousand electric shocks through his body. The release was all-encompassing and he shuddered. Dimly, he heard a sharp cry. Felt her pulse around him. Felt a scratch of nails down his back. He savored the pain as it pulled him back to her. He rolled, then pulled her into the shallow of his shoulder.

And for the first time in a long time, he wasn't sad.

She wasn't sure what woke her. Nick was asleep, his slumber well earned. She shifted and stared at him, his face relaxed. The dark shadow of his beard was growing in. Her skin was marked with a red rash from persistent scratchy kisses. Well worth it. His nose was straight, and a long forelock of hair fell in front of his closed eyes. He was unguarded in sleep, but just as difficult to read. He hadn't said any of the things she'd wanted to hear. But she didn't care. Empty words were the last thing she needed; she'd heard them, and said them, enough times before. No, she'd take the actions any day, and what actions they had been.

She wasn't a virgin. Far from it. But she hadn't ever had sex like that before. Her body tingled at the mere memory. He'd woken her twice during the night, and worshipped her. *Worshipped* felt like an appropriate word; his ministrations had brought her close to God. It was scary now. Having another thing she didn't want to lose. No, she self-corrected. She didn't have him. *You can't lose what you don't have.*

If she was careful, they could do this. She could help Alix and be with Nick. She could fulfill her sister's dreams and live this one for herself, too, no matter the doubts she'd had before. Everyone had secrets, and it wasn't like things were going to get serious between them.

This revelation was a good one.

He opened his eyes, the warm brown awakening her cravings. "You look good enough to eat."

His hand, moving under the blanket, trailed up her leg.

"I'd think you'd need a fast after all the feasting last night?"

"I'm a glutton for punishment." He grinned, dipping his head beneath the sheets.

Her hands twisted in the fabric. She pressed her head back into the pillow, squeezing her eyes shut. She wasn't going to think about anything but his tongue. Not that she could have had she wanted to.

"Where do you think you're going?"

She stilled. She'd thought he'd fallen back asleep. Surely the man needed rest? She slipped on her shoes and twisted to face him. "I've gotta get back to my own bed."

"Speaking as your boss, I think you might have other duties to attend to," he joked, rubbing the still-warm spot on the sheets she'd occupied a few minutes earlier.

"Speaking as your niece's roommate, I better get back. I don't want to sneak in after she's awake. Plus, I think you're out of condoms." Her revelation was quiet, but daring.

A shadow passed over his face. "You're right. You should go."

Her heart sank. She wasn't sure what she'd been expecting him to say, but *you should go* stung. He looked at his watch.

"Shit, it's already seven." He was out of bed like a flash.

Standing naked in the daylight, the sight of him weakened her. "Looking good, Mr. Hartmann." She whistled.

"Watch your mouth, miss." His eyes promised a playful threat, and he pulled on a pair of briefs that only heightened his allure.

"I better go," she said.

"See you at breakfast?" He spoke as he pulled on gym clothes. "I'm just gonna find the gym, then I could meet you ladies in an hour and a half?"

Rose nodded, and let herself out of his room. The bed separated them, so there was no kiss goodbye. She didn't want to seem needy. It was fine. She'd had a thousand kisses.

Alix was still asleep when she entered the neighboring room. She sank onto her bed, and opened the drawer of her night table, pulling out Mary's clunky phone. *I've done something.* She didn't speak her admission aloud. Didn't need to. Voicing it didn't make it more or less true.

A quiet knock interrupted her confessional. She opened the door to find Nick.

"You forgot something." His voice was warm and husky.

"Did I?"

He took a step closer, raising a hand to her face. He lifted her chin and met her mouth with his. The kiss was short, sweet and deliberate.

"That's better," he breathed as he pulled away from her.

She hadn't wanted to seem needy, and yet here she was. Needing.

A sound from inside the room—Alix stirring?—made her heart race. And suddenly the *something* she'd done felt like a mistake. The kind of mistake her sister would never have approved of.

Nick studied her, gym bag on his arm. "What's up, buttercup?" he asked.

"This." She gestured at the space between them. "I

think we need to remember why I'm here. For Alix."
For Mary.

He stepped back. Something like hurt flashed in his eyes before it was quickly replaced by nonchalance. "I get it. Let's cool things off. Sure."

She nodded, lips pulling into a thin line. Nick spun and walked away, leaving Rose with the distinct feeling the cooling off was much easier said than done. With the taste of him fresh on her lips, she swallowed, acknowledging after the night they'd shared, a second course might be even more tempting than the first.

Eleven

Samantha stood to the left of him, tapping her foot in a sharp aggressive beat against the floor. *Tap*, *tap*, *tap*.

"What?" He looked over to her, his tone a victim to the annoyance flushing through him that hadn't abated in the two days since they'd returned to the ranch.

"What yourself," she snapped back.

Being around Samantha served only to remind him of all the things he liked about Mary. Surely the decision to *cool off* was premature, but at the same time, her reaction begged the question he'd been artfully avoiding for forty-eight hours: Why had he nearly sacrificed everything to heat things up with her? And why was the suggested cooling off feeling like more of a punishment than a good idea? Surely he could focus on work and her. Why couldn't she manage Alix, then on her off time… His mouth went dry as he escaped once again into the memory of her curls spread against his chest. No, the distraction was devastating to his productivity, and if Alix, or anyone else for that matter, were to find out about their tryst, the consequences would be far reaching and expensive. Even for a Hartmann. Especially for this Hartmann.

Exhaling, he turned his attention to the email in front of him. It was a huge deal. China making a move in beef commodities.

"I need to talk to Daniels. Can you get Jeff on the phone?"

The directive shot her into action. "Of course, give me a moment."

The intercom on his desk buzzed. "Jeff Daniels on line one, and you're to return a call from Kellerman."

Nick clicked his phone to line one. "Nick, what can I do for you?" Jefferson was a family friend, issued from blue-chip stock.

"We need to chase Chinese dollars. With the new tariff strategy being announced, I want to see Hartmann beef with a bigger presence in Asia. Where are we with the joint venture proposal and the Shenghen brothers?"

"Things are good. Feng's jet touches down in two weeks, nothing a discreet gala couldn't firm up?" Jeff's voice trailed off.

"You want the brothers to come here?"

"Yeah. We can give them a Stetson, show them why Hartmann beef is the top end of the market and offer a Wild West you can taste in the brisket..."

"Look, I don't have time to host a party right now." Nick's tone reverted to his terse standard.

"As if you've got a huge part to play hosting anything. Call Josephine. She can pull together black-tie faster than most people can find their own underwear."

"All right. Have your team coordinate with Samantha. We'll do it." Nick smiled.

One down. Now to call the lawyer.

"I got your message. What can you tell me, Saul?"

There was a brief pause on the line. "It's not good,

Nick. There's been an official petition for custody, an aunt apparently." Nick heard the shuffle of papers through the phone and set his jaw in grim determination.

"There's a lot we can do. The fact there's a will, that you assumed custody directly and of course your brother's written directive—I wouldn't say it's a real threat." Saul spoke as though he were working through a bullet point list.

"My money-grubbing sister-in-law can't keep her nose out of it, is that it?" Nick felt his temper rise.

"Shouldn't be a problem—we're filing a countersuit today. We'll right the ship." Saul didn't sound concerned, so hopefully the custody suit was nothing.

"Right, please keep me closely apprised." He disconnected and made his way to the second living room. All the talk of Chinese beef and tariffs and the call with Saul had left his head buzzing. He longed to anchor his thoughts.

"You're confusing the armies again, love. The South was the Confederate Army, I'm pretty sure..."

From his position, leaning against the doorframe, he had a clear view of Mary flipping through a huge textbook. She lifted a finger to her mouth, licking it, then flipped another page, eyes scanning until she pushed her finger down and tapped it against a block of text. "See here? I was right." His stomach tightened at the sight of her pink tongue.

"You don't gotta sound so pleased with yourself, Mary. I can read, you know." Alix gave her tutor a good-natured shove, which Mary met with a smile.

"Darn right you can, you're a machine!" She smiled again, then, noticing him, colored pink.

"I'm gonna have to agree with Mary—you're definitely not an ordinary teenager." He smiled at Alix and, to his surprise, she smiled back. He accepted the smile as an invitation to join them, and sauntered in, taking a seat beside his niece. "So I had an interesting call today," he started.

"Tease," Alix accused.

He smiled. "Easy, I was just getting started." His hand snaked out and tousled her hair. "We're hosting a gala. A small one," he hurried to correct.

"Gala?" Mary mouthed the word, but no sound came out.

"Yep. I've got a new joint venture on the table, with a Chinese group, the Shenghen brothers." He was speaking to Alix, but looking at *her*. Hard not to as she was channeling her thousand-watt smile in his direction.

To hell with cooling off. He had to figure out a way to get the woman on a date. After hours, of course.

"Get to the gala already," Alix insisted. "What do we wear? Will there be other teens there? Is it like a masked party or…" She was speaking rapidly, tripping over her words in the excitement over a soiree to break up the monotony of homeschooling.

Nick laughed and shook his head. "I'm afraid it's gonna disappoint you."

Alix snorted. "Not likely. I love parties." Her eyes shone with sincerity.

"Maybe we could find a way to help. Plan it, I mean. We could work it into a lesson. Make a budget, calculate returns, cost per serving. I'm sure I can think of something." Mary's tone matched Alix's, but her train of thought was interrupted with an ecstatic squeal.

"Yes! I want to—yes, yes, yes! We are gonna plan a sick party!" Alix jumped to her feet.

"Ah-ah-ah," Mary tutted. "Maybe this offers a lovely opportunity for a little research? Maybe we could write an essay on joint ventures? Or East Asian investment in the commodities market?"

"Mary, let's discuss how to make the gala a learning opportunity."

"I'd love that," she answered, eyes widening in his direction.

"I've got meetings until six. Maybe you can stop by. My room. After dinner," he finished.

"Yes, sir." She winked. "Anything for a gala."

Alix fell back onto the couch, busy on her phone. "We gotta have the most epic food. It's all about the Instagram opportunities now." She was muttering to herself, swiping wildly at her screen.

He was in for it. Both women were excited, and he had somehow managed to hand over the largest business deal of his career to the naive fingers of his niece and her delicious tutor. Clearly, he also had a lot to learn; he just hoped the price of the ensuing education was palatable.

Twelve

Nick.

He could hear her. Taste her.

He wondered if his skin had some sort of memory, programmed to want her. He'd dreamed of her sneaking out of his bedroom again. He could have sworn his sheets still smelled like her. And he couldn't seem to stop thinking of her hair against his pillow, as arousing as the creamy velvet of her inner thighs.

He shook his head. This distraction was precisely why she'd been right about cooling things off. Seven generations of Hartmanns had run this ranch. He needed control of all his faculties if he was going to keep this land, and more if he was going to transform it. To expand the empire of their holdings, he needed more than control; he needed mastery of every faculty he had.

Doubling down on a newfound commitment to his goals, Nick was pulled back to the present. Lunch, here with Ben.

"Earth to Nick." Ben waved a beer stein in his direction.

"Right. Sorry." Nick shrugged.

"Nick, I can't hold her off any longer. This is going to happen. Best you just accept it." Ben's frustration coursed through his speech and beer licked over the edge of his glass as he placed it forcefully on the high-top table, front of house, at Chez Gregoire.

"I peeled myself away from the ranch for a front seat to your whine-fest?" Nick swallowed the last dregs from his own pint and ran a hand through his hair, pulling the loose strands from his face. "Snap out of it. Three weeks is nothing in the scheme of things." He was aware of the exasperation in his tone, but he couldn't be bothered to mask it.

"Three weeks of trying to convince Josephine she'd cause more stress than good by interceding? Talking the woman off a ledge on a moment's notice?"

"How bad is it?" Nick asked.

"Pretty bad. She won't stop calling—haven't you listened to any of her messages?" Ben hunched forward and lined up his cutlery in even parallel lines across his place mat. "Apparently you won't return her calls?"

"Oh, Benjamin, you're the son she always wanted." Nick laughed, but it was hollow. Ben's reputation for calling Josephine back minutes after any trace of a missed call was well-earned. To be fair, Ben had been a fixture around the Hartmann residence growing up, having lost his own mother at age eight. He'd latched onto Josephine and had never let go. One would think the discord in the Hartmann home would have dissuaded him, but no.

"You're lucky to have her. You should call her back." Ben had hackles up at the mere insinuation he went too far in his admiration of the Hartmann matriarch.

"Fine, you've made your point. I'll call her." Thankfully, the waiter arrived with refills, and as both men ordered the house special for lunch, the tension dissipated.

"You're quiet," Ben noticed.

"Lots on my mind." Nick reached for his glass and took another sip of his pale ale.

"Such as?"

"I've been playing a game of voice-mail tag of my own." He put his cell phone on the table, covering it with his hand. The damn thing was a curse. It gave the illusion of communication, but he was still the same victim to his sister's schedule.

Ben eyed the phone and raised an eyebrow.

"Evie. I've been trying to get ahold of her, but it's been a desert, communication-wise."

It was impossible to miss the twitch in Ben's jaw. They'd been best friends long enough for Nick to see through the charade of nonchalance his buddy put up when it came to his sister Evie. Sure, he didn't get the obsession, but he'd never kicked into that hornet's nest. It was a no-go zone in their friendship, probably the only one.

"That doesn't seem like her," was all Ben acknowledged.

The *salade Niçoise* arrived, and both men tucked in.

"I guess," Nick said through a mouthful of tuna, swallowing it down before continuing. "I guess she's a bit sore about the ranch. Pausing the sale, I mean." He knew he'd find an ally in that argument with his buddy.

"Yeah, well, I can't say I blame you. Hartmann Homestead's been in the family for ages."

"I guess her acting career wasn't the slam dunk she had hoped for," he added.

"I could fly out there, explain it to her, calm, like, you know, show her your point of view, maybe get her to call you back? Does she know about the Chinese interest you've drummed up? About the gala? There's a lot of opportunity here now."

This was going precisely the way Nick intended.

"Aww, I couldn't ask you to do that," he said through a wide smile.

"No, really, I wouldn't mind. Stallion I've had my eye on is going to auction out west next week."

"I think if Evie would listen to anyone, it'd be you."

"Say no more, consider it done." Ben smiled. "You bringing a date to the gala?"

Nick shook his head. Satisfaction couldn't come close to describing the feeling washing over Nick in that moment. Evie was the last piece of his puzzle, and what he had said was true: if she'd listen to anyone, it would be Ben. As for a date? There was only one person he was interested in, but he wouldn't fall into that trap, despite his appetite.

Nick brushed his hand through his hair and pulled into the barn. Rowen, his favorite stallion, was saddled for him, waiting for a ride. He needed a moment of calm. A moment to reconnect. Then he'd tackle the problem he'd been putting off.

Once out of pasture, they settled into a relaxed gait, putting some distance between the house and themselves. Twenty minutes out, he tapped on his phone and touched his Bluetooth headphones. "Siri, call Mom."

He wasn't sure what he expected and smiled in surprise at her quick answer.

"Took you long enough," she said. A dutiful practitioner of call screening, Josephine Hartmann only answered when she felt like it. 'Course, it helped that she'd been trying to get in touch with him for three weeks.

"Sorry, Mom. Things have been a bit busy, you could say." Rowen's gait slowed, and the horse pulled down to snack on some dandelion. "Whoa, boy," he muttered under his breath, squeezing his thighs together.

"Excuse you?"

"I was talking to Rowen, sorry." He cleared his throat.

"Never thought I'd see the day my own son refused to call me back," she started to rant.

"I'd have thought you were used to it by now, what with Austin's allergy to family communication."

"Nice, Nicholas. Nice."

"Right, sorry. What did you want to chat about?" Best keep her on track, he figured.

"Maybe I wanted to know when would be a good time to see my only granddaughter? Or if my son would be open to dinner with a lovely daughter of a friend I met at bridge club? Could it be I want to talk about the ranch, and why the broker called me about the suspension in the listing?" She was talking without pause, and Nick rolled his eyes.

"I'm not looking for a date. Alix is handful enough, thanks." He clipped out his words, instantly regretting them. She wasn't a handful. She was a sad kid.

"You've heard, then? About the petition? That woman, Francesca, she called me, full of threats."

"She doesn't have a leg to stand on, Mom." The sun fell lower in the sky, and he pressed forward at a faster pace in an effort to leave the bugs behind him. The canter had him moving with the horse and it was easy to lose himself as the wind rushed past his ears.

"Don't be so sure. She mentioned a second will to me. A letter from her sister?"

Nick cursed. "I'll call Saul in the morning." Hopefully, it was nothing a little more money couldn't fix.

"I'm shocked I haven't been invited to visit. Didn't it occur to you that I might be able to help with the handful?" Josephine sniffed.

"Alix doesn't need a sitter, Mom, but you're more than welcome to come and boss around the household staff if you'd like."

"How about tomorrow, then?" She was to the point, which made the proposal tough to skirt.

"Yeah, fine. I can't wait." He disconnected and stared to the horizon.

A squeeze of his thighs, and Rowen picked up the pace, taking them down the path to his own thinking rock, miles from the house, from the blonde tutor he couldn't stop thinking about and the niece he'd never known he wanted but couldn't bear to lose.

Thirteen

Whatever it was, it wasn't good.

Her stomach had turned over the moment Alix passed the envelope to her, smug smile plastered to her face.

"I think this is meant for you?" To Rose, the girl's tone sounded accusatory.

She accepted the envelope, addressed to Miss Rose Kelly, and retreated double-time to her room. *That Ellen. Bloody instigator.* Only *her* relative would bother penning an actual letter in this digital age. Mary and Ellen were so similar in that vein that Rose couldn't hold the oddity against her cousin. She supposed it was a good thing her sis hadn't been more technological, or she wouldn't have been able to step into her life here in Montana.

The post had arrived moments into breakfast, but she'd lost her appetite when a gleam of curiosity registered on Alix's face. Nick hadn't been there; with the gala imminent, he wasn't around much these days. Just as well, it was becoming more and more difficult to keep from remembering their one night together when he entered a room.

Had Alix noticed?

Heaven. Could she not have twenty bloody minutes without thinking about him?

She kicked her feet ahead of her and stretched on the coverlet of the bed. The letter was cheery enough. She scanned the page, the ordered penmanship easy to read, and paused on the salient points of her note: *things are fine at the flat, heaps of mail for you, scanning them to your inbox. Included a pic of your pen pal, heaps more letters here. I told you—you should have canceled.*

It was the type of message she could have sent via text, but *no*, she'd had to address it to Rose Kelly and mail it. At least it had been Alix giving her the letter and not Nick himself, or worse, his conniving secretary. Rose looked at the picture her cousin included. A kid whose eye surgery she hoped to sponsor. She smiled with a renewed determination to earn out this contract.

She pulled her leaden feet off the bed and answered the quiet knock at her door, surprised to find her young charge wringing her hands. Gone was the previously smug mailwoman and before her was a fresh-faced sixteen-year-old, stripped of all attitude. *What was up?*

"Alix, I thought we were meeting at nine?"

"Yeah, I know." The girl shifted from foot to foot. Her hair, worn long, trailed past her shoulders and fell in front of her face, an auburn curtain shielding her expression from closer inspection.

"Can I help you with something?" Rose opened the door wider.

"My grandma is coming tonight. Nick just told me." The girl stood, feet rooted in place, and cautiously looked up.

Perhaps Rose wasn't an Oxford-educated tutor, well, not any tutor at all for that matter, but she did have a knack for people, and she saw straight through the tough-girl act Alix often wore. "Why don't you come in, have a cuppa with me. I've got a cinnamon chai brewing, it's lovely."

"Sure, yeah, okay." Alix made her way to the oversize armchair beside the bed, and sank into it, punching back the pillow before wriggling into the duvet across her knees.

"Would you say you're close to your gran?" Rose poured a steady stream of freshly brewed tea into the second mug and offered it to her guest.

"Close?" Alix scoffed. "No, not close. I've met the woman, like, twice? I barely know any of the Hartmanns."

"What about your mom, Katherine? Did she have any family?" Rose was careful to keep her tone soft, and she purposefully avoided looking at Alix, instead focusing on the coverlet.

"My mom? Yeah. She has a sister. Francesca. I have a cousin I kinda know, Wendy. She didn't have to go to boarding school."

"Sure. You know, when I was a kid, I dreamed of going to boarding school. It's really cool in London, the old buildings, secret passageways. I used to wish my door was a swinging bookcase I could hide behind."

Rose was rewarded with a laugh from Alix.

"I was a bit worried that you don't have any mates around here," Rose continued, tapping a finger on the edge of the mug with nervous energy.

"Mates? You mean like friends?" She shook her head. "I didn't love boarding school. No hidden staircases or anything where they sent me." Alix smiled, but the smile was tight.

"If you didn't like boarding school, why were you there?" It was the question Rose had wanted most to ask.

"My parents. I wasn't exactly a planned baby. My mom never wanted kids. And when I turned eleven, I was sent to my first sleepaway school. Anyway, it's the same story I bet you've heard a lot of poor little rich kids tell." Alix was chewing on her lip.

"Right, well, you've got that behind you now." She didn't want to go into all the stories she *didn't* have. "I've always wanted a big family, but it was just my sister and me for as long as I can remember. I also have a cousin. She's pretty annoying."

Another laugh. Perfect. Rose took another sip of tea and continued. "I'd love to meet your gran. Do you think you want to..." Rose let her voice trail off, a classic trick she'd used time and time again behind the bar.

"To do what?" Alix brightened at the intrigue.

"I was thinking maybe a little makeover for tonight?" Rose smiled. If Alix were anything like her sixteen-year-old self, a makeover was a great plan.

"Like, a big makeover?" She spoke with cautious optimism. Rose knew when to seize a victory.

"Yeah, we need to elevate our looks, anyway, with a posh gala only four days away. I was thinking, we pop into town—" she ventured a wink "—and maybe get a little update to our wardrobe? I've had two paydays pass and haven't spent a cent. I mean, I can't donate it *all*..."

"Yes. I'm totally into this idea." Alix now wore a wide smile and had jumped to her feet. "When are we leaving?"

"Let me have a chat with your uncle. I'll need to borrow a vehicle. How do you think we can spin this as educational?" Rose was now chewing on her own lip, eyes shining with a sense of shared rule-breaking. And because she had an excuse to get back in front of Nick.

"You're the tutor," Alix flipped back, skipping the few steps to the door. "Aren't you?" she added as a saucy afterthought.

"Right, yes, of course I am. I was just trying to decide if shopping was more tied to variable algebra or maybe, um, social studies. Give me a few minutes to read through some notes and get the okay from your uncle for a pair of keys."

How he had been talked into a girls' day out was still beyond him. He had a multimillion-dollar empire to run, an export offer to pull together, but here he was, driving the forty minutes into town, just because she had asked.

She. Alix. She. Mary. It didn't matter; he'd have taken the commute for either of them, and the two beauties knew it.

"So what is it exactly you're doing?" Country music filled the back seat of the car, and Alix was nodding her head to the beat of a song on her phone. Just as well, it gave him a chance to talk to *her.*

"Variable algebra, in a real-time setting. Makes it more approachable."

He laughed. "Do you think speaking in a posh accent validates your lesson plans? Just admit you wanted to shop." He rolled down the driver's-side window and let his arm lie relaxed on the outer edge of the car, allowing himself to wonder for a moment if perhaps she wanted to spend the afternoon with him as badly as he wanted to spend it with her.

They'd been cooling off for weeks now and somehow he was even hotter than before their night together. The cooling off wasn't working for him; if anything he wanted her more than ever.

"Shopping? It's Tuesday. This is a lesson plan," she insisted. She met his gaze and then licked her lips. The glimpse of her tongue left his body tight with desire.

"Quite the tutor you have yourself, Alix. I hope you appreciate her," he said over his shoulder, and the teen perked up with the comment.

In the passenger seat, Mary smiled, then ran a hand along her leg, slowly, deliberately, pulling the hem of her dress up. He was going to need more than a cold shower to dampen this inferno. She was playing with him and he knew it, but he didn't mind. He liked it.

"Sure, I love algebra now. Favorite course of mine, variable equations…all that." Her eyes sparkled and her animated reply provoked a grin from Nick.

"I'm clearly at your mercies, ladies." He laughed.

The easy chatter in the front seat had time flying by, and before he was ready to let the womenfolk out of his sight they arrived downtown. He pulled in front of a high-end salon, and dropped the women off, promising to collect them in three hours for a lunch date. He could meet with Saul while they got the shopping out of their system.

"Take this, then." He offered a black credit card to Mary, but Alix swiped it before her fingers could close around it.

"Probably better if I manage the card? She's so British. Might be shocked by our comfort in propping up the local economy."

"Sure." He laughed. "Just be sure to get something black tie for you each—we've got the gala."

"Cool. Yes. Black tie. We are so in." Alix tucked the card into a Prada wallet and slipped the wallet into her purse before turning to Mary. "Coming?"

Nick slid the car into Park, and Alix hopped out.

"I'll join you in a moment," Mary called after her, getting out of the car herself. Her skirt fluttered in the wind, and Nick's breath caught at the long expanse of leg offered by the breeze. She caught his gaze, and played with the hem again just long enough to hypnotize him.

"Yes, you get started. I need to discuss something with Mary," Nick added, willing himself to look away from her legs.

Mary shook her head and took a step toward the store, but Nick hopped out of the car and motioned to the side street to the left of the store entrance. The sun shone hot on the back of his neck, and to his relief, she followed him to privacy.

"I had an idea..." With a few steps more, he moved into her space, nearly pressing her against the brick facade of the building. He wanted more, needed more, and he hoped she did, too. He was about to find out.

"Someone could see us," she hissed.

"In the alley? At nine thirty on a Tuesday? No, we have a few minutes." His hands ran down over her body, exploring the sweep where her thigh joined her ass in a glorious curve. She widened her stance, welcoming him.

"You left before I had my breakfast," he accused. "Are you still wanting things to stay cool between us? I'm hungry..."

She shook her head, and his mouth covered hers with expert efficiency. One finger pushed against the elastic of her panties, and she let her head fall back against the wall.

"I want you, Mary." The woman was addictive, and he was pretty sure she knew it.

"Not in the alley. Tonight," she managed in a ragged breath.

She wanted him, too. A fierce longing swept through him at her response.

He covered her mouth again. She melted into him, meeting every parry of his tongue, and pressing her chest against his.

She twisted and was free of his grasp with a quick twirl. She took another step out of the shadows, before turning and looking at him. With a slow deliberation, she put her hands under her skirt. Shimmying, she stepped out of a cotton lavender thong. "Why don't you hang on to these for me?"

A few steps and she was back in front of him, and

while he was too shocked to move, she tucked the small scrap of fabric into his back pocket. "Tonight, cowboy," she promised.

When she suggested a makeover, she hadn't meant a *Pretty Woman* moment, but Alix was clearly in her comfort zone shopping with a black credit card.

Rose turned to find Alix laden with a variety of dresses. "I—I can't possibly try on all that," she stammered, especially since she was now shy a pair of knickers thanks to her class act in the alley. She backed up toward the door.

"Oh, no, you don't. I wouldn't be a good friend if I didn't insist you try on that dress." Alix pointed at the gown at the back of the shop, and Rose flushed.

"That's the spring collection, the nicest couture in town." The sales associate perked up, clearly encouraged at the prospect of hitting her sales quota for the month with one sale.

But it wasn't the silk dress that had driven Rose's heart into her throat. *I wouldn't be a good friend if I didn't insist you try on that dress.* A very small corner of Rose felt a rush of pride. She and Alix were connecting. "Right. I'll try it on, but no promises."

Moments later, she peeled back her thin cardigan. The dress was quite something.

"How is it?" Alix was calling through the velour curtains, her voice dampened by the thick fabric.

How was it? The silk clung to her body, the sheen of the fabric reflecting light in all the right places. The silk, as light as butterfly kisses against her skin, was an inky blue so dark she had thought it black until a twist to inspect her rear offered a quick glimmer of navy. The cut? Designer. Rose was far from a fashion victim, but even to her untrained eye, she could tell the dress was expensive. Classy. Effortlessly sexy.

Everything she wanted to be when she saw Nick tonight.

"I'm coming in," Alix pronounced. "Wowza." She stopped after pulling back the curtain. Her bravado vanished, and she looked up at Rose, insisting, "You're, like, really beautiful. For serious."

It was difficult not to smile at the pronouncement, and instead of denying the compliment, she accepted it. "I guess I have to buy it."

"My uncle is going to love it," Alix answered, pulling the curtain closed before Rose could confirm or object to the knowing wink she heard in Alix's words.

The price tag fluttered as she rehung the dress on the wooden hanger. The dress was nearly two thousand dollars. For a slip of silk. Taking it off, she broke the spell of insanity.

"It's lovely, Alix, but I can't accept this dress from your uncle. I'm sure he didn't mean—"

"If you're trying to talk yourself out of that dress, forget it." Alix whipped back the curtain, rings sliding, and snatched the dress from the hook, dashing off.

"Excuse you?" Rose howled after her, tripping out of the dressing room before bothering to fasten her cardigan. Alix was already at the cash register.

Rose slapped her own credit card down on the counter. "I'll pay for this, Alix," she said.

For a moment, she didn't feel a twinge of regret at the largest purchase of her life, and instead felt only excitement. *Her friend* loved it. *Her friend's uncle* would love it, too. And the private tutor gig did pay pretty decently. She could afford the dress and the surgery sponsorship as long as she managed her other expenses.

Alix stared a moment at the Visa card, eyes widening, then stepped back from the counter. "If you're gonna insist, but it's no big deal. You've seen the ranch. I mean, this dress is a blip on the radar for us." She snapped her fingers to emphasize the fleeting effect the purchase would have on their bills.

Rose faced her charge and doubled down. “Sometimes, the dress means more if you buy it yourself. Plus, each time I pay down this outrageous bill, I’m gonna think of you.”

The assistant picked up her card and slipped it through the machine. A moment too late, Rose realized the pause on Alix’s face might have meant she had read the credit card name holder: *Rose Kelly.*

Fourteen

The lawyer was talking, but Nick wasn't listening. All he could think about was the alley. The brick wall. The woman who had rocked his world with a scrap of fabric. The thong burned a hole in his pocket and in his mind. That was the problem with Mary. She was unpredictable. He had to stop thinking about her, focus on the lawyer. On the ranch. Which he would do, after tonight.

"You see, you have nothing to worry about. Any petition Francesca can offer we can overcome, particularly with your mother's endorsement." Saul was nodding as he spoke, and with great effort Nick dragged his attention back to the task at hand: Alix.

"Great. So we're all set, then?" He flexed his fingers and tapped them on his thigh.

"For now, there's nothing more we can do. You're the proxy, and it's been validated by the federal court. The vote is yours until she's of age, that is to say the next two general assemblies."

A two-year clemency. He could get her to fall in love with the ranch in two years, especially if he managed to avoid falling himself. He just had to keep his eye on the endgame.

"Thanks. That sounds great." Nick rose and left, eager to return to his role as chauffeur.

If there had ever been a doubt Alix was a Hartmann, it was put to rest today. Per her text, the girls were waiting at an ice cream parlor; both were laden with shopping bags and finishing a frozen yogurt each.

He waited in the truck, observing a few moments before waving to greet them.

"Nick, you're not gonna believe what we got for Saturday." Alix was jabbering before even entering the truck.

"Really, your niece has such lovely taste—the girl could be a fashion designer herself," Mary added for good measure. Then she looked up at him and while maintaining eye contact recrossed her legs. His breath caught in his throat.

She bit her lip, and he swallowed. Addictive indeed.

Bags deposited in the back, Mary opened the passenger door and scooted into the front seat. She had a new shade of azalea pink lipstick, and it matched the pink hue flushed to her cheeks.

"It's easy to pick out nice outfits when you look like a model," Alix flipped back.

The kid was right about one thing: Mary Kelly was model material. He swallowed, wondering what she had picked up at the lingerie store. Immediately, he questioned the importance of this dinner tonight, figuring he could subside easily on a hearty round of dessert.

The forty-minute drive back to the ranch passed in a flash as both women regaled Nick with tales of their shopping, coffee date and their mishap in the shoe store.

Mary, sitting in the front seat, kicked off her shoes and put her feet up on the dashboard.

"That's dangerous," Alix complained.

"You know me, I like to live dangerously from time to time."

Nick could swear she was talking only to him. Her skirt slid up her thigh, struggling to find purchase. He could almost see—

"…tons of stuff," Alix jabbered on from the back seat, launching into a recap of everything she'd tried on and bought.

He didn't say anything, just eyed Mary. She shook her leg, the movement causing her skirt to slide. He couldn't look away.

"Watch the road," she teased.

He managed to keep his eyes on the road the rest of the way, with willpower he hadn't known he possessed. The sun was high in the sky as the crew arrived back at the house.

"What's your plan for this afternoon?" Nick ventured.

"Fashion show?" Alix suggested hopefully.

"Not on your life. We gotta do a bit of work today," Mary interrupted.

"So you didn't manage as much variable algebra as you had hoped on your excursion?" Nick couldn't help himself.

Mary blushed. "Not as much as I had hoped."

"Speak for yourself," Alix added under her breath.

Nick opened the door, and stood back, letting the women pass ahead of him. He hesitated before making his way left, back to the home office. "Don't forget, my mom is coming tonight."

Alix was skipping down the hall, but to her credit, she paused and yelled, "Yeah, sure, we'll be there," over her shoulder.

With Alix out of the room, Mary held out her hand. "You can give them back now." She flushed.

He smiled. "Not likely."

"Come on, Nick. I was just joking around earlier."

"Don't try and hide it in a joke." He lifted a finger to his lips. "Shh, let's just talk about what you're wearing tonight."

"Just give them back." She held her hand out.

He caught her hand and raised it to his lips, pressing a kiss to her wrist. He could feel her pulse quicken, and decided to press his advantage. "Tonight, be naked under your dress."

He left before she could answer.

Back at his desk, Nick started going through a barrage of emails, but he kept wondering what his mom would think of the new tutor. How would he handle the two women alone? He might need some backup.

"Buddy?"

"I'm on my way," Ben answered before even being invited.

"How did you—"

"Jo called me. She wanted to know what to bring as gifts for Alix and her tutor."

"The tutor? Ah, Ben, what did you say to my mom?" Nick spun on his chair and ran a hand through his hair. Just what he needed…

True to his word, Ben arrived not long after their call, spit-polished and ready for a night with the matriarch. Nick made a mental note to buy a nice bottle of Scotch for his friend. First, dealing with Evie; now, taking on his mom? Nick struggled with the thought that perhaps he'd been a bit selfish lately when it came to his friendships. As soon as the gala and the custody battle were behind him, he was going to up his game as a committed wingman.

Josephine Hartmann was the picture of elegance. She was sixty-five but didn't look a day over fifty. A credit to her stylist, a disciplined habit of drinking eight glasses of water a day, never smoking and a sharp tendency to only buy clothes cut for her figure. She arrived promptly at six, entering the ranch after an awkward knock was left hanging in the air.

He rushed to the door, offering a hand to take his mom's coat as she breezed in, pecking an air-kiss to each of his cheeks.

"Where is she, then, darling?" The tone was arid and cool. His mom had a way of keeping him and his siblings on their toes, and despite himself, a wave of guilt rushed through him.

"I'm sorry, Mom. I should have told you, but I've just been feeling a bit…" His voice trailed off when his mom put a cool hand on his arm.

"It's a lot, son. All this. It's a lot. Stop putting so much pressure on yourself. You're doing a good thing. But try to remember, I'm on your side through all this. I support you, my dear, *most* of the time." She gave a quick squeeze and lifted her chin. "So? Where is she?"

Nick led the way to the living room, where Ben was entertaining the women. Chesapeake furniture featuring heavily carved wooden elements scattered the room under cashmere plaids and large down pillows, and a cheery fire in a ten-foot-wide fireplace threw a gold cast over the room. Alix and Mary stood together facing the fire, backs to them. Alix had a hand snaked around Mary's waist, and the two stood in static stillness entranced by the flames.

Mary's hair, lush ringlets, fell just past her shoulders, worn loose. Nick cleared his throat and both women spun to face him. She wore a butter-yellow sundress with a Peter Pan collar. It wasn't a sexy cut, but from the blush on her face he guessed at her nakedness underneath and determined he'd never seen a hotter ensemble.

"Mary, Alix, I'd like you to meet Josephine, the official head of the family." He stepped forward to present his mom.

Josephine and Alix stood like two dogs, sizing each other up. Alix, breaking first, lowered her head, and his mom took a step forward in answer.

"Alix, I've waited quite a long time to see you," Josephine began.

"Not like it was much of a mystery where I was," Alix answered.

"Alix." Mary beat him to the punch, a quick rebuke, delivered with hawklike precision.

"Sorry," Alix mumbled under her breath. "I just meant, if she'd really wanted to know me, she hardly needed to wait until my parents died."

"Nick was telling me things are going better with Francesca?" Ben offered in a bid to interrupt and lighten the mood.

"Aunt Fran?" Alix perked up.

"Well, it seems there's a second claim on your guardianship. Nothing we can't sort out, Alix, so don't worry about it." Nick threw a dagger with his eyes and Ben smiled sheepishly.

The mention of Francesca added a thick layer of tension to the room, and Nick fidgeted. "So, I think Pierre has quite the spread waiting for us. Anyone hungry?" Sure, they generally started evenings like this with drinks, but he figured liquid courage was not the answer to tonight's tension.

"So early?" His mom raised an eyebrow, but in lieu of an answer, Nick marched the troupe toward the dining room.

The dining room was lit by over fifty candles, and the room basked in the same gold glow that had met them in the living room. Sure, there was no fireplace, but they didn't miss it for all the splendor of the room.

"Lovely," Mary whispered as they rounded the corner.

Josephine took her habitual seat at the head of the table,

and Nick sat to her right, Alix opposite. "Sit here," Nick invited, drawing the chair next to him out a few feet.

With dessert came the inquisition. *At least they made it past the main course.*

"Your sister has been calling quite a bit," his mother started. Nick noticed that Alix leaned forward, nosy kid.

"Well, Evie isn't too pleased with me at the moment."

"And why wouldn't she be pleased?" his mother asked, as though she didn't already know, an irritating quality that brought him right back to his childhood.

"I've a feeling you've got a good idea." He shot a glance at Alix, who was working on her pie as though it had wronged her in some way, jabbing to spear each chunk of apple.

"You've delisted the ranch," his mom added.

"I hardly think now's a good time to discuss it." Typical Josephine, everything was on her agenda and timeline.

"If you'd answer my calls, we could have discussed it earlier. For now, I'd like to know why you're going against your siblings' wishes?"

Beside him, Mary sputtered some of her drink.

"My job is to make decisions. Dad saw to that. Perhaps Austin wanted to sell, sure, but this ranch is our heritage, and now Alix can make that decision herself." He looked at her and smiled and, for once, she met his gaze directly.

"Convenient, then, isn't it?" His mom couldn't help herself.

"Convenient?" He didn't bother veiling his tone. This was thin ice. "As her guardian, I'm in a position to help make decisions to best preserve her interest until she comes of age."

"Such as cloistering her here, away from any counter-opinions? Away from her education?" Josephine's regal facade slipped for a minute, and her forehead betrayed her emotions with a few lines screwing up in anger.

"Away from her education? I hired the best tutor money

could buy. She's being educated by a pro, and I'll not apologize for it." He threw his hands down on the table. "Now can we enjoy our dessert or not?" He glowered at his mother.

Josephine eyed Mary, a fresh victim for her inquisition. "Nick tells me you're an Oxford graduate? Top of your class? What made you want to be a tutor?" It was the first question Josephine had directed toward Mary all evening, and Nick could feel the tension roil in the woman to his right.

"Yes, right, Oxford. Yes, it was a brilliant school."

"Sure is. Only the best for our Alix, right?" This time, the question was directed to Nick, who, in lieu of an answer, just nodded his assent.

"Do you find Montana living up to your hopes? As the top graduate, I was wondering why you'd choose to come here rather than Dubai or maybe Singapore. I know in-demand tutors with a wide-spectrum curriculum capability are heavily recruited."

Mary forked a piece of pie, and pointed to her chewing mouth, taking a moment to swallow before answering. She took a sip of water, then ventured a cautious, "I love Montana actually." Her cheeks pinked, and she added, "You know, I had no appetite for a haughty sheikh or oil baron's child. I became a tutor to make a difference. It's been important to me since my own parents passed away."

In the candlelit room, Nick noticed a softening around his mother's mouth and smiled. Amazing, Mary had even thawed his mother.

Mary continued. "I got the call with the job offer, and my answer came on autopilot. I like to feel needed." She looked down at her hands, twisted in her lap, and before he could stop himself, Nick reached under the table to take one in his. Her hand was small in his. Then, suddenly, her thumb pressed over the crest of his hand. If she was feeling for his pulse, the quickening would be impossible to ignore. As it stood, he didn't even try to hide it.

She made no eye contact with him, and just continued to stroke his hand under the table.

"More wine, anyone?" Nick offered, feeling a second wind of energy overcome him.

"Definitely." Ben pushed a glass forward, as though a strong dousing of alcohol could salvage the night.

"I'm glad you're not in Dubai." It was Alix, eyes shining, who spoke.

"Yes, indeed," Josephine added, and from the corner of his eye, he saw the small smile spread across her face.

"Me, too," Mary added.

"Me three," Nick finished.

All in all, it was a pretty smooth evening. She was the spoonful of sugar everyone needed; albeit a peculiar tutor, she was the perfect fit. He squeezed her hand again and felt the reassuring squeeze back.

He could barely wait to get her alone, and was driven to distraction with the wait. With the want.

Rose wasn't sure what she'd been expecting. She hopped up on her bed, head spinning from the evening's dinner. What had his mom thought of her? He'd taken her hand, unprompted. That wasn't sexual, but it sure felt intimate. Her head hurt from trying to make sense of it all.

She nearly missed the soft knock. Without the hushed, "Mary, it's me, are you awake?" she mightn't have answered.

"Nick?" She opened the door, revealing her favorite cowboy dressed in a relaxed T-shirt and snug jeans.

"Is it later yet?"

"I sure hope so."

"Did you want a nightcap?" he asked.

Would she like a nightcap with him? Damn right she did.

"Lemme just grab a shawl." She turned and made for her bathroom, spritzing another shot of perfume in passage.

Such was how they ended up back in front of the fire, in his office.

"Whiskey?" he asked as he poured one for himself at the wet bar. The floor-to-ceiling wood paneling, oversize leather furniture and ten-foot-high wall of leather-bound books in his office would leave the set designer from *Beauty and the Beast* envious and inspired.

"Yes, of course," she answered.

He brought the two drinks with him as he joined her on the sofa. "So now you've met my mom," he ventured.

"Sure did, she's lovely."

"You're lovely." He reached a hand to tuck a stray curl behind her ear. "Your hair is like spun gold," he said softly, and pulled at another curl, watching it spring back into place. "I've wanted to touch it all evening. Touch *you* all evening. Every day since we left Jacks's rodeo."

"Are you hitting on an employee, *sir*?" She smiled back. *Please keep going.*

A shadow of indecision flickered across his face. She wasn't the only one who knew they were skirting close to a very blurry line. But he clicked his glass against hers and vanquished his doubts. "I am. I *so* am." He lifted his glass in cheers.

She sank closer to him on the couch, drawn magnetically. For a few minutes, they sat in silence, basking in the glow from the fire, focused on the heat between their touching bodies.

"I'm glad you're not in Dubai," he added. His hair, a mess of long dark locks, reached his shoulders. She pressed her eyes shut. The man had her dreaming of the things he could do to her.

"I'm glad, too." She swallowed, licking her lips, her tongue acting of its own accord.

"You know full well what you're doing to me," he said matter-of-factly, sipping his whiskey as he studied her.

"Do I?"

"Don't you?"

She leaned into the question, crossing into his space again. He smelled divinely masculine. Like the woods.

She had been so good. She had tried to cool things off, but the yearning persisted. And now, she was connecting with Alix, fulfilling her sister's dreams… She deserved this. She nudged closer to him and parted her lips.

"Mary." He kissed her. Hot, and full of promise.

She pulled away. "Don't talk." The last thing she wanted to be right now was Mary.

His hands, on a mission to torture her, pushed her against the back of the couch, the leather a cool contrast to the wet heat spreading through her.

"Your wish is my command."

As he kissed her, he touched her, trailing fingers over her arms, up her legs, pausing at the buttons at the back of her dress. "Off. I want this off." He fiddled with the small buttons, which seemed even smaller against his large fingers.

She didn't answer, just stood and made quick work of unbuttoning her dress. She hadn't planned this—why hadn't she planned this? She'd known she'd finish here, well, not here per se, but with him, naked. Her lack of planning with her wardrobe resulted in a thin white cotton bra, no underpadding, no underwire even, just a simple white brassiere. Against her pale skin, it seemed wholly inadequate for this rancher CEO. She should be in Agent Provocateur or some other fancy lingerie. The top of her dress fell to her waist, held in place by a belt. She brought both hands to cover her in a flash of modesty. She wasn't wearing any underwear, on his orders. He whistled, pushed up from the sofa and took a step closer to her, then another, until there was no space between them.

He pressed a kiss into her neck, and another in a hot trail to her ear.

"Have I told you, Ms. Kelly, I find you devastating?"

She smiled.

"Devastatingly attractive, my God. It feels religious, being here with you now." Another hot kiss, this time aimed lower, his mouth trailed over the thin cotton of her bra before tucking the fabric beneath her breast and feasting on the treasures beneath.

"Nick." She managed a strangled cry of his name and squirmed beneath him. "I want to touch you." She pulled his shirt over his head. Hot ridges of muscle begged to be touched and she marveled at his physique. Damn. It didn't get old, this sight. Her fingers followed every ridge, starting with the hard chest and moving down, tracing his abs, and swirling in the light sprinkle of hair that dipped into his waistband.

"Let's go." He broke away, his hand flying to his belt, pausing her exploration.

"Go? Not likely, Nick. I'm just getting started." Gone were her inhibitions; she was buzzing with attraction.

She'd fallen.

Who knew how much longer she'd live in this fairy tale before her karmic bill came due?

"I'm hardly going to ravish you on this couch." His delivery held little conviction, and with her one free hand, she managed to unhook the buckle of his belt.

His jeans slid away. He was hot against her, and she leaned into him, pulling him closer. "I want to feel you," she said, biting down on the bump of muscle on his shoulder.

"Did you spend the day bare?" he asked, catching her hand in his.

"Wouldn't you like to know?" She flirted back, bringing her hands back to his chest.

"Yes, very much." He lifted the hem of her dress. She

felt his rough fingers explore her, taking in the satisfied look in his eye when he stroked her, no barrier between them. “Good girl,” he crooned.

“Sometimes.” She kissed him, finishing with a nip to his lower lip.

“Go to bed with a vixen, don’t be surprised if you get bit, is that it?”

“I don’t see a bed here.” She bit him again.

“You’re too sexy for your own good.” He gripped her head, tangling a hand in her curls.

“What about your own good?” She pressed a kiss on his chest, and looked up.

“My welfare would be greatly aided by a little less talking and a little more loving.”

She shuddered. Loving. The word slipped out, innocuous and unassuming on his lips, but she couldn’t ignore it. It was too close to being real, even if he hadn’t meant it that way. It was the difference between smiling and laughing. Of loving and sex. Right now, she’d happily smile if it was with him. But not more. *More* was not something she knew how to do. The correction was necessary. “They don’t call this loving back where I come from.”

Frowning, she tightened her lips. She couldn’t lose herself, not while she had so much on the line. But maybe she could smile and mean it. Lord knew she wanted to.

“Well, maybe you’ve been doing it wrong.” He grinned. “Come, let’s go to my room. Spend the night with me.” He kissed her, and she felt herself smile against his lips. “The whole night.”

She wanted to. With everything that she was. To not have to wake up and sneak away as she had at the rodeo. But no. She could sleep with him, but men you fell asleep with? They meant trouble.

“Sounds like a good way to get hurt.” She was surprised she’d said it aloud. She hadn’t meant to. His hands stilled, and he brought a single finger to her chin, tilting it toward him.

"Well, I couldn't have that now, could I? You're right, let's stick to—"

"What was it I said before? You talk too much." She couldn't bear to have him belittle what they had. They weren't friends, and she didn't want to be a benefit.

"Maybe you should talk. Tell me what you want."

She looked at him and felt a pang in her chest. "I want to taste you," she admitted.

"Where?" His voice was rough.

"You know where." She took a step forward, gripping him. The pulsating heat was a lit match to the fire inside her. He twitched in her hand.

"What do you want?" he asked. She felt his hand on her arm, a gentle pressure as she sank to her knees.

"I want you inside me. Fast. Hard. I don't want it to stop until…"

"Until what?" He sank to the couch nearby and she scooted forward maintaining her proximity.

"Until I explode."

She didn't wait for a follow-up question, instead taking him in her mouth. It wasn't something she usually liked to do. But now? There was something undeniably erotic, feeling his hardness with her tongue. Knowing he wouldn't move. His hands went to her hair, pulling, tightening in her curls. It hurt a little, a sharp pain she liked, driving her tempo forward. One hand moved on his shaft, the other caressed his muscled thighs. He was so innately male. She felt a flexing tremble in his thigh and doubled her efforts. At this moment he'd surrendered to her. He was hers, but that surrender had a cost—her own surrender in kind.

"Enough," he breathed through gritted teeth.

She had no intention of stopping and didn't slow. He was close and she knew it. Then a strong hand stopped her.

"Vixen," he panted, before kissing her.

She bit him again, but just lightly. "What are you going to do about it?"

She could see the smile. Feel it as he covered her in wide kisses. Feasting on her chest, her nipples tightening as he consumed them. Consumed her.

He took her then, without prelude or discussion. Her slick need for him was all the further encouragement required. He woke in her a selfishness she'd missed. A selfishness she only dreamed of but had never known. Gone was the concept of waiting, to explode together. Instead, she cried out on her own, melting in a chorus of sharp delight. But he didn't stop, just fueled her to spiral higher, reaching new heights. He paused before he came, endearments on his lips. He spoke with a reverence she wondered at.

Was she imagining it? It felt perfect.

"Tell me something no one else knows about you," she asked from her new vantage point on the rug by a dying fire.

"What do you want to know?" He trailed a finger over her ribs, lazy and without purpose. Just to touch her, she supposed. It didn't matter, she liked it.

"Tell me…" She paused. "Tell me why you're fighting so hard for this ranch."

His finger stilled.

"You never mention your dad. Is that part of it?"

"It's always part of it, isn't it?" His voice was quiet and she turned to look at him.

It was her turn, and she trailed a finger on him now, as though touching him would make it easier to talk.

"My mom said it was never about me. When he left."

"Your dad left?" she clarified. The revelation was new.

"For seven years. To find himself." Nick swallowed hard. "I was fifteen. Twenty-two when he came back.

But he missed the better part of Jackson's adolescence. Not to mention the girls'. Who knows, maybe Austin wouldn't have been such a jackass if he hadn't shouldered all that…" His voice trailed off.

"And?" She kept her voice small on purpose. As though a louder intonation would scare away his confessions. He rolled toward her and kissed her softly.

"I guess he left for him, and came back for us. When he left, I swore I'd be the man this ranch needed. The man our family needed. Austin never cared about the ranch, or admired Dad. I've learned to put the ranch first, always. I've made a lot of mistakes, but I'm gonna keep this land."

She nuzzled against him, and watched as the dying embers turned to ash. It was hard not to wonder if she counted as one of his mistakes.

Fifteen

"Damn thing's not cooperating," he muttered as he fiddled with his tie.

Maybe it was the sight of the sumptuous couch, where only four days ago he'd experienced nirvana, pressed against the supple leather with his British minx. They hadn't discussed it. Hadn't so much as mentioned the tryst, or the revelations following. She was infuriatingly distant, escaping with Alix at every opportunity, sequestering them both in the kitchen for hour-long chats with the chef about the costs of different menu items. Sure, he understood the need to make lessons relatable, but the avoidance was a tad extreme.

His phone buzzed. "Nick here," he answered, glad to set his maddening tie aside.

"Hey, it's Jeff. They arrive in Bozeman just shy of thirty minutes."

Thirty minutes, plus forty more for the drive, so he had about an hour to pull everything together. "Thanks, Jeff, you arriving on time?" He balled up his tie and chucked it away. The slip of fabric vivid on his bland desk.

"Sure am, not missing a Hartmann party. Not enough of them to look forward to as it is."

"Right, then, see you at seven." He hung up and Samantha breezed in. "Saul's office called, and he emailed over this will. I guess Fran's lawyer sent it." She handed him the fax and pursed her lips. "Let me just..." She took another step closer to him, snaked the tie off his desk and looped it around his neck.

"Er." He straightened.

"Lemme just," she whispered, leaning forward, tying his tie. Another step into his space. He stiffened. Somehow it felt wrong, the intrusion.

"Listen, Samantha, can you schedule a time for us to chat? I'd like someone I can trust at the head office. High time you were promoted."

She nodded, expression impossible to read.

He reached for the printed email. A second will, apparently Katherine's. Naming Francesca as Alix's guardian.

"For all we know, Francesca wrote this herself. Make sure no one sees this tonight."

Taking his dismissive tone as the cue it was, she spun on her heels and left without acknowledging the promotion. Just as well. Sure, it was true, with all the work she'd taken on after Austin's death, she might be due a raise, but how could he give it to her without giving her the wrong idea? He resolved to ask Ben, and made a mental note to bring it up the next time he saw him.

The sky was summer bright, and at six thirty, the cool of night had not yet fallen. The ranch was transformed. Josephine and Rebecca, the staff events coordinator, had outdone themselves once again, and the lawns were lit with thousands of candles, each encased in a handblown glass dome and suspended from random branches along the mile-long winding driveway.

The west wing of the ranch was similarly bedazzled. A staff of forty waiters, dressed in matching black uniforms, waited with limitless glasses of sparkling wine and champagne. Platters of canapés and mini deconstructed ribs along with other modern interpretations of classic American foods circulated among the guests.

"Anyone seen Ben?" he asked a passing waiter dressed with a blazer atop his fitted shirt, a team leader. He'd said Ben, but he'd meant Mary. Her name was always on the tip of his tongue, always top of mind.

"No, sir."

Just as well. He saw dozens of people he needed to meet with, starting with the mayor of Bozeman. He assessed the room before entering, then his eyes focused on her. Sakes alive, she was a stunner. A vision, really. Her curls piled atop her head, a messy spill of blond, the smell alive in his memory. He wondered if she smelled like lavender tonight. Her dress was simple, a blue-black silk that clung to her curves. Impossibly thin straps held up the sweetheart neckline, and the dress fell to the floor with a designer's considered simplicity. She leaned back, tilting her head, and laughed. The movement carried a leg forward and he swallowed. A white thigh pushed through a sky-high slit in the front of the gown. He felt a tightening in his body, an anticipation of what it might be like to run a hand across that leg, following it higher to its apex. He needed to get her out of here, somewhere alone, now.

Making a beeline toward her, he distracted himself in an effort to cool his body, focusing on her entourage—namely, the two Chinese men she was charming. No. The Shenghen brothers? Like moths to a flame, they were attracted to her because…well, because of course they were.

She was like the moon, and had a similar gravitational pull on him. He stopped for a moment. That was it. He had fallen for her. Like gravity. He couldn't fight it. He watched her work the room and it occurred to him, maybe she was the missing piece he needed. Maybe she would stay and be the partner he'd never had. One he deeply wanted.

"You lot are too much." Rose smiled, aware of the importance of her company.

"Ms. Kelly, it is you who are too much." Both men spoke with a trace of a British accent, and flirting with them felt somehow familiar.

She tilted her head back, smiling wider. "I'm afraid you're a bunch of flatterers, the lot of you." She reached for an arm and gave it a squeeze. Gazillionaires or not, men were men, and Rose was strangely in her element.

She had arrived before the first guest, flanked by her charge. She and Alix had made a tour of the party, both a tad gobsmacked by the glamorous transformation of the ballroom. Sure, to her, it had been glamorous to start with the floor-to-ceiling windows gave way to a view unparalleled by any Rose had seen in her life. But after Rebecca was through with it? The same glass balls suspended from the fruit trees outside were suspended from the ceiling, in sweeping arcs of artistry casting the soft light of a thousand candles through the room. Chandeliers were lowered to create an ambience of comfortable intimacy, and the yellow light reflected off the many bedazzled dresses of the guests. Oversize bouquets of flowers six feet across released heady perfumes of jasmine and lily. The room was the picture of opulence and even her rich-kid student was silenced.

The ballroom was now invaded by glitterati, celebs flying in from both coasts, from top bankers to a rapper Alix idolized; the amalgamation of guests was the who's who of the society pages. The "small gathering" now welcomed at least two hundred people.

Nick's mother, dressed in an Egyptian-inspired chiffon dress, was pretty as a peach. Alix stiffened upon seeing her.

"Your dress is rather loud." Josephine's eyebrow shot up as she took in the hot-pink ensemble on her granddaughter.

"Thanks," Alix said, deliberate in her misinterpretation of the comment.

"I didn't mean it as a—"

"It's lovely to see you again, Mrs. Hartmann," Rose cut in. She put on her best smile, retucking a stubborn curl behind her ear.

Josephine snaked a glass of champagne off a passing tray. "You look—" she paused and cast her eyes in a deliberate once-over of Rose "—presentable."

The matriarch spat out *presentable* in a tone that left it sounding like an insult, but Rose was British. Polite insults had been bred into her people for generations. "As do you." She smiled back.

"Did you check on the canapés?" Alix broke the tension with her question.

"Canapés? There's a caterer—I'm sure everything is to the Hartmann standard." Josephine arched her eyebrow again and beckoned a waiter to her side, replacing her now empty glass with a full one.

"Maybe we should check," Alix said.

Rose nodded. *Canapés* was their safe word, and she had committed to getting Alix out of any situation that would necessitate its use.

Once out of earshot, they huddled behind the four-piece jazz band. "She's the worst," Alix hissed.

"That's maybe a bit harsh," Rose interjected.

"You look presentable." Alix mimicked her gran with a fair copy and the two giggled.

Rose saw two men speaking in what Alix's research had proposed was likely Mandarin to a small group just as an aide came in their direction.

"Mr. Shenghen." She bowed into a deep curtsy.

"No, I'm his aide, but he'd like to meet you."

He'd like to meet you. In this dress, she believed it. A huge part of her wanted to turn and run, but this was a massive business opportunity for Nick. For the ranch.

"With pleasure." She followed the aide and quickly found herself engaged in questions from the elder of the two brothers.

"Still fresh from the UK, I presume, as I don't hear a trace of the Western accent quite yet," he commented. But gone were her witty answers.

She saw Nick, towering a few inches over the heads of most of the crowd. No man had a right to look that good. He stood suave, confident and sexy as all hell. Once his eyes caught hers, they narrowed, and he made his way over to them.

Swallowing, she bit her lip.

She robotically nodded in reply, adding an obliging, "Yes, indeed."

"Feng, Liu." Nick's voice interrupted them and the men fell into a rapid succession of handshakes.

"Your tutor has been enthralling us with stories of the Wild West," Liu Shenghen started.

"Has she now?" Nick moved closer to her, and she took a step back, foot hitting the edge of the wainscoting. She'd reached a wall, both literally and figuratively.

"You're from the same stock. She's an Oxford grad, did she mention?" Nick smiled, an invitation to pick up the ball and run with it.

Of course she'd landed at the one ranch in Montana that would host a black-tie event with renowned alumni from her fake alma mater. Because that was her life. *Rose's life.* But now? Her ruse was important, to save face for Nick.

The brothers had graduated with honors from the business program, and they had a volley of questions.

"What did you study? Did you board? Wasn't the library wonderful?"

"Easy, gentleman." She laughed in an effort to brush them off.

"Amazing to have hired an Oxford-educated tutor at the last moment," Feng marveled. "Some men have all the luck."

Nick slid one hand behind her on the small of her back. His palm, a hot brand she was proud to wear.

"What faculty were you in?" Liu asked.

She swallowed the last drops of champagne, tipping her glass vertically with a flourish. "Education," she answered. That sounded right. She was pretty sure that's what Mary had studied.

"I did a minor in Education," Liu cut in with excitement.

Her stomach flipped and she faltered against the steady hand behind her.

"Brilliant. Did you have Mr. Peabody?" She picked the most British name she could think of and just leaned in.

The brothers exchanged glances, shaking their heads.

"I'll always remember being dropped off for Michaelmas Term—best part of the year, I say," Feng concluded.

"Yes, I used to spend all summer looking forward to September." Rose shot another winning smile at her audience. This was getting easier.

"You mean October?" Feng clarified.

"Don't try and trip me up." She laughed, nervous.

A few more blundering references to Harry Potter and she felt sick to her stomach. The last joke about house dinners did not land well. Champagne and lies were a dangerous combination.

"Who did you say your favorite professor was?" Feng asked, an edge growing in his tone.

One Oxford professor, surely I can think of one Oxford professor. "Mr. Johnston-Man?"

"Johnston-Man?" Feng scoffed. The brothers switched into a rapid conversation in Chinese, the elder brother gesturing with his hands, then turning to her. "Are you saying, miss, that you attended Oxford College?"

"What are you implying?" Nick jumped in, voice terse.

"I don't believe you, but I am curious as to why you'd lie about it. Shall we continue the farce?"

"Excuse you—" Nick started.

"You know she attended Oxford *Brooks* College?" It was Alix who calmed the group, saving the day with a reference to another college.

The lined faces of the men relaxed. "Brooks? Ha, what a story," said Liu, signaling for another refill. "Quite the misunderstanding."

What a story indeed. Rose flashed a strained smile at her charge. "Canapés."

Sixteen

"You didn't go to Oxford."

A waiter sped past Nick in a vain effort to offer some privacy. It didn't matter.

She stood, shoulders back, blinking three times in quick succession. "No." Blink. Blink. "Not really. I guess I didn't."

Somewhere in his mind, Nick recognized his anger was disproportionate. Yes, lying was bad. Yes, he was her employer and there would be consequences. But what he felt now? It was akin to rage. He'd trusted her, fallen for her…

His voice shook despite his efforts to keep it measured. "*Not really?* Pick a side, Mary, either you did or you didn't."

Mary stood, and teetered back and forth.

"Didn't, then." She sounded proud of herself, perhaps for not hesitating with her answer.

He reached for her arm and pulled her toward the corner alcove. They were tucked away from prying eyes and ears, and he doubled down on his effort not to scream at her. Even through his rage he wondered, why did she have to smell so good?

"So you lied about your experience, then? Is that it? You lied?"

She pulled her arm away and rubbed a hand over her elbow where he had pulled her. But she didn't complain; instead, she brought her chin up a notch to look him in the eye. "I guess. I mean, I've *been* to Oxford. So I *went* to Oxford. I didn't *study* there, but I never claimed to."

He shook with fury. She was trying to dance around the facts with a technicality? He pressed his hands to his sides. His fingers bit into his thighs as he clenched and unclenched his fists. "That isn't the same damn thing at all."

"I guess not," she said, shoulders falling as her strong front faded. She backed up into the window seat of the alcove and sank down. Her head dropped onto her hands.

"You guess not?"

"Are you just going to repeat everything I'm saying?" Her voice quavered and her eyes filled. A curl came untucked from the pinned tower of flaxen curls on her head.

"Until I hear an apology."

"I want to explain but…" Her shoulders slumped. "Do you think I'd be better for Alix if I had a degree from a fancy-pants school?" The question was soft. He could hear the hurt in her voice. Well, that was too damn bad.

"Don't even try to turn this around on me."

"Don't try to defend myself to my lover who's so quick to think the worst of me?" Her voice caught on the word *lover* and wavered.

"Your lover? Twice, we've been together twice."

"I'm just an employee now?"

"Why don't we start with liar?" He could see that his words cut her and he continued nonetheless. All he could feel was pain and anger. He couldn't have risked the ranch on a liar. Be in love with a liar. "You've embarrassed me tonight. Badly." He paced. "You knew how important this was to me. How important Alix is to me. Anyone finds out her education is compromised and I could lose her, Mary. Lose her, lose the ranch. My sisters, Francesca—everyone is waiting for one fuckup. One mistake, and I think I just made it."

Her sharp intake of breath sliced him open.

"I can't do this right now. Can't see you right now." Then he parted the curtains and left them swishing behind him.

He was in a foul mood.

Nothing worse than being in a foul mood with a room full of people to entertain, or worse, impress. He didn't much like impressing people on a good day. Nick prowled the ballroom, shrugging off invitations and niceties as he made a beeline for the bar. "Scotch neat, the Macallan 45." He rattled off his drink order on autopilot and leaned into the leather-bound bar.

"You mean the Macallan 45, *please*," a female voice corrected. He spun and came face-to-face with the last person he expected to see, one he hadn't dared invite based on their last parting. Evie Hartmann, his sister.

"Evie!" For a moment, the room was empty, and it was just him and his little sis, together again. "It's…been a long time."

She stood back, and he took her in. Evie was twenty-eight and breathtaking. Tall, lithe and slim, she wore a sleeveless gold lamé dress and looked like a movie star from the 1950s.

"Long enough for you to change everything," she said evenly, and smiled at him as she delivered the cutting blow, reminding him she was an actress, ready and capable to deliver a line whenever the situation called for one.

"I hardly orchestrated the… Well, let's just agree it's all been very sudden, all this change." He took the Scotch off the bar, and passed it to Evie. "I'll take another," he said, then with a sidelong glance at his sister, added, "Please."

As per his usual, Ben was only moments behind Evie, and had arrived with two glasses of champagne. "I got us each a…" His voice trailed off as he took in Nick, sipping Scotch next to his sister.

Evie reached for the champagne. "Thanks." She smiled.

Nick didn't like it, not one bit. He knew his sister for the heartbreaker that she was. Ben was too nice for her. But that was another problem for another day.

"Why did you come?" Nick drilled down to the point, his humor not sufficiently improved enough by her presence to shrug off the cloud of melancholy Mary had left him with.

"The listing agent called me." Smooth jazz flooded the room now that the band had dispensed with their break, and he struggled to hear her. "You suspended the sale? Didn't even pick up the phone to call me?" She was mad.

"I had a lot on my plate."

"Mom told me. Precisely why I'm pissed." She clamped a hand on his shoulder and squared herself to him. "You didn't call me *once* after our brother died."

"I was probably busy listening to all the voice mails you'd left me," he snapped sarcastically.

"If you're trying to figure out which Hartmann has the harder head, after a lifetime of experience, I still don't know." Ben's affable tone did little to calm the siblings.

"Too busy making friends with the niece to think of your sister? Or were you preoccupied with another set of legs?" Evie was back to being mean.

"This place is Alix's birthright, and I'm not about to parcel it up to sell to the highest bidder."

"Easy, Nick, no one's trying to sell anything," Ben said.

"This isn't over between you and me," Evie said.

But before she could issue more threats, Ben extended a hand and said, "I think you owe me a dance."

He'd let Ben deal with Evie. He'd had enough of temperamental women for the evening.

Rose stayed in the alcove for nearly forty minutes. Not crying, barely. She'd deserved the lecture. Deserved the inquisition. Deserved worse.

"You're a liar," she whispered, pinching herself, hard, finding comfort in the sharp pain. She closed her eyes, and when she reopened them moments later, she wasn't alone.

"Canapés," the small voice ventured. Rose's head jerked up.

"Canapés," she answered.

Alix stood, one hip cocked in an awkward posture, and grinned. "I did good, huh?" she asked, referencing her save during the conversation with the Shenghen brothers.

Rose smiled. "Yeah, you sure did." In a way, it was a relief to drop the facade. To put her energy into just *being*, versus trying to constantly maintain a state of perfection. "You wanna sit?" She moved over and made a bit of space on the window seat. Alix sat and Rose dived in. "I guess you know—"

"Everything," Alix finished.

There was a window in the alcove, and though the space was lit only by the stars, it was bright enough to see a corner of Alix's mouth turn up in pride. *She was so like her uncle.*

Alix shifted in her seat, and brought her big brown eyes to an inquisitive focus on Rose. "Everything…except why?"

"Then let me start at the beginning."

And so she did. Rose told Alix about a young girl who very much looked up to her sister. About an older sister who inherited an even bigger responsibility the night their parents died. About how that older sister died. She told Alix about the kids in India, her sister's legacy. She admitted that maybe the wrong sister died. A truth she'd never spoken aloud.

The one despair she didn't voice was the loss she'd earned tonight. She'd lied to Nick, when he'd been unbelievably honest with her. She didn't deserve him. But she wanted to—needed to—deserve him.

What would Mary do? And could Rose do it on her own?

"Yeah, but how did you end up here?" Alix's voice was quiet but steady.

"It's simple, really." Rose smiled, confident in the one part of this decision she'd made on her own. "I came for you."

Seventeen

She'd left the letter on purpose, putting it where he'd be sure to find it. He reckoned as much, anyway. Alix wasn't the type of kid to leave her things around; the girl was so private he'd worried at first about the lack of adolescent sprawl at the ranch. So when he retired after the gala to pour a congratulatory drink, he had been shocked to see the letter there, on the center of his desk. The placement, so deliberate. The white envelope addressed, Alix Hartmann. The letter, open underneath it.

Alix,
We haven't spent much time together.

I'd like the opportunity to get to know you better, a lot better, in fact, and my lawyer tells me at sixteen you're old enough to make the choice yourself. This is something he and I would very much like to discuss with you.

Your aunt,
Franny

Wow. Just wow. *We haven't spent much time together.* What did that even mean? From the interactions between their lawyers, he could guess at Franny's endgame. But why had Alix left the letter for him to read?

If there was one person who might have insight as to the why, it was Mary. But he couldn't go find her now—he looked down at his watch and cursed, three a.m. already? And not after the words they'd exchanged earlier this evening.

There was nothing to be done until morning. Nothing but drink more. Alone.

The first glass had gone down smooth. He read the letter again. Thought about his brother, now dead. About Katherine, the woman who'd betrayed him, who'd—indirectly—given him Alix. Thought about the woman he loved, who'd lied to him. Third glass. Another read. Another glass.

"Nick?"

Was he hallucinating? It was Mary.

"I'm glad you're awake."

Was he?

"I'm sorry—" her voice cracked "—I'm sorry about the lie." He heard the rustle of silk as she moved to stand behind him.

The fire, lit by some overeager staff member, was now coals. Nick was transfixed by the live embers, still emanating waves of heat.

"The letter on the table—Alix left it here for me to read. Franny is openly challenging my bid for custody. You, Alix—everything is falling apart." *Everything except the deal.* He had a handshake agreement that would triple the profits of their ranch. Under his guidance, they'd become one of the most profitable cattle ranches in America. An empire, with no one who wanted it. An empire, and only him left to appreciate it.

"I didn't go to my brother's funeral. Did I ever tell you

that?" He didn't move from the couch. The room was so quiet he heard the silk slide against the leather and imagined her shoulders rising to affect the pull of fabric.

"Why not?"

He directed his attention from the memory of her shoulders back to the fire. He spoke robotically, mouth set in grim determination. "I was mad at him. Still. Sixteen years later and I was mad."

"That's quite the grudge." A hand furtively descended to his shoulder.

"Katherine was my first love, but was a wild child. Wanted to leave Montana, not just for school, but forever. We fought and she broke up with me. Went with Austin to prom, even though she was my prom date."

"You'd said."

"We'd been together four years. And she slept with him on a whim that night. She said she loved me, but she lied."

Mary didn't say anything, so he continued.

"She got pregnant. I can't call it a mistake—that baby was Alix. But I couldn't forgive her. Couldn't look at Austin. And I missed out on it all."

She swallowed, and he heard it. She had to understand. Had to see why he could never forgive her.

"You let me believe the lie, so I can't trust you. I won't… I don't even know you now."

"I guess you don't," she said with a calm so quiet he twisted to look at her. "But you could get to know me. Where I went to school, why I pretended to go to Oxford. That can't be the deal breaker here." Her voice was quiet, hopeful and heartbreaking.

"We're past deal breakers, Mary. You're a risk now. A liability." This ranch was all he had. And Alix? The one person who stood a chance at helping him keep it. If Franny were to find out that he'd misrepresented Alix's education to the courts?

"I guess you know what you want, then," she said

flatly, then spun on her heel and left. She was a dichotomy. She was light. And for a moment, he'd believed he could have her.

All the more fool he. Some people, himself included, were not built for love.

She awoke before her alarm, unsure whether to blame a busy mind or her fitful sleep. Perhaps one element was responsible for the other; she couldn't know which was to blame.

Except now? For her? She knew exactly who to blame.

Rose pulled her covers off and slipped on yoga pants and a sweatshirt, the first ensemble that came to hand. Hesitating, she circled back to her dresser and grabbed for her swimsuit. One last swim before she left. It seemed appropriate, even if she hadn't earned it.

The walk to her spot at the creek was cathartic. The damp in the air smelled fresh, and the birds sang with an optimism that gave her hope all wasn't lost. She needed her five minutes, then she'd make a plan.

A plan to deserve him.

A plan to convince him that she was a risk he wanted to take.

She arrived and dialed, phone pressed to her ear, tears held back. She waited for the answer, for the recording she cherished. Then a damning beep greeted her, followed by the accursed, "I'm sorry, the number you have called has been disconnected. Please check and try again."

Disconnected? How was that even possible?

The question floated in her head, and she bit the inside of her cheek hard because she knew. The copper taste of blood startled her, but she bit down harder. By reflex, she kicked her foot against the base of the rock, then cried out in pain. It hurt. *Good.*

She hadn't paid the phone bill. Too busy falling for a rancher, preparing for a ball. Hot tears streamed down her face. "I'm sorry, Mary," she said to no one in particular. "I guess I haven't changed at all."

No sense in staying here. She now knew it with the certainty that she knew her own name. She'd failed Alix, who stood to lose the guardian and home she'd come to love, all because of her lies. She'd failed the kids in India, failed Mary's memory. She deserved to lose this place, this man. She'd go back to being a barmaid; at least she couldn't crush anyone's hopes and dreams that way.

One last swim and then she'd say goodbye.

He had almost blown it off. Almost rolled over and given in to his hangover, when the shriek of his alarm ruined his dream. And what a dream it had been! Mary, squirming against him, hot body pressed against his. But he'd pulled himself out of bed and to the creek. The cold of the swimming hole doing little to ease the memory of her. He closed his eyes. Mary was his lover in a dream, and in waking? She was a liar.

When he opened his eyes, he blinked. She was there, at the edge of the creek bank.

She wore a simple one-piece, black and efficient. It did the job with little room for vanity, but damn, even in the modest swimsuit she was a vision. A lying vision, sure, but a vision nonetheless.

She stepped into the water, ankle-deep, and shivered. After a moment's pause, she dived in.

He swam toward her, questions hot on his lips. "Didn't think I'd see you again so soon."

She didn't seem surprised to see him there. "I came to say goodbye," she started.

The statement came as no surprise. She had to leave. They were at a moral impasse, and as much as he longed to pretend it didn't matter, it did.

"Goodbye, Mary," he said simply. Nick fought the impulse to reach for her, beg her to stay. She didn't make a move to swim away just yet. He scoffed—why would she? She'd only just arrived for the swim.

"It's Rose."

The admission came from nowhere. "Rose?"

She nodded. "Mary was my sister," she choked out.

"Your sister?" He wanted to scream.

She'd been telling a bigger lie than he'd imagined. But why come clean at all? She was leaving. What did it matter if he knew everything?

"Mary died. Because of me. She was picking me up from a party, and a drunk driver… I guess it doesn't even matter. I came here because I wanted to help. I wanted to be good, like her. I read about Alix—I thought I could be there for her, two orphans. Support her, but I've messed it all to hell. I'm so sorry, Nick."

The lies were too much.

His love for her? An exquisite torture, because he felt it still.

She'd played him. And still he wanted her.

"Why did you tell me?" he asked.

"I had to," she said simply. "I love you."

The admission was directed toward the woods. She didn't look his way as she said it. Instead, she stepped out of the creek, picked up her sweatshirt and pants and walked away.

Eighteen

She'd endured a crap flight, mostly due to the fact that she'd taken the first available connection to Denver, then spent seven hours waiting for a puddle-hopper to Heathrow. It was easier waiting at the airport, staring out of focus into space, than being at his ranch fighting the feeling that she was already home.

"Here's the post." Ellen gestured toward a huge stack of envelopes as she welcomed Rose back. "I'm dying to hear all about your cowboy adventure." Ellen was smoking. Inside the flat.

"Could you not?" Rose gestured toward the cigarette.

"Sorry, did you want one?" Ellen grabbed her purse and dug through it.

"Do I want one? No." She was tired. Tired and devastated. "What I want is a nap."

Ellen got the hint. "I'll take this outside. We can get together for lunch?"

"Perfect." Rose yawned. Her arms stretched above her,

and as she let them drop back to her sides, they slapped the protruding kitchen countertop that came within a meter of her entrance. How quickly she'd forgotten the "smallness" of her kitchen, particularly when faced with the vast beauty of Montana.

After five minutes stretched atop her covers, it dawned on her that she couldn't sleep.

Hope you got home okay. Thinking of you, Rose!

The text was from Alix. Checking in. She smiled at her phone and sent back an affirming, Yes, everything fine, just long. I'm knackered now but will catch up after a quick nap.

Nothing from Nick. She supposed it wasn't unexpected. They had slept together twice. Never had a simple qualifier made her feel so unimportant.

She swung her feet from the bed to the floor and made her way to the stack of correspondence with a newfound urge to be organized. She'd tackle the overdue bills and make a real plan. It probably wasn't Nick she missed, but wanting to make a difference, and she could surely find a way to do that.

It wasn't Nick she missed.

If she said it enough, maybe she'd start to believe it.

Perhaps she hadn't earned enough to sponsor all twenty-seven kids, but she had saved enough to sponsor more than half, and it was a good start. She would find another way to earn the rest of the money.

After the tenth bill, her optimism about the savings she'd tucked aside began to flicker. While she did see many opportunities to curb her spending, the large stack spoke to more than her financial obligations. Well, this was the start of it, then, of being a real grown-up. *I'm my own conscience now.*

Midstack, she pulled at a cream-colored envelope, the

return address marked as Royal London Insurance. Her sister's life insurance.

Her hands shook as she opened the envelope. The letter inside was simple. Sorry about her loss. They've processed the claim. She was the named beneficiary. The sum of… "Blimey." She dropped the letter.

No, that couldn't be right. Eight hundred thousand pounds?

The forty quid Mary had set aside every month? Quite the investment indeed.

She reached for her jacket, and drove to the only place in London that made sense to her right now.

When she arrived, she stared at the headstone. It felt the same yet different. She was closer to Mary, physically, but she missed talking to her sister in the quiet of the Montana woods. The dampish cool of the stone she sat on and the alluring promise of a hard shoulder only a few minutes' cry away. Still, that was then, this was now. She had to stay in the now.

"It's an awful lot of money. What am I meant to do with it all? Did you think, if a tragedy struck, I'd be happier with the cash? Reward for good behavior?" Her voice rose and a woman ushered a young girl quickly past her to another part of the cemetery. "What should I do, then? With more money than I'd earn in ten years?"

"Those things ever talk back to you?"

She jumped at the voice. It was a gardener, or at least a man who looked like a gardener, tending to the plot a few rows behind her. He was several decades her senior, his face weathered by too much time in the sun.

"No," she admitted.

"You know what you're gonna do? With your awful lot of money?" he insisted.

She was incredulous. "You were listening?"

"You weren't whispering," he defended. "Blokes like

me have to pass the time as best we can, isn't that right?" He smiled at her and her defenses slid.

"I'm sorry." She pointed to the headstone. "I just wish I could talk to her."

"Don't apologize." He rose from his plot, but to her relief turned away from her. "I still talk to my wife. I take her with me everywhere."

"But you're here," Rose said, unsure of where this conversation was going.

"Did you ever think, all we gotta do is just live honorably?" He took another few steps, then waved at her before leaving.

Live honorably. She knelt at the head of the grave and brushed the headstone free of debris. The odd twig and a few leaves had gathered at the base.

"I'm gonna make you proud, Mary," she promised.

It started to rain on her as she walked back toward her car. She was so tired her vision blurred, and a lone tear fell on her cheek. Tears? Rain? Fatigue? It didn't matter.

I have an idea I wanted to talk over with you. Can we chat?

It wasn't smart, her idea. But as she stood, in the rain, feeling more alone than she had ever felt in her whole life, she pressed Send and sent her missive into the waiting inbox of Saul Kellerman.

Nineteen

"Please scan and send this to Jeff." Nick passed the Chinese distribution agreement to Carly, Samantha's replacement.

Samantha was doing well in her new position, and he was relieved that she'd seemed to move past her crush on him. Relieved because it felt like less of a big deal now that he was entirely unable to move past his own feelings regarding a certain British tutor.

He couldn't stop thinking about Rose. If Samantha could forgive him for his mistake, surely he could do the same?

He spun on his chair, taking in the view of the countryside he loved so dearly. He wanted to be riding, not stuck here, managing the minutia. He needed to ride the land while he still could. Who knew where the custody battle would leave him.

Not for the first time, he frowned. If he lost the custody battle, he'd lose more than the ranch. He'd lose Alix, just like he'd lost Rose. The thought of losing both the women he'd come to love suddenly a thousand times worse than losing the land he'd been fighting for.

Rose said she'd come here to help Alix. Her eagerness to do something good for her sister's memory had led to mistakes.

He studied the horizon, his own mistakes—with his brothers, his family, with Alix…with Rose—playing like an old-time movie, burning into the back of his brain. Overhead, an eagle flapped easy wings as he flew, then a second eagle joined, and the two birds hunted in tandem. Two souls, on the same journey.

Maybe love didn't mean not making mistakes. Maybe love was forgiveness. More than that, a commitment to stay regardless of mistakes. If Austin had stayed, where would they be now? One thing was for sure, if Nick had forgiven him, they'd be better still.

He wasn't sure how long he sat like that, thinking about Austin, and swallowing the regret at waiting too long to forgive, but when Evie entered, flanked by their mother and Ben, he pulled himself together. He decided that this time *he'd* forgive first.

It would hurt less than losing the chance to love.

"We are concerned," his mother started.

"*Concerned* feels like a strong word," Ben corrected.

"Strong? Not strong enough, I'd say." Evie stepped in front of the two others and put a large manila envelope on his desk. Department of Education was written in large capital letters.

"We think it would help everything, in particular the custody battle plainly on the horizon, if Alix sits an assessment test."

"Assessment test? She's had the best tutor money could buy." He paused, realizing he meant it. Maybe not academically, but while Mary—Rose—had been here, Alix had transformed from a sullen teenager to a member of the family, and he knew to whom the credit was due. Alix had even left the letter from Franny to help in the custody battles she knew were looming.

"Are you sure you're not being unduly influenced by the tutor?" This time it was Josephine.

Nick didn't answer. He picked up the envelope. He could see the point. If Alix did well on the test, it would solidify the argument that she belonged with him, here. That he'd made good choices for her, as her guardian. No one had said it—no one had accused him outright of sleeping with the tutor—but the doubt was there. Rose was too pretty. Too tempting. No one thought he'd hired her for Alix, and while they might be right with regard to how it had ended, that certainly wasn't how it had started. It had all started for Alix.

"I don't want to talk about this without Alix. As far as I'm concerned, she gets to be a part of this conversation."

"I'm here." Her voice was small, but she stepped in from behind the door to his office. She was dressed simply, in jeans and a T-shirt. For the first time since she'd arrived at the ranch, her hair was pulled back off her face, in the same messy-bun style Rose had worn every day. It made her look both younger and older at the same time.

"She's gone, anyway—Rose, I mean."

"I thought it was Mary?" Evie asked.

"Anyway, she's gone now." Alix's eyes were downcast and she stared at her feet.

This admission caused a flurry of commotion, which Alix interrupted. "I'll take the test, then, whenever. Like, now is fine for me—not like you can study for an aptitude test."

"Right, that's a good point," Nick added.

"It's going to go well, Uncle Nick, don't worry. Rose did a good job."

Uncle Nick. He smiled for the first time since Rose had left.

"I wasn't worried, Alix."

The two weeks since Alix had taken the test were excruciating.

He thought about Rose every time he closed his eyes. Every time he sat on the couch, or ate dinner. Thinking about her was as natural as breathing, the impulse as hard to deny. She had been the light in his day, and everything was a crushing gray without her. He needed her back. Lies be damned.

She'd come clean when she hadn't needed to. Admitted to a bigger deception than he'd suspected. Why would she do that?

Because she loves me.

Could he forgive her?

He didn't have a choice. He loved her. But he had to wait for Alix's test results before he could leave to get her back. Rose wouldn't want him to abandon Alix when she was uncertain that she could stay.

Nick paced the hall, footsteps clicking on the polished granite floors of the foyer. The mail was here. An official-looking envelope, arriving via express service. Speedy turnaround one of the perks of a pushy lawyer and a private assessment center.

Alix's laughter echoed through the hallway as the side door pushed open and she entered with Evie. His sister was a poor substitute for Rose, but it was…nice having Evie at home again.

"Your results—they're here," he called down the hallway.

Alix's voice echoed back, "Let's read 'em over breakfast?"

They all made their way into the dining room, and once they'd sat down, she reached for a roll and dug into the food. Her face was windburned from horseback riding and she looked happy.

Nick nodded at the envelope. "Well, then?"

"You don't seem worried," Evie added, smiling.

"I'm not worried." Alix scooped a scone from the passing platter, and added it to her plate, nestling it beside the pyramid of new potatoes.

"Love the confidence, girl." Evie smiled.

Nick, impatient, opened the envelope and read aloud.

Mr. Hartmann,
Per the Montana Connect Assessment Center aptitude test and curriculum grid, it is our finding that Miss Alixandra Hartmann exceeds state standards in both Mathematics and Language Arts, with an elevated result in critical reasoning.

Please get in touch regarding tailored learning opportunities befitting her advanced placement level.

Regards,
Aurora Sinclaire

The room was thick with silence, apart from the sound of Alix's smacking lips. "These eggs are something else," she said through a mouthful of breakfast.

"Manners, Alix," Nick managed to say, head spinning from the short letter, and fingers shaking as he flipped through the attached report. *Exemplary. Exceeds peer result. Above average logic and verbal reasoning...* Every section scored with high marks. "How do you explain this?" He hoped Alix could make sense of it. The headmistress from her former school had described her as a disengaged troublemaker.

"Rose. She just made me want to try." She sliced another bit of egg.

"But I never saw you reading. You're always listening to music, disconnected..." He tried not to sound incredulous.

"Audiobooks, I'm listening to audiobooks. And podcasts on the economy."

"The economy?" Evie asked, similarly open-mouthed in shock.

"Well, yeah, but I also listen to podcasts on mental math, speed reading strategies, tons of other stuff..."

"So this whole time you've been working on advanced subjects?"

"I guess," she said, mumbling through her food. "Rose really inspired me to get curious. I wanted her to stay."

"Okay, well, I guess that's perfect." He smiled.

"Perfect?" Alix brightened. "She's coming back?"

"If she says yes." Two weeks without her was more than enough to convince him he couldn't manage a day longer. He smiled. "But I meant that with results like these, there's no question she was a good hire. That I made a good choice for you. And that you'll be able to stay."

She smiled back at him.

He was going to keep Alix. And the ranch—he had a plan for that. And Rose, too, if he could convince her to give him another chance.

But first, he had to break the news to the rest of his family.

He was nervous. It was a big step, but a necessary one. No turning back.

But he was sure. Leading this family involved change. And before he could ask Rose to spend her life with him, he needed to mend the fences he'd carelessly broken over the years.

"Thanks for meeting me. I decided I would list the ranch—well, part of it, anyway. If y'all want. We could parcel a section. With the profits we're due to get over the next twenty-four months from the export deal, earnings are through the roof. The company can buy out the personal shares of whoever wants to sell. So if you all wanna sell. I can—" his voice cracked "—I can accept that."

The women sat in stunned silence.

"Where is this coming from?" Alix asked.

He looked at her. Fresh-faced, clever, independent. He wanted her to love this ranch, yes, but he felt ashamed that his initial motive had been a calculated one. He trusted her to make up her own mind about what was right.

"Some might think I took you in because I wanted your vote." He reddened. "Well, I did want your vote. But more than that, I want you. You're my family. And you're smart. A lot smarter than any of us gave you credit for. You get a say in what you want."

Alix pushed her chair closer to him. "Uncle Nick," she said plainly. "I'm not going to sell."

Evie spoke next, following Alix's overture with a light cough. "You know, I'm kinda liking Montana these days. I was thinking maybe I could take over the old house? You know, official-like?"

Nick felt a wide smile spread across his face. "You wanna stay?" Incredible that he'd gone from being the only Hartmann to care about this ranch to one of many.

Amelia spoke for the first time. "I'm not selling, either. Now that I'm divorcing..."

His head spun. "Wait. You both want—"

"We *all* want to be included in how this ranch is run," Josephine corrected, smiling. "It's our legacy. Our *family's* legacy. Thanks for making us a part of the process."

Nick rubbed a hand over his eyes, giving himself a second to blink away his surprise, eyes hot with emotion. He opened his mouth to speak, then shut it, instead studying his family. Evie, arm slung over Amelia's shoulders, hand rubbing her back with a steady and reassuring pace. Josephine, focused on Alix, who beamed back at him, eyes dancing and mouth wide in a smile. Jackson would always have his back, but to feel the support of the other members of his family was a dream come true. All the Hartmanns aligned, and just one person was missing from the equation. An English rose.

Twenty

When Nick arrived at the door of her apartment, unshaven and mildly disheveled, he knocked before he could think twice.

He was here for her, and he didn't want to waste one more moment waiting.

"You're late," she said simply after opening the door.

"I came as fast as I could," he answered. "Can I come in?" He took his hat off and held it to his chest like armor.

Alix had opted to stay in the café next door, and Nick was grateful that she understood the tact he would need to dig himself out of his current predicament. While he was ready to grovel, he preferred to do it without witnesses.

"I guess." Rose stepped back and let him in.

Her flat was disordered, mostly due to the cartons filling every available space.

"Moving?" he asked, gesturing around.

"Yep," she shot back. "I'm downsizing. In my new job, I plan to travel."

"New job?"

She shifted against the doorframe. "Would you like a cuppa?" Rose waved toward her kitchen.

"I would," he said, more to appease her than because he wanted tea.

She turned, and in two paces was in the corner of her flat designated as a kitchen.

"Where are you off to, then?" He shifted. He hadn't come for small talk, but couldn't seem to find a way to say what he'd come to say.

"I've still got a bit to figure out, but I'm starting a charity."

"A charity?" He edged closer to her and put his hat on the small counter dividing the cooking area from the dining area.

"Look, Nick. I know I messed everything up. But getting to know Alix, getting to know you…getting to *matter* to someone? It helped me, Nick. And now? I just want to do it again."

He bit down on his lip. *He had a chance.*

She continued, fingers squeezing into fists and clenched at her sides. "I took the life insurance money. From Mary. I had no idea about the policy, but it's enough to make a difference. I've incorporated a nonprofit. I want to offer inner-city kids a chance to reconnect with nature. To heal, away from the pressures of the city, to commune with horses, to swim in a creek… Saul Kellerman is helping me set it up. He mentioned there might be some land for sale. In Montana." She pushed a curl back from her face, tucking it behind her ear, and for a minute he swore his pulse stopped.

She looked at him, raising her eyes to meet his. "I'm so sorry, Nick. I didn't take the job to fall in love with you, but I fell…hard. And yes, I lied about my name and my education, but I have never been more myself than I was with you these past few months. How I felt about you? It's the most honest thing I've ever felt in my life. I love you. Love your land. I love Alix." Her voice caught.

He took a step toward her, but she held up a hand to stop him. "I want to be near you. Show you I'm good. Earn back your trust. I'm ready to invest everything I have. Everything I am." The timbre of her voice fell, and she added a soft, "Do you think it will ever be enough?"

He stepped closer to her. Crossed that invisible line between holding grudges and the willingness to forgive. Crossed into her space. "You're enough. You're so much more than enough." He took a final step, feeling his chest brush against hers, unable to stand any closer without crushing her toward him. "I'm sorry, too," he managed gruffly. "It took me a little while to make things right with the family. Or start to make them right. I mean, I'm the first to admit everyone makes mistakes, but I wanted to fix some of mine. I've made enough of them."

"You can say that again," she whispered, then paled. "I meant, that everyone makes mistakes." She followed the sentiment with a playful pat to his chest, but he caught her hand and pressed it over his heart.

He wasn't going to let himself off the hook that easily. He didn't want to. He wanted to give her everything she deserved, and that started with the truth.

She stiffened, pulling back from him. "Why are you here, Nick?"

"It's simple," he started, realizing for the first time that it was.

Sure, he'd made things right with his siblings, but he'd be here even if that wasn't the case. He'd rather be here, with her, than anywhere else in the world alone.

"I've never loved anyone as much as I love you. You took Alix, my kin, my friends, and you made us a home. You made us a family. You're complicated, genuine, beautiful, delightfully defiant, endlessly sexy and… I need you. I love you. Utterly. Completely. I didn't care when I left, didn't care if I was gonna be too late, I had to come. I had to try. I had to tell you. You want to know why I came?" The words escaped him, traveling on the last breath he had. That was the thing about it all. If he could use a last breath for anything it would be to say, "I love you." So he did.

She nodded, eyes shining.

"And so?" he continued. "Do you think you have enough charity left in you to forgive a fool of a cowboy?"

"It depends." She smiled and let her hands circle his neck. "Does a *Rose* by any other name taste as sweet?"

Nick Hartmann was thirty-two. He might not know everything, but somehow he'd gotten everything he ever wanted. And when it came to the answer to this age-old question, first posed by Shakespeare, he was confident.

She did.

* * * * *

ONE NIGHT EXPECTATIONS

LaQUETTE

To my ride or die and fellow Brooklynite,
my agent, Latoya Smith.
Thank you for helping me show the world
what two little brown girls from Brooklyn can do.

One

"I said what I said."

Amara Angel Devereaux-Rodriguez sat at her desk on a Zoom call with her grandfather, internally reeling from the five words he'd just spoken. His tone was casual, as if he was sitting at home with his feet up reading a newspaper, not discussing contracts totaling more than a quarter of a small country's GDP.

But that was what made her grandfather so good at what he did. He was so unassuming, he was deadly. By the time opposing counsel figured this out, he'd already have the deal signed, sealed and delivered.

"You can't do this, Granddaddy." Her voice was calm but her clenched teeth and stiff body language accurately relayed her displeasure. "I've put in too much work for this company for you to pull the rug out from under me like this."

He was unmoved as he sat in the den at Devereaux Manor, dipping his gaze to read the document he was holding. Only when he was finished did he pull off his readers and look up, finally acknowledging her presence on the video call.

"Can't?" He raised a brow as he sat up straight in his chair. "As lead counsel for Devereaux Inc. and your boss, I can do whatever I want. Just because I'm out of the office spending time with your uncle Ace while he's sick doesn't mean I'm not still in charge. My decision is final. I'm not retiring until after this Falcon Development deal is closed."

She folded her arms, trying her best to suppress the anger boiling inside. "I have closed more deals and made more money for this company in the last three years than any other lawyer here, including you. You were poised to sail off into the sunset and give me the reins. Then all of a sudden you're changing your plans and pushing me to the sidelines. What the hell, Granddaddy?"

She realized two seconds after she'd said it her mouth had written a check her ass couldn't cash. David Devereaux might've been her sweet grandfather, but he didn't tolerate disrespect from anyone. And by the way he was slowly leaning into the screen, she realized shit was about to get very real.

"That right there is the reason I'm not handing the reins over to you yet. You're brilliant and determined. But you don't know how to get what you want without bulldozing your way through every problem."

"My methods have never been a problem before, certainly not when I was making this company more money than it could count. I fail to see the problem now."

"The problem…" He paused and stared into the screen. She could tell the moment his features softened and his shoulders relaxed that he'd gone from seeing her as an insubordinate employee to his only grandbaby.

He calmly leaned back in his chair, folding his long arms across his chest. He was tall and lean, wearing the navy blue Brooks Brother suit he adored. Even though he was working from her uncle's home, the power suit dominated any corporate space he was in, whether it was the office or on the computer screen.

The same kind, dark brown eyes that had always shone with pride in Amara were tinged with sadness that moved something in her, even though she tried hard to ignore it.

"The problem," he continued, "is that your all-or-nothing approach doesn't work for some deals. Your greatest strength and weakness is that you always go in for the best financial deal. Money is great, but it ain't everything, baby girl. And the fact that you don't know that yet troubles me. It's gonna land you in a world of trouble. Success comes from the heart, not the bank account. And because you don't understand that, you let Falcon stipulate that we're responsible for securing the building permits from the city council in exchange for a better financial return for Devereaux Inc."

She shrugged. He was always going on about heart. Heart didn't pay the bills, though. Only cold, hard cash did that.

"I fail to see the problem. We're getting more money in exchange for dealing with the permits ourselves. It's bureaucracy. We have experience cutting through red tape. What's the issue?"

He shook his head as he looked up to the ceiling like he was asking for celestial grace to deal with her.

"You're right. Bureaucracy usually wouldn't pose a problem for us. But the particular area where we're building is smack-dab in the middle of Lennox Carlisle's district. If you'd bothered to learn anything about the councilman, you'd know he blames companies like ours for gentrification and running residents out of this neighborhood. And now he's running for mayor on the same issues. That's why Falcon made it a contractual obligation for us to get the permits instead of them. Carlisle has been slapping Falcon down every chance he gets. Now we can expect similar treatment. But your zeal to secure the bag blinded you to that. So here we are."

Amara flinched as if he'd struck her. Sure, this city councilman hadn't factored into her thinking when she inked the deal. But she was meticulous when it came to wheeling and dealing. If this bureaucrat was so problematic, she would've known about it.

"This isn't a big issue, Granddaddy. It's a minor detail."

"The fact that you don't see this as a problem is why I can't have you leading this deal. Carlisle can't be swayed by the trappings of wealth like other politicians. And since your focus is always money, he'll never give us what we need if you take the lead on these negotiations. He needs heart, Amara, and you don't speak his language. My decision is final. I want you nowhere near this deal."

"You'd never do this to my mother. If she were still practicing here—"

"If she were still practicing here," he interrupted, "I wouldn't have to tell her this. She'd know it already. Your mother retiring from practicing law was the worst hit this company has ever taken. If she and your father weren't so happy traipsing around Brooklyn so carefree, I'd still beg her to return. She understood that you need both heart and skill to win. I'm still waiting for you to learn that lesson."

She thought to defend herself for a hot second, until she saw disappointment cloud his eyes. Nothing she said would matter. Especially not when he was yet again comparing her to her mother. No one could reach the pedestal Ja'Net Devereaux-Rodriguez had been perched on since she graduated law school decades ago. Least of all Amara, the daughter who had her brains, but not her grace.

"I don't have time for this. I have to call Jeremiah and get him down to the office. Martha's up to something and whatever it is, it can't be good. We have to be prepared if she tries to disrupt the vote to appoint Trey CEO today."

Amara wasn't just using a diversion tactic, either. The

company her great-uncle Ace Devereaux had turned into a billion-dollar enterprise was in crisis now that he was ill. His fiercest protector, Jeremiah Benton, whom Ace had taken in as his ward when Jeremiah was sixteen, had been leading the business, trying to keep Ace's sister, Martha, from staging a boardroom coup and destroying everything he'd built. And now Jeremiah had a new ally in Trey Devereaux, Ace's granddaughter who'd recently rejoined the fold after years of estrangement. Trey was up for appointment as CEO in accordance with Ace's rules of succession. Which ruffled Martha's feathers, to put it mildly, since she thought she was owed the job.

Amara inhaled slowly before getting in the last word with her grandfather. "You'll regret this." Her voice was full of calm and control, as befitted her upbringing. But before he could respond, she ended the call.

She wouldn't allow him to raise her blood pressure over this. Devereauxs didn't get mad. They got even. She just had to figure out what that looked like in this situation.

"If all you're going to do is stand there staring at me and not help me to stop Jeremiah and Trey from stealing this company, you can scatter like the rest of the scared little roaches that just left this room."

Amara stood in the mostly empty conference room staring at her great-aunt Martha. The impromptu board meeting that Amara had worried so much about had taken place a few moments ago with pleasing results. Well, pleasing for the company and those trying to save it. Not so much for Martha after the board had voted Trey and Jeremiah in as co-CEOs.

"Aunt Martha," Amara began carefully, "I know today's events were…disappointing for you. But I think if you took the time to get to know Trey, you'd feel a lot more confident with her and Jeremiah running the company. I know you can't see it now. But this is best for Devereaux Inc., for the family."

Martha stood up slowly, splaying her fingers flat on the large conference room table. "Best for the family?" Her voice was eerily calm, making the hairs on Amara's neck stand on end. "Sweet Amara. You most of all should understand that what's good for the business and family never seems to be good for the women doing all the work."

"What are you talking about, Auntie? Trey is a woman in this family."

"Trey is a puppet being used to keep my brother's antiquated succession rule in place long after he's dead and gone. Those of us who would breathe life into the company, take it in a new direction, are always sidelined."

Amara tried to make sense of Martha's words. "Auntie, it's been a long few days dealing with Ace's unexpected hospitalization and now this. My brain is too tired to piece together the meaning of your riddles."

Martha's smile sent a cold chill down Amara's back. The older woman casually grabbed her clutch and placed it under her arm.

"Amara, you're smart, determined, and you buck against every rule my brothers have established for how this business is run. You more than anyone should understand what I'm talking about. Everything you've ever wanted has been denied you because you don't do things the way your grandfather wants, while he praises your mother, a woman who did everything exactly according to his rules."

She stepped closer to Amara, placing a hand softly against her cheek and offering her a soft, sincere smile that shook Amara to her core.

"Do you enjoy being treated as an afterthought in the family? Do you feel content to live in the shadow of you mother's accomplishments?"

Amara didn't answer, partly because Martha's questions were rhetorical. But mostly because she feared what her answer would actually be.

"Grandniece, if you don't fight for what you're owed," Martha warned, "you'll find yourself in the same place as me, villainized, rejected and forgotten by those who are supposed to love you."

"Aunt Martha," Amara interrupted. "I'm not you."

"You're the me of your generation, grandniece. And if you're not careful, you'll end up dedicating years of your life to this family and to this company with nothing to show for it."

"I think you're exaggerating a bit, Auntie."

Martha lifted a brow, giving Amara that "young'un, you don't know what you're talking about" look.

Silent, Martha placed a gentle kiss on Amara's cheek and exited, leaving her there to comb through everything the woman had said.

She didn't want to admit it, but Amara saw the parallels between Martha and herself. The worst part however wasn't admitting Martha was right. The worst thing was the fear that her pain might one day make her just as bitter and resentful as her great-aunt.

"Amaretto sour, Ian, and your best bag of pretzels." The friendly bartender at The Vault threw Amara a nod as she secured her phone inside her assigned locker and headed for the empty stool at the end of the bar.

If you were wealthy with any hint of celebrity, a membership at The Vault meant you could have a drink or five and not worry about it ending up in the tabloids. Electronic devices were prohibited, and the Brooklyn VIPs and power players entering the premises had to relinquish their phones in order to gain entry and be served.

"Rough day?"

Rough didn't begin to describe it. "If you call losing the promotion you were primed for because your boss sees you as too aggressive to get the job done right, yeah, it's been a rough day."

"Damn, someone at work actually played the aggressive Black woman card with you?" He shook his head. "Sounds like you deserve a double, then." He poured a healthy dose of the cocktail in her tumbler and slid it to her with a large bowl of pretzels. "Let me know if you need a refill on either."

"Definitely a refill on the drink. An order of hot wings would be great, too."

He gave her a thumbs-up and put her order in.

Relieved to have a moment of solitude, she looked at her drink and the bowl of pretzels and sighed. How cliché was her existence that she was sulking about the developments at work, nursing her wounds with alcohol and carbs at a bar. But Ian was right. Her grandfather had played the aggressive Black woman card and the more she thought about it, the more it pissed her off.

Being born to an African American mother and an Afro-Cuban father, she'd long ago learned how Black women were stereotyped. What was throwing her here was that it was coming from her own family.

Amara had never wanted to work anywhere else but Devereaux Inc. Why would she? It was a "for us by us" situation where she didn't have to navigate the misogynoir present in many corporate spaces. She could display her brilliance and excel without having to deal with bullshit. Except her grandfather's refusal to step down and allow her to lead was another kind of foolishness altogether.

She was the best Devereaux Inc. had to offer, and it still wasn't good enough for her to get the promotion she deserved.

"How did I end up here?"

"Not sure." A smooth, deep voice pulled her attention

away from the pity party of one she was trying to have. "But I can't say I'm necessarily mad you are."

There was a smart-assed retort on the tip of her tongue until she looked up and saw the face that went with the voice. The man had golden-brown skin, hazel eyes, and a thin, dark brown goatee framing thick, full lips. She was so busy soaking up his good looks she couldn't find the sour retort she'd usually have waiting for a weak line like that.

But there was something more than his good looks that captivated her. He was vaguely familiar.

He stretched out his hand as he offered her a wide, easy smile. "I'm Len."

When she didn't immediately respond, he dropped his hand while dipping his head in an apologetic nod.

"I'm sorry, I didn't mean to bother you. I'll leave you to your drink."

She looked into his eyes, and recognition hit her. This was Lennox Carlisle, the very person at the center of her work woes. She searched his eyes, waiting to see if he recognized her as well. But to her surprise he didn't seem to.

"It's fine," she responded. "I've just had a long day. I didn't mean to be rude."

"Wanting to be left alone with your own thoughts isn't rude. And just because I wanted to speak to you doesn't mean you're obligated to give me the time of day. I apologize for interrupting you."

He stood up, tapping the counter to get the bartender's attention. "Hey, Ian, anything she orders tonight is on me."

"That's not necessary."

He shrugged. "It's not. But everybody deserves a break here and there. Hope your day gets better."

He smiled once more then turned toward the long hallway that led to the restrooms and offices. She watched his retreating form, not exactly certain of what had just happened, but not exactly put off by it, either.

While her grandfather had proven himself to be a misogynistic jerk, this stranger had offered her a small measure of kindness that somehow sparked hope inside her. Hope for what? She had no clue.

But she was curious to find out.

Two

"Hey man, where you at?"

Lennox looked up at the sound of Carter's voice. His best friend was sitting on the edge of the desk in the middle of the room.

"Sorry," Lennox answered. "My head was elsewhere."

"I know," Carter replied. "I told you, no work when you're within these walls. Stop worrying about your next debate and relax a little with your boy."

Lennox slid into a relaxed slouch on the small sofa, spreading his arms across the back.

"I wish it were work that has me so preoccupied." When his friend lifted a questioning brow, Lennox sighed, closing his eyes as he dropped his head back against the sofa cushions.

Carter and Lennox's friendship went as far back as junior high school in Bedford-Stuyvesant when Carter's Puerto Rican parents moved their family from the Bronx to Brooklyn. Besides blood, there wasn't anyone Lennox trusted more, which was why Carter Jimenez was the only person he could let his guard down around.

"Sorry, man. I ran into this woman at the bar..."

"Someone you know?"

Lennox shook his head. "I don't think I've ever seen her here before."

"Considering you haven't spent an enormous amount of time here since I opened three years ago, that's not so strange."

Lennox chuckled. "The low-key shade isn't necessary. It's not like you're at my office every other day."

Carter shrugged. "You're a politician. Who wants to hang out in your stuffy office with people who lie like they breathe? My place of business is the hottest spot for folks like you to chill without cameras flashing in your face. Everybody wants to come here."

He wasn't wrong. If Lennox could spend more time here than at his office, he'd definitely do it. But when you were trying to keep the little guy from getting squashed by big corporations, there wasn't a whole lot of time for chilling at your best friend's lounge.

"So, what's up with this woman? She one of your constituents?"

"No clue. Apparently, she was having a rough day."

Carter folded his arm as a devilish grin curled his lips. "Let me guess, she wouldn't happen to have been gorgeous." When Lennox didn't answer Carter let out a howl. "Man, stop acting like you're worried about this stranger's welfare. If you saw something you like, shoot your shot."

"Says the man who's been single for—" A cloud of sadness shrouded his friend's face and Lennox instantly regretted his careless tongue. "Man, I'm sorry. I didn't mean to—"

Carter ran his hands up and down his thighs, taking a deep breath before settling his gaze back on Lennox.

"Don't apologize, Len. You're right, I shouldn't be giving dating advice. Mich has been gone for four years and I still haven't found the nerve to start dating again. She was my world."

"You've had a lot to deal with, Carter. Losing Michelle in a tragic accident and having to raise a one-year-old by yourself, that'd be a lot for the strongest shoulders. The fact that you've been able to do that and start a successful business, it's more than I could've handled under the same circumstances. Speaking of my goddaughter, how's Nevaeh?"

Lennox thought of Carter's five-year-old daughter, who pretty much ran the man's life, and his too whenever he was around.

"I think she's been talking to my mother too much. Mommy was grilling me about working too hard and not having someone special. Ever since then, Nevaeh has been pointing out all the pretty men and women she thinks I should date."

Lennox shook his head and laughed. He could definitely see Nevaeh doing something like that. A few months ago Nevach had walked in on a conversation Carter and his mother were having about her friend's son who was bi sexual and single. When they realized the girl was in the room, Carter didn't even blink. He simply sat her down and explained in very age-appropriate terms that he was attracted to both men and women.

That was the thing Lennox admired most about his friend. When it came to his daughter, his default was to do what needed to be done. That meant he never shied away from the hard or awkward parts of being a parent.

"Mrs. Jimenez is a mess. Remind me to stay away from her before she starts in on my nonexistent love life."

"Well, considering you've been sitting in my office for the last half hour thinking about someone you saw at my bar, I'd say she has less to worry about when it comes to your love life than mine."

Lennox waved a dismissive hand. "Nah, man. My campaign is in full swing. Now is not the time for me to get involved with someone."

"Who said anything about getting involved? I'd settle for a few hours of pretty awesome sex."

"Same, dude," Lennox moaned. "Same."

Carter stood up, tipping his head toward Lennox as he headed for the door. "I'm down a server tonight, so I gotta get back out there. Chill for as long as you want."

"Thanks, man." Lennox slid down farther on the couch and sighed. "When you get a chance, could you send a beer back here?"

Carter nodded as he stepped out of the office and Lennox was left to enjoy the silence. Campaign season was all about movement and noise. And if he were honest, that was the part he hated most about running for office.

Nothing was more fulfilling than working hard for the people in his district. But now that he was trying to do that on a larger scale by running for mayor, it meant so much of his focus had to be about how well he performed the campaign song and dance.

"Don't complain," he mumbled. "No one's forcing you to do this."

No one except the trifling son of a bitch who currently sat in the mayor's office. His opponent had done nothing for the five boroughs during his term. Especially certain neighborhoods in Brooklyn that were being gentrified at far too great a rate for the original inhabitants to remain unaffected.

The first twinges of a tension headache prickled at the back of his neck. He closed his eyes and took a few cleansing breaths to bring things back into focus. "Today is a no-work day. Just chill."

Between now, the primary and then Election Day, he wouldn't have too many more of these moments where he could just be and do nothing. So, he'd better take advantage of it while he still could.

The image of the woman with the light brown skin sitting at the bar slid across his mind. She was gorgeous. Even from the bar stool he'd been able to see large, rounded hips and thick thighs. The flex of her calf in those impossibly high black patent leather heels didn't hurt the sexy picture she'd made, either. But when she turned to him with fire smoldering in her eyes, that was when he knew he had to speak to her.

There was an intelligence, a keen awareness there that he couldn't resist. And as gorgeous as the rest of her looked, it was that special something written across her face that read "try Jesus, not me," letting you know she wasn't to be messed with, that made him want to know everything about her.

But now wasn't the time. Not just because she didn't appear to be in the best mood, but because his life was about to turn into chaos. He'd be under the microscope for the next few months. What was it his campaign manager, John, said?

Don't do anything stupid, keep your dick in your pants, and you might just win this thing.

A light tap on the door intruded on his thoughts. His friend always had the best timing. A cold beer was just what he needed to get his mind right.

He got to his feet and in two long strides was at the door, swinging it open. "Thanks, man. I was just about—"

His mouth stopped working momentarily when he saw the beautiful woman he'd been obsessing about standing before him, leaning into the doorframe.

"You were just about to what?"

He let his gaze openly slide down her full-figured form and didn't bother to try to hide his appreciation. "I think I should be asking you that. What are you doing back here? Are you lost?"

She shook her head, never once dropping her gaze as she continued to flash her slightly sinful grin.

"Nope," she replied. "Ian is getting slammed out front, so I offered to bring you the beer you ordered. I didn't know it would be you. But I'm not exactly upset it is."

He tilted his head, taking in the full picture of her and trying hard to remember John's edict about keeping his dick in his pants.

"Speaking of not being upset, when we spoke earlier, you didn't seem to be in the best mood."

"A strange man was kind to me for no other reason than he could be. Who knew that kind of courtesy would improve my mood?" She stood up to her full height. In those sexy stilettos he'd admired earlier, the top of her head came to just beneath his chin.

"Since your mood's better, would you like to come in and keep me company?"

"I don't want to intrude."

"You're not," he answered, then stepped aside, letting her in. When she sat down on the couch, he remained standing at the now-closed door.

This isn't smart, Lennox. You don't know this woman from Adam.

He didn't. But that didn't seem to stop him from sitting down next to her on the couch.

She handed him an unopened longneck before speaking again. "I told Ian to leave it closed so you could be certain it wasn't tampered with."

Courteous and aware that accepting open drinks from strangers could be hazardous. He was liking her even more.

He didn't respond. He simply took the offered bottle and stack of napkins, twisting the metal cap off and taking a long drink. Was he thirsty? Yeah, but by the way she smiled at him while leaning back and crossing one thick leg over the other, he could see they both knew this was more about distraction than needing a drink.

Lennox put the beer down on a nearby end table and stared at the woman sitting next to him. Trying hard to remember John's warning, he fought with himself about what he should say next. Lennox was in no way afraid to talk to a woman as fine as this. But when you were trying to become the mayor of New York City, you had to think twice about what you said as well as did.

He extended his hand to her, "Thank you, Ms.…"

She tilted her head, her sultry gaze sliding down the seated length of him, leaving a fiery burn in its wake. But instead of making him back away like the cautious, level-headed professional he was supposed to be, it made him lean in closer.

She took his offered hand in a firm grip and smiled. "Angel," she said. "My name's Angel."

"Angel is a lovely name. It's my pleasure to make your acquaintance."

She continued to smile at him, holding his hand and letting her thumb pass over his knuckle. It wasn't necessarily an overt gesture of attraction. But coupled with the flash of fire he saw in her eyes, he was pretty sure they were vibing on the same wavelength.

"Well," she said, breaking the silence. "I don't want to interrupt you any further. I suppose if you're back here and not at the bar, you probably weren't looking for company."

She stood up, and he followed suit, stepping closer to her than he probably should have considering he didn't know anything about her beyond her name.

"I did come back here to get away from the crowd. But that's not the reason you should leave."

She folded her arms, pushing her full, round breasts up, and he couldn't find enough decency anywhere in him to look away.

"I'm not sure I get your meaning," she responded. "What's the reason I should leave?"

He hesitated for a moment, pulling his lip between his teeth to keep the words on the tip of his tongue from spilling out of his mouth.

"Aww, don't get shy now, Len. Speak your peace."

He nodded, loving the fierceness she wore like a second skin.

"You should leave because I'm tempted to find out if this thing that makes me want to bend you over that desk is mutual. Because if it is, I don't think I have enough give-a-damn to ignore it."

There, he'd given her the truth. And if she was smart, she'd take her leave, and this would never become more than a little flirting in the back of a bar.

But when she stepped into his space, so close that all he needed to do was shift slightly and his body would be pressed against hers, he groaned.

"You'd better know what you're doing, Angel."

She narrowed her gaze as her full lips curved into a sultry smile. "Is Len short for Leonard?"

Her question seemed out of place, but instead of using that brief moment as an excuse to step away, he shook his head. "No, it's short for Lennox."

"Good." She moved in closer, wrapping her hand around the base of his neck. "I'd like to make sure I'm calling you by your proper name if this ends up being as good as I hope it will be."

Lennox's entire body tightened. Given her provocative words, coupled with the firm yet tender feel of her hand against his bare flesh, it was a wonder he didn't explode right then and there.

"Make sure you know what you want, Angel." His eyes locked with hers, finding a blaze of fire that rivaled the inferno burning inside him.

"I always know what I'm doing, Lennox. I was just waiting for you to catch up so I could get what I want."

He smoothed strong hands up her sides and placed a firm grip on her waist, pulling her against him. He waited a second to see if there was any resistance, but when she leaned into him, pressing herself against his already twitching cock, all he could do was smile.

"And just what is it that you want from me?"

She tilted her head with her sexy grin still caressing her lips. "A one-time offer for you to—how'd you put it?—find out if this thing that makes me want you to bend me over that desk is mutual."

He groaned as he positioned his lips less than an inch away from hers. All it would take to set this off was the slightest lean and he'd finally know what those plush pillows felt like pressed against his mouth.

"That's all it can be, Angel. I don't have room in my life for more at the moment."

"No worries, Lennox." The way she said his name with such authority made his heart beat harder against his chest. "I've had an unusually difficult day and a little mindless fun with you would certainly help me unwind. But beyond this moment, I don't have the spoons to heap another thing onto my plate right now. So, can you handle a few moments of bliss with me and nothing more?"

He stepped around her slowly, walking to the door and twisting the lock to make certain they weren't interrupted.

He stared at her, looking for any signs of unease or discomfort. When she smiled, lifting a coy brow and leaning back casually against Carter's mostly empty desk.

"You ready to do this, Lennox?"

"Hell, yes."

It was the last coherent thought he had before he stalked toward her and finally allowed his lips to touch hers. Fire shot through him. When she slipped her fingers around the sensitive skin of his neck, cupping it, pulling him closer, making sure he couldn't escape, it was an accelerant that made the hungry flames licking at every inch of his skin burn brighter and faster.

She slipped her hand beneath the lapels of his jacket, pushing it off his shoulders and down his arms. She broke the kiss, staring at him as if she needed to commit every line on his face to memory. He stared back, needing to do the same.

Their movements quickly turned frantic and desperate. While he was pulling up her pencil skirt, hitching it up just enough that he could freely lodge himself between the cradle of her legs, she was unknotting his tie and unbuttoning his shirt. Then they switched, him working his way down her buttoned shirt, splaying the two flaps to take in the perfect vision of her luscious breasts in a breathtakingly sexy black lace demi bra while she unbuckled his belt and pants, slipping her warm hand inside and boldly cupping his sex.

She looked up at him, winking as she gave him a squeeze, and everything in his world narrowed into the feel of her hot palm searing his flesh. The tension of his day bled out of him, replaced by the hungry tension of arousal.

This was exactly what he needed. Fun with a partner who knew what the hell she wanted and wasn't afraid to grab it. Literally.

He moaned as he gave in to the tantalizing slide of her closed palm up his length. He allowed her a few more strokes. Then he pulled her hand away, placing it flat on the desk and leaning in to steal a desperate kiss.

"That feels great. But too much more of that and neither of us will get what we want."

She nodded, tugging her skirt up a little higher, wrapping her legs around him. "Then quit stalling, let's get to it."

Never taking his eyes off her, he slid his hand over her smooth, tanned skin until his thumb rested at the juncture between her thighs. He hesitated for a second, taking her chin between the fingers of his free hand.

"Are you sure this is still what you want?"

She took the hand he had latched on her thigh, moving it over her mound and pressing against it until he was cupping her sex with his whole hand.

"I'm sure."

He let out the breath he was holding. He pushed aside the black patch of lace covering her, finding slick heat beneath it. The moment his fingers made contact with her flesh, they both gave into a deep and satisfying moan, its vibrations shaking through his entire being.

He latched his mouth on to hers as his fingers continued their exploration, parting her flesh and slipping one, then two fingers inside of her. She rewarded him with a slow swivel of her hips and wrapped her arms around his neck, using him as her anchor as she rode his fingers, hanging on to the very edge of what he hoped would be a memorable orgasm with the greatest show of resolve he'd ever witnessed.

Determined to break her, he swiped his thumb over her clit with his fingers still buried inside of her and it was the final chink in her armor. Every place where their bodies touched, she wrapped herself around him, squeezing him in what had to be the most sensual embrace he'd ever experienced.

Watching her come heightened his arousal, his length hard and insistent against his abdomen, aching for the same chance at release he'd just given her.

When she finally came down from her climax, he untangled himself from her long enough to find the condom he always kept in his wallet. He wasted no time pushing his clothes down just enough and slid the condom on as quickly as he could.

Sheathed, he placed himself at her opening, wrapping his arm around her waist while his opposite hand traveled up to her breasts, tweaking one pebbled nipple between his fingers as he slid slowly home.

And that's exactly what bottoming out into the depths of her body felt like.

They fit better than lock and key. No awkward groping, no off-beat rhythm. From the moment his flesh touched hers they were in sync with each other's movements.

It didn't matter how fast and hard he thrust, creating

the beautiful slapping sound of slick flesh against flesh. It didn't matter how slowly he slid in and out, taking the time to savor her kisses, worshipping her mouth as well as her body. Whatever their tempo, she was right there with him, providing the answer to every movement he initiated.

And when she clenched around him, drawing out his orgasm as she succumbed to a second climax of her own, their mutual release was the perfect end to the moment they'd shared. The moment that couldn't be repeated.

Spent, trying to regain enough energy to pull his body away from hers and the dexterity he needed to right his clothing, he thanked all the stars in the sky that this would never happen again. Because if it was that good when they were perfect strangers, it frightened him how good it would really be if they knew more than each other's first names. Her sex could be addictive. And right now, he didn't have the luxury of being strung out on anyone. Not if he wanted to win.

When he was finally able to slow his labored breathing, he pulled out, looking down to remove the condom when shock mixed with equal parts fear spilled down his spine.

"What's wrong?"

When he looked up at her, he could see his panic reflected in her deep brown eyes. He swallowed, finally finding the courage to speak three chilling words.

"The condom broke."

Three

"Lennox, did you hear me?"

The sound of his campaign manager's voice snatched him from his thoughts.

"Len?" John Christos, a tall, lean man of Greek decent with almost black hair and blue eyes, stared at him, waiting for an answer.

"I'm sorry, John. I'm just preoccupied."

"With what?"

Oh, nothing. Just sitting here wondering whether I impregnated a stranger four weeks ago.

Lennox closed his eyes as the thought dragged across his mind. When he met John's assessing gaze, he turned in his chair to face the window.

"Nothing I care to share at the moment. Let's get back to work."

When he swiveled back to John, he saw a strange mix of pity and compassion painted across the man's face.

"Lennox, I know these last four weeks have been brutal. The nonstop rallies, the appearances, the debates, all while still handling your duties as city councilman. It's a lot. But all the work you've put in has led to a twelve-point lead in the polls. The primary is yours if you can just hold out for a little longer."

He dragged a deep breath in through his nose, trying to quell all the alarm bells ringing in the back of his head. Everything John stated was fact. If his campaign kept up its current momentum, he would be the next mayor of New York City. Which was why he was so pissed that he'd let a moment of weakness possibly derail that.

"You can do this, man," John continued. "I don't back lost causes. If I agreed to run your campaign, you know it's because I believe you'd win."

Lennox met John's gaze with a smile. The man was known as the best in the business for that very reason. Lennox was lucky to have him running the show. Which was why he knew he also needed to come clean. If this shit blew up in his face, blindsiding John wouldn't help Lennox or his campaign.

"I know I can do this," he whispered. "But I don't know if I'll get the chance."

John's brow furrowed as he straightened in his seat. "What happened?"

"About a month ago, I met a woman at Carter's place."

John took a sharp breath. "Why do I already know I'm not going to like how this story ends?"

"Because you're smart," Lennox answered. "Smarter than I was."

"Please tell me it was consensual, and she wasn't an employee, or in any way directly connected to your campaign."

Lennox's body tensed as he glared at John.

"What?" He spat the words through clenched teeth. "You really think so little of me?"

"It's not about what I think. It's about how she felt and

whether or not she believes you violated her boundaries. So, I'll ask you again. Was the sex consensual?"

As offended as Lennox was, he realized John was right. It wasn't about him. It was about whether his partner felt safe in that moment.

"It was. We both verbally agreed to the sex before, during and after the act."

"But?"

"The condom broke."

John's stiff posture relaxed a little, and his stern expression was softened by compassion.

"So, you're worried about a health scare and unwanted pregnancy?"

Lennox rubbed at the dull throb starting to thump at his temples.

"I had blood work done a couple of days ago. My doc says everything came back negative but wants me to be tested at the three and sixth-month markers to be certain."

"And the pregnancy?"

"This woman was a perfect stranger, John. Other than her first name, I have no idea who she is. I gave her all of my contact information. I told her to call me if our time together resulted in pregnancy."

"Has she?"

Lennox shook his head slowly, wishing the lack of contact from his mystery Angel eased his mind as much as it should.

"Have you called her?"

"She wouldn't give me her info."

John stood, running his hand through his short dark waves before he started pacing. This was classic problem-solver John. He thought better when he was moving, and with all Lennox had just dropped in his lap, the man probably needed to run a couple of laps to figure out how to fix this situation Lennox found himself in.

"Doesn't Carter's lounge require membership? Even if you're a guest of a guest, they have to submit ID, right?"

Lennox nodded. "True, but I'm trying hard not to ask my friend to violate the privacy of one of his members for my personal issues."

"So, unless this stranger tells you she's carrying your baby…"

"I'll never know."

John stared back at him, his face relaying the words the man had yet to speak.

You are so screwed.

"Cousin?"

Amara had just parked in front of Devereaux Manor when her phone rang. Turning the ignition off, she settled back into her seat before responding to her beloved cousin Stephan. These weekly phone calls had become their new tradition since Ace was rushed to the hospital last month.

"He's still with us, Stephan."

There was an audible sigh of relief on the other end of the line.

"I speak to Uncle Ace on our weekly Zoom calls. He never lets on to how he's really doing." Stephan's voice was barely a whisper but the worry in this tone came through loud and clear. "I promised him I'd be home in time for Trey and Jeremiah's wedding next week. Do you think I should get home sooner?"

"Steph, if you can get away, I'd tell you to get home now. That old man is a fighter, but I don't know how much longer he can keep this up."

The line went quiet for so long, she looked at her screen to make sure they hadn't been disconnected.

"Steph, you still there?"

"Yeah," he answered, sounding slightly distracted. "I'm just making some arrangements."

"Want me to send the family jet for you?"

She heard keys tapping on his end, followed by what sounded like shuffling papers.

"No," he answered quickly. "The jet is in New York. It'll take seven hours to get here and another seven to get me back home. There's a commercial flight leaving in two hours. I'll be in New York by eleven tonight your time."

She couldn't help but smile. Out of all of her cousins, Stephan was the most like Ace. Strong, decisive and able to make an effective plan even in the face of crisis. If her cousin had wanted it, she was certain Ace would've chosen him as his second-in-command. Not that Jeremiah and Trey weren't equally qualified. But the way Stephan always figured out what the best path was in an instant, that was something he inherited from their uncle.

"I'm glad you're coming back, Steph. There's a lot of upheaval going on and your calming presence will definitely help."

Truer words had never been spoken. Amara had made a huge mess of things. Sleeping with Lennox Carlisle was a huge mistake.

You knew that when you entered that office at The Vault. Why would you do this in the first place?

Hurt.

That was the simple answer. Her grandfather's lack of faith in her leadership skills found the wound she'd secretly hidden all these years. As much as her grandfather didn't believe she measured up to her mother as a lawyer, deep down, Amara had always feared it was true. And having her grandfather snatch the one thing that would've proven she'd surpassed her mother's successes made her ache for comfort in the worst way.

She'd thought the drink, the pretzels, and the hot wings would be enough to make her feel better. But when Lennox offered her kindness and unquestioning support, she'd forgotten all the reasons she should stay away from the man and given into her need to just feel good for once in that moment.

Fortunately, she never had to see Lennox again since she'd been taken off the deal. Otherwise, this bad situation she'd created for herself would be a whole lot worse.

"You mean with our long-lost cousin and new CEO? Is Trey a problem? 'Cause you know I don't have an issue coming in and wrecking shop."

A hardy, deep laugh slipped through her lips. Considering all the stress the family had been under recently, it felt good to let go for a brief moment and enjoy Stephan's sense of humor.

"Trey is actually kinda badass. I like her a lot. I think you will, too. But just so you know, you might wanna watch how you talk about her. Jeremiah is pretty much sprung. He might not take too lightly to you coming after his woman."

Stephan chuckled, and Amara felt her smile widen. "Listen, Jeremiah knows the most important trait of surviving in the Devereaux clan is having a thick skin. If Trey hasn't already learned that lesson, she's about to get schooled."

"She's good people, Steph. She's also really good for the company and Ace."

"Unlike my mama, you mean?"

That was an understatement. Martha had attempted to steal Devereaux Inc. from Ace. And as angry as she was about losing to Trey and Jeremiah, Amara had a bad feeling the woman wasn't done waging war on the rest of the family yet.

"She blames Ace for a lot of her pain, Stephan. You know that. If you're coming home, maybe stop in and talk to her. Tell her Randall's death and your leaving wasn't his fault. Try to get her to see Ace and settle this nonsense before it's too late."

Losing Stephan's older brother had been a blow to the entire family. But to their mother, Martha, it had decimated her life.

"I'm coming to New York to see my uncle and attend my cousins' wedding. My mother's nonsense will have to wait until another day," he said in a clipped tone. "I'll hit you up when I land, Cousin. Tell that old man I'm on my way."

"I will, Cousin. See you soon."

She dropped her phone into her purse and stepped out of her car. As she looked up at the grand white pillars at the front entrance of the mansion, a familiar ease spread through her. Although she and her parents hadn't lived at Devereaux Manor, she'd spent so much time there growing up, learning from her grandfather and Ace as they built Devereaux Inc. into an unstoppable force that would last for generations.

She'd never been happier than the times she'd sat at those two wise men's feet, soaking up all they had to teach a young, impressionable girl about dominating the business world.

But today, her shoulders were heavy with worry as she considered that the dynamic of her family could quite possibly change forever, and she was powerless to stop it.

Get yourself together. You've got to be strong for him.

After taking another moment to compose herself and still the tremors that threatened to reveal just how afraid she was, she rang the bell.

A few seconds later, Ace's home health aide Ms. Alicia's bright smile greeted her as she ushered Amara inside.

"Ms. Amara," she beamed. "Your uncle was just asking about you a little while ago."

"I guess that's why my ears were burning." Amara smiled and gave the woman and tight hug. Alicia had been with Ace only a couple months but she was already an irreplaceable fixture in the family. "Is Uncle Ace up for visitors?"

Alicia shook her head. "Visitors? No. Family? Always. You can go right on upstairs to his bedroom. He sent the rest of the family out to get some rest. You'll have him all to yourself until the others start trickling back in."

Amara gave Alicia another hug and walked upstairs, tapping on the heavy wood door before she slowly slid it open.

There, in the middle of the room, Ace sat up in the king-size four-poster bed that seemed way too large for his frail form. He looked so much smaller, so delicate. It was heart-breaking. She was about ready to collapse into a puddle of tears until she saw the bright sparkle of joy and mischief in the older man's eyes and suddenly, she forgot about his infirmity. In those eyes, she saw the strength and love that had carried her throughout her life, and somehow that was enough to help her hold on to her composure.

"Tío," she half sang as she walked toward him with her arms stretched wide, *"te extrañé."*

To make sure that she was fluent in Spanish, her Afro-Cuban father had spoken exclusively to her in his native language when she was a child. To support that decision, Ace learned to speak conversational Spanish so he could converse with his only grandniece.

"You just saw me yesterday." He waved a dismissive hand in the air. "How can you miss me already?"

She sat down on the edge of his bed and he gathered her into his arms. She could feel his bones as he hugged her, which saddened her more than she could say. But the blessing of still being able to be held and loved by this man kept the shadows of grief away.

"You are my favorite uncle," she beamed. "I miss you every moment we're apart."

He pulled away from her, placing his long hands on her cheeks and caressing the skin there with his withered thumbs.

"And that is exactly why you will always be my favorite grandniece."

She lifted her eyebrow, knowing full well he told every single family member they were his favorite, but still loving the special feeling it gave her every time she heard him say it.

"You'd better not let Lyric hear you say that. You know she thinks she's your favorite."

He placed a gentle kiss on her forehead and leaned back against the headboard of his bed.

"She's my favorite niece. You're my favorite grandniece. There's no comparison."

"You're very lucky I'm you're only grandniece." She wagged a finger at him. "Otherwise, I might be offended."

He chuckled softly, patting her hand as he stared into her eyes. "I love all my babies. Nothing makes me happier than all of you being around. Having four of you here has done my heart glad."

She could see the slight bit of sadness twinkling in his muted brown gaze.

"He's coming home, Uncle."

She didn't have to say who *he* was. The spark of acknowledgment in Ace's eyes and the resulting expectant smile said he knew exactly who she was talking about.

"Is he?"

She nodded. "Yes, Stephan will be on a plane in two hours. He should probably get to Brooklyn sometime around midnight." She lifted her brow as she tilted her head. "He would've been here earlier if you hadn't told him to stay in Paris."

Ace squeezed her hand and gave her a timid smile filled with remorse. "I knew if I asked, he'd come. There's so much pain for him here. I didn't want my boy to suffer just so I could have the pleasure of holding him in my arms one last time."

His words chipped away at her resolve, and she couldn't hold back the hot tears that spilled onto her cheek and slid down her face. With trembling hands, she held his face and made sure his gaze locked with hers.

"Here me now, Jordan Dylan Devereaux. You're worthy

of any sacrifice we have to make to keep you happy and proud. You've been the bedrock of this family and championed for each one of us. There isn't anything you could ask of us that we wouldn't give you. You're that important. *Lo entiendes?*"

He tugged her into his embrace, stroking her hair as he had when she was a child in need of comfort. *"Sí sobrina,"* he whispered softly in her ear. "I am such a lucky man to have the five of you in my life. When each of you were given to me, I promised Alva I'd do everything in my power to protect you, love you and support you in any way you needed me to, all in exchange for your happiness. Trey and Jeremiah are taken care of. After speaking to Lyric, I think she might be halfway there herself with that producer friend of hers, Josiah. I'm especially happy about that because she was widowed so young when Randall died, too young to be alone for the rest of her life. Now it's just you and Stephan."

She sat up, gently pulling out of his embrace and looking at him with playful suspicion. "Uncle Ace…"

He shook his head. "I know you don't need a man to complete you. You are fierce, powerful and one of the most beautiful creatures to ever walk on this earth."

Amara couldn't help smiling. Even frail and sick, the old man was a slick flatterer.

"I don't want you to have someone because I think you're incomplete," he continued. "I want you to have someone who will do for you what I have always done—love you, support you, protect you."

He rubbed her hand and smiled back at her. "So, niece, if you want me to remember how much I'm loved, you have to do me this one favor. Remember the love I've had for you your whole life, and when it comes again in a new form, recognize it and let it in."

Every part of the independent woman in her wanted to rebuff his words. But somehow, coming from him, coming from the depths of the love he'd always shown her, she couldn't deny how tempting Ace made love sound.

She took a breath and closed her eyes to gather her strength before continuing. "Don't worry about me, Uncle Ace. I'll be just fine. Besides, my work for Devereaux Inc. keeps me so busy, there's very little chance of me finding the kind of love you want for me."

He readjusted the pillows behind his back before responding. "Speaking of work, I talked to David."

Amara shook her head. "Uncle Ace…"

"Let me finish, chile. David was wrong and I told him so. There's no one who's worked harder than you have. You deserve to be his successor."

She huffed, trying her best not to take her frustration out on her beloved uncle. "My grandfather has made his decision, and he obviously doesn't have faith in me. There's no use arguing about it."

"Don't be so sure. As much as your grandfather accuses you of being unable to see the big picture, I reminded him of a few times throughout his career when he acted much in the same way. Give him some time, niece. He's a little slow on the uptake sometimes, but he eventually gets there."

She shook her head and gave him a soft smile. "I came here to check on you and give you comfort, and here you are making me feel better. How does that work?"

He chuckled and patted her hand. "It doesn't matter if I'm sick. It's still my job to take care of my babies. It's a responsibility I will always fulfill."

She picked up his withered yet remarkably strong hand and kissed it. "I love you, Uncle."

"Not more than I love you, baby."

Four

"Amara?"

At the sound of her grandfather's voice, she lifted her gaze to find him standing in her office doorway.

"Do you have a few minutes to talk?"

There was something about the almost solemn quality to his voice that made fear wrap around her spine, pulling her straight up out of her chair.

"Is everything all right? Is it Uncle Ace?"

The tight lines of her grandfather's face relaxed and he rushed into the room, standing next to her and pulling her into his arms.

"No, baby. Ace is still with us. I'm sorry if I worried you."

Relief bled through her. Knowing you were losing someone in no way meant you were prepared for their eventual departure. And this moment proved to her she would probably never be ready to get that terrible news.

He released her and gave her a wry smile as she nodded and returned to her seat, gesturing for him to take the chair on the other side of her desk.

"What's going on, Granddaddy?"

"Your uncle ending up in the hospital was a reality check for me. I don't have a lot of time left with my brother, and I want to spend whatever remainder I have at his side. I know I accused you of being too impetuous to be my successor."

"Has your opinion of me changed?"

He chuckled and shook his head. "No. You are impetuous. But you're also one hell of a lawyer and you know Devereaux Inc. like the back of your hand. I would like to see you temper your approaches a little. However, that shouldn't be a reason to keep you from the position you've clearly earned. We have a solid team, and you're smart enough to listen to them to figure out when caution is needed."

She felt a glimmer of hope. Too afraid to let it grow for fear of disappointment, she sat up straighter in her chair and braced herself for his next words.

"What are you saying, Granddaddy?"

He took a breath and stood, extending his hand for her to shake. "I'm saying, I'm taking a leave of absence to spend time with my brother and making you acting lead counsel of Devereaux Inc."

Amara tugged her lip between her teeth, fighting desperately to restrain her show of excitement so she didn't end up jumping up and down and clapping like a seal.

"I promise to make you proud, Granddaddy. You won't regret this."

"I know you will. Consider this your audition for the job. It's your chance to show me you're the best choice for the position. Don't blow it, Amara."

"I won't."

He smiled at her, but she could still see the wariness in his eyes. He didn't have to worry she wouldn't mess this up.

"Good. Now, cut out some time in your schedule to come have a cup coffee with me so I can get you caught up on this Falcon deal. You're set to meet with Councilman Lennox Carlisle tomorrow morning."

Amara's body tightened and the bottom of her stomach felt like it dropped a few stories. Instantly images of her and Lennox locked in a quick and dirty embrace flashed across her mind.

"Are you all right?" Her grandfather's concern dropped the curtain on her memories. Her hotheadedness had made her indulge in petty and self-indulgent revenge that was now coming back to bite her on the ass.

The responsible thing to do would've been to come clean. She knew this. But when she looked into her grandfather's face, she couldn't reveal the truth. She'd worked so hard to get what she wanted, to prove her worth. No way was she allowing a momentary lapse in judgment destroy all her dreams and hard work.

She'd spent four weeks worried that she might be pregnant. Her period arriving—albeit lighter, earlier and shorter than usual, a fact she attributed to her stressing out over the situation—should've been her opportunity to let this go. But now, the universe was serving her just desserts, making her face the mess she'd made.

"Nothing's wrong. I'll have my assistant check my calendar and we'll set a time." She looked up at him with a grateful smile on her lips. "Thank you, Granddaddy."

He leaned down and pressed a gentle kiss on her cheek before leaving the room. She stood in the middle of her office thinking back to her time with Lennox, pushing back the fear she could feel rising from the pit of her stomach. She couldn't let it overwhelm her. Not now.

She put her head down on her desk and closed her eyes as she tried to get a hold of herself. With nothing but work to connect them now, she had to focus on the job at hand. Because no one, not even the sexy man who'd brought her to earth-shattering climaxes in a short amount of time, would keep her from doing what she did best: protecting Devereaux Inc.'s interests.

A loud knock made Amara jump in her chair. She blinked a few times until she realized she was still in her office, sitting at her desk.

"So, you get the big promotion you've been working your butt off for and you celebrate by falling asleep at your desk, Cousin?"

Amara followed the familiar voice until she found Stephan seated on the edge of her desk.

"Technically, I'm just the stand-in while Granddaddy is on leave. Besides, there's no time for celebration when you've got as much work on your desk as I do." She stood up and stretched, then grabbed two armfuls of the man sitting on her desk.

"Cousin," she crooned. "I missed you. I wish you were here under better circumstances."

They hugged tightly, hanging on as if they were much-needed lifelines for each other. "Have you seen Uncle Ace since you got in last night or did you go straight to your place?"

"I stayed at Devereaux Manor last night. I plan to stay there for the duration of my trip. I've missed two years' worth of moments with Uncle Ace because of bullshit. I'm not going to miss any more of the time he has left."

Amara pulled back to look into Stephan's dark eyes and ached at the sadness she saw there. He'd lost his only brother, Randall, two years ago, and now he was poised to lose another loved one so soon after.

"I can only imagine Uncle Ace was thrilled when he saw you."

"Uncle David and Ace were asleep when I let myself in. I grabbed a quick bite from the kitchen and spent the night curled up in the chair at Ace's bedside. It wasn't the greatest thing for my back after a transatlantic flight. But getting to see the big grin on Uncle Ace's face when he saw me, that was worth every ache I have."

She laid a hand over his and smiled. "You're such a good man, Stephan."

He just nodded, silently looking her up and down.

"I thought I'd see if you wanted to have dinner with me, but all you seem ready for is an evening nap. Everything okay? You not getting enough rest at home?"

She went to speak but found herself fighting off a big yawn. "I sleep fine. I don't know why I'm so tired all of a sudden."

She'd never been one to take naps. But she yearned for at least twenty minutes more of the impromptu catnap Stephan had interrupted.

"I guess it's the stress of prepping for this Falcon deal. I closed my eyes for a minute, and I wake up to you giving me a hard time."

He waved a dismissive hand at her. "Girl please, since when are you stressed about doing deals? You've been beating folks outta their coins since we were in diapers. Remember when you convinced Ace that taking us to the new ice cream shop downtown was an educational outing because we'd get to explore your scientific hypothesis that black cherry was indeed tastier than strawberry?"

She looked up at him, basking in the glow of his warm smile. "A theory I still stand by, thank you very much."

"My point is—" he poked his finger against her shoulder as he laughed "—if you can do that, this Falcon deal should be a breeze. Stop stressing and come treat your handsome cousin to dinner like he does for you when you visit him in Paris."

"I guess I can feed you."

He jutted his jaw in her direction. "You'd better. Usually, Jeremiah or Ace would have a full spread waiting for me the moment I entered Devereaux Manor. Last night, I had a ham sandwich. And it wasn't even hand-carved ham. I'm talking your run-of-the-mill deli slices. You know I'm too boujee for all that. You need to take pity on me."

"Poor baby," she cooed. "Let's go get you something suitable to eat while I give you all the family updates and you tell me about all the fine men in Paris that are begging for the slightest bit of your attention. I need to live vicariously through you."

After nearly blowing her life to shreds by sleeping with Lennox, that was the only kind of action Amara was interested in. Stephan had always been able to make her laugh and keep her mind off her problems. More than ever, she needed him to use his superpower tonight.

Because tomorrow would come all too quickly, and she'd finally have to deal with this very messy situation she'd created. Resigned to her plan to distract herself, she stood, grabbing her Louis Vuitton OnTheGo MM tote before looping her arm through Stephan's and giving him a wide grin. "It really is good to have you home, Cousin."

Five

Amara sat in the back seat of the platinum Mercedes-Maybach tapping her fingers against the armrest as her driver took them over the Brooklyn Bridge. A few minutes later, they were weaving through Manhattan traffic, past City Hall, until he pulled up to the curb in front of 250 Broadway.

She grabbed her briefcase and gave the chauffer's shoulder a squeeze. "It's a bus stop. No need to get out, Mr. Parker. I don't want you getting a ticket."

She watched the momentary flash of resistance in his eye. He'd worked for Devereaux Inc. probably since before she was born, and he absolutely hated it whenever she opened the door for herself and hopped out.

Today, however, she had too much restless energy and she needed to work it out of her system. She'd use the few extra seconds alone to collect herself before she faced off with Lennox Carlisle.

As she approached the entrance to the office building,

she took a breath, smoothing her hand over any imaginary wrinkles in her black strapless jumpsuit. She'd paired it with a white, wide-collared blazer, and black-and-white color block heels, presenting the perfect picture of a business executive with just enough flair to be noticed and not ridiculed.

Her clothes were her armor. The first thing people saw that showed them exactly who they were dealing with: a boss who had the power of Devereaux Inc. behind her.

A quick glance at her reflection in the glass doors and she knew she looked like a force to be reckoned with. But inside, she felt like a fidgety intern nervous about her first round of negotiations. That wouldn't do. Especially not in front of a man who knew what she looked like naked.

Well, partially naked, if she remembered correctly. And she definitely remembered that night correctly.

Those few minutes in that secluded office at The Vault had been the best sex of her life. Hot, uninhibited and so damn good she could still feel his scorching touch.

She shook her head, forcing the fluttering nerves in her stomach to subside as she squared her shoulders and made her way inside. A short time later, she was opening the door into the reception area of his office where she was greeted by an Asian man in his mid to late twenties with a welcoming smile.

"Hello, I'm Thomas, welcome to Councilman Carlisle's office. How may I help you?"

"Good afternoon," she said, offering a pleasant smile. "Amara Devereaux-Rodriguez on behalf of Devereaux Incorporated. I'm here to see the councilman."

Thomas nodded and stood, directing her to a small waiting area. "Please have a seat, Ms. Devereaux-Rodriguez. I'll let the councilman know you're here."

She sat down and placed her briefcase on the floor next to her, then crossed her legs to get comfortable. She took in the room. It looked like any other municipal office in the city, with its assembly-line art covering the white walls and gray metal desks and filing cabinets.

"Ms. Devereaux-Rodriguez." Thomas's voice pulled her attention away from her thoughts. "I'm afraid the councilman is in the middle of urgent business. He says he's not certain when he'll be able to receive you. Perhaps we should reschedule for a later date."

She tilted her head to the side and watched Thomas. His face was relaxed, with just enough faux concern that he appeared remorseful for the message he was delivering. But he didn't know who he was up against.

"Oh, I'm fine with waiting. I've cleared my entire calendar this afternoon just to talk to the councilman. Please tell him I'll be here whenever he's free to see me." She leaned down to pull her iPad mini out of her briefcase. She opened the keyboard folio case and positioned the device on top of her thighs, preparing to tap at the tiny keys.

When she looked up again, she watched Thomas nervously swallow. She gave him a knowing wink before returning her attention to her tablet.

Sucks to be you, Thomas. Go tell your boss I called his bluff.

"Sir, I don't think the Devereaux Inc. rep is gonna fall for your usual diversion tactics. She's basically set up shop in the waiting area as if she plans to be here all day."

Lennox groaned as he leaned back in his chair. He didn't have time for this. He was knee-deep in campaign work, which wasn't going well because he was too distracted thinking about Angel. Would he ever see her again? Would she be willing to see him again? And the most distracting thought of all, did they conceive a child together four weeks ago?

His mood taking a decided plunge, he glared at Thomas. "I don't care if she sets up shop or not. Let her. I'll wait her out. Eventually she'll get annoyed enough, or hungry enough to leave."

He returned his attention to his computer screen, silently dismissing Thomas. He knew what this rep wanted, and there was no way in hell she was getting it. Devereaux Inc. was in league with Falcon Development, and he wouldn't let them push another resident out of Brooklyn to gentrify it. Nope, not today, not ever.

New fire sparked in his chest, and he was able to clear his mind of all distraction. He set about handling the people's business, checking one thing at a time off his to-do list.

By the time his stomach reminded him that he'd skipped lunch, he looked out his window to find dusk settling over the city. A quick look at his watch and he realized he'd been working three hours straight.

Lennox buzzed for Thomas to come to his office. When he did, he was carrying a large pizza box with a couple of paper bags on top.

"Is that from Artichoke Pizza?" His stomach growled at the thought of his favorite pizza place. When Thomas confirmed with a grin and a nod, Lennox moaned in anticipation. "This is why I will never fire you. You always anticipate what I need before I can even ask for it. Thanks, Thomas."

There was a mischievous grin on Thomas's face that made Lennox suddenly aware he was in trouble.

"Don't thank me," Thomas replied. "Thank the rep from Devereaux Inc. When she saw we were all working late, she placed an order for the entire office."

Lennox took the pizza box, too hungry to care who'd ordered it. He opened the box, seeing the darkened brown crust of a well-done artichoke and extra-cheese pie.

"At least you told her what to order."

Thomas shook his head. "No, she didn't ask me what to order. Apparently, she's done some research on you."

He pointed to the two bags Lennox had pulled off the top of the box.

Lennox opened one of the bags to see two cans of Dr. Pepper in one, and a bag of buttery garlic knots in the other.

He narrowed his gaze as he looked up at Thomas. He was intrigued now, which was exactly what he'd bet the Devereaux rep wanted. He chuckled to himself, amused by the lengths to which this person would go for an audience with him.

"Tell her she's got until I finish my last can of Dr. Pepper to speak her piece."

If the grin on Thomas's face was any indication, he was certainly enjoying this game of chess between Lennox and the Devereaux rep. He nodded and headed for the door.

Without preamble, Lennox tore into a slice, folding the triangle in half like any proper New Yorker would. That first bite was heaven, and he didn't censor the almost obscene moan of sheer gratification that slipped from his lips.

"I hope you saved a slice for me?"

He looked up and choked. Once his coughing fit stopped, he swallowed the food in his mouth and grimaced as it hit his stomach like concrete cinderblocks.

"Angel?"

She smiled, stepping closer to him and extending a hand. "Amara Angel Devereaux-Rodriguez, lead counsel and negotiator for Devereaux Incorporated. Good to see you again, Lennox."

Six

Amara steeled herself against Lennox's cold glare. She hadn't exactly expected him to welcome her into his office with open arms once he saw who she was. But the hard anger she saw creeping into his eyes surprised her.

"You?"

And here we go.

"I prefer Amara. But yes, it's me. If we're done with the reintroduction, perhaps we can focus on business."

He stood, splaying his fingers on the long conference table in the middle of the room. The angles in his face were sharp, and she was sure she'd cut herself on them if she were foolish enough to try to touch him.

"Business? You have the audacity to saunter into my office to talk business on a major deal after screwing me senseless under an assumed name?"

"Lennox," she said firmly, trying to get a handle on the situation. "If you would just calm down—"

"Calm down?" He spat out the words as he stood to

his full height and closed the distance between the two of them. "Unless you're going to tell me you didn't know who I was when you let me bend you over Carter's desk, I don't think there's a chance of me calming down. So, *Amara*, is that the case, or is it safe for me to assume I was set up?"

He watched her for the slightest inkling of guilt or remorse. But what he found in the depths of her dark brown eyes was fire and strength. It was the same power he'd witnessed the one and only time they'd previously met. Its lure had seeped into his blood and made him do something incredibly stupid that could cost him everything. And even now, when he was pissed off beyond all recognition, he could still feel the thrum of arousal coursing through his body as she stood before him, calm and unbothered by his ire.

"Well, are you going to answer me? Or should I take your silence as your official response?"

"The answer is yes and no."

A derisive chuckle escaped his throat as he crossed his arms. "Well, I can't wait to hear this story. It's gotta be a good one if you think you're going to justify your actions."

She lifted a questioning brow as she tilted her head. "My actions? As I remember it, I didn't take anything that wasn't freely given. I was sitting at the bar, and you approached me."

He slowly shook his head from side to side while keeping his eyes locked on hers. "That is a weak-ass argument, and you know it. It doesn't matter who approached whom first. What does matter is you knew who I was, and you let me sex you anyway."

He saw a slight chip in her composed facade and, for just a second, he wanted to take back his harsh words and comfort her. But then he reminded himself that he was the victim in this situation, and he had a right to be mad as hell.

"I want to know why? Were you trying to set me up for some sort of extortion scheme?"

She took a deep breath, smoothing her hand against her curls that were pulled into a severe bun. After knowing what those curls looked like wild and free, what they felt like against his skin and between his fingers, it offended him to see them locked away under the guise of professionalism.

"I knew who you were." Her statement had a matter-of-fact quality to it that both soothed him and pissed him off. It calmed him because the lawyer in him liked facts. They were easier and less messy to deal with. But the human part of him, the man who'd had the pleasure of knowing what sliding inside of her body felt like, raged at the fact she could speak about their encounter with so little emotion.

"I'd had a really rough day at work. My boss denied me a promotion and basically affirmed what I've always known to be true—he didn't think I was good enough to do the job. That's especially hard to swallow when your boss is your grandfather, and the only person he thinks is worthy is the same person he's always compared you to, your mother.

"I was feeling raw and angry and then you walked in and you were kind to me and you agreed with my perspective without knowing any of the details. After a blow like the one I'd suffered, seeing that kind of trust made me feel better, and I wanted more."

She took a breath, but kept her eyes locked with his. "I'm ashamed to admit it, but I selfishly dismissed the conflict of interest because I knew no one would ever know if I took something for myself this one time."

He felt the sting of her confession like a slap. From the moment he laid eyes on her, he'd wanted her. Finding out he was a means to an end messed with his head more than it should.

"So, I was a hate-fuck to piss off your grandfather. But somehow your plan of never having to do business with me failed. Why are you the person here tonight and not some faceless suit from Devereaux Inc.?"

She reached out for the table as if to steady herself. Was this an act to get her out of the hot water she'd landed them both in? Or was this real?

"Are you okay?"

She closed her eyes and nodded, pointing to the chair beside her. When he nodded, she sat down, crossing one thick leg over the other as she leaned back.

He pulled out a chair, crowding in on her. Sure, he could stop being a jerk and give her some space. But this woman had purposely played with his damn career. He wasn't about to let her off the hook.

"When you're born into the Devereaux family, your place is pretty much decided from conception. My grandfather and my mother ran the company's legal department until my mother had me and decided motherhood was more important than corporate law. Being a stay-at-home mom and wife became her joy in life, and she never wanted to go back to practicing law. My grandfather idolizes her, and he's never gotten over the fact that she won't be around to take over at his retirement. Long story short, in his eyes, I don't measure up to the standard my mother set."

She tapped her fingers against her thigh, a move he was sure she did absentmindedly. But to him, it just brought back the memory of how good those elegant fingers felt against his naked flesh.

Focus, Lennox.

"My great-uncle is dying of cancer and had a major setback recently that landed him in the hospital. As his brother, my grandfather decided his place was at Uncle Ace's side. As a result, I'm now the interim head of legal. And when he dropped this deal in my lap, I couldn't tell him I had to step down because I'd compromised myself and the company by recklessly sleeping with the city councilman responsible for the permits we need."

He let his gaze slide down the length of her, trying to gain perspective. Her strength and power had called to him when they met. Which was why it bothered him so much that such a formidable person seemed so broken before him.

"Why doesn't your grandfather recognize your worth? Do you have a habit of making bad deals?"

She shook her head. "No, I'm focused. I know what I want, and I have no qualms about reaching beyond the limits others have placed on me. But to my grandfather, that looks like impulsive recklessness. If I were a man, he'd call me a trailblazer. If I were my mother, he'd call me brave. But because I'm neither of those things, he can only see me through his narrow perspective."

She leaned forward, placing a warm hand on top of his. "I'm sorry for putting you in a compromising position. It was never my intention. But I have to ask, where do we go from here?"

He switched the position of their hands so his now engulfed hers. He still couldn't help taking in the inviting warmth her touch brought. "Well, in my mind, how we proceed depends on how you answer my next question."

She narrowed her gaze as she leaned forward. "What's that?"

"Are you carrying my child?"

Her tongue felt heavy, so she swallowed to try to loosen it from the roof of her mouth. She tried to pull her hand out of his, but he held on tighter, forcing her to meet his determined gaze.

"I'm not pregnant, Lennox."

She searched his gaze for the relief she assumed would be there. Instead, she found a flicker of something sad and reserved in his eyes that puzzled her. Could he be disappointed?

"Are you sure? Did you take a test?"

She shook her head. “I didn’t have to. My period arrived right on schedule.”

He released her hand then, leaning back against his chair. His expression was inscrutable, but whatever he was thinking was weighing heavily on his mind if the distant look in his eyes was any indication.

“This isn’t the best situation, Angel.”

The way he’d comfortably slipped back into using her middle name, the name he’d called while he’d given her pleasure beyond her wildest dreams, made the skin at the nape of her neck tingle with excitement.

“I realize that, Lennox.”

“No, you don’t. It’s not just a matter of impropriety. I’m in the middle of a campaign. Something like this gets out and my bid for mayor is over.”

She nodded. He was right. This could destroy his career. And out of all the things she’d wanted from their one night together, him losing an election was never one of them.

“It was one night, Lennox. Neither of us should lose everything we’ve worked for because of it. I think if we can agree to keep things professional, we can both get what we want out of this deal.”

He stood up, leaning against the large conference table as he looked down at her, making her feel consumed with a single glance.

“Could you so easily forget what we shared, how we were together?”

Her throat felt tight, and her body burned from within. Forget? No, she doubted she’d ever be able to wipe what they’d shared completely from her mind.

“As good as that night was, I can’t let it negatively impact Devereaux Inc. I’ll do whatever I have to, to make sure we both get what we want, Lennox.”

Something flashed in his eyes. She couldn’t tell if it was anger or acceptance. After several long moments of holding her gaze, he looked down at his polished shoes.

"The only problem is, we don't want the same thing, Angel. You want to build new, expensive buildings that will displace so many of my constituents. I can't let that happen."

"So you're saying you're turning down my proposal without even reading it?"

"Oh," he answered quickly, "I've read it. It's impressive. But I can't sign off on it. You want gentrification, but the only thing I'm interested in is urban renewal. So, if you want those permits, you'll redesign your proposal to suit my desires."

She frowned. "You're splitting hairs. What's the difference between the two?"

"Clear your schedule for tomorrow and I'll show you the difference."

Intrigued by his suggestion, she stood, walking past him, plucking a paper plate from the stack on the other side of the table. She opened the pie he'd abandoned when she walked into his office and placed two large slices on her plate.

She took a bite of one, savoring the flavor and perfect texture of the well-done slice of pizza. Then she walked back to where he was leaning against the table, reached past him, picked up her bag and nodded. "I'll see you at noon."

She walked toward the door, only to be stopped by the liquid sound of his deep baritone. "I don't have your address to pick you up."

She didn't turn around. She grabbed the doorknob and smiled to herself. "I still have your number. I'll text it to you. See you tomorrow, Councilman."

"Oh," he called out before she could step through the doorway. "Make sure to dress comfortably. Wouldn't want you ruining a perfectly good pair of Jimmy Choos."

She looked over her shoulder and had to tighten her grip on the doorknob to steel herself against his brazen, half-cocked grin. It was the same smile he'd worn when he exercised such knowing control over her body in that office at The Vault. She'd fallen prey to it then. But never again. Not when everything she ever wanted hung in the balance.

"No worries, Councilman. I'll be ready." She nodded one last time as the silent *for you* hung in the air. No matter how much she wanted to, she couldn't drop her guard. If she did, she knew he'd destroy her.

The only problem was she knew how beautiful and satisfying that destruction could be.

Seven

Amara stood in front of the mirror turning this way and that, trying to figure out if her outfit was casual enough. She had an entire bedroom as a walk-in closet in her Clinton Hill brownstone, filled with designer clothes for every occasion. Elegant evening gowns made specifically to fit her deep curves, power suits to show people how formidable she was before she spoke a single word, and casual wear that often cost as much as the couture items in her possession. But after Lennox's comment about her Jimmy Choos, somehow everything she put on felt like too much.

He hadn't said anything that could be seen as an outright insult. But the smirk on his face coupled with the way the designer's name fell from his lips somehow gave her the impression that dressing up for him today would be out of place.

After changing several times, she finally settled on a pair of high-rise capri jeans, Stan Smith Adidas and a cute halter top. She piled her dark curls on top of her head in a pineapple, pulling a few tendrils out at her temples to cascade against her face. A simple pair of gold hoop earrings and a little Pat McGrath lip gloss completed her outfit.

"This is as casual as I know how to get, Councilman," she said to her reflection in the mirror. "Hopefully it meets your approval."

Why do you care if it doesn't?

She didn't have time to answer her own question before the doorbell rang. She grabbed her Louis Vuitton wristlet, popped her ID, credit card and lip gloss inside, and headed for the door.

"Right on time, Council—" She couldn't finish her sentence, the sight of him stopping all conscious thought and forcing her to focus on one thing: how absolutely fine this man was.

He wore a simple navy polo shirt that stretched tightly against his muscular chest and arms. His khaki shorts fell below his knees, displaying his strong tanned legs, sprinkled with fine dark hair.

"Were you peeking into my closet this morning, Angel? It seems we're matching."

She pulled her eyes away from a slow perusal of his body to meet his gaze, but still couldn't figure out what he was talking about.

"Our footwear. We're both wearing Stan Smiths. I wouldn't have thought a blue blood like yourself would know anything about these classics."

She blinked a few times, as she tried to force her brain/tongue connection to start working again.

"As you said," she finally began, stopping briefly to clear her throat, "they're classics. It doesn't matter what tax bracket you're in, some things are universal."

An awkward moment of silence passed between them as they just stared at each other in the doorway. She smiled, more to herself than him, thinking that this was more than an uncomfortable silence. They were both obviously checking each other out.

So, it ain't just me. Good to know.

"Shall we?" She made to leave but he tilted his head, then lifted his hands. He held a brown bag in one, and a drink tray with what appeared to be two cups of coffee in the other.

"I brought breakfast. We'll need the energy for what I have planned today. You mind if we eat here and then start our day together?"

How she'd managed to miss both the smell and sight of the food was beyond her. Because from the moment she'd opened the door, all she'd focused on was him, that's how.

"Sure," she managed to answer. "Follow me."

She led him through the large foyer, down the long hall to the kitchen in the back. She offered him one of the stools at the counter.

He sat down, pulling out what appeared to be sandwiches wrapped in foil. She hadn't been hungry, but the moment she peeled back the aluminum wrapping and the divine aroma of scrambled eggs, bacon and butter overwhelmed her senses, she was suddenly starving.

"This smells heavenly." She nearly sang those words. "Thank you, Lennox. This was very kind."

"Nothing like bacon, egg and cheese on a buttered roll from the bodega to start your day."

She picked up half of her sandwich, biting into it without any pretense. Fried breakfast food wasn't really her jam, but hell if this wasn't the best thing she'd ever tasted.

"My God, this is good."

"I take it you don't frequent the bodega on the corner much, do you?"

She couldn't bother with trying to speak. Instead, she shook her head as she chewed on her next delicious bite.

He kept a knowing smile on his face; it seemed that he was enjoying watching her eat. She went to pick up one of the cups of coffee to wash her food down, but there was something unpleasant about the smell that made her pull back.

"Is something wrong? There's cream and sugar in the bag if you want."

She replaced the cup and shook her head. "No, I usually take it black, but for some reason it doesn't seem all that appealing today. I've got apple juice in the fridge. Do you want some?"

"I'm good with water if you have it. If the coffee doesn't suit you, that's probably a hint I shouldn't be drinking it, either."

She nodded, turning around and quickly grabbing their beverages from her fully stocked fridge.

She handed him his bottle of water and twisted the top off her juice, taking a long drink from it. When she was done, he was still staring at her with a strange smirk on his face that she couldn't read.

"What?"

He shrugged, leaning forward on the counter. "Nothing. It's just, most of the people I spend time with are always so careful about appearances. I rarely get to see someone enjoying simple pleasures such as good food. A woman who will actually eat in front of me like a normal human being is a rarity in my professional circles. It's refreshing to watch."

She stood still, trying her best to decipher whether he was being honest or sarcastic. But then her gaze landed on the remaining half of her sandwich, and she figured her time was better spent enjoying her food than trying to decode the man sitting at her kitchen counter. She'd figure him out later. Right now, her sandwich was calling her name.

"So, tell me what you see."

She looked at him with a raised brow as she tried to figure out what he was getting at. They were standing on the corner of Gates and Clinton avenues, around the corner from her family's residence and business.

"I see Devereaux Manor right here. It's the jewel of the block. But when you turn the corner onto Gates Avenue, I see dilapidated buildings being torn down and rebuilt to match the splendor of Devereaux Manor. The new construction will bring a nicer-looking neighborhood and boost the local business district."

He nodded, but there was something in the depth of his gaze hidden that suggested he didn't share her perspective.

"Let me guess," she hedged. "You see something different?"

He turned around in a circle with his arm held out as if to put their surroundings on display for her.

"You're right." His tone was neutral without the tinge of judgment she'd expected. "We don't see the same thing."

He stepped in front of her again, meeting her gaze, forcing her to engage even though everything about his eyes warned her that retreat was her best bet.

"I see an area where kids used to play, where the old folks who carried the history of this neighborhood could sit and share their knowledge with the younger generations. Where you see business revitalization in all the new upscale stores popping up, I see places that are removing the personal element from shopping, replacing the traditional small businesses where merchants were also your neighbors. Like the bodega where I picked up breakfast. The owners have been part of this neighborhood for generations."

Lennox's comment seemed to suggest that she might live in Clinton Hill, but obviously she was missing something.

"I see a neighborhood where people could shop close to their homes for their necessities while paying reasonable prices for their goods," he continued. "Gentrification is robbing them of their ability to do that."

She tore her gaze away from his, trying to picture the oasis he was attempting to paint with his words. But to her, no matter how she tried, she couldn't see things through his eyes.

"There are so many specialty and boutique shops whose merchandise come with a higher price point, it's impossible for the working class, let alone residents on fixed incomes, to acquire basic goods."

The gentle conviction in his voice pulled her gaze back to his, tethering her to him, making her think about what he was saying, and feeling the impact of his words, too.

"Where you see shiny new buildings, I see higher rents designed to draw in people in higher tax brackets while it forces the people who've lived here for generations out of their homes and the very neighborhood they helped build and sustain."

His words came down like a cartoon mallet on top of her head. But this was no cartoon. If she believed Lennox's perspective, she was bringing untold doom to Clinton Hill.

She took a deep breath as they continued their walk, trying to reconcile what Lennox was saying with the development plans she was tasked with executing for Devereaux Inc. She might not have grown up poor, but she loved Clinton Hill just as much as the next resident. Lennox seemed to be insinuating otherwise, and the more she thought about it, the more it angered her.

"I'm not trying to harm Clinton Hill. I resent how you're insinuating that I am. This project will bring millions of dollars in revenue to this neighborhood. And not just to the rich people. Everyone in Clinton Hill will benefit."

After a few more stops on their tour, they were back in front of her doorstep. The awkward silence they'd initially shared returned, but for wholly different reasons.

"Angel." He whispered her name, sending tingles up her arms. Her entire life, she'd only heard her middle name spoken when one of her parents was calling her by her entire government name when she was in trouble. But the decadent sound of it on his lips made it feel like she never wanted to be addressed by any other name again.

"I wasn't insinuating you don't care about Clinton Hill. I just think your perspective is skewed because you've only ever experienced it as the heiress to a billion-dollar legacy."

She huffed, rolling her eyes. "You say that like it's a sin."

He shook his head, stepping closer to her, leaning against the iron safety railing on the stoop. "It's not a sin to be wealthy, Angel. I spent a lot of years in corporate law working myself out of poverty. Having money is really nice. I just want you to look at the total picture."

She held up a hand to stop him. "Lennox, even if I agreed with you, which I don't, it doesn't matter what my perspective is. As the head of legal at Devereaux Inc., my job is to get these permits from the city and get this project underway. I can't deviate from that objective."

He nodded, giving her a side glance and a half smile that highlighted the deep dimple in his cheek.

"What if there was a way for us to both get what we want? Would you be willing to think about the big picture then? We've both spent a lot of years negotiating. We know how this works. The best deals have compromise built into them. So, what do you say to me picking you up again so we can gather more intel to make this deal equitable?"

His words created small flutters in her stomach that bordered on uncomfortable. Agreeing to meet with him again was definitely the wrong move for Devereaux Inc. But she couldn't look away from that dimple, and found herself nodding against her better judgment.

"Good," he responded. "I'll call you with details."

He made his way down her steps and turned just before he reached the gate. "Oh, and Angel, I promise you won't regret this."

He gave her a playful wink and disappeared through the gate and down the block. And the only reply she could come up with was, "For both our sakes, I'd better not."

Eight

"Is that my favorite son I hear coming through the door?"

Lennox stopped in his tracks the moment he heard his mother's greeting. Up until his father's death, the moment either he or his sister walked through the door, Della Carlisle had celebrated their arrival exactly the same way.

But since they'd lost his father, and his mother had lost the love of life, she'd barely done more than give him a cursory hello when he entered her home.

He walked down the hall of the two-family building he'd purchased for her and his baby sister when his father died. This purchase had been more than a financial investment. It had been a safeguard, a way to make sure someone was always around to keep an eye on his mother. As hard as she took his dad's death, he didn't trust that she'd be okay alone.

When he found her in the kitchen plating up food, he leaned down and kissed her lightly tanned cheek.

"How's my favorite girl doing today?"

"Better now that my baby boy is here to spend time with me."

He tilted his head, while trying to stifle the smile on his lips. "You know I'm the oldest of your two kids, right?"

"Doesn't matter." She dismissed him with a wave of her hand. "You're always going to be the baby boy they placed in my arms all those years ago."

He regarded her carefully. She sounded like the mother he'd adored before she'd lost the other half of herself. But he was so afraid to trust this newfound exuberance.

"So, what's with all this food. Looks like fried catfish and grits? You haven't cooked like this since..."

"I know," she responded softly, her pain palpable.

Determined not to spoil her mood, he quickly sat down, minding his manners and waiting until his mother said grace before he tucked into what he knew was going to be a fantastic meal.

He was halfway through his first piece of catfish before he could pull his gaze up from his plate.

"Mama, you put your foot in this. This catfish is so good."

"Glad you like it. I was inspired to make it."

"By what?" He brought his focus back to his plate, scooping up a spoonful of grits as she continued.

"I dreamed fish last night."

He momentarily forgot how to chew and swallow, causing the grits to skid a little too close to his airway and kicking in his gag reflex.

"You all right, baby?" his mom asked while he tried to get through his coughing fit. "Raise your arms up so you don't choke."

He wasn't all right. Not by any stretch of the imagination. Growing up, he'd always been told that dreaming fish meant someone was pregnant.

"Like I said, I dreamed fish," she continued. "And you

know that means another baby is coming into this family. So, you got anything you want to tell me?"

His coughing finally quieted enough that he could speak. He could feel his brows knitting together as he looked her. "Me? What about my sister? She's the one that has a wife living upstairs with her."

His mama kept her gaze leveled at him. "I asked your sister. It ain't her."

"Well, it ain't me, either."

He grabbed his empty glass and filled it with iced tea from the nearby pitcher. He drank half the glass in one gulp, trying to get himself together.

"Layla and Mina have decided they're gonna wait a little longer to expand their family. So that leaves you."

It couldn't be. Angel had said she wasn't pregnant. There had to be some mistake. But as he remembered his mother's fish dreams had accurately predicted the last seventeen pregnancies in his very large extended family, panic settled in.

"Mama, I don't know what you're talking about. I'm not even seeing anyone."

"Well, somebody lyin', 'cause according to my dream, I'm sho' nuff about to be a grandmother."

The food he'd been enjoying a moment ago sat heavy in his stomach and he couldn't manage another bite. Instead, he stood from the table and went about washing the dishes as his mother finished her plate. When he was done, he hugged her, made excuses about work and headed straight for his car to make a call.

Two rings later, momentary relief bled through him as the call connected. "Hey, Lennox. What's go—"

"Angel, I need to see you immediately. Are you home?"

"Yeah."

"Don't go anywhere," he said with more force than he intended. "I'll be there in less than thirty minutes."

He ended the call with an abrupt tap of his thumb and

started the ignition. Pulling out into traffic, he kept a repetitive litany on loop in his head.

Please let my mama be wrong for once.

A heavy, persistent knocking alerted Amara to Lennox's arrival. She rushed to the door, opening it wide to see Lennox midknock. The angular lines of his face were pulled tight, and his shoulders were high as if he was having difficulty breathing.

"Lennox, come in." He pushed past her, standing in the foyer looking back and forth as he tried to figure out which direction to go in. He didn't wait for her to guide him through the house; once he looked to the right and saw her living room, he stalked into it, pacing back and forth.

"Lennox, you're scaring me. What's wrong?"

He slid his hand over his bald head as he kept pacing.

"Lennox, please."

He stopped, his panicked gaze latching on to hers, ratcheting up her concern.

"I think you're pregnant. And I need you to take a test to confirm it."

She stood there with her mouth open, shocked by both his words and his demand.

"Lennox, I've already told you I'm not pregnant and there's nothing for you to worry about."

"Yeah, except my mama dreamed fish, so I need you to be certain."

She stared at him, her eyes blinking rapidly as she tried to process what he was saying.

"Your mama dreamed fish? Did you really just burst into my house because of some superstitious wives' tale?"

He put his hands on his hips, confirming she'd jumped to the right conclusion. She was torn somewhere between being annoyed and falling into a fit of laughter. "I told you, I'm not pregnant. So, your mother's dream notwithstanding, you have nothing to worry about."

"You don't understand, Angel. My mother's fish dreams are never wrong. She never gets the interpretation, or the expecting parent, wrong. In this case, she's saying it's me. And since you're the only person I've had sex with recently, that means you're pregnant."

She didn't know if it was the conviction in his tone or the abject fear she saw in his wide hazel eyes. Whatever it was, she was beginning to get nervous.

"We need to go pick up a test right now."

She shook her head. "Lennox, you're a mayoral candidate and I'm a Devereaux. We can't just walk into Duane Reade and buy a pregnancy test. It would be all over the gossip rags before I could swipe my card at the register."

"Then what do you suggest?"

She walked over to him, grabbing his hand and leading him to a large sofa in the middle of the room. "I'll order one online and have it overnighted. By tomorrow I'll take it and put your mind at ease."

"You're assuming it's going to be negative. What happens if it isn't, Angel?"

The hell if she knew. Truly, she couldn't let herself think that far ahead. The timing of a pregnancy right now would complicate both their lives and careers in irrevocable ways. Ways she wasn't sure either of them was ready to face.

How the hell did I get here? As quickly as the question arose, her mind answered.

Because you screwed a sexy man you know you had no business touching. The question you should be asking is what are you gonna do now.

Nine

The package arrived.

We'll know in the morning.

He'd waited for those texts all day. He was about to respond when he watched those maddening three dots appear on his screen, followed quickly by a new message.

Do you want to be here when I take it?

His thumb hovered over his phone, poised to respond. Of course, he wanted to be there. But after the way he'd barged into her house yesterday demanding she take a test, he wasn't sure she'd want him around. Honestly, it would serve him right if she didn't.

If you want me there, I want to be there.

Be here by six. Bring BEC sandwiches with you, please.

The price of entry?

Absolutely.

At least she was in good spirits. They were certainly going to need their senses of humor if the results came back the way he expected.

Amara smiled as she stood in her kitchen rereading her text conversation with Lennox. Even through text, she was reminded of what had attracted her to him in the first place.

Aside from how fine he is, you mean?

Well, his looks certainly hadn't been a problem that night at The Vault. But she'd been taken in by not just his appearance, but his presence.

As a confident woman who understood her power, it wasn't often she came across a man who was equally self-possessed, enough to not be threatened by her confidence. If memory served, Lennox had thrived off her strength that night.

Amara, stop thinking about this man like that. This is serious.

Serious was an understatement. According to Lennox, his mother's fish dreams were never wrong. Amara was aware of the mythical fish dream. She'd heard several variations of it from both the Black American and Afro-Latinx sides of her family. But there hadn't been a baby in their branch of the Devereaux clan since she was born. So, to her, this kind of thing was all superstition with very little evidence of actual truth. The idea that Lennox's mother could be right shook her to her core.

Could she even picture herself as a mother?

Financially of course, there was nothing stopping her from raising a child. But was this what she'd imagined for her life, especially at this stage of her career now?

She was finally getting everything she wanted. Her grandfather was handing her the reins. And as much as they'd discussed contracts and negotiations, she couldn't recall if he'd ever expressed his views on single motherhood. Would they be old-fashioned? Would he think her irresponsible for having a baby out of wedlock? Would that be enough to make him change his mind about promoting her?

Four weeks had passed since she'd been with Lennox. Other than miraculously being cured of her normal addiction to coffee, a fact she'd attributed to her dropping into bed by nine every night for the last two weeks, she had no symptoms whatsoever. No nausea, no cravings, and most importantly, her period had come right on schedule.

Or had it?

She scoured her brain, trying to recall some random piece of information from her high school health ed classes.

"Implantation bleeding?"

A cold chill spread through her as she thought of her last health ed teacher explaining it. *It's bleeding that occurs at the beginning of pregnancy caused by the embryo implanting itself into the womb. Sometimes pregnant women mistake it for their period.*

"No. It couldn't be."

She continued to muse until she heard the doorbell ring. With the nerves in her stomach beginning an inconvenient two-step, she opened the door to find Lennox standing there holding up a familiar brown bag with large grease spots on it. More than expensive gems or designer clothes, she couldn't remember ever being so excited by a visitor's gift.

"Price of passage." Lennox smiled as he waved the bag back and forth in front of her. "Since you seemed to like the first so much, I got you an extra one for later if you want it."

She snatched the bag and opened it, taking a long sniff of the glorious aroma. "I could kiss you."

He chuckled as she stepped aside and let him in. "Kissing me is what got us into trouble in the first place."

He wasn't wrong. That kiss had set her ablaze. Any thoughts she'd had about restraint went out the window once her lips touched his.

"I was about to say something slick." She shrugged. "But it would be a lie. It was a pretty great kiss."

He chuckled, nodding in agreement, then clapped his hands together as they stood facing each other in the foyer. "So, do you wanna eat first or take the test?"

Smiling as she watched him, she could tell by the way his hands were shoved in his pockets and he was shifting his weight from one foot to the other that he was anxious.

"Come on. Let's put you out of your misery. I'll take the test now and we can eat later."

She headed for the stairs and motioned for him to follow her. They'd already slept together; him being in her bedroom was no big deal at this point. She directed him to the bench at the foot of her king-size bed. She stood there, looking into his eyes, wondering how the next few minutes could alter the course of both their lives.

"Angel." He took her hand and gently ran thumb across her knuckles. "No matter what that test says, I'm here. You're not alone in this."

Used to doing everything for herself, the idea of having someone to hold her hand as she ventured into unfamiliar territory was a comfort she didn't know she needed.

She nodded and closed her eyes, needing to break the connection. She'd seen this man partially naked and had shared her body with him. Yet somehow, this moment was so much more intimate. And standing there as Lennox's gaze reached beyond her defenses made her feel vulnerable in a way that wasn't necessarily comfortable for someone who prided herself on being a corporate conqueror.

He released her hand and she headed into the en suite bathroom. The test was sitting on her double vanity looking like a ticking bomb that had the possibility of blowing her career to tiny bits. She picked it up carefully, her fingers gingerly caressing the sides as she tried to steel her nerves.

No sense in dragging this out, girl. Pee on the stick and find out for certain if you'll be a mother or not.

Lennox sat on the bench, leaning over with his forearms on his knees, praying that for once, his mother's dreams were just superstition and not premonition.

He wasn't afraid of having children. He'd always imagined he would become a father and pass down the things his parents had shared with him to a child of his own. But the timing, and his precarious connection to Angel, made things complicated in ways he wasn't prepared to deal with. Most notably, for his mayoral candidacy.

The door to the en suite opened and Angel reentered the bedroom. He locked gazes with her, his brows lifting in expectation of an answer.

"It's still processing." The test sat atop a paper towel in the palm of her hand. "I'm too anxious to watch this little digital timer tick by myself, so I thought I'd make you suffer with me."

She shared a shaky half smile with him that made his heart constrict inside his chest. He'd known from the moment he'd laid eyes on her that she was fierce and capable. But right now, she was anxious, and protective instincts he didn't know he possessed started flaring up.

He opened his arms to her and waited until she finally laid down her armor and sat down next to him, sliding into his embrace.

"Are you afraid?" When she didn't respond he smiled. "It's okay if you are. I certainly am."

"Let me guess," she replied. "Knocking up a one-night

stand you never had any intention of seeing again wasn't on your bucket list?"

He chuckled at how she used sarcasm to deflect emotion and filed that bit of information away in his things-I'm-learning-about-Angel file.

"Getting you pregnant may not have been on my agenda, but I'd be lying if I said I didn't want to see you again after the night we shared."

"Really?" Her reply grated on his nerves a bit and he couldn't tell why. He didn't make a habit of following up with one-night stands. But for some reason, he didn't like the implication of her question when applied to the night they'd spent together.

"Are you saying I was so easily forgettable for you?"

"A powerful man needing his ego stroked. Who would've thought it?"

"You're deflecting, Counselor. Answer the question."

She paused a moment, but he could feel her mouth curving into a smile against his chest.

"I might've had a thought or two about you before I walked into your office."

"Well, depending on what that stick you're holding says, we might be spending much more time together than either of us ever anticipated." He placed a gentle kiss atop her head and cupped her cheek with his hand as they sat there quietly for the next few minutes, waiting to discover their fate.

Her watch buzzed, making her stiffen against him. He loosened his hold on her, but slid his hand down her arm and interlaced their fingers. She looked up at him and steadied herself with an audible breath before she opened her palm and turned the pregnancy test wand over to view the digital screen.

Right there in bold digital print, one word confirmed what he'd known since his mother had informed him of her dream. Angel, a woman he hardly knew, a woman currently seeking to do business with his office, was pregnant with his child.

He felt her stiffen in his arms and it made him tighten his hold on her. Whatever was going through her head he needed her to know he was her anchor.

"Tell me what you're thinking, Angel."

She turned to him, blinking just before her tears spilled down her cheeks. "I… My thoughts are all over the place. I'm terrified."

Yeah, he was scared out of his goddamn mind, too. But there, mixed in with the fear, was something else, something bright, uplifting and unexpected. But that didn't mean Angel was feeling that, too.

"Is that all you feel? Fear?"

She gave him a shaky smile as she shook her head. "If you're asking what I think you are, however we created this child, I'm not considering terminating the pregnancy."

He squeezed her tighter. "Thank you for sharing that with me. And for the record, whatever your decision, I would've supported you."

Quiet cloaked the room as they both tried to get their emotional footing.

"Is it weird that despite our situation, I'm happy, too?" she finally asked.

Lennox felt his smile growing wider. His campaign manager was going to have a fit once Lennox shared this news. But he didn't care. He was gonna be a father and nothing else seemed to matter in that moment.

"We're having a baby, Angel."

She sighed, closing her eyes and leaning into him. "We're having a baby, Lennox. What are we going to do?"

Her question stoked his apprehension again. The hell if he knew what the next steps were. The sound of his heart beating so loudly beneath his ribs made it difficult for him to think anything other than, *Oh shit. Oh shit. Oh shit*, on a repetitive loop. He closed his eyes, blocking everything else out, and then the solution came to him.

He turned to her, squeezing her hand to get her attention. She asked him again. “What are we going to do, Lennox?”

And with a wobbly smile of his own he said, “We get married.”

Ten

"Hell no."

She spoke the words as easily as her own name. Probably a little too harshly, from the way Lennox recoiled in response.

"Angel, we have to."

"Actually, no, we don't. We don't know anything about each other, Lennox. We can't get married. Why would we?"

"Angel, we're having a baby."

She stood up, pacing back and forth to help her think. What the hell was he thinking? "Yes, I'm aware. But this isn't some 1950s drama. I don't need a husband to have a child and maintain my respectability. I don't give a damn about what anyone else thinks. And in case you haven't noticed, I'm a Devereaux. I'm more than capable of taking care of a child financially."

"Personally, I don't care what people think, either. But professionally, this could be career suicide. I have to think about that. As for your identity I'm well aware of who you are...*now*." His eyes narrowed into two tiny accusing slits as he leveled his gaze at her.

"So this is my fault?"

He tilted his head slightly. "That we created a baby? No, we both bear that responsibility. That I slept with you in the first place? Yeah, that's your fault. You knew who the hell I was and how problematic things would get if we found ourselves in a situation. I wasn't given the same courtesy of knowing your identity. If I'd been aware, there's no way in hell we'd be here now."

The cold glint in his eyes made her shiver. "Lennox, I've already explained..."

"That you were in a bad way and exercised poor judgment, and that you had no intention of ever seeing me again. Yeah, I got that part. But that's not how life has worked out. I'm campaigning in the primary to be the next mayor of New York City. The incumbent is a man who keeps pointing out that I'm unmarried, suggesting that I have no ties to ground me, making me too flighty and unsettled to get the job done."

Lennox stood with his legs wide and his arms folded against his chest, making a sexy yet imposing picture. "Up until now, constituents haven't bought into his BS. But the moment it gets out I'm having a baby with someone my office might end up doing business with, my bid for mayor is over. You withheld information that kept me from making an informed decision. You were wrong and you owe me. You're going to marry me."

Unbothered, Amara put her hands on her hips and jutted one out. Two could play this "I shall not be moved" game.

"I'm *going* to marry you?" she spat, slightly amused but mostly pissed off by his edict. "Last I checked, marriage was a voluntary agreement. You don't have enough leverage over me to make me pour you a glass of water, let alone marry you."

Something hard and dangerous sparked in his eyes as he stepped closer into her personal space.

"I wonder what David Devereaux would have to say about that?"

The mention of her grandfather's name made an internal tremor quake throughout her body.

"If I remember correctly, when we met, you were upset because your boss was giving you grief about being too reckless at work. Sounds to me like he wouldn't be too thrilled if he knew how we ended up here."

She folded her arms across her chest. "That sounds like you're threatening me."

"Call it whatever you like. But if you don't agree to marry me immediately, I'm going directly to David and telling him about the unethical game his granddaughter played and how it's going to cost me a campaign and Devereaux Inc. millions, because there's no way I can give permits to a company with such an unprincipled leader."

He took one step closer, closing the last sliver of distance between them. "I wonder how quickly the old man would end his temporary leave and snatch control away from you if he knew all that."

She could feel her throat tightening as she tried to swallow and tamp down both her anger and fear. Amara had no doubt her grandfather would end her trial period as head counsel in a heartbeat.

"What happened to all that smooth talking about you being here for me, Lennox? You've strangely gone from comforting me to blackmailing me. How's that work?"

"I *am* here for you." His words were softer but still managed to hold a sharp, frigid quality that put her on the defensive. "I want to be here for you. But I need the same kind of support from you. Neither of us need lose our careers over this. Marrying protects us both."

"I see how it protects you." This situation was definitely more advantageous for him with respect to his career. But there were too many variables where hers was concerned. "How does this protect my job? Are you saying you'll give me the permits if I marry you?"

His brow furrowed, registering mild shock. "I would never promise you something like that. Us having a child together is conflict of interest enough. When we marry, I'll have my assistant set up a third-party panel who will handle the entire process. Whatever they decide will be final. So even if the outcome doesn't go your way, you'll have to abide by it."

She shook her head. "That's not fair, Lennox. This marriage would give you exactly what you want by protecting your career. Why would I agree to something that doesn't provide me the same assurances?"

"Again," he responded, his smooth features schooled into an inscrutable expression, "perhaps you should've thought of that when you slept with me under false pretenses. I didn't get the chance to make a choice about putting my career on the line by sleeping with you. Seems fitting the tables are turned now. Don't you think?"

He's got you there, girl.

Fire bubbled inside of her. He was right, of course. But that didn't mean she had to like the fact that he had no qualms about putting her in her place so succinctly.

She dropped her gaze, trying to find a moment of reprieve from the intensity of his. "But we don't love each other, Lennox. Hell, I'm not even sure if I like you all that much. How's a marriage going to work between us? We're going to make each other miserable."

He lifted her chin, locking eyes with her again. "We knew enough about one another to create this child. The rest will work itself out."

She stepped back, trying her best to put distance between them to keep her thoughts clear. When he was this close, touching her even in the most benign way, her brain shut off and her body completely took control.

"I'll ask you again, what about love, Lennox? I come from a family where marriage is sacred. Love is our bedrock. We'd be making a mockery of that."

"I'm not looking for love, Angel. My parents adored each other so much that when my father died, my mother became a broken shell. She gave up on life and just sat back waiting for death to claim her so she could be reunited with my dad. That sounds romantic, but it's the most painful thing I've ever lived through. I won't allow that to happen to me."

He pulled his hand down over his face and took a steadying breath. Although the hard exterior was still there, she could see tiny cracks in his resolve that made her ache for him.

"I can offer you companionship, partnership and kindness. I can't offer you love."

The hard glint in his eyes didn't make her afraid. Sadness, that's what she felt clawing at her as she watched him. She knew they didn't love each other. They'd just met. But the fact that he couldn't even be open to the possibility made her sad that her child would never know the joy of growing up with parents who adored each other like she had.

"If love is off the table, what are your terms?"

He seemed to relax, his shoulders dropping slightly as he prepared to answer her. "One, we stay married for as long as I'm in office. Two, we reside in the same household. Three, whenever we're in public, we play the role of devoted spouses and parents. Four, as long as we're married, there will be no outside relationships. We're faithful for however long we're tied to each other."

She could feel her forehead pinching into a sharp point. "You could end up being in office for eight years. What are we supposed to do about sex?"

He quickly threaded his fingers through her hair and seared her lips with a kiss. Her mouth burned from his touch, and when she moaned, trying her best to deepen the kiss, he tore his mouth away from hers and stared down at her. "If we need sex, we come to each other. It doesn't matter to me how this marriage came about. If I take you as my wife, you're mine, Angel. No one else touches you besides me. I won't be made a fool of by anyone, least of all a cheating wife."

Amara didn't scare easily. But the harsh tone of his voice had her wondering if for once she'd bitten off more than she could chew. Because the way he'd said the word *mine* made her afraid and more than a little aroused. Either way, she realized things were getting out of hand.

Especially when his fingers tightened in her hair, and he pulled her against the hard planes of his body. She'd never been a woman who cared much about hard pecs and abs. But there was something about the firm foundation of Lennox's body that felt like hallowed ground to her. And as he wrapped his arm around her waist, locking in their position, she noticed instantly that his pecs and abs weren't the only part of his body that was hard, a fact she was most grateful for at the moment.

Much like the first and only time they were together, her clothes seemed to somehow fall away of their own accord, and she was pressed against hot flesh, her arms instinctively wrapping around him, determined to hold on.

Lennox must have somehow read her mind, understood that her need to be closer to him was much more than simple attraction. It was desperation. Like dehydrated ground soaking up rain, she savored every kiss, every touch until he hoisted her up, carrying her to her bed and lowering her to the mattress.

She quickly realized she wasn't the only person desperate for their bodies to connect. As she lay back on locked elbows, she watched him rip his clothing from his body, until he was naked in all his beautiful glory. Even though she knew he was a threat to everything she was trying to protect, she didn't run away, didn't put up the slightest bit of fight. She wanted this, and she couldn't see past the haze of her desire long enough to care about how this was going to wreck her life later.

He covered her body with his, satisfying her need to touch him and be touched by him. But it wasn't enough. Even with his lips on hers, on the curve of her neck and shoulder, her collarbone, and then slowly moving down the line of her décolletage, she ached until his mouth finally met the turgid peak of one nipple while his fingers continued to travel down her abdomen, between her legs, until they were slipping through her wet folds.

"Damn, I've barely touched you and you're already dripping." He pulled his fingers to his mouth, licking the evidence of her arousal away before leaning down and kissing her, demanding she open for him, letting her taste herself on him.

All she could do was surrender because it was the most potent and enticing thing she'd ever experienced. When he pulled away slightly, still brandishing that wicked smile of his, she burned from the hold he had on her. She secretly reprimanded herself for the lack of dignity she was displaying.

She narrowed her gaze, frustrated by his obvious gloating as well as the delayed action.

"Don't flatter yourself." She managed to find enough air in her lungs to speak quickly. "Increased sexual desire is a symptom of pregnancy."

A wicked gleam in his eye now accompanied his exasperating smile.

"If that's what you need to tell yourself to help you sleep at night."

She was busted. She knew it and so did he. Which was the problem with this thing between them. Amara wasn't used to being at a tactical disadvantage. When it came to Lennox, she always seemed to find herself at his mercy, and that just wouldn't stand.

"Shut up and fuck me."

His eyes slightly widened, and she realized she'd caught him off guard. Before he could recover the upper hand, she locked her knees around him, flipping the two of them over so that she was on top and in control.

She leaned down, grabbing a foil packet from her nightstand. "Until we're comfortable foregoing them."

Just because she was pregnant didn't mean either of them was ready for unprotected sex. Without delay, she wrapped her hand around his girth. Stroking him up and down, letting her thumb caress the tip, thoroughly enjoying the full-body shudder he exhibited, she sheathed him in the condom. She grinned, reveling in the fact that she wasn't the only one affected by their explosive need.

She slowly lowered herself onto him, satisfied moans escaping them both with each inch she took into her body. The stretch was significant, but so titillating she had to fight with herself not to rush this process.

Soon she was seated, so full of him she could hardly tell where she ended and he began. She kissed him as she swiveled her hips, drawing the movement out, delighted by the almost painful grip he had on her hips as he tried to make her speed up her movements.

She refused to be rushed. This was too good, and she would enjoy it for as long as she could. When they weren't in bed, she spent too much energy trying to get the upper hand in a situation that was quickly getting out of control. But here, with her body clenched around his like they were molded to fit perfectly together, nothing else mattered. Not her job or her fear of losing the promotion she'd earned. Not the fact that her life was about to change irrevocably. And certainly not the fact that marrying Lennox was a bad idea, considering they barely knew each other.

She didn't have to think about any of that, as she swerved her hips then sat up so that she could experience the decadent pleasure of sliding up and down his length with her muscles clenching so tightly she could feel the erratic rhythm of his pulse. All she had to do was savor how good he felt inside her body as she climbed higher and higher, toward the climax that seemed just out of her reach.

He must have somehow realized her struggle, or maybe he was going through a similar one of his own. He sat up, wrapping one arm around her waist while the other hand went to the back of her neck.

In one fluid motion, she was on her back with one leg over his shoulder as he lodged himself as deeply as he could. He leaned forward, deepening his stroke, his cock sliding in at just the right angle to touch that elusive spot that would give her the release she was begging for.

"Please," she muttered, not giving a sliver of a damn at how needy and desperate she sounded. With one side of his mouth lifted in a grin, he placed a soft kiss on her calf before glancing down at her.

"Please what?" He ramped down his pace, swiveling his hips as slowly as she had, returning the torture she'd so happily doled out to him.

She was too close to tell him off. No way was she doing anything that would make him deny her what her entire being was aching for.

"Please fuck me, Lennox." Her voice was a whispered cry that was equal parts pitiful and frustrated. "I need…"

"You need me." His voice was steady and forceful. It was a declarative statement, as if he knew this was an undisputed fact. "Say it," he commanded in a low growl. "Say you need me."

And there in that moment, when they battled like titans over whose will would reign supreme, her need grabbed hold of her so strongly, she knew he was the decided winner of this round.

"I need you, Lennox. Please."

She waited for the gloating, the bragging rights her concession handed him. But instead, there was relief in his eyes. He lowered her leg, leaning forward, burying his face in her neck as he whispered, “I need you, too. Can’t do this without you.”

Those words broke the dam holding back the wave of her climax. Like a tsunami crashing over her head, the powerful undercurrent of her orgasm dragged her beneath the rough waters of pleasure as he plowed into her with deep, strong strokes until she finally stopped struggling, and went willingly into the depths of satisfaction.

And when she thought she’d drown alone, every muscle in his body clenched as he joined her in bliss.

As they swam back to reality, their breathing labored and their chests heaving, he fell onto his side, grabbing her and pulling her into his embrace.

“Do you still have questions about what we’ll do if either of us needs sex?”

Doubts? No. At this moment, all she had were guarantees. And the biggest one ran through her mind as her gaze met his. *This man is going to dismantle your entire life.* And as she watched a smile creep onto his face, all she could think was: *And you’re going to let him.*

“Fine,” she whispered. “I’ll marry you.”

Eleven

Amara stood behind the railing and looked out over the ocean view balcony. Two days ago, Lennox had texted her travel information for an impromptu trip to Port Antonio, Jamaica. He'd taken care of all the arrangements, and as soon as she entered the property, she'd been whisked away to a beautiful private villa that boasted clean lines, minimal furnishings and open space.

Once the bellhop had escorted her to her room and left her bags lined up neatly in front of the wide closet doors, she headed straight for the patio. Marveling at the deep blue water, white sand and verdant greenery, Amara instantly felt her apprehension bleed away. She'd been on edge ever since Lennox told her they were flying down to Jamaica to elope.

A knock on the door pulled her from her musings. She traversed the large bedroom and living area quickly, looking through the peephole to see a warped image of Lennox standing on the front porch.

She opened the door, stepping aside and letting him in.

"Glad to see you made it here safely." His tone was reserved. She led him to the living area and sat down next to him on the love seat.

"How was your flight?"

She wasn't sure how to answer that question. The pilot had gotten her to Jamaica safely, but flying alone on a private jet meant she'd had roughly four hours to dwell on how out of order things were.

"Angel?"

"My trip was thankfully uneventful." He raised his brow, encouraging her to continue. "The attendant mentioned how the last time I took the jet to the Caribbean, my parents were with me." He remained quiet, waiting for her to continue when she was ready.

"My parents and I are very close. We take impromptu family vacations all the time. The attendant just made me start thinking about how I'm going to explain all of this to them. They'll be thrilled to know they're going to be grandparents. But I think it's going to hurt them when they find out I married without their knowledge."

"And that's making you feel guilty?"

Guilt didn't really describe it. More than anything, she felt disappointment in herself for robbing them of sharing in this moment.

"During the father-daughter dance at my quinceañera, my dad told me how proud he was of the woman I was becoming and how the next father-daughter dance we had would be at my wedding."

Amara had never been an overly sentimental person. But knowing how much her father had looked forward to this and how she was intentionally taking it away from him weighed on her conscience more than she'd imagined.

"It seems that my moment of selfishness—that's how you put it, right?—is negatively impacting more than just you. This might be a pattern. You sure you want to go through with this wedding plan of yours?"

"This wedding is happening tomorrow evening, Angel." His words were direct, but she could see a brief flash of empathy in his eyes.

"Are you close to your parents?"

"Very," he responded, shifting on the sofa as if he needed to get comfortable before he could speak. "My dad passed away a few years ago. He was my best friend. My mom is thankfully still with us. She's this tiny little spitfire who still manages to get my younger sister and me to do exactly what she wants. Even my sister-in-law is wrapped around her finger."

"How do you think your mother's gonna feel about all of this?"

"She'll be pissed," he replied. "But I hope telling her about the baby will keep me from getting disowned."

There was an awkward pause. She presumed he was thinking about the consequences of their plan, too.

She looked around the room. "Thank you for the beautiful accommodations. Please send me the bill and I'll have you reimbursed."

His features tightened and she wondered what about her statement offended him.

"Angel." His acrid tone made her stiffen. "I may not be as rich as the Devereauxs, but after spending fifteen years as one of New York's top-paid corporate lawyers, I think I can afford to pay for a nice trip here and there without going broke."

"I didn't mean any offense, Lennox." Her apology was quick and true. "It would never dawn on me that a man I'm not really with would go through so much trouble for me."

He stretched his arm against the back of the love seat and leaned a little closer. "Angel, that's where you're wrong. We are together." He reached down and pulled her hand into his, resting both against his thigh. "Our union is definitely unorthodox. I'll give you that. But even though there's an expiration date on this marriage, I promise you, I intend to honor my vows to you for the duration. I hope I can count on you for the same."

Suddenly overwhelmed by emotion, she nodded in response, pulling a genuine smile from him.

"Good. Because I see no reason for us to hurt each other and be unhappy while we're together. So, get used to me doing nice things for you." He slid his hand to her stomach and splayed his fingers wide. "You're carrying my child. For that reason alone, I'll see to it you never want for anything."

Part of her delighted at his nurturing instincts. But another part wished that he wanted to spoil her for no other reason than she deserved it.

"Everything all right?"

"It's fine. Thank you for your generosity. I promise I'll make sure to enjoy our time here."

"Good," he replied. "I'm glad you're seeing things my way. Because first thing tomorrow morning, a masseuse, a hairstylist, a makeup artist, a nail technician and a personal stylist will be here to pamper and dress you, so you'll be the most beautiful bride to ever step on sand."

He placed a gentle kiss on her lips and granted her a kind smile as he pulled back. Before she could figure out what he was doing, he kneeled down in front of her, reaching into his pocket and retrieving a small velvet box.

"As I said, our union may not be conventional. But that doesn't mean it has to be any less significant. For as long as you choose to be my wife, I'll honor you, Angel. And that means if we're going to do this, we're going to do it right."

He opened the box, revealing a very large princess cut diamond with smaller round diamonds and rubies alternating on the band. She was about to say this was way too much for a fake marriage, but once she saw the ring sparkle, the words never came.

"Amara Angel Devereaux-Rodriguez. Will you do me the honor of meeting me on the beach tomorrow evening and becoming my wife?"

Excitement mixed with something unfamiliar spread through her until tears were spilling from her eyes. It had to be this pregnancy, because she couldn't remember being so easily brought to tears before in her life.

"Yes, Lennox."

That was as much as she got out before he slipped the ring on her finger and brought his lips to hers. And as she lost herself in the high of his kiss, she pushed the fear trying to remind her that this wasn't real to the back of her mind. It wasn't smart. But this moment was too perfect to allow reality to intrude.

He broke the kiss, smiling as he stood. "I'll see you tomorrow on the beach. I'll be the guy standing next to the minister staring at you in awe."

He turned toward the door to leave, and she called his name. "Where are you going?"

"I have a room at the main hotel." He stared directly at her, his intense gaze making her feel like she should brace herself for whatever he was about to say next. "I didn't know if you'd be comfortable with me staying here with you."

This was the same man who'd threatened to expose her poor judgment to her grandfather unless she agreed to marry him. If she hadn't seen the concern in the depths of his brown eyes, she'd question how her comfort could matter to him at all.

"Angel." He turned to her, his features softening as he spoke. "Even when I push you to consider the greater good, that doesn't mean I don't care about what happens to you. Although I expect us to share a residence when we return home, you don't have to worry about me making other demands because we're married. Whether this is a marriage in name only is solely up to you."

A nervous bubble of laughter slipped past her lips. “I’d say the horse is already out of the barn on that one. Besides, didn’t you just say we *are* together?”

“Yes, I did.” He offered a casual shrug before tilting his head. “This is a partnership. An unconventional one, but still a partnership. I won’t lie and say I don’t want to share your bed, Angel. The two of us together are like fire and gasoline. I don’t think there will ever be a time when I don’t want to touch you.” His eyes narrowed into slits, and she could feel the heat radiating from his intense gaze in the core of her chest. “But us being together doesn’t mean I automatically have free range of your body. If you want more, you’ll have to say so.”

Those words were a challenge. A challenge she should ignore. This situation was messy enough. Him giving her an out on the physical intimacy was a boon she should gratefully accept. But she had never been known for letting things be, so she saw no reason to start now.

She stood up, folding her arms over her chest as she met his gaze. “All of this sounds really good, Lennox. But forgive me if I’m having a hard time buying it. Weren’t you the same man who told me one of the rules of this marriage is if we want sex, we have to come to each other?”

He stepped in front of her, closing the space between them.

“I won’t presume I’m owed sex because we’re married, Angel. But for as long as this marriage lasts, I am the only person you will have sex with and vice versa. That is not up for negotiation. Do you understand me?”

Part of her wanted to curse him out for the ultimatum he was throwing down. He had no right to demand anything from her. But the tight set of his lips and the look in his eyes made her rethink the smart-ass comment hanging from the tip of her tongue. For the first time, Amara realized something about Lennox that made fear trickle down her spine. In this gorgeous, powerful man, she just may have met her match.

She swallowed, taking a step back before she nodded. "Understood."

Twelve

Amara lay on the left side of the large empty bed with her eyes closed, hoping that if she remained still, she could stop the minutes from ticking and avoid the fate that awaited her later this evening. She turned over onto her back, pulling a smooth breath into her lungs. Lennox wasn't a monster. His actions last night proved it. He'd brought her to this island paradise, pledged his fidelity to her, and comforted her when she admitted her misgivings about marrying without her parents by her side.

But somehow, all his goodwill made this day even more difficult. It felt good. Too good. Good enough that she had to keep reminding herself this was fake, all a part of the show they were putting on. Getting caught up would be the worst thing she could do.

Realizing she couldn't hide from life or Lennox, she dragged herself out of bed and headed for the shower. Slightly soothed by the powerful spray of hot water against her skin, she quickly toweled off, grabbing the satin robe she'd placed in the bathroom last night before stepping in front of the large double vanity in the middle of the room.

Amara wiped the condensation from the foggy mirror as she stood trying her best to recognize the reflection staring at her.

"How did you end up in this mess, girl?"

She waited for her reflection to answer her, to in some way make it make sense to Amara. But somehow, the woman in the mirror remained silent, refusing to answer her question.

She looked down at the large engagement ring Lennox had placed on her finger last night. It was impressive, even by Devereaux standards. And that proposal, goodness, even knowing their union was a sham, she was moved by his declarations.

Amara heard a knock. Tightening the belt on her satin robe, she headed toward the door. Lennox had said her glam squad would show up early. However, she'd thought she'd at least have a chance to have breakfast before they arrived.

"Wow, I must need more work than I thought if you're here this early." She opened the door, ready to greet the people who would make her wedding-ready. But instead of a team of strangers holding garment bags and makeup trunks, she found Lennox standing in front of the door with her parents.

"Surprise!" Her mother and father yelled as they surrounded her, hugging and kissing her. Stunned into silence, she looked up at Lennox to find a conspiratorial grin on his face.

Why would he do this?

He must have understood her unspoken question, because he waited for them to move farther into the villa before he addressed it.

"I know we said we wanted an intimate ceremony. But knowing how close we both are to our parents, I didn't feel right about going through with it without telling them."

Once her parents stepped aside, she opened her mouth to speak, but he held up a hand, interrupting her. "I hope you're not too upset with me. I just wanted to make this day as perfect for you as I could."

Quite frankly, she was so overwhelmed by the sight of her parents, she didn't know how to define her emotions. She was shocked, for certain, and probably more than a little ticked off he'd done this without her knowledge. This wasn't a regular wedding. Throwing her parents into the mix could have uncontrollable effects on this whole charade.

But deep in his eyes, there was something soft and comforting that brooked her anger and made her feel all warm and emotional. She'd like to blame it on pregnancy hormones, but the truth was she didn't know if this was a result of pregnancy or if this was just Lennox's power over her.

"Mi amor," her father said softly to her mother. "Do you see this? I may have had my reservations when a total stranger called us and told us he was marrying our daughter. But only someone who loves her terribly would do something like this for her."

Amara dropped her eyes, too ashamed to meet her father's gaze, and slightly afraid he'd see through their lies.

"Mr. Rodriguez, as I mentioned, I take full responsibility for waiting until the last minute to notify you. I was wrong for making plans that didn't include our families. I just hope you won't hold it against me and will give me the chance to prove my worth as Angel's husband."

"Angel?" her father repeated with a gentle smile on his face as he walked toward Lennox. "That's what you call my daughter, Angel?"

"Yes, sir," Lennox answered. "That's what she is to me."

Right there, she watched her father melt and fall in love with a man she was only tied to by convenience. And

Amara knew her mother wouldn't be far behind from the way she was quietly dabbing her eyes.

They went out to the patio where a breakfast feast had been laid out. It took up most of the table.

"I assume this is more of your doing?" She smiled as Lennox shrugged, taking his seat next to her, directly across from her parents.

"It's our wedding day. Keeping a smile on your face is literally the one job I have."

"And you're very good at that job," her mother added. "From the look on my daughter's face now. Tell me, how'd you get so good at that?" She leaned forward, raising a brow. Her voice might have been liquid sunshine, but Amara recognized this look for what it was. It was the precursor to the inquisition that always followed. "Obviously you haven't been seeing my daughter long, otherwise we'd have known about you. So how does a man I'm just meeting today get so adept at making my only child this happy?"

"Mamí..." Amara attempted to stop her mother's line of questioning when she felt strong but gentle fingers slide down her arm.

"It's fine, Angel. If I were in your parents' shoes, I'd have questions, too." She watched Lennox carefully, sitting back against her chair and hoping he knew what the hell he was doing.

"Your daughter and I met a little over a month ago at The Vault. The plain truth is, I couldn't take my eyes off her from the moment I saw her. Once we spoke, and bonded over what it's like to be young, Black and gifted, I couldn't let her go."

Okay, Lennox. Score one for the Nina Simone reference. My mama will eat that up.

Her mother nodded and sat back in her chair, taking a sip of water from her glass. "Attractive, generous, smart enough to recognize gold when he sees it, and cultured?

You seem almost too good to be true, Lennox. Or are you simply giving me campaign face right now?"

Amara waited for Lennox to flinch. But he didn't so much as bat an eyelash. Instead, he spread his arm across the back of Amara's chair as he leaned closer to her.

"Mrs. Devereaux-Rodriguez, I'm the same whether I'm on the campaign trail or not. I'm all about protecting and supporting my people, working hard to see them thrive." He looked at Amara, and the fire sparking in the depth of his eyes pulled her in, tricking her senses into believing this could be real, if only for this moment. "That's even more true when it comes to my future bride and..."

He stopped short, tilting his head to silently ask her if he should continue. She couldn't help herself: she smiled, momentarily forgetting about how this situation came to be and focusing on the only bright spot. The fact that she and Lennox were thrilled about her pregnancy made the rest of it seem, well, unimportant.

She nodded, and he took her hand in his before turning to her parents again. "...and the child she's carrying."

Amara giggled when she saw the stunned looks on her parents' faces. For the first time in her life, she witnessed her mother and father struck speechless. Too delighted to hold back any longer, she chuckled as she watched confusion pass between them. "Mamí, Papí, you're going to be grandparents. I'm pregnant."

"You're grown, Amara," her mother began as she stood next to her, going through the selection of jeweled headpieces the stylist had left. She'd never thought about all these little details for a wedding because she'd never thought about marrying. "You have to make this decision on your own."

"Mamí, they're all so beautiful. How am I supposed to choose?"

Her mother sighed before giving her a look. "I wasn't talking about the headpieces, and I think you know that. Are you sure you're not rushing into this because of the baby?"

She should've known surprise and happiness wouldn't keep her mother quiet for long.

"Neither of us feels compelled to get married because of the baby. Not for the reasons you're thinking anyway. This marriage is strictly about Lennox and me. The baby is a happy gift. We didn't plan on becoming parents, but we're both thrilled this little one is coming."

Her mother nodded, her eyes filling with tears. "If this is what you want, then that's all I care about." Clasping her hands around Amara's, her mother beamed with happiness. "My baby's gonna have a baby. And I'm gonna get to pick out my granny name."

Amara chuckled. "What's wrong with grandma or abuela?"

Her mother jutted her chin in Amara's direction, giving her the same sassy smile Amara often wore. "I'm too sexy and fabulous to be a grandma or an abuela. I need something befitting like noni, or big mama. Maybe even something sophisticated like ma'dea."

"Well," Amara said as she wiped the wet streak from her mother's glowing face. "One thing is obvious to me. Whatever this baby calls you, you're going to end up spoiling it rotten. Aren't you?"

"I spoiled you, didn't I?"

It was true, Amara had never known anything but her mother's love and support, and adoration.

"You sure did."

"Well, considering how wonderful you turned out, I think me spoiling this baby will be just as effective."

Amara took in the sight of her mother glowing as she talked about the baby. And in that moment, she realized Lennox had done her a huge favor in bringing her parents here.

"I'm really glad you and Papí are here, Mamí."

"So am I, baby. So am I." Her mother cleared her throat. "Now, enough of all this sentimental crying. We've got to pick out the perfect headpiece for my perfect baby girl."

Amara knew she wasn't perfect by any stretch of the imagination. But knowing her mother still saw her that way, even after discovering news of her secret wedding, that really was more than she could ever ask for.

Amara stood in front of the mirror taking in her reflection. Of all the outfits she'd ever dreamed about wearing, never had she imagined herself quite like this.

She'd chosen a fitted crepe trumpet gown covered in Swarovski crystals with a plunging neckline and a keyhole back. Every curve on her size sixteen body was on full display and she'd never felt sexier in her life.

She turned to the side to see the small train move and get a glimpse of how the overall design of the dress complemented her shape. She picked up the card that Lennox had sent with the dress and read it again.

I know you probably would have preferred to choose your own dress. Even though our unexpected nuptials didn't leave you enough time for that, I wanted you to have something you'd like. A quick search, and countless pictures of you in LaQuan Smith's clothing, and I decided to take a chance and see if he could help us out. When he heard it was for you, he said he had the perfect piece. I can't wait to see you in whatever he came up with. I hope it makes up for all the things you'll miss because we didn't have a year to plan a proper wedding.

See you on the beach,
L.

The way she looked in this dress more than made up for any loss due to their speedy wedding. Lennox was right, LaQuan Smith was her favorite designer, and this dress fit like he'd made it specifically for her.

Her hair cascaded down over her shoulders. A diamond comb her mother wore on her wedding day tucked some of her dark brown tresses behind one ear.

"Look at my baby!"

Amara turned around to find her mother staring at her with tears threatening to spill from her loving eyes.

"You are a vision. Lennox will be speechless."

She gave her mother a warm a smile and looked behind her. "Where's Papí?"

"He's waiting downstairs to walk you down the aisle. I think he was afraid he'd start crying if he watched you get dressed. He's happy that you're happy. But it's still hard for him to give away his baby girl."

What could she say to that? *Don't worry, Papí, this is only a temporary marriage, and your baby girl will be yours again in four to eight years?* She remained silent, taking a deliberate steadying breath.

"Well, I guess it's time for me to get this veil on and get downstairs." No matter her reservations, a deal was a deal, and she couldn't back out now. "Time to become Mrs. Lennox Carlisle."

Thirteen

"My baby's getting married!"

Lennox's mother hadn't been able to contain her excitement since she'd arrived in his hotel room. She ambled over to where he stood in front of a mirror, trying to remember how to tie his necktie.

When she reached him, she placed her hands lovingly on either side of his face, rubbing her thumbs against his cheeks. The tears he saw glistening in her hazel eyes made his chest swell with emotion he wasn't quite sure how to define.

"Mama, don't start crying. You'll ruin all that pretty makeup you have on."

"It's either cry from happiness or wring your neck for lying to me about not seeing someone. You kept a whole girlfriend from me, Lennox. I owe you a behind-whoopin' for that."

He leaned down and placed a quick kiss on her smiling

face. "But you won't, because I'm also responsible for you finally becoming a grandmother."

"My baby's having a baby and marrying into a celebrity family. How can I be mad? I'm so happy for you, Lennox. Your daddy, if he were here, he'd be so proud of his boy. Falling in love, starting a family, settling down with the woman he loves, building a strong foundation for the next generation…it's all he ever wanted for you."

"Mama, Amara and I aren't some fairy tale." This wasn't a marriage in the traditional sense. But looking down into his mother's happy face, he realized she had no knowledge of that. To her, her baby boy really was having a whirlwind love affair. He didn't know if this strange feeling was because he was lying to his mother or because in some small way, he was actually happy this was happening. As for his mother, he understood how significant this was for her and decided to just feel happy that he could give it to her. It didn't matter if it was under false pretenses. This was her moment, and he would let her have it.

"Mama, I know Amara and I originally planned to do this alone. But I'm glad you're here."

"I'm glad I'm here, too." She took hold of the loose tie ends and made a beautiful knot. "Otherwise, who would make sure you're camera ready while you wait at the altar?"

Who indeed? There was no one like his mama.

It's gonna break her heart when this finally comes to an end, and it will be all your fault.

It was true. It would be his fault. But he still couldn't bring himself to tell the truth and take away the light shining in her eyes. Not when he'd ached to see it return.

Lennox stood in front of the wedding arch, which was completely adorned with a mix of tropical flowers and white roses, and stared out at the rippling blue waves of the Caribbean Sea. He shoved his hands in the pockets of his cream linen pants, wondering how he'd ended up here.

Of course, he knew the events that had led to him standing at the altar, waiting to make a legal and binding commitment to a woman he barely knew. But what he didn't know was how he'd come to the point where this wedding was anything more than a formality.

He'd like to say it was just because he was playing a role to benefit his mother and Angel's parents. But as he stood here, waiting for the ceremony to begin, he realized the flutters in his stomach weren't caused by dread. No, this was something akin to anticipation, excitement even.

He'd meant it when he'd told Angel this marriage would be real, and they would be together. He would honor the vows he spoke today until their marriage came to the agreed-upon end. He intended to treat Angel with the same respect and care his father had always shown his mother. She was gifting him with a child. In his mind, she deserved no less. But he was beginning to think he actually *wanted* to marry Angel.

Why, though? It can't just be about the baby.

He didn't have time to explore that thought, and honestly, he wasn't certain he wanted to. The sound of approaching footsteps pulled him from his musings and forced him back into playing his role as expectant groom. Except, strangely, it didn't feel so much like playing a role at this moment.

"Lennox," Angel Rodriguez called to him just before reaching the arch. "May I have a moment?"

"Of course, Mr. Rodriguez."

"Do we really need to be this formal? You're about to become my son-in-law and the father of my first grandchild."

"Well, since I refer to your daughter as Angel, I feel like family gatherings might get a little confusing if I call you by your given name."

Angel Rodriguez's mouth spread into a wide grin, the same one his daughter wore when she was amused by something. There was warmth there. Considering the situation, Lennox appreciated it.

"Lennox, I won't beat around the bush. I know the reason you and my daughter are marrying so hastily is to protect your career."

Lennox was poised to speak when the older man held up his hand to stop him. "I'm not here to argue the point, Lennox. My daughter has never mentioned anything about wanting to settle down. Her only goal has been to run the legal department for Devereaux Inc. But if she's doing this, she must care a great deal about you. Knowing she doesn't give her heart easily, if she's willing to give hers to you, that speaks volumes to your character."

Lennox stood, staring at the man in awe. He was obviously a proud and protective father, and Angel was lucky to have him. And that made Lennox realize how much he missed sharing a moment like this with his own father.

"Thank you, sir. That means more than you could know."

His future father-in-law nodded and stepped closer to him, slowly raising his hands to Lennox's tie.

"Ven." He waved his hand, beckoning Lennox. "Let's straighten your tie. It wouldn't do for you to greet your new bride looking less than perfect."

Lennox complied, stepping closer and letting the older man fiddle with the silk around his neck.

"You might wonder why my wife and I aren't losing our minds about this quickie marriage. Well, in the Devereaux clan, quickie marriages are sort of the norm. You and Amara are no different in that regard. My wife and I married less than six months after we met. It would be hypocritical of us to oppose your union."

Lennox continued to watch the older man's painstakingly slow movements as he fixed Lennox's tie.

"We don't know each other, Lennox. But I hope to change that. I want to be the same kind of father-in-law to you that David Devereaux has been to me. I too had lost my father by the time I married Ja'Net. *Mí papí* held such a special place in my heart, I never thought I'd be able to love another man in that same way. But David filled a void and gave me a way to be a son again, to lay my burdens at my father's feet again."

He finished with the tie, smoothing it, making certain it was tucked neatly inside of Lennox's light gold vest before smoothing his hands on his shoulders and giving them a firm squeeze.

"My baby is my heart, Lennox. And as long as you love, honor and protect her, you'll be mine as well. Which means I'm here for you too if..." He bowed his head slightly. "If you want me to be, that is."

Lennox's throat was tight. He hadn't felt this much emotion since he'd watched his father's casket lowered into the grave. He'd never thought he could think of another man as a father after losing his own. But at this moment, he certainly didn't mind the offer of a surrogate.

"Sir—"

"Papí." The man reprimanded Lennox with a pointed finger and a fake glare. "Papí, Pops, Dad, or some derivative thereof. Whatever the reason you and my daughter are marrying, it doesn't matter. If she's marrying you, you are family. End of story."

Lennox gave him a wavering smile and reprimanded himself. He was such a jerk. Not just because he'd pushed the man's daughter into an impossible corner, forcing her to marry him. But because as he stood there with this proud man welcoming him into the fold, all Lennox wanted to do was accept everything he was offering him.

The worst part was when Angel's father stepped back and held his arms open, waiting for Lennox to make a decision. Without hesitation, he selfishly accepted everything being offered, even if he was taking it under false pretenses.

"Thank you, Papí."

They embraced until the officiant joined them in front of the arch, telling them the bride was ready.

His soon-to-be father-in-law ended their embrace with

an encouraging pat to the arm before he disappeared to join his daughter.

And if the father had just thrown him for a loop, catching the first glimpse of the man's daughter as she stood at the top of the balcony stairs damn near knocked him over.

When he'd contacted LaQuan Smith about sending a dress, he'd had no idea the designer would send what Lennox could only describe as a work of art.

Angel stood alone at the top of the stairs, the picture of elegance, sophistication and outright sex appeal. The form-fitting dress with its deep, plunging neckline kept his rapt attention. Even if he'd wanted to look away, he couldn't.

As she descended the stairs and met her father, and the two of them walked slowly toward Lennox on the white sand, he was struck by an unexpected zing of pride. This fierce and self-possessed woman would be his wife. And as much as he knew this marriage was a business decision, he couldn't help but realize how fortunate he was to align himself with someone who understood her own power and unapologetically basked in it.

They might not be in love, but with Amara Angel Devereaux-Rodriguez by his side, he knew they'd be unstoppable.

Fourteen

"Are you sure you can't stay longer?" Amara asked as she hugged her parents tightly. "We've only just eaten the wedding cake."

Her mother pulled back, smiling at her. "Sweetheart, the cutting of the cake is the traditional end of the wedding. Besides, you're officially on your honeymoon. You don't need your parents underfoot. We wouldn't want to scare Lennox off when we just got him."

"Well..." Amara relented. "Can we at least have breakfast in the morning?"

"Sorry, Mija," her father answered as he placed a quick peck on her cheek. Your mother and I need to be stateside as early as possible. We're leaving before dawn and giving Della a ride back with us. You and Lennox had better enjoy this time together. You know all hell is going to break loose as soon as the Devereauxs find out. Speaking of, when do you intend to tell the family?"

"Can we get past Trey and Jeremiah's wedding next

week? They're so excited about their ceremony and Lyric has worked her butt off putting it together in so little time. I'd feel bad about stealing their thunder and making it about Lennox and me."

Her mother lifted a brow, throwing a pointed look in her direction. "So, your plan is to hide your husband for a week? Why?"

"Mamí, the primary is only a few weeks away. I don't want to heap that kind of circus on Trey and Jeremiah. When they get back from their honeymoon, Lennox and I will get the entire family together and tell everyone. I promise."

Never one to interfere in her daughter's private life, Ja'Net simply nodded to bring the subject to a close. The room was abuzz with happiness and family, making her forget how problematic this entire situation was.

All three parents remained a few minutes more to say proper goodbyes to the newlyweds. But when Lennox closed the door to the villa with a resolute click, suddenly, the weight of their reality bore down on her. She was Mrs. Lennox Carlisle for the next four to eight years if her husband became Mayor of New York City.

She cringed at the way she thought about their marriage. Referring to it like she was doing a bid in Sing Sing was a little melodramatic, even for her. Except for when he'd threatened to expose her irresponsible behavior to her grandfather, he'd been nothing but generous and supportive. And considering she was the one who'd been dishonest at their initial meeting, she couldn't say she deserved anything other than his scorn.

He took slow steps back into the living area then just stood there with his vest open and his loosened tie hanging around his neck, his hands casually stuffed inside his cream linen pants. Watching him, she could almost pretend this wasn't what it was—a business deal and nothing more.

"Thank you again for getting our parents down here.

Your mother is a gem. I'm so glad I had the chance to meet her."

He scanned her face, looking at her through narrowed eyes. "You make it sound like you're never going to see her again. News flash—you just married her only son and are carrying her first grandchild. You couldn't keep Della Carlisle away with a restraining order at this point."

For some reason, his statement didn't stir as much panic as it should have. She had honestly enjoyed the time she'd spent with his mother today.

"She looked really happy. My parents, too."

She dropped her eyes, fiddling with the heavy diamond wedding set encircling her ring finger. He took her hand in his, causing her to stop twisting her rings and look up at him.

"Our parents being happy about us somehow makes you unhappy?"

"I'm relieved, for sure." She looked up at him and found the weight of his gaze to be too much. She walked to the balcony, hoping to put some distance between them. How could she explain her feelings when she didn't exactly understand them herself?

"Angel?"

She felt his heat before his whisper tickled the base of her neck and sent chills down her spine. He'd followed her onto the balcony.

"I'm not unhappy. I'm just worried about what happens when we divorce."

"We signed a prenup and custody agreement before we married. We know exactly what happens when this marriage ends."

He was right, they had. Their lawyers had been furious to have to jump through so many hoops with so little time to get everything ready. They'd even had both of them sit for a video addendum pledging that neither of them was under any duress.

He moved closer, his body pressing slightly against hers. "Are you cold?"

He took her silence as acquiescence and wrapped her in his embrace. God help her, the feel of him, even when he wasn't necessarily doing anything sexual to her, made goose bumps pebble on her exposed skin.

"I was talking about our parents. I don't think either of us fully appreciated how many people we're going to hurt with our lie."

He slid his hands up her arms and across her shoulders, his thumbs lingering at the base of her neck, rubbing the tension there.

"Angel, I don't know about you, but I hadn't intended on sharing the intimate details of our marriage with our parents. There are some things that should be kept strictly between spouses."

Her nipples pebbled beneath the expensive but thin crepe material of her dress with the barest touch from him. If she were smart, she'd find a way to untangle herself from him. But since she wasn't keen on tumbling over the balcony railing, there was nowhere to go but his arms.

"What do you mean?"

Lennox tightened his hold on her and placed a gentle kiss at the curve of her neck that made her shiver.

"If I must be blunt, I wouldn't share what happens in our marriage bed, so why would I feel compelled to tell them about the sensitive nature of our arrangement? You are my wife, Angel. No matter how that came to be or how it will end, you *are* my wife, and this marriage is very real. I thought we had this conversation already."

She turned around, finally finding the strength to look up into the amber fire in his hazel eyes. "Not that you could, but you promised you wouldn't force me to consummate the marriage unless I wanted to."

He wrapped one hand slowly around her waist, pulling her closer against the bulge tenting his pants. "I am a man of my word. Unless you say otherwise, I will say good-night and head to my room. But that hungry look in your eyes makes me doubt you'll give me my marching papers."

"Cocky, aren't you?"

He shrugged, taking her hand in his and kissing it. "If I remember how we burn everything down around us when we make love, I think I have plenty of reason to be. But if you want me to leave, just say the word."

He took one step back, and before he could take another, she held tight to both ends of his tie, pulling him against her.

"It's dark and it's a long walk across the resort. I wouldn't want you to get lost on your way back to your room. Perhaps for safety's sake, you should spend the night here, with me. After all, as your wife, your well-being should be paramount to me."

His gaze slid down her face, her neck, and continued down the deep vee of her dress, leaving every inch of skin it touched flushed with desire. Then he lifted his hand to her cheek, stroking the skin gently with his thumb.

"Whatever helps you sleep better at night."

She closed her eyes, trying to steady her heart rate while she fought with herself about what would happen next.

She should tell him to leave, start things as she planned to finish them. But his touch was as intoxicating as the most potent drug, calling to her even when common sense told her to run far, far away.

But when she opened her eyes to find fire burning in his, any thought she had of denying him, denying herself, fell away.

He stepped back, and she placed a hand on his chest, enticed by the rapid pounding of the strong heartbeat beneath it.

"Stay."

She didn't speak another word and was grateful Lennox didn't require her to.

He put his hands on both her shoulders, turning her

away from him, gently undoing the intricate fastenings that secured her wedding gown. He tenderly held the fabric as he slid it carefully down the length of her body and waited patiently for her to step out of it when it pooled around her ankles.

Eager to have his skin pressed to hers again, she reached for him, but he held up a finger then picked up her dress and carried it across the room, laying it carefully on the couch.

When he returned, he stopped and took in the full picture of her standing in a silk thong and stilettos. Amara had never been self-conscious about her body. Her curves were a natural part of her, and she had no reason to feel ashamed about them. But as Lennox stared at her, she raised her arms to cover her naked breasts.

Lennox's pinched brow was the only indication of his frustration. He gripped her chin, forcing her to meet his gaze.

"Never hide yourself from me. Everything about your body turns me on."

She kept her arms wrapped around herself, covering her chest. "I don't have issues with my body, Lennox."

"Then why…?"

She dropped her gaze as she tried to figure out the answer to his question. Nothing about it made sense.

"You're a lawyer and a politician, so you should know why. Playing your cards close is a means of survival for people like us. I never have a problem controlling the narrative. Showing people only what I want them to see. But the way you're able to see through all of my defenses, it unnerves me."

"Why? You think I'd hurt you?"

She shook her head without hesitation. Everything she knew about Lennox indicated he was a principled man. Even forcing her to marry him had been so he could continue the work he was doing for the people in his district.

"Not intentionally," she answered. "But this uncontrollable thing between us that makes me do reckless things just to have a taste of what you're offering, I'm afraid of what I'll sacrifice next just to have it. I'm afraid of losing control."

He shook his head. "Angel," the deep rumble of his voice vibrated through her as he leaned close enough to kiss her, "I don't think you're afraid to lose control. I think it's what you want."

She opened her mouth to speak, but nothing came out. She'd spent years negotiating and litigating for the Devereaux empire. But nothing in her arsenal prepared her to respond to a statement like that from a man like him.

"You've always had to think ten steps ahead and do three times as much just to get your grandfather to see your worth. Now you're finally in the position you've always wanted and you're trying to manage everything to secure your place. But there's only one problem, Angel. You can't manage me."

While she tried to gather her wits, he removed his vest, shirt and tie. Before she could anticipate what he was doing, he sealed his mouth to hers in a punishing kiss that left her lungs breathless, and her lips bruised.

"I'd wager to say that's what brought you into Carter's office that first night. That's what keeps this thing burning between us." He devoured her mouth again, pulling her into his arms, holding her tight as he walked her back until the bend of her knees touched the armchair and she soon found herself seated. He ripped his mouth away from hers, leaving them both panting.

"So you're one of those men who gets off on dominating women, making them do your bidding?"

With unwavering confidence, he stared down at her. "Subservience doesn't do a thing for me. Docile, demure women may attract some men, but not me. I only keep strong people in my circle because they push me to be better. That rule applies to the women I'm attracted to as well."

He kneeled before her, spreading her knees until he was

pressed between them. He took her hands into his, placing each on an arm of the chair and pressing them into the plush cushioned leather.

"I don't get off on bossing you around, Angel. When we're together like this, the only thing I care about is giving you what you need. And more than anything, you need to stop thinking, managing, manipulating and just feel."

He tapped the backs of her hands with his fingers. "Keep your hands on the armrests. If you move them, I stop."

Her gaze lasered in on the almost sinister smile he wore. "Stop what?"

"This," he responded as he hooked her thighs over his forearms and pulled her to the edge of her seat before dipping his head, placing a gentle kiss against her sex. Even through the silk of her thong, she could feel the heat of his mouth on her, drawing out the first ripple of pleasure.

Her natural response was to splay her hands on his bald head and pull him forward until his face was buried between her folds. And by the mischievous stare he was giving her, he knew it, too. He kept staring, silently daring her to lift even one digit from where he'd placed them.

"Can you give up control long enough to let me please you? Or do we have to fight and fuck like usual?"

Anger-charged sex certainly had its benefits. But there was something about the hungry look in his eyes that promised if she let him have his way, she'd know pleasure like she'd never experienced before.

He took her silence for the acquiescence it was, removing her thong, rubbing his hand slowly up and down her sex as he tugged his bottom lip between his teeth.

Anticipation prickled along every inch of her flesh, making her body tremble even though he'd barely touched her. By the time his tongue slipped between her folds, and he buried two fingers inside of her, she was halfway to climaxing already.

She nearly reneged on her agreement to cede control

in this moment. But when the tip of his tongue laved her clit and electric heat spread from her core to the whole of her being like lightning-charged water, she was lost. Each dip of his fingers, scissoring inside of her, caressing her walls with expertly targeted strokes, brought her closer and closer to release.

She felt the uncontrollable shudders, the twitch of her legs. She felt her body tighten around his fingers, the zing of satisfaction building every time the firm, hot flesh of his tongue slid over her sex. She felt it all while crying out against the torture—while begging him to never stop.

She needn't have worried about him stopping, though. He was relentless. That was the only way she could describe the way he pleasured her, never letting up, never slowing down, never missing an opportunity to completely destroy her.

Tension coiled inside of her, her muscles tightening as she dangled over the precipice of completion. And with one final swipe of his tongue, with one final stroke of his fingers stretching her perfectly, she tipped over into bliss, still clutching the arms of the chair, screaming, letting go in a way she'd never before allowed herself.

When the powerful spasms of her climax began to lessen, and conscious thought returned, she wasn't sure if it was a good thing or not to be married to the person that knew how to break her like this. Not when he knew how to own her so completely with so little effort, and especially when she couldn't seem to find the willpower to walk away.

Amara stretched and purred like a cat, cracking her eyes open just in time to see the first rays of the sunrise. Her movement stirred the hard wall of flesh lying behind her, and a thick, corded arm draped itself around her waist, pulling her into a heated cocoon.

"Morning."

Lennox's voice, full of sleep, was rich and deep, and the

caress of his breath against her ear made the idea of leaving this bed and his embrace painful.

"What do you want to do today?" he asked.

She laughed at that. They'd been at one of the most exclusive resorts for the last four days. The farthest they'd made it out of her villa was to the private beach for their wedding, and one impromptu evening walk that led to sand getting in places it wasn't supposed to be.

"You mean besides having sex?"

He tightened his arm around her and placed a gentle kiss against her ear.

"You say that like it's a bad thing."

She turned in his arms and instantly regretted it. Until now, their playful banter had felt fun and flirty. But when she met his hazel eyes, everything about the moment they were sharing felt heavy.

"Do you want to go out and see the sights?" He grabbed his phone from the nightstand. "I can make arrangements if you want."

There was something strange in his voice that concerned her, making her raise her hand carefully to his cheek.

"Is there a reason you'd rather stay inside?" She gave his jaw a stroke as she smiled at him. "Besides the obvious, I mean."

"I'm not ashamed of my wife, if that's what you're insinuating. The primary happens soon. If I win, that means constant campaigning for the next five months. I'm sure your desk isn't exactly clear, either. We might not have a quiet moment to ourselves again until the election."

There was something more, something unspoken in his words but still there in his tone. Whatever it was, it made her lean in and kiss him. It was a sweet kiss, meant more to comfort than ignite the passion that sparked so easily between the two of them.

"If you're okay with spending the day inside, so am I."

He snaked one hand around the back of her neck and

placed the other at the small of her back, pulling her on top of him. They'd both fallen asleep naked, which made straddling him so much more fun. Grateful they'd finally had that conversation about foregoing condoms the morning after the wedding, she could already feel the slick of her arousal as her folds came in contact with his already hard length.

The few days they'd spent in this paradise, tucked away on a private beach in the Caribbean away from the world, existing on nothing but fun, relaxation and plenty of sex, had been bliss. If she refused to think about the truth of her situation, she could almost forget this wasn't a proper relationship.

She closed her eyes, wrapping her body tightly around his as hope unwisely grew. Perhaps this relationship, or whatever they were doing, could become more than an arrangement with an expiration date.

Just as that thought began to take root, Lennox's phone rang.

He groaned into her neck before pulling away, groaning again when he looked at the screen to see who was calling. "It's my campaign manager. I have to answer this."

She simply nodded, slipping from the bed and grabbing her silk robe from the foot bench before heading into the bathroom. She glimpsed herself in the mirror on her way to the shower stall. Her lips were kiss-swollen and her curls were in disarray. Though completely debauched, she'd never looked more relaxed and satisfied in her life. But before she could revel in that satisfaction, Lennox knocked on the bathroom door, pulling her away from her thoughts.

"I have to return. One of my opponents in the primary backed out of a Robin Roberts in-depth interview for *20/20*. If I want the slot, I've got to be ready to film by tomorrow morning."

And like a balloon stuck by a sharp pin, her bubble of satisfaction popped.

She swallowed and put on her best smile, the one that told the world everything was fine, even when she knew it wasn't.

"Well, I guess we'd better get packing, then."

He assessed her carefully, then nodded as he left the bathroom. She went back to the mirror, watching as disappointment clouded her eyes and she realized something that should've been obvious from the start. This marriage was a business transaction. If she didn't hold fast to that particular truth, she'd find herself in more trouble than a marriage of convenience, a threat to her career and an unexpected baby could bring. If she wasn't careful, she'd lose her heart.

Fifteen

"And I think that does it for the interview prep."

Lennox gave a friendly smile to the young man sitting across the table from him in the studio's green room with a clipboard and a pen in his hand.

Lennox zeroed in on the man's work badge to double-check his name. "Thank you, Brian."

Lennox was usually good with names and giving his attention to people when they were speaking to him. But ever since he'd had his driver drop off his new bride outside of her brownstone, he'd had trouble focusing.

He absentmindedly twisted the large wedding ring on his hand. He tried to pretend it was just because wearing the piece of metal against his skin was new. But the truth was, he'd found himself doing it consistently since he and Amara had parted ways.

"Is that real or just for decoration?"

Brian's question pulled him out of the cloud of thoughts

filling his head. "It's real. I took a few days off and my fiancée and I got married in the Caribbean."

Brian nodded, granting Lennox a wide grin. "Congratulations," he said brightly as a glint of something akin to excitement mixed with hunger sparked in his eyes. "Are you willing to discuss your recent nuptials during filming with Ms. Roberts?"

Lennox kept his features cool as he pondered the question. Amara wanted to wait until after her cousin's wedding this week to break the news. But the media being as relentless as they were, he wasn't sure they'd be able to keep this quiet. Perhaps the best way to control the story was to share the information on his own terms.

"Sure," Lennox said easily. "I have nothing to hide. Just one question. When will this air? There are people in our family we haven't told yet and we'd like to share the good news with them first before it's all over the airwaves."

"Tomorrow night." The man scribbled something else on his clipboard and gave Lennox a farewell nod. As soon as Brian left, Lennox pulled out his phone and dialed Amara.

"Hey, is everything okay?"

Her greeting was strange. "Everything's fine. Why would you think there was a problem?"

"Because you just dropped me off. Did you need something?"

There was a cool tone to her voice that he'd noticed since they'd boarded the charter jet back to New York. With no time to discover its source, he simply cleared his throat and continued.

"Nothing's wrong. My wedding ring was just spotted by Robin Roberts's assistant and now they want to talk about our wedding during the filming. The show will air tomorrow."

"But I wanted to tell my family after Trey and Jeremiah's wedding this weekend."

"I know that, Angel. But we either control the story ourselves or risk some paparazzi breaking the story in a salacious way. It's still early. How about you gather your clan today and we tell them about the wedding and the baby?"

She was quiet, and that unnerved him. "Angel, you still there?"

"Yes, I am. Fine, I'll talk to my family."

"No," he responded. "We'll talk to your family, together."

"I'll make the arrangements."

She ended the call without a goodbye and the coolness of her tone raked against his nerves. Whatever this was about, he didn't have time to deal with it now. Brian had returned and was motioning for Lennox to follow him out of the greenroom. He just hoped this wasn't a sign to come of what married life would be like.

Lennox parked in front of Devereaux Manor, shutting off the ignition before turning his gaze to Amara. Aside from rubbing her right thumb repeatedly over the back of her left hand, she hardly moved.

"Is everything okay?"

She met his gaze calmly. "Sure. Why do you ask?"

He pointed to her hands in her lap. "Either you're practicing strumming a guitar on the back of your hand, or that's a nervous tell."

She immediately pulled her hands apart, the action allowing him to see her bare ring finger.

Something ugly flashed in him. He twisted in his seat to face her, fighting hard to keep the dark and dangerous storm brewing inside him from taking over.

"You wanna tell me what's up with that?"

"What's up with what?"

He reached across the console, taking her left hand in his and rubbing his thumb across her bare marriage finger.

"This," he answered with his teeth held tightly together. "Where are your rings, Angel?"

"I haven't lost them, if that's what this is about."

"It's about the fact that we're married and you're walking around with nothing on your finger as if we're not."

She pulled her hand away from his and waved it dismissively in the air. "Expensive jewelry doesn't make us married, Lennox. The little piece of paper we brought back from Jamaica does."

When he failed to respond, she blew out an annoyed breath and dug around in her purse for a few seconds. Then she pulled her hand out, opening her fingers to reveal both her rings cushioned against her palm.

"See, you don't have to worry. They're here."

Silently, he plucked the rings from her hand, turned them over and effortlessly slid the rings over her knuckle and into place.

"For however long we are husband and wife, you will wear my rings and I will wear yours."

"You can't possibly be upset about this. We both know this isn't a real marriage, Lennox. I don't see the need in keeping up pretenses every moment of the day."

The muscle in his eye jumped as if someone had punched him. He could tell from the relaxed look on her face that the punch she'd landed wasn't intentionally thrown. Hell, even he questioned why this was upsetting him so much. But logic be damned, it did bother him.

"This marriage may have an expiration date, but for as long as it exists, it's real. I expect you to wear these so that people across the street can see that you're otherwise spoken for. I will not be made a fool of in public, Angel. You'd do well to remember that."

Shocking himself with such an unusual display of possessiveness, he dropped her hand and settled back into his seat, staring out at nothing and taking a deep breath. When he felt he had control of himself again, he turned back to her, nodding.

"Shall we?"

A spark of fire flashed in her deep brown eyes, turning them a chestnut brown. He'd seen the same fire every time desire blazed between them. But as she twisted the rings on her finger and gave him a cool nod, her mask comfortably settled back over her face. He realized this wasn't passion, it was controlled anger, a warning he might want to proceed with caution.

Amara was a formidable opponent in business and a formidable partner in bed. But no matter how powerful she was, he would not, in any way, allow her to dismiss their marriage in front of anyone.

For the briefest moment he considered he'd possibly come on too strong. But he couldn't relent. He was a proponent of teaching people your boundaries so there was no confusion later. She'd gotten them into this with her lies of omission, so she would meet the expectations he'd laid out to her before they married. Because he would allow no one, absolutely no one, to make him look like a fool. Not even his beautiful wife who tempted him beyond good reason.

"Cousin!"

Stephan was the first one she saw when she walked into Devereaux Manor with Lennox two steps behind her. He surrounded her with a tight hug and kissed her cheek. She lingered in the hug longer than she should have for two reasons. First, soon enough, Stephan would return to Paris, and she'd miss his wonderful hugs. The second and most significant reason was that she needed his support. She knew no matter what she said today, her cousin would back her.

She stepped out of his embrace and made eye contact with the other cousins in the room. Lyric stood near the fireplace smiling at Amara with a wide, comforting grin. Jeremiah and Trey were on the opposite side of the room sharing their warmth and support for her with twin smiles and raised glasses in their hands.

Watching those four people, she knew that whatever

resistance she met today, the four of them would have her back. And then she looked to her right and saw the greatest boon of all: her uncle Ace sitting in an armchair with wide-open arms, waiting for her.

She went to him, fortifying herself with his love, taking an extra squeeze before she let her eyes meet her grandfather's questioning gaze. David Devereaux knew something was up, but as her mother placed a gentle hand on her grandfather's shoulder, silently telling him to back off, Amara understood she could and would do this.

"Everyone, thank you so much for dropping everything and gathering here. It's been an odd but significant last few days, and I wanted to share some new developments in my life with the people I love."

She didn't have to look behind her to know that Lennox was standing close. She could feel his distinct heat enveloping her. It was heady and empowering, helping her forge ahead with their plan.

"I know this will seem strange to most of you, considering how focused I've been on work. But, as my parents and the elders of our family have always told me, work isn't enough. Family, I'd like to introduce you to Lennox Carlisle, my husband and the father of my unborn child."

The room was silent. Considering the Devereauxs always had something to say, concern began to make the skin on her arms prickle. She didn't know how he'd sensed it, but Lennox chose that moment to place a gentle hand around her waist, drawing her in and placing a sweet kiss on her temple.

She looked up into his hazel eyes as everyone in the room stared at them. He was silently telling her, *Don't focus on them, focus on me.* It was the best advice, because as long as she stared into his comforting gaze, she didn't have to deal with her grandfather's glare.

"Oh, my goodness!" Lyric squealed, running over to the two of them and grabbing them into an excited hug.

"Congratulations, Cousin! I'm so happy for you. But first things first, let me see the rings."

Lyric's celebratory mood broke the uncomfortable silence as the rest of her cousins watched her carefully, but slowly began to surround them and offer congratulations. Everyone except her uncle Ace, who blew her a kiss and gave her a knowing wink, as if he'd finally gotten the treat he'd been longing for. And then there was her grandfather, sitting next to Ace, watching her through hooded eyes with not a single glimmer of happiness, glee or even surprise. Apparently, this wasn't over by a long shot.

Stephan stepped in front of them, giving Lennox a strong handshake before leaning over to Amara, wrapping her in one of his tight hugs.

"I don't know what's going on," he whispered in her ear as he nearly swallowed her in his embrace. "But whatever it is, I've got your back. When you're ready to tell me, you know I'm here."

She latched on to Stephan like the anchor he was, the anchor he'd always been, holding her up when the ground beneath her seemed to fall away. She gave him one more squeeze then stepped back, feeling the slightest bit better.

"Damn, girl, I thought Jeremiah and I were moving fast. You've got us beat," Trey teased from her spot near the fireplace. Amara hadn't known her new cousin long, but in the short time she'd been around, she and Amara had become family in more than name only. "I don't know about anyone else, but I need details. When, where and how did all of this take place without any of us nosy folks being the wiser?"

"Lennox and I took one look at each other, and we just knew." That was the most truthful response Amara could come up with. But she'd never imagined in such a short time she'd end up pregnant with his child and married to him.

"We didn't want to wait, but I didn't want to steal your and Jeremiah's thunder with your wedding coming up this week," Amara continued. "So, we eloped to

Jamaica and married in a small ceremony on the beach with the ocean and the sunset as our backdrop with our parents by our sides."

Lyric sighed loudly enough that everyone in the room turned to her. Her face was bright with wide eyes that sparkled as her eyelashes fluttered.

"That's so romantic!"

"It absolutely was," Amara's mother responded as she stood up and walked to the doorway. "In celebration, I had a replica of their wedding cake made. Lennox's family should be here shortly. Della texted me a little while ago to say she and her daughter and daughter-in-law will arrive soon. We'll cut the cake when they get here."

"How did you have time to do all of this, Mamí?"

Her mom blew a kiss her way before leaving the room, and the tension twisting the muscles at the base of Amara's neck loosened just a bit. Lennox chose that moment to slide his hand down her back, leaning in to place a kiss on her temple.

"Why don't you have a seat? A lot has happened in the last few days. I don't want you tiring yourself out."

She looked into his eyes and saw what looked like genuine concern. And for the brief moment that their gazes connected, she wanted to believe all that worry and consideration was for her. But the small voice pulling at the back of her brain wouldn't let her reach for that hope. Not when she knew there was an expiration date on their union. This marriage was about the baby and his career. There was no room for her or what she wanted. Not that she had any clue what that was.

"I'm gonna go check in on my mom for a sec. You wanna join me, or are you okay with being in the middle of the lion's den?"

He chuckled softly and nodded. "Believe me, I've dealt with worse. I'm a politician, remember. Schmoozing tough crowds is kinda my thing. Go check on your mom. I'll be fine."

Amara left the room, feeling every eye following her as she went through the archway into the hall. By the time she found her mother in the kitchen, her fingers and limbs tingled with relief.

"Mamí, you didn't have to go through this trouble to get us a cake."

"Hush," her mother chided, never once taking her eyes off the cake as she removed the protective box. "My baby just got married. If I can't play the mother of the bride at a big wedding, then I'm surely going to do it here amongst family."

Amara flinched at her mother's comment. "Are you upset we didn't have a big wedding?"

Her mother stopped her fiddling and looked directly at Amara. "Baby, how and when you married was completely up to you. I'm just glad I could be part of it. As long as you're sure this marriage is what you want, I'm thrilled to play any role I can in celebrating it. You are still sure this marriage is what you want, aren't you?"

Amara was about to reassure her mother when the familiar baritone of her grandfather's voice vibrated through the room.

"That's certainly a fair question, considering this marriage happened out of thin air."

"Daddy, leave that child alone."

Amara raised her hand to stop her mother from leaping into mama bear mode. "It's okay, Mamí. It's understandable that Granddaddy has questions."

"I have quite a few questions, Granddaughter. Namely, how the hell did you end up married to the city councilman we need to make this Falcon deal happen?"

"I went out for a drink and ran into Lennox. We hit it off. Once we spent time together, we realized our connection went deeper than business."

Her grandfather's face was pulled into tight lines. She could see suspicion clouding his eyes.

"And the deal? In your zeal to be together, did either of you think about the conflict of interest you were willingly walking into?"

"Yes, Grandfather." The formal name slipped from her lips, and she could see him brace against it. Too bad if he didn't like it. She didn't like being interrogated about her personal life, so they were even as far as she was concerned. "We thought about it and came up with a reasonable solution. We will use a third-party review panel to decide if we get the permits or not. It's the only way we can ensure that things happen in a fair manner."

Her grandfather narrowed his eyes into tiny slits as he tried to see the holes in her lies. Her story was solid, and she knew it. But that didn't mean David Devereaux was buying any of it.

He stepped closer to her, placing his hand carefully on her forearm as he looked down at her.

"Marriage is sacred, Amara. It's not something you should take lightly. Whatever it is you've gotten yourself into, I hope it doesn't come back to haunt you. You've got so much more on the line now than a business deal. The decisions you've made affect that little one you're carrying, too. Make sure you know what you're doing."

Everything in her wanted to flinch at his warning, but she refused to give him the satisfaction. She already questioned her decisions and how they would impact her baby. She didn't need him reminding her of how she'd screwed up yet again.

"Did you question how fast Trey and Jeremiah decided to marry? The only difference is they apprised the Devereauxs of their relationship. We know what we're doing. This is our decision, and it doesn't require anyone else's approval."

There was a cold glint in her grandfather's eye. "If that's your final word on the matter, then I guess I'll have to accept it. But hear me, Amara. If for one moment I think Devereaux Inc. is in danger because of the decisions you've made, I won't hesitate to remove you and reinstate myself as lead counsel. Do you understand me?"

Fire burned beneath her skin but she had to remain in control at all costs. This was a power play, and she couldn't afford to lose.

"I've earned this position. You didn't give it to me. If you didn't question Jeremiah's ability to lead as co-CEO upon discovering his involvement with Trey, don't question mine regarding my husband. Devereaux Inc. will thrive under my leadership in the legal department. Just stand back and watch."

She stiffened her spine ramrod straight and stepped out around her grandfather into the hall. She would prove him wrong, no matter what it took. Because the best motivation in the world was for someone to tell her she shouldn't or couldn't do something. She would make David Devereaux eat his words. Even if the personal cost was more than she could bear.

Sixteen

Lennox looked from one side of his living room to the other. Every surface was covered with laptops and papers, every seat was taken, and the volume of the television above his fireplace was so loud, it was as if Anderson Cooper was personally yelling at him from the CNN newsroom.

He rubbed the tight muscles of his neck, trying to stave off the tension headache he could feel coming on. He had no one to blame but himself. He knew that lack of sleep, too much caffeine and too little food always resulted in a pounding headache that made him miserable to be around.

"Hey." Carter tapped him on the shoulder before handing him a cup of coffee and sitting down next to him. "You okay?"

Lennox sipped his coffee, hoping that if he focused on his drink long enough his friend would forget his question.

"I know you heard me."

No such luck, apparently. Lennox pushed aside some

of the papers cluttering the end table next to his chair and gently rested the coffee mug on it.

"I'm fine, Carter." He gave his friend a practiced smile before he began twisting the wedding band on his finger. He'd never been one for jewelry. Other than his class ring from law school, he rarely wore any. But somehow the thick, smooth platinum band felt so natural to him, he found himself touching it, making sure it was still where it was supposed to be ever since Angel had put it there.

"Nah." Carter shook his head. "I've seen fine and this ain't it. What's up?"

"If you haven't noticed, I'm kind of busy waiting for primary results to find out if I'll actually make it as a candidate for mayor."

Carter sipped his coffee, then nodded slowly. "I had. But we both know you've got nothing to worry about with the primary. This race has been yours since you entered it. The only thing that could've derailed it—" he jutted his chin out in the direction of Lennox's wedding ring "—you handled. So, if I could hazard a guess, I'd say it's more personal than professional."

Carter made a show of looking around before he met Lennox's gaze again. "Where's Amara? I was hoping to get to meet my best friend's new surprise wife. Everything okay on the home front?"

Lennox looked around to make sure all of his campaign staff were otherwise occupied. Most of them knew he'd recently married, but none of them knew the circumstances and Lennox wanted to keep it that way.

He picked up his mug, stood and beckoned his friend to follow him to his study.

He waited until Carter closed the heavy door and they were secure inside the dim space with its mahogany walls. He sat on the edge of his desk as Carter sat on the leather couch against the wall.

"Things not so perfect in paradise?" Carter began, picking up right where he'd left off in the living room.

"Angel and I are fine."

"Well, you're still using her nickname, that's a good sign. But if you're fine, where is she? She's your wife. Don't you think it's strange that she's not standing by your side as you wait for the results?"

Lennox took another sip of his coffee as he thought about the answer to that question. Yes, he and Angel were husband and wife. But their relationship wasn't exactly traditional. Other than his expectations of fidelity, and the duration of their marriage, he hadn't added any terms that concerned situations like these.

"Angel has a job, too. She's head of corporate legal at Devereaux Inc. I can't expect her to just drop everything and come babysit me while I freak out about the results."

Carter lifted a brow as he tilted his head, giving his full attention to Lennox. "Of course, you can. She's your wife. If you need her here, she should be here."

"If she wanted to be here, she would be. I'm not about to force her to do anything she doesn't want to do."

You didn't have a problem forcing her to marry you when it suited. Why the hesitation now?

He ground his teeth as his conscience reminded him of his actions.

"Knowing you, Lennox, you didn't even ask her to take the day off to be with you."

His friend had him there. No matter how much he'd wanted her to stay before she walked out the door this morning, he couldn't give in to that desire. It would mean he needed her, the way his mother needed his father. And his mother had lost everything when his father died; Lennox couldn't afford to be dependent on Amara like that.

"Carter, I appreciate you trying to help, man. But I know what I'm doing. Angel and I are fine. I'm fine."

"You keep saying that, but somehow I'm not convinced."

Carter stood up, heading for the door. "Call your wife, man. If for no other reason than it will look strange to any reporters that may happen by."

Lennox took one final look at his friend, nodding his head as he grabbed his phone. Carter turned to him once more, pointing an accusatory finger at him.

"Oh, and Nevaeh said she wants to meet her new *tia*. If you know like I know, you'd better make that happen. Nothing will ruin your world like a five-year-old who's mad with you."

Lennox chuckled as Carter left. Nevaeh was definitely a handful on her best day, and she'd rip him to shreds if he crossed her. But that little one was his heart. As her godfather, it was his job to keep a smile on her face.

Feeling a little less unsettled, Lennox sent up a silent prayer of thanks that his friend had given him an excuse for calling his wife. At least now he could pretend it was all about preserving their ruse for the media and not about the fact that he needed her by his side. Because never, not as long as he drew breath, would he allow himself to admit he needed her for anything more than his professional image and physical satisfaction.

Amara watched as Lennox's name flashed across her cell phone's screen. A heady mix of anticipation and apprehension swirled inside her. Today was the primary. Today, they'd know if the people would choose him to represent their party in the upcoming mayoral race.

She tapped the screen connecting the call, clearing her throat to stabilize the tremors in her voice.

"Hey, how's it going?"

"That's a strange way for a wife to greet her husband, don't you think? Shouldn't you know how I'm doing? Oh wait," he interrupted himself. "That would mean you actually seeing me, which you haven't done since we announced our marriage to your family."

"Lennox, I can't just drop everything. I work, too. Or did you forget why I agreed to this marriage in the first place? Also, my cousins are getting married this weekend. I'm busy."

"I wasn't suggesting that you aren't." He blew out a long breath. His voice sounded slightly less irritated when he spoke again. "I'm sorry, Angel. I was being an ass. I'm just…"

"You're on edge about the primary, right? I'm sure you've got a roomful of people around you to help you relax. Make them earn their keep."

He was quiet, too quiet. She held her breath, waiting for his response.

"You're right, there is a roomful of people. But none of them is my wife."

There was something in the way he said the word *wife* that cut through her. There was a longing there that made a gentle ache spread through her.

"Well, I know we agreed I'd be officially moved into your place by the wedding, but I guess I could stop packing long enough to come over while you watch the returns."

Again, more silence, then another breath. "Thanks" was all he said before he disconnected the line. But that simple word felt heavy, filled with so much unexplained emotion that even after the call ended, she was still standing there trying to process what exactly was happening.

Guess you'll find out when you get there.

Amara found Lennox on his balcony with the sleeves of his white button-down shirt rolled up to the middle of his forearms and his hands shoved in the pockets of his slacks.

She could see the tension vibrating off him in waves. Lennox always came off confident and self-assured. Save for the time he tried to convince her to take a pregnancy test because of his mother's premonition, this was the first time she'd ever seen him look less than in control.

She stepped closer to him, placing a light hand against his bare forearm when she stood next to him. “The last I checked, you were ahead. Has that changed?”

His stiff shoulders dropped as he released a soothing breath. “No, I’m still ahead.”

“Then what’s wrong? You sounded tightly wound on the phone, but this is way worse than a little angst.”

“Did I ever tell you how I got into politics?”

She shook her head.

“I was a corporate attorney for many years. It paid me very well, as you know from firsthand experience. But it left me empty.

“My father was a local politician with a focus on the city councilman’s office. That might sound shortsighted, but his heart was only ever in helping the people locally in his beloved city. We were pushed out of our home by a big conglomerate who didn’t care that we were a poor family barely hanging on. They just came in, threw their money around and brought in more people with lots of money to take our place. It took us years to get back on our feet. But it sparked a fire in my father to fight for a voice in what happened to his neighborhood. So, he ran for smaller offices until he finally became the representative for his neighborhood.”

Amara hadn’t known any of that. It explained why Lennox was so hell-bent on keeping companies like Devereaux Inc. on a tight leash.

“And now you’ve protected his neighborhood and are moving on to taking care of his city. You should be proud, Lennox.”

He turned to her, scanning her face as if he were searching for something. Then he leaned down, pressing his mouth against hers. The kiss was more comforting that sensual, yet it still made her heart pound hard underneath her rib cage.

“What was that for?”

He pulled his thumb across her bottom lip before looking out across the cityscape.

"For being here. I've been in my head a lot today. Thinking about what happens next if I win the primary race." He huffed, closing his eyes for a brief second before returning his gaze to hers. "My father's political career started because he wanted to create a better situation for my sister and me. When I entered this race, I would've said I was doing it to continue my father's legacy."

"That's changed?"

He shrugged, leaning against the railing. "I'm about to become a father. Everything has changed. I want to make a difference in this city for all my constituents. But mostly, I want to make a better one for the child you're carrying. I have this sudden need to make everything better before the baby gets here. And all day I've been wondering what will happen to my child if I fail. Knowing this baby is coming raises the stakes of this primary and the election in the fall. There's so much more on the line."

So this was what his moodiness over the phone was about. She found herself stepping into his embrace, wrapping her arms around him as she laid her head against his chest.

As surely as she knew her own name, she knew that she and this baby were lucky Lennox was its father. He was annoyingly condescending, controlling, and downright rude at times when he dealt with her. But he was also tender with her in ways that made her feel precious.

Her head warned her about falling for this man. All of his concern was for the child she carried and not for her directly. But even knowing that wasn't enough to stop her from diving headfirst into the rippling ocean that was Lennox Carlisle. More than anything, she wanted to be swallowed whole by him.

"Lennox," she whispered so softly she didn't think he could hear her. But when he tightened his arms around her, she knew he had. "Whether you win or lose, this baby is going to be lucky you're its dad. Despite all the rough patches we've had, I'm glad I get to coparent with a man who cares this much about the community he lives in."

He peered down into her face with unanswered questions burning in his eyes.

"Angel—"

He didn't have a chance to finish as a loud commotion erupted from inside the apartment.

"Boss!" A man Amara recognized as Lennox's campaign manager made his way through the small crowd until he was standing directly in front of them. "CNN just projected you as the winner of the primary race. You're in the running for Gracie Mansion!"

She looked up at Lennox just in time to catch a grin so wide and bright spreading across his face that her breath caught in her chest, and she felt the slightest bit dizzy.

She tried to pretend it was pregnancy hormones that had her feeling so light-headed. But then that ever-present voice in the back of her mind tapped her on her shoulder like a little devil, or angel, she couldn't tell which just yet.

You know doggone well this ain't got a thing to do with that baby. Go'n and admit. That man's happy smile just made you swoon.

Amara girl, the voice bellowed in her head. *You'd better watch out.*

She'd certainly better.

Seventeen

"Amara?"

Lennox perked up when a woman in floral scrubs called his wife's name.

"Are you coming with me?"

Lennox looked up at a now standing Angel as she gazed down at him with a furrowed brow.

"I wasn't sure you'd want me to."

A generous smile lifted the corners of her lips, calming some of the anxiety he'd experienced since arriving at her ob-gyn's office.

"Lennox," she whispered as she extended her hand to him. He stood, grabbing her hand and letting her lead him through the doorway to the examination room.

Once they were there, the nurse led Angel behind a partition while he sat in a chair next to the exam table, taking in all the instruments and machines.

He took a deep breath, attempting to steady himself, trying to decipher what he was actually feeling. From the moment they'd discovered her pregnancy, Lennox's heart had ached with anticipation of this child's entrance into the world. But he hadn't counted on the fact that Angel would want him by her side every step of the way.

He was grateful for the chance to participate, thrilled to learn about the development of their child firsthand, but there was something unsettling about being here that kept intruding on the joy and excitement of this moment.

Angel rejoined him dressed in a cloth hospital gown. As soon as he saw her, his chest tightened. It was at that moment he understood what that thing was that kept picking at what should be one of the happiest moments of his life. It was fear. Fear of this bonding exercise that would make it harder to walk away from her when he had to.

Refusing to think more about it, he swallowed the lump in his throat, standing and extending his hand to her as she lay back on the exam table.

A smiling woman with a short pixie cut and a white lab coat entered the room. She stared at Lennox as if she were attempting to figure out the answer to an equation. "Hello Amara and..."

"I'm Lennox Carlisle, her husband."

The woman nodded and extended her hand to him. "I'm Dr. Bautista. Forgive me for staring, but you look very familiar."

Angel chuckled, relieving some of the tension in the room.

"He's running for mayor. You've probably seen his face on posters all over Brooklyn."

The doctor nodded again, shaking his hand, then taking her seat on the stool next to the exam table.

"Today I'm going to do a transvaginal sonogram to confirm proper placement and development of the fetus as well as gestational age. According to the information on your intake form, you believe you're approximately eight weeks along?"

"I'm fairly certain." Angel looked up at Lennox and winked, drawing a knowing smile from him.

"All right," the doctor continued. "Let me wash my hands and we'll get started."

Lennox returned to his seat and watched silently as the doctor went through the process. He had no idea what to expect, and as blotchy images began to form on the dark monitor, he stiffened with anticipation.

Angel took a deep breath, drawing him out of his own musings. She was nervous, too. Honestly, she had a right to be. She was doing all the heavy lifting in this scenario. It was his job to reassure her and support her through these moments.

He slid his hand into hers and noted some of the tension left her. Her calm spilled back over onto him in a feedback loop, solidifying their partnership in ways he couldn't explain. They really were in this together. Success or failure, this was all on them as a team.

The doctor pointed at the monitor and smiled.

"Amara and Lennox, it's my pleasure to introduce you to your little one."

Lennox stared at the screen, trying to decipher the mixture of black and gray spots and then, suddenly, a tiny gray tadpole jumped out at him.

"Is that…?"

"Yes, it is." The doctor smiled as she looked up at him. "And if you think that's a neat trick, just wait until you hear this."

Dr. Bautista fiddled with some of the controls on the machine's keyboard and suddenly a sound like a miniature jackhammer filled the room.

Lennox looked down at his wife in awe. Angel's eyes looked like liquid glass as tears spilled from them. His own heart rate picked up and he wondered if he could withstand this level of excitement.

"Lennox, do you hear that? It's our baby's heartbeat."

"It sounds strong." He smiled down at her, too drawn in by their shared happiness to let any misgivings about their relationship mar this precious moment. Not caring that they weren't alone, he leaned down, placing a grateful kiss on her lips.

He realized his face was wet with what he thought were Angel's tears. But as he pulled away from the kiss and fresh hot drops slid down his face, he understood they were his.

As a politician, he'd learned long ago to keep his emotions hidden in public. But in this moment, the cloak of respectability and restraint fell away as he touched his forehead to his wife's and celebrated.

The doctor cleared her throat, interrupting to give them all the details of her findings and what the next steps were. When she was done, she slipped quietly from the room.

As soon as Angel sat up, Lennox sat down next to her on the table, pulling her into his arms, kissing her, hoping each press of his lips articulated all the things he couldn't say like *thank you*, and *I'm happier than I've ever been in my life*, and *I love you*.

That last one made his brain snap to attention, doing its best to swim through the dopamine haze. He pulled himself back, ending the kiss, locking eyes with Angel as if he were seeing her for the first time. And in part, he truly was.

He'd never thought love would be a word he associated with her. But looking at her, the realization filled his heart and pumped out into his blood vessels, seeping into every cell of his being. He was in love with his wife.

So, his mind began, *what are you gonna do now, Lennox?*

Panic clawed at him as he pulled Angel into his embrace and held on as tightly as he dared without risking hurting her.

I have no idea.

Lennox was quiet. He'd been quiet since they'd left the doctor's office and all through the ride back to his home.

"Is everything all right?" she asked as they walked through the door.

He turned around with raised brows and met her gaze. "Sure," he replied. "Why wouldn't it be?"

She shrugged, assessing him, trying to see past his defenses.

"You've just been quiet since we left my appointment. Are you having regrets? I know the sonogram probably made this child real to you in ways you hadn't anticipated. It certainly has for me."

He stepped closer to her, placing a gentle hand on her cheek.

"Angel, my feelings about this baby haven't changed. If anything, seeing the sonogram and hearing our baby's heartbeat made me even more determined to be here with you."

Her heart felt like it had grown too big for her chest wall, pushing against the confines of her ribs. She saw hope floating in the depths of his eyes. Hope she reminded herself she couldn't chance reaching for. This wasn't about her, only their child.

"I'm more committed to this baby than ever."

Those were the words any mother should want to hear from their child's father. But somehow they only seemed to highlight the painful truth of their relationship. He wanted their baby, and Amara was a convenient afterthought.

She pulled her gaze from his, afraid he'd see the disappointment she felt clutching to the edges of her good mood.

"Glad to hear it." She looked down at her watch, finding the excuse she needed to end this awkward moment. "I've got to get to work and finish up some things."

"Will you be returning here tonight, or are you still pretending you're packing?"

The smile on his face was contagious and she nearly laughed aloud. "Everything I'm bringing with me is already here. I just need to know what bedroom you want me in."

He nodded, turning down a long hall and beckoning her to follow him. At the very end of it was a set of double doors that he opened up, ushering her inside.

"This is the master. You can have it."

"Have it? Is this where you sleep?"

He pushed his hands into his pockets. "It is, but it's the only room with an en suite bathroom." When she threaded her brows together to silently ask why that mattered, he continued. "According to the literature I've been reading, frequent trips to the bathroom are to be expected. With all the prep for the primary, I haven't had a chance to move my things into the guest room, but I'll try to get it done soon."

"This is very kind of you, Lennox. But are you sure?" She looked around the room, her gaze colliding with the large platform bed sitting in the middle of the room.

She pulled her eyes away from it quickly. The one thing she didn't need was the image of Lennox spread out in this bed with nothing but a sheet covering up all that golden skin of his.

"You don't have to worry, Angel. I promised the only thing I'd demand from you as your husband was that we share a residence and present a united front in public. Anything else that happens, happens because we both want it. I'll never take what you're unwilling to give."

She swallowed as she looked at him. His face was pulled into tight lines, emphasizing how serious he was about the subject. If only he knew she wasn't as unwilling as he believed.

Amara wanted her husband. But since he hadn't approached her for sex since they'd returned home, she'd figured their little honeymoon romp was over.

"And what if I'm willing?"

He let his gaze caress her like an appreciative hand.

Her nipples pebbled beneath her shirt. Hello, pregnancy-enhanced libido.

He must have noticed the turgid peaks beneath the soft

cotton of her shirt, because his gaze burned through the material, searing her without the benefit of touch.

"What is it you're trying to tell me, Angel?"

She never had a problem articulating her thoughts. She saw no reason to beat around the bush now.

"I'm saying, I want sex. And I explicitly remember you telling me if I needed it, you'd gladly supply it. Are those still the terms of our agreement?"

He didn't answer, at least not verbally. With two long strides he was in front of her, threading his fingers into her hair and pressing his lips against hers. His other hand snaked up her side and he ran his thumb across her nipple. Her sex clenched, eliciting a deep moan that made her wonder who else was in the room with them, because there was no way such a hungry needy sound came from her.

She briefly recognized how easily all sense of decorum and decency disappeared. Later she might lament how little it took for her to succumb to her baser needs whenever he put his hands on her. But right now, all she could focus on was the fire his kisses were stoking in her.

If she was honest, she'd acknowledge the joy she'd experienced when they'd witnessed their baby for the first time, heard its heartbeat, had changed something between them. Watching what they'd created thriving inside of her, it was like a heavy lock clicking into place, binding her to Lennox on every plane of her existence.

And once he'd kissed her, each press of his lips filled with so much joy, she lost what little control she had over her heart.

Now, she was swooped up in her husband's arms and carried across the expanse of the large room. He placed her on his bed, stripping her of all her clothes as if he was tearing through wrapping paper to get to the present inside.

His hands roamed frantically over her body, burning her flesh with his touch.

She reached for his length, delighted he was as hard

as granite beneath her fingertips. She loved foreplay, but right now, the only thing she wanted was her body wrapped around his.

He didn't make her wait. With no hesitation, he placed himself at her entrance and pushed until he was stretching her wide, touching her in all the hidden spaces only he seemed to know how to reach.

"Damn, baby," he moaned in her ear once he was fully seated inside her. "You never have to ask me for this, Angel."

He began a slow rhythm with his hips, one that teased and tortured her, drawing a keening sound from the depths of her being. It was too much and not enough all at the same time, keeping her in this constant state of need that both excited and frightened her simultaneously.

Out of bed, they couldn't be more different. He was a political do-gooder, and she was a corporate vulture. Their worldviews clashed. But in this bed, while she touched him everywhere her fingers could reach, while he owned every inch of her, they were in perfect sync.

And yet still, she wanted more.

"Please, Lennox."

She couldn't say exactly what she was asking for, couldn't have defined if she'd tried.

He stared down at her, his eyes aflame with a passion mirroring hers. She might have been afraid of it if she didn't feel the same uncontrollable desperation herself.

"You have no idea what it does to me to hear the sound of my name on your lips while I'm buried inside you."

Without warning, he pulled her up and turned her over, the motion throwing off her equilibrium while exciting her at the same time.

Her sex tightened and she lamented the emptiness his absence left. Fortunately, she didn't have to wait long before he was buried inside her again. This time, there was no slow rocking. Instead, he slammed deep inside her from the first stroke.

He laid a strong hand at the base of her neck, pushing her down to deepen the angle until her head rested against the pillow, and when he moved again, his cock slid across that magical knot inside her and the world turned upside down.

With no warning, she climaxed, every muscle she possessed seizing up.

"That's it." He leaned over her, still pounding into her, extending her orgasm, breaking her into tiny pieces from the inside out. "Let go. Let me give you what you need."

He pulled himself upright and she thought he might be kind enough to give her a momentary reprieve to compose herself.

He did not.

Instead, he clasped his fingers so tightly around the deep curves of her hips she knew there'd be bruising there tomorrow. But she didn't care, because he was sliding back into her, reigniting the flame she'd barely survived the first time around.

And like before, the feel of him, the way he played her body like a master when he reached around, sliding the rough pads of his fingers over her sensitive clit, sent her careening off the jagged edge of a cliff into blinding pleasure that made her body quake uncontrollably.

When her body spasmed around him this time, his pace increased; his thrusts were more forceful, but his rhythm faltered. And as she broke apart for him again, he crashed into his own orgasm, gripping her so tightly, mixing the slightest bit of pain with her pleasure just before he collapsed. His body covered her like a hot weighted blanket that soothed and comforted her while she tried to piece herself back together.

He gathered her in his arms, kissing her mussed hair. Just as she began to drift off into post-coital sleep, she felt his arm draped across her waist as he pulled her closer to him and whispered, "Mine."

Amara shuddered, delighted by the possessiveness of this moment, but afraid this was all just endorphins making him say something he didn't mean. As she snuggled closer to him, placing her hand atop his, with every ounce of her being, she wanted his declaration to be true. Refusing to dig deeper, she closed her eyes and began to drift off to sleep, ignoring her plans to return to work.

Yeah, she'd told herself she was going back. But she figured since this was her first time ditching work for good sex, she was entitled to stay curled up in her husband's embrace.

Halfway between sleep and consciousness, Amara silently luxuriated in the feeling of heavy warmth pressed against her. She thought about getting up but didn't want to risk disturbing the serenity that lying in Lennox's arms gave her.

She finally opened her eyes when he pressed a light kiss to her bare shoulder. She turned around and when their eyes met, for the briefest moment, the joy she felt building inside was reflected in his gaze. But before she could fully appreciate it, the warmth left his eyes and a cold glare remained.

"I still have some things I need to take care of today."

She lifted up on her elbow to look at the wall clock. "It's almost eight o'clock. Business for the day is over."

"Not when you're a public official." He disentangled himself from her and got out of bed, putting on his underwear and grabbing the rest of his clothing off the floor. "The fridge is fully stocked if you're hungry."

She was still reeling, trying to figure out how they'd gone from being so cozy to the wide chasm that seemed to be broadening with every article of clothing he picked up.

When he reached the door, he nodded, stopping briefly

and looking up at the ceiling before returning his gaze to hers.

"Thank you for allowing me to come with you to the doctor's today. I'd like to attend all your appointments, if you'll allow it."

"Of course," she replied.

"Let me know as soon as you book them, and I'll juggle around my schedule to make sure I'm available."

There was something strange about the way he stared at her, as if he wanted to say more.

She sat up on the bed, pulling the covers over herself, needing a barrier between them.

"Lennox, whatever my hesitation about this marriage, I've never attempted to keep you out of the loop when it comes to my pregnancy. You don't have to ask me to be a father to your child. I appreciate the consideration you're showing me, but there's no need to ever question if I want to share this baby with you."

The stiff set of his shoulders relaxed a little before he nodded and gave her a small smile.

"Thank you for that. This baby really does mean the world to me."

It was the last thing he said before leaving, and once again Amara was left walking a tight line between delight that Lennox wanted to be such an involved father and disappointment that his only focus, even after they'd spent the day making love, seemed to be the child she was carrying and not her.

Eighteen

"Earth to Lennox."

Lennox looked up into his friend's questioning gaze.

"I'm sorry, Carter. My mind was drifting."

Carter gave him an inscrutable look and then started wiping the bar down. "You know, despite being a guy who was lucky enough to recently marry a gorgeous woman—and, my friend, Amara truly is gorgeous—a man who has a baby on the way, and who just won the primary race for the office he's seeking, this is the second time this week I've caught you looking hangdog in the face."

Carter was right. Lennox was a lucky bastard who should be at home counting his blessings instead of hiding in his friend's bar avoiding his wife. So why wasn't he?

Because he was a coward. A coward who was becoming more deeply ensnared by the woman he married.

"Angel is gorgeous, and after seeing the baby for the first time, I'm happier than I've ever been."

"Then why are you sitting in my bar instead of at home loving your wife?"

When Lennox didn't answer, Carter regarded him carefully and then nodded his head as if he'd cracked the mystery of Lennox's broken way of thinking.

"That's it, isn't it? It's the loving her part you're having difficulty with?"

Carter and Lennox had known each other too long and been through too much to lie to each other. So there was no use in denying Carter's assertion.

"All I keep thinking about is how destroyed my mother was when my dad died. She may as well have been in the grave with him. What happens when Angel walks away from me? What happens if something happens to her, and I'm left behind? I mean, I know it sounds irrational, but you of all people should understand why my fears are valid."

Carter spread his arms out and braced his hands on the bar. "I do understand what you're thinking. I've lived it. And if I hadn't needed to live to take care of Nevaeh, I don't know if I would've made it when Mish was killed in that accident. But knowing all I do, knowing all the pain I'd eventually suffer after she was gone, I could never regret the love we shared. If I could, I'd choose to love her over and over again."

Lennox wished he was as brave as his friend. But he wasn't. Being that caught up in someone else scared the hell out of him.

"Before I came here, I was holding Angel in bed after spending most of the day making love to her. And everything felt so right. She turned around and I looked at her, and all I wanted to do was forget about the rest of the world and never leave the safety of that bed."

"Then why did you?"

"Because if I stayed with her that way tonight, I'd do it again the next time and the next time. I'd never be able to let go. So, I got up, dressed and came here."

"Man, listen," Carter scoffed. "For a man with a bunch of fancy degrees, you're not that bright."

Lennox shrugged. "What the hell are you talking about?"

"You've got a boss babe in your bed, and you voluntarily leave her to come sit at my bar and work out your issues? Make it make sense, man." When Lennox waved a dismissive hand, Carter continued. "Let me give you a friendly piece of unsolicited marital advice. Don't mess around and become the subject of an early aughts hip-hop and R & B collaboration track."

"Now I'm really lost. That cleaning fluid you were spraying on the bar top must be getting to your brain."

Carter shook a scolding finger at him. "You know what I'm talking about. The tracks where fellas are trying to be hard and mess around and lose their women and then the R & B crooner has to come on and sing a soft hook to beg for forgiveness."

When Lennox didn't respond, Carter pulled out his phone, scrolled a few times. Suddenly, LL Cool J's 2002 hit "Luv U Better" blared from the elevated speakers mounted in the corners of the main lounge. And to piss Lennox off further, Carter started dancing behind the bar as he sang the lyrics, making a point to look directly in Lennox's face as he did so.

By the time LL, Marc Dorsey and Carter reached the bridge, Lennox felt like trash, which he was certain was the point of his friend's little performance. The only problem was now he was more confused than before. Because he'd never considered he could lose Angel by his own lack of action. What the hell was he supposed to do now?

Amara woke up in the cold bed, alone and distinctly aware that something was wrong. But she was a problem solver, and she would deal with this situation no differently than any other challenge.

She twisted in the sheets, her body still tender from the way Lennox had made love to her until she was a mess of limp limbs. When she'd recovered enough to move, she'd turned around in his arms and found a brief glimpse of reciprocity in his eyes. It wasn't just the physical. It was something stronger that tethered them, making her feel connected to him in a way she hadn't since the night they'd met. And if the fire in his eyes was any indication, he'd felt it, too.

But before she could grab hold of it, it had slipped through her fingers like a silky ribbon, too elusive for her to grasp. Within a second of that iron curtain coming down, he was picking up his clothes and leaving the room. She'd waited for him to come home, thinking they could talk about it, but as midnight crept up, she'd lost her battle with sleep.

After showering and dressing in a red wrap dress that hugged her curves and ensured every eye in the room would be on her, she took one last glimpse in the mirror, running her fingers through her layered waves, so her hair framed her face just right.

She walked down the hall to the nearest guest room and knocked on the door. When she didn't get an answer, she slowly opened it to find Lennox's bed empty and made. Either he made it before he left, or he'd never actually come home.

When she got to the living room, she heard voices coming from the kitchen. She smoothed her hands down her sides and took a breath before she walked through the swinging door that led to the large modern space. Lennox was standing on one side of the counter talking to his campaign manager.

"Morning, Angel." His voice was smooth and light, as if nothing odd had occurred last night. He walked over to her, kissing her lightly on the cheek and leading her back to the counter. "You remember John Christos."

She put on a polite smile and extended her hand to the man. "Good morning, Mr. Christos. It's a bit early for campaign strategizing, isn't it?"

His blue eyes sparkled with mischief, and she realized that if his presence weren't an inconvenience at this moment, she'd probably get along well with this man.

"Sorry, Mrs. Carlisle. Even though Lennox has won the primary, we can't sit back. We've got to keep up with the momentum. I'm glad you're here. It gives me a chance to make sure you're up to speed."

She lifted a brow, smiling over his attempt to finesse her. "You mean find out if I have any skeletons in my closet that could derail his run."

Again, that sparkle of mischief shone bright in his eyes, causing a chuckle from everyone in the room.

"Lennox, you're in trouble with this one. I don't think you're smart enough to handle her."

"You ain't lying there," Lennox mumbled as he placed a glass of orange juice in front of her.

She ignored Lennox's quip and addressed John. "I don't have a lot of time to break down my background. My family is one of the oldest and wealthiest families in Brooklyn. We're in the business of making money, but we don't make a habit of doing shady business."

She took a sip of the juice before she continued. "I've spent most of my adult life helping my family enlarge its fortune. There hasn't been a lot of time for me to get involved with anything that could be considered scandalous."

"And what about this latest project your company is working on with Falcon Development?"

"When Lennox and I realized who was on the other side of our respective titles, we set up a third-party panel to consider Devereaux Inc.'s application for the permits. My rep tells me we have a few days before we have to submit our final proposal, and then we'll have a final decision. Whatever they decide, both Devereaux Inc. and the city have agreed to abide by."

John scribbled a few things on a notepad before lifting his gaze back to hers.

"Good. Sounds like everything is on the up-and-up. Hopefully there won't be any surprises. If anything does come up, please don't hesitate to let me know. Getting ahead of a scandal is always the key."

She nodded and gave him a cordial smile. "Understood."

She turned away from John and leveled her gaze at Lennox. He stood next to her, but other than the brief kiss he'd placed on her cheek when she entered the kitchen, he hadn't made any physical contact with her yet. She figured it was because they had company. But part of her couldn't shake the feeling he was still avoiding her.

Her plans to clear the air with her husband were ash with John sitting in the middle of the kitchen. Nevertheless, they still needed to talk.

"Hey, do you think we can meet up for lunch today? I need to run something past you."

"We can talk now."

She glanced briefly in John's direction before meeting Lennox's eyes again. "Can't. I'm going to stop in to see Uncle Ace before I head out to run some errands today. With everything that's been going on, I haven't had the chance to spend any quality time with him. I also have a final dress fitting for my bridesmaid's dress for Trey and Jeremiah's wedding."

Lennox nodded. "Okay, where do you want to meet up?"

"Could you pick me up from Trey's apartment? That's where the tailors and seamstresses are meeting the bridal party."

"Sure." He leaned in, giving her a respectful peck on her lips. "I'll see you this afternoon."

She nodded her farewell to John before making her way through the kitchen door, grabbing her bag and keys from the coatrack in the foyer and leaving the apartment. Hopefully, when she returned, things would be much more settled between her and her husband. Otherwise, she wasn't so sure how they were going to be able to keep their promises to each other. Not if they didn't deal with whatever this was now.

Lennox watched as his wife disappeared behind the swinging kitchen door. As his gaze lingered on her retreating form, he had to force his body not to react. It was an amazing feat considering the way the stretchy material of her dress cradled her lush body.

"That takes one worry off my list."

Lennox pulled his gaze away from the door and looked at John. "What?"

"When you told me you'd married the woman who was carrying your child, I worried that you were rushing into a loveless marriage to salvage your career. Those kinds of setups almost always backfire, and it would've led to an even worse situation for me to have to clean up."

Lennox watched John carefully, trying hard not to give too much away. "And after meeting my wife you're no longer worried about that?"

"Nope, not after seeing the way the two of you were looking at each other. You two are going to burn the camera up on this last leg of the campaign. Even if you weren't leading the polls by fourteen points, the sight of you two together would convince people to vote for you. We need to figure out how we can strategically use this to our advantage. Let's just hope whatever Amara has to say to you doesn't derail all the plans germinating in my head."

Lennox leaned on the counter to try to help him hold his temper. "Again, what the hell are you talking about?"

John stared blankly at him, blinking slowly as if he were trying to process Lennox's words.

"As taken as your new bride is with you, no good has

ever come from the phrase 'we need to talk.' Whatever it is, I have the feeling she only spared you because I was here. Did you hog all the covers last night?"

Lennox wished it were that simple. That would mean he'd actually slept with his wife last night.

"You're reading way too much into this. There's nothing wrong."

John lifted both eyebrows. "You're sure? Because it didn't seem that way to me."

Lennox swallowed as his mind replayed the exchange with his wife. Of course, he knew what she wanted to talk about. He'd all but run out on her last night after spending most of the day buried inside her. Suddenly, he could hear Carter's warning from last night ringing in his head. Had she already decided to toss him away?

Refusing to give in to the panic, he took another swig of the juice Angel had left and met John's skeptical gaze.

"My marriage is fine. You have absolutely nothing to worry about."

Lennox just hoped he was right.

Nineteen

"Stunning."

Amara turned to Trey, who was sitting on the large bed in the center of the room. Due to the estrangement of Trey's father and grandfather, she hadn't grown up in the fold with Stephan, Lyric, Amara, and Ace's ward, Jeremiah. But once she'd blown back onto the scene like a mighty wind, she'd quickly carved out a unique place for herself among the Devereaux cousins.

"You like it?" Trey's question lingered in the air.

Amara returned her gaze to the full-length mirror, admiring the way the champagne one-shouldered gown hung on her curves. She wasn't exactly showing yet, but her pants were beginning to feel a little snug. She'd worried the dress wouldn't fit. But she was pleased with the way the fabric clung to her skin, creating a lovely silhouette.

"I do. You made a great selection, Trey."

Trey stood from the bed and came to Amara's side. "I don't think that glow you have going on has anything to do with my bridesmaid's dress selection. Pregnancy and marriage seem to be agreeing with you."

"The pregnancy is. But the marriage part is up for debate."

When Amara refused to meet Trey's gaze in the mirror, her cousin tugged at her shoulder, bidding her to turn around and face her.

"What's that supposed to mean?"

Amara hesitated to speak the truth of her marriage to anyone. When you came from a family where failure wasn't an option, it wasn't always easy to admit when things were going wrong in your world. But the soft concern she heard in Trey's voice made Amara want to lay all her troubles bare. Maybe because Trey wasn't as entrenched in Devereaux culture yet it felt easier to share. Whatever it was, Amara took her hand and led Trey back to the bed she'd previously sat on.

"Everyone knows my marriage and this baby were a bit of a surprise to Lennox and me. We didn't plan on any of this. But that didn't stop it from feeling right."

Trey leaned in, giving Amara her complete attention. "Are you saying you regret your decision to marry?"

Amara shook her head, then nodded. She didn't know the answer after last night.

She recounted the events that had transpired, as her cousin sat there quietly taking in each new detail.

"I'm really sorry you're going through that," she said when Amara finished. "Have you talked to him about it? It could just be as simple as adjusting to his new role of husband and expectant father. I don't think you have anything else to worry about with him."

"What makes you say that? The man literally left me in bed the minute things seemed like they were becoming more than just physical."

Trey gave Amara's hand a gentle pat as she spoke. "I watched him when you two announced your marriage at

Devereaux Manor. Except for when you left to help your mom with the cake, he never left your side, and he kept a protective hand on you almost the entire time. When you left the room, he didn't stop watching the entryway. Those aren't the behaviors of a man that doesn't care about his pregnant wife."

"If he cares so much, why'd he leave when we seemed to be getting closer?"

"Intimacy is scary."

Trey's response rang true in Amara's heart. Fear of loving Lennox had plagued her and caused her to withdraw into herself, too.

"Talk to him, Amara. I'm sure whatever it is, once you two have a chance to hammer it out, things will get right back to normal."

"For someone who just found her way into this family, you sure do give great cousin advice."

Trey leaned in, touching her cheek to Amara's and squeezing her in a sideways hug.

"I'm great at everything I do."

Amara chuckled and reveled in the comfort of her cousin's embrace.

"If I couldn't tell by looking at you, that famous Devereaux confidence leaves no doubt you're one of us. I'm really glad you're my cousin. Thank you for the advice, and for letting me take part in your special day."

Trey gave her one more squeeze before she pulled back, sharing a broad smile with Amara. "I'm glad you're my cousin, too."

"Amara! Get out here now!"

Both Amara and Trey stood quickly when they heard Stephan calling them into the living room. Without changing back into her street clothes, Amara was the first to make it down the hall, finding Jeremiah, his best friend Josiah, Lyric and Stephan standing in the middle of the living room.

"What happened?"

Stephan moved to her side and pointed to the television where Abby Phillip sat behind the CNN anchor desk with a breaking-news runner ticking across the bottom of the screen.

"This just in. Documents have surfaced suggesting a backdoor deal signed off on by New York City mayoral hopeful Lennox Carlisle with his new wife's company, Devereaux Incorporated, in what some would call a serious mismanagement of his current office. The project is expected to displace longtime residents, in direct conflict with the candidate's campaign pledge to increase the availability of affordable housing."

Amara's jaw dropped as she watched photos of her initial proposal for the permits fill the television screen.

"Please tell me those are fakes," Trey said in a clipped tone.

"Those documents are from the first proposal Devereaux Inc. put together, before Lennox and I knew we'd be working together. After we recused ourselves from the process, the terms of the deal would have changed to limit the impact on the neighborhood and prevent further gentrification."

"Did you accidentally send the originals to the third-party panel? Have they been considering the wrong deal all this time?"

Amara tried to pull her chaotic thoughts together long enough to scan her memory for anything that could reasonably explain this situation.

"Trey, that couldn't have happened. My team reworked that proposal from scratch to make it more favorable for the city, to get them to agree to our terms more readily. Lennox did not have any say over the new proposal. The only people to see the original proposal were the members of my team, and Lennox, when I handed them to him at our first meeting in his office. And before you even ask it, there's no way he'd do something like this. It's significantly more damaging to him than us."

"How did this get out, Amara?" Jeremiah asked. As co-CEO of the company, he certainly had a right to an answer. But as the report kept alluding to some sort of collusion, she couldn't focus on what Jeremiah was saying.

"Amara, did you hear me?"

"I heard you, Jeremiah," she answered with a sharp glint of annoyance in her voice. "I don't know, and I can't stand here trying to figure it out right now. I gotta get to Lennox."

She turned down the hall, taking the bridesmaid's dress off quickly as she went, praying she didn't rip it to shreds as she tried to get out of it. When she was finally changed, she grabbed her purse and headed downstairs. She was in the process of calling a car to pick her up when the blacked-out SUV Lennox used for official travel pulled up to the curb.

Lennox's driver exited the SUV and turned to face her. "Mrs. Carlisle, the councilman sent me for you."

He opened the back door for her and she got into the vehicle. Once she was settled and her seat belt was secured, the driver slowly pulled into traffic.

As she combed through her mind to try to figure out how those documents were leaked, her phone vibrated in her purse.

Her stomach sank when she saw her great-aunt Martha's name flashing across the screen. It could not be a coincidence that she was receiving a call from the woman now.

"Aunt Martha, now isn't such a great time. I'll have to call you back later."

"What's wrong, niece?" the woman crooned a little too sweetly over the phone. When Amara didn't answer, the woman cackled like a cartoon villain before she continued. "Let me ask you this. How does it feel to watch your dreams blow up in your face? Can you accept that everything you've ever wanted has been cruelly snatched away?"

Amara felt rage welling up in her chest. She took a silent breath, pressing her anger down until she was certain she could speak without her voice cracking.

"I don't know how you did this," she began, "but I promise you, if this negatively impacts my husband's career, I will end you."

"Niece, how I did this is unimportant. Just know I still have friends in high places, and I know exactly where to dig to find out the dirt the Devereauxs are trying to hide."

Amara closed her fist so tight she could feel the bite of her nails in her palm. Even as the black sheep of the family, Martha still wielded more influence than most. That was especially evident considering the mess she'd managed to stir up.

"We're family, Martha. Why would you seek to destroy me? Why would you try to compromise the company, your family's legacy, with such a decisive blow?"

Martha laughed again, the shrill sound spilling like ice down Amara's spine. "It's called efficiency, dear. I just killed two birds with one stone. The Devereaux family turned against me, and I won't stop until I've paid every single one of you back."

Amara spoke through clenched teeth. "Be careful, Auntie. This is a war you don't want. There's nowhere you can hide. I'm coming for you."

"Bring. It. On." The line went dead after Martha spoke those three words.

Amara was too heated about what Martha had done to be insulted by the fact that the woman had hung up on her. As she returned her phone to her purse, the driver pulled over and parked in front of Lennox's office.

When she stepped into Lennox's office, she took a cursory look around. The room was full of people she marginally recognized from Lennox's house the night of the primary. They were all hovering around her husband as he sat holding his head in his hands.

Her protective instincts were already on full alert after

speaking to her great-aunt. Seeing him look so helpless there made her want to lash out at the world.

She slammed the door behind her, getting the room's attention. "Everyone out now." Her tone must have conveyed she wasn't in the mood for nonsense today, because they all scurried out, including John, the campaign manager.

Finally alone with her husband, she walked toward Lennox, placing a hand on his shoulder for comfort. He quickly grabbed it before looking up at her.

"Angel." His voice was rough, filled with more despair than anger. "I don't want to ask you this, but I have to. Please tell me you didn't do this."

She flinched as if he'd struck her. The truth was, he may as well have. The question was like taking a sledgehammer to glass, breaking her heart and turning it into tiny shards of glass in one decisive blow.

"I don't want to believe you had anything to do with this. But my team traced the emails that contained the leaked files. They came from your address."

She was hurt, because her first thought had been to run here and protect him while his first thought was to believe trumped-up evidence against her. It stung more than she could bear.

For all her doubts about their relationship, she was still holding on to the hope that they could make this work. But when she saw the expectant look in his eyes as he waited for her response, she understood that Lennox would always prioritize their child and business over her feelings. And after their child was born, she didn't think Lennox would have even the slightest bit of love left over for her.

If she couldn't have her husband's love, his trust, she would at least walk away with her dignity. She pulled her hand away from his, slowly letting it drop to her side as she stiffened her shoulders.

"If you need me to confirm that, then you don't know me as well as you should."

He stood, remorse filling his expression for a brief second, but it was too late. The damage had already been done. He didn't believe in her, and from the looks of it, he never would.

"I'll admit I messed up in sleeping with you without telling you who I was. But I haven't lied to you once since we've been together. I've done everything you've asked of me to make this situation right, including legally binding myself to a man who will never love me, even when I knew I was falling in love with him."

Lennox was silent for a moment, seemingly processing what she'd said. But in true Lennox fashion, when he finally spoke, he ignored matters of her heart and stuck to the business at hand. "Angel, you can't expect me to ignore this breach. That information came from somewhere. I sure as hell wouldn't gain from it being exposed. It would be irresponsible of me to pretend the possibility doesn't exist that you leaked this."

"Well," she continued, "I should've seen that coming. That's all you've ever seen me as, some flighty, irresponsible woman who would sabotage everything she's ever worked for to get what she wants in the moment. I had one lapse in judgment in sleeping with you and not telling you who I was. For you, that somehow equates to me trying to destroy your career?"

"I didn't say that, Angel." He squeezed her hand again, as if it would somehow diffuse her anger. Little did he know, she wasn't the slightest bit angry, just hurt.

"You know what? I'm done being your sacrificial lamb. I'll remain married to you for however long you need me to. After all, that was the agreement I made. But from this moment on, the only thing you and I will share is our child. If you need me, I'll be back home in Clinton Hill where I belong."

Without another word, she stepped away from his desk and walked straight to the door. With each step, it felt like a sharp, serrated knife was plunged into her chest, ripping at her insides. But no matter how much she wanted to crumble, she wouldn't give him the satisfaction of seeing her broken.

Not now, not ever.

Twenty

"Hey, you doing okay?"

Amara shifted in her chair, trying to force the muscles of her face into a friendly smile. She'd been doing that all day as she helped Trey get ready for the wedding, posed for bridal party pictures, and stood at the altar with the bride and groom as they exchanged vows.

But now, as Stephan stood in front of her at the reception, asking about her well-being, she couldn't muster enough strength to put a smile on her face and put Stephan's obvious concern to rest.

She picked up her glass of apple cider in a mock toast, tipping it toward him. "Of course, I am."

He pulled an empty chair from the table and positioned it in front of hers. Leaning in, he took her hand, trying his best to convey the concern written all over his face.

"Don't pity me. This is all my fault."

"How do you figure that?"

She took a deep breath, trying her best to offload the

weight of all she'd been concealing over the course of her relationship with Lennox.

"Lennox certainly thinks so."

"Did he accuse you of doing this?"

She shook her head, recalling the conversation she'd had with Lennox. "Not technically. But he did ask me to confirm I hadn't done it."

"That couldn't have felt good."

"It didn't," she admitted. "Although, after everything I've done to him, I can't really blame him."

Stephan tilted his head and scanned her face for clues to her meaning.

Too tired to hide her transgressions, she succinctly recounted the summarized version of how she ended up pregnant by and married to Lennox Carlisle.

"Cousin." Stephan spoke cautiously as he digested all she'd shared.

"I know, Stephan."

He dropped his head, shaking it.

"How did Lennox take it when he found out who you are?"

She laughed heartily. "He was pissed and demanded I marry him, or he'd go to Grandfather and tell him what I'd done and refuse to even consider Devereaux Inc.'s permit application."

Stephan sat back in his chair, blowing out an exhausted huff as he watched her.

"Amara, I'd love to go all protective cousin for you and snatch Lennox by his collar. But what you did, the situation you put him in, I can't say that I blame him for the way he reacted. What were you thinking?"

"I wasn't," she admitted. Why lie? Everything had disintegrated into dust, there was no use protecting the illusion now. "But surprisingly, that wouldn't be the last stupid thing I did."

He pinched the bridge of his nose before settling a knowing gaze on her. "You fell in love with your fake husband, didn't you?"

"And now, for the second time in as many months, his affiliation to me is screwing up his professional life. He could lose everything he's worked so hard for because Martha wanted to prove a point to me."

She could see the muscle at his jaw tighten at the mention of his mother's name.

"You have a lot to answer for where Lennox is concerned. But my mother's vindictive streak isn't one of them. Have you determined how she was able to make this happen?"

"She found someone in our IT department to exploit, a man who was desperate for the money to pay for medical treatment for his sick daughter. The truth is, after finding out why he did it, I couldn't really be mad with him. I fired him, of course. But I also contacted the hospital and made myself the guarantor for her medical bills. That baby shouldn't suffer simply because her father had the misfortune of falling into Martha's clutches."

Her cousin reached for her hand and this time, she held on tightly, needing his strength more than she ever had in the past.

"This isn't your fault, Amara. The fault lies with my mother. She did this. Not you."

"It doesn't matter," she answered as she struggled to keep the pain out of her voice. "I risked Lennox's job for selfish reasons, and then my family banged the nail into his professional coffin. He could be impeached for this, Stephan."

"No one ever said loving a Devereaux would be easy, Cousin."

She lifted a brow, wondering how many celebratory cocktails her cousin had downed before joining her.

"You mean 'loathing.' Love has never lived in this relationship."

"Sometimes it's hard to see the truth of things when you're too close to them. Trust me, distance can bring great clarity."

She could see the shadows of his demons flitting across his eyes and knew her cousin was speaking from experience.

"Amara, I watched him watching you the night you brought him to meet the family. That man is sprung and possessive. This might not have started out as a love match, but the way that man was looking at you, there's more than convenience and duty binding him to you."

Her heart fluttered. She wanted to grab hold of the picture he was painting, but doubt wouldn't let her.

"Trey said the same thing. I wish you both were right, Steph..."

He held up his hand. "Just stop, Amara. Stop and listen to me. If I were you, I'd shut down this personal pity party and get my shit together so I could fight for my man. Because if I had a man looking at me the way Lennox looks at you, I'd go to any length to keep him."

"I don't know how to keep him." She struggled to keep her tears at bay but lost the battle. "Even before this happened, things weren't great. He treated me well. But he was always adamant love would never be part of the equation."

"Listen." Stephan leaned in and wiped her tears with a gentle thumb. "As a gay man, I have a unique perspective. Being a man and loving men, I can tell you something you might not know. Men are stupid and we have no idea what we want or need."

She narrowed her gaze at him and then slipped into a fit of giggles that led to more tears.

"You're a mess. You know that, right?" she finally said as she got ahold of herself.

"Yeah, but you still love me, though. So listen to me. If you love Lennox, you've gotta make this right for him. You're a Devereaux, and with the exception of my mean-ass mama, we protect our own. You've just got to ask yourself if you love Lennox enough to consider him one of us."

She loved Lennox, there was no question about it. But had he ever truly been hers? Did he belong to her and by extension to the Devereauxs?

Then she remembered something her uncle Ace mentioned when he brought Jeremiah, a kid off the street, to live with him at sixteen. He'd told everyone Jeremiah was family. And when she asked how, he answered, "By love." He was right. Loving Lennox was the only qualifier she needed to claim him as one of her own. And Devereauxs never had, never would abandon one of their people. And she decided in that moment, she wouldn't start now.

Satisfied, he'd gotten through to her, he gifted her with a knowing smile. "Glad you're seeing things my way. Now, let me go get Lyric to help you fix your makeup, because you are looking a hot mess right now."

"You know you're sounding like you share your mama's mean gene, right?"

"That's a low blow, but you ain't wrong. At least I use my powers for good, though."

"A fact I will forever be grateful for." She stood up and pointed at him. "Go ahead and get Lyric so she can hurry up and fix my face. I feel like there's a Cupid Shuffle with my name on it waiting for me on the dance floor."

Twenty-One

"Len, this can't go on."

Lennox sat at his desk, staring out a nearby window at nothing in particular as his campaign manager continued his diatribe.

"If you don't address these allegations, this could end up turning into an official investigation for collusion."

Lennox hung his head in defeat. "There was no collusion. You know that. Any investigation will show that I went above and beyond what's required to avoid any conflict of interest."

John stopped pacing in the middle of his room, dropping in the chair on the opposite side of Lennox's desk.

"You're right. But by the time you're absolved, you'll have already lost the election. You've already dropped three points in the polls. We have to do something now before it's too late."

John was right, of course. He needed to act. But since

his Angel had gone, he couldn't seem to focus on anything but his pain.

He chuckled at the irony of it all. He'd fought so hard to avoid this pain, doing everything in his power to keep his distance so he wouldn't fall in love with her. And yet he'd still managed to let things deteriorate so badly that he'd pushed himself right into despair.

"John, I know you're right. But my mind isn't on this right now. Angel moved out and she won't talk to me so we can work this out."

John's face bore compassion, which only made Lennox feel worse.

"Lennox, you can't ignore this anymore." John handed him a printed piece of paper. Lennox scanned through it to see a very truthful, yet cautious public statement.

John watched Lennox carefully as he spoke. "The press is already gathered in the lobby. All you have to do is go downstairs and read it."

He huffed, waving the statement in the air. "Let's get this over with."

Lennox stood at the podium in the lobby, looking out into the sea of cameras and reporters. Before he could even speak, they were hurling questions at him, each feeling like a body shot thrown by a champion fighter.

"Please, hold your questions until the end," Lennox said calmly, using every trick he knew to keep himself still and focused. "A lot has been said in the last week and I'm here to set the record straight. There was no collusion. Everything about the application process Devereaux Inc. underwent was aboveboard."

He took a breath and before he could speak again, a reporter interrupted. "Councilman, if there was no collusion, can you explain the details of the emails leaked to the public?"

"He can't." The room went silent as a familiar voice

boomed from one side of the atrium, hitting Lennox square in the chest. "But I will."

He scanned the space, and saw his wife moving through the crowd, making her way to the podium. When she got to him, he covered the microphone with his hand and leaned closer to her ear. "What are you doing here, Angel?"

"Saving your ass. The question is, will you let me?"

They held each other's gaze much longer than professionalism allowed. But to hell with professionalism. His wife was here, and all he wanted to do was cherish this moment, no matter if it was playing out in front of the cameras.

He stepped aside, and she took her place in front of the microphone. Suddenly, he saw all the things that had drawn him to her on that very first night. She was strong, self-assured. And by the way she turned slightly and gave him a sexy wink, whatever it was she had planned, he knew she'd end up owning the room.

"Good morning, everyone. As I was saying, Councilman Carlisle can't give you the details of the proposal. What was released was an initial deal memo we used in-house as a springboard for any negotiations Devereaux Inc. engages in.

"Devereaux Inc. is a for-profit company. As such, it's always our desire to make the best deal possible for the business. But this deal memo was a draft. It was never signed by me or anyone at the company. As many of you may know, the councilman and I recently married. Our relationship began prior to Devereaux Inc. filing the permit applications. While I had previously worked on the Falcon deal, at the time of our wedding, I wasn't assigned to it. But then I became lead counsel of Devereaux Inc. due to a family emergency. We saw the potential for conflict of interest and took immediate steps. The city set up a third-party panel to evaluate the permits and both the councilman and I recused ourselves from the negotiations to avoid any impropriety. But I'm here today to set the record straight and make Devereaux Inc.'s position clear."

She raised her head to glance out at the audience. Once she captured their attention, she continued.

"Devereaux Inc. was the victim of a targeted internal breach. My email was compromised by an employee who has since been terminated. Neither the councilman nor his office had any involvement in this."

Angel acknowledged one of the many reporters who were frantically waving their hands in the audience.

"Mrs. Carlisle. You're married to the councilman. Why should the public believe you?"

"That's simple," Angel answered, as smooth and calm as ever. "Because it's the truth. And if that's not enough, I have a signed affidavit from the third-party panel established to process and rule on the permits."

"So if this deal memo was just a draft and never submitted for formal consideration, what are the actual terms of the application submitted?"

Angel continued, unfazed. "I'm glad you asked that question. I have a signed affidavit from my second-in-command, Sergio Dennison, stipulating that after further study, he and his team amended their proposal to make sure Devereaux Inc. was providing the most benefit for both the business and the neighborhood slated for construction.

"On behalf of Devereaux inc. Mr. Dennison has committed to investing in the existing small businesses in the area and making sure residents aren't pushed out by this development. He further proposes that Devereaux Inc. reserve fifty percent of the project's rental units for lower-income families. An elaborate park and garden area for families and seniors to enjoy a bit of nature will be created. And finally, he's included plans for two brand new community centers and funding for their maintenance and programming. The panel's affidavit includes the full proposal, so the details can be found there."

Because he'd recused himself from the process, Lennox hadn't previously known about the new deal terms.

As Amara listed them all, he had to lock his knees to keep himself from dropping where he stood.

She had heard him, heard everything he'd said about urban renewal.

"Devereaux Inc. is dedicated to helping better our community in line with the councilman's vision," she continued. "We think we've finally come to a solution that will bring much-needed dollars and employment to this part of Brooklyn without discarding the people who have built it from the ground up. Thank you for your time."

Angel relinquished the podium to him, giving him a gracious smile as she stepped aside. Wanting to talk to her, but knowing he had a job to do, he gave her arm a squeeze, hoping it conveyed his gratitude.

He returned to the podium, finishing things up as quickly as he could. In his mind, her willingness to help him had to mean she was ready to address their problems. He wouldn't allow himself to believe anything else. And when he realized Angel had somehow disappeared, he wasn't deterred. He wanted his wife back, and now he knew he finally had a chance.

Twenty-Two

Amara rushed toward her office door ignoring her assistant, who was trying to get her attention. "Whatever it is can wait. I just need a moment."

Two steps inside her office, and she knew what her assistant was trying to tell her. Her grandfather was sitting on her couch with one leg crossed over the other, making him look like thc stately gentleman he was.

Too exhausted from the emotional upheaval of seeing her husband for the first time since the permit story broke, she didn't have the energy to listen to him recount all the ways she'd messed things up.

"I've had a long day, Grandfather. So if you're here to tell me how I've gone too far once again, I'm really not up for it. This deal might not be as lucrative as the original proposal, but it was the right thing to do for the community. And I'm going to make sure Devereaux Inc. fulfills every promise."

He remained silent for a long moment, until the tension in the room reached the breaking point.

"I agree with you," he finally said. "This was the right deal to make."

She went to the couch and sat down. Trying to figure out the angle he was working, she crossed her arms and gave him a skeptical look.

"You agree with me?"

"I do," he replied easily, nodding. "You've been driven by monetary success for so long, I was afraid you'd eventually end up destroyed by your greed. But the proposal you spoke about today, that took heart and confidence. Two things you must have equally in order to be both successful and responsible. This was the lawyer I was trying to mold you into being. I'm so proud of you."

Confusion welled up inside her. She'd waited so long to hear him speak those words to her, and now that he was, her brain was having a hard time wrapping itself around what was unfolding right before her very eyes.

"You're proud of me? After all this time? But this wasn't even my deal. Sergio and his team put this together."

His relaxed posture stiffened as he watched her, as if something she'd said struck a nerve.

"That may be technically true," her grandfather responded. "But you were the leader that gave him and his team the space to work and you listened to their recommendation. So yeah, I'm proud of you. All that took courage."

She must have remained silent too long because he asked, "Why is it such a surprise that I'm proud of you?"

"Because you've spent every day of our working relationship telling me how I don't compare to my mother as a lawyer."

The light in his brown eyes dimmed as he processed what she was saying to him.

"Is that what you believed? That I didn't think you measured up?"

"Yes."

She went to stand, attempting to put a bit of distance between them. But he laid his warm hand atop hers as sadness filled his gaze.

"Amara, if that's how I made you feel, I'm terribly sorry. It was never my intention to make you believe you were lacking in any way. I simply thought I was giving you something to aspire to. I didn't realize I was causing you pain."

The sincerity in his voice made her breath hitch, and the tears began to fall. And just like when she was a little girl who cried when she'd fallen off her bike onto the unforgiving concrete, he pulled her into his arms and rocked her back and forth.

"You are the best of us, Amara. That's why I've always been so hard on you. Not because I lacked faith. But because I was nearly blinded by the brilliance of your potential. All I can ask is that you forgive an old fool for pushing you away when all I wanted to do was nurture your innate talent. Please forgive me."

Of course, she wanted to. Accepting his apology meant she could finally allow herself to believe he had faith in her.

She pulled back, and he must have seen the doubt in her eyes, because he gifted her with a gracious smile before speaking again.

"Amara, what have I always told you?"

"Words are meaningless unless they're in a contract or backed up by action." He'd drilled that into her over and over again. His motto had been the foundation for so many of the contract negotiations she'd won for Devereaux Inc. Which was why Lennox's accusation cut so deep. It was proof he really didn't know her. And if he didn't know her, there was no chance he could possibly love her.

"Exactly," her grandfather replied with a wobbly smile. "So let me get on with why I came here today. You've proven yourself ready for the job and all the things that come with it, both good and bad. I turned in my retirement forms today. As soon as they're finalized, I will name you as my permanent successor. The person most qualified to take on the job."

If she hadn't been sitting, she might have fallen over. Hell, she still might. This moment was the culmination of everything she'd ever wanted. And even as happiness filled her, there was still an echo of darkness surrounding her heart because she couldn't share this with the man she loved.

When her grandfather left, Amara stood at the window of her office in Clinton Hill, trying to make sense of all that had happened today. She'd done something good for her community and her business, pulled Lennox back from the professional brink and won the promotion she'd worked so hard for. She should be pleased with herself. Instead, her mind kept focusing on the one thing she'd managed to lose in all of this: her husband.

Before she could sink further into despair, she was distracted by a knock on her door.

"Come in," she answered without turning away from the window. She didn't need her visitor to see her misery, which she didn't have enough energy to cover up at the moment.

"Angel."

The rich tone of Lennox's voice sent a tremor through her body. Slightly afraid she'd managed to conjure him up, she turned around to find him standing near her desk.

He was still wearing the navy Brooks Brothers suit from the press conference. But his tie was gone and the first button of his collar was unbuttoned. Whatever this visit was about, it wasn't business. He'd never negotiate without his full corporate armor in place.

"Please forgive me for just popping up. Your secretary told me I could come in. I guess you haven't announced that you left me?"

"I told you, I'll keep up the pretenses of our marriage in

public for as long as you need me to. I just can't live with a man who has so little faith in me."

She saw something akin to regret flitter in his eyes.

"Not to be rude, Lennox. But what are you doing here?"

He chuckled as a sad smile crept onto his face. "I'm here for a couple of reasons. The first, how did you get Falcon to agree to everything you promised at the press conference today? They're taking on extra building I'm sure wasn't part of the initial deal."

"Devereaux Inc. will cover the cost of building the additional structures. Because the terms I negotiated between Falcon and Devereaux Inc. are so favorable, we still stand to make a healthy profit from the deal. We can afford the added expense."

"And the powers that be at Devereaux Inc. are okay with this?"

"Exceedingly so," she answered. "My grandfather's actually naming me as his permanent successor. I got the job I've always wanted." She narrowed her gaze and scanned his face. Something was off and his questions, though seemingly benign, made the lawyer in her suspicious.

"What's all this about, Lennox? If you're here because you're worrying that this will somehow backfire on you, don't. The city will get everything I promised on behalf of Devereaux Inc. You didn't have to come all the way down here for that."

He stepped closer to her, until she could smell his sweet and spicy cologne, drawing her into his powerful orbit.

"No, that's not why I'm here. According to John, I've recovered from my drop in the polls. I'm still in the lead to win this thing. John says it's because you're a miracle worker. I'm sure if you ever got tired of working for Devereaux Inc., he'd definitely take you on his team."

"He couldn't afford me." She tilted her head as she waited for him to get to the point.

"I came down here because I wanted…needed to see my wife."

When she remained silent, he closed his eyes for a brief second, before returning his amber gaze to her.

"I was wrong, Angel."

"About accusing me of sabotaging you? Yes, you were."

"Yes, I was wrong for that. But I was wrong for so much more. Namely, keeping you at arm's length when all I wanted to do was pull you closer."

He cupped her cheek in his warm palm, the mere touch causing her to involuntarily moan.

"I'm sorry that I was so afraid of being hurt by you, I refused to give in to what I could see so clearly."

His words, coupled with the warmth of his touch, were like an elixir for every pain she'd experienced during their marriage. But she couldn't help worrying about whether this was just temporary relief that only masked the symptoms or an actual cure that would revive her wounded heart.

"Why are you saying this to me? I don't understand, Lennox. From the moment you found out I was pregnant, you've offered me everything except your heart. You clearly stated love wasn't on the table and I stupidly went along with it even though I knew I was falling in love with you. What's changed now? Because I can't go back to loving someone who will only run from me the closer I try to get to him. I won't condemn myself to a life of having to put myself back together every time you reject me. So, tell me, what is it you intend to gain from this visit?"

His usually stoic expression cracked and his mask slipped just the tiniest bit, the same way it had the day of her sonogram.

"I came to beg my wife's forgiveness for treating her so terribly and being careless with her heart. I came to tell you I'm done with letting fear rule me, and if you'll have me, I'll spend the rest of my life worshipping you. I came to say that I love you, and although that scares the hell out of me, the idea of losing you is a fate worse than death. I came to beg you to take me back even though I know I don't deserve you."

Hot tears welled up in her eyes, scorching her skin as they slid down her face. Could this day really grant her all the things she wanted at once?

"I want to believe you, Lennox. But I'm afraid. This entire marriage has been about your career and our baby. And as much as I know you already love this child, I want you to love me for me, and not because you see me as some human vessel for your baby."

He slid his gaze over her face before he responded. "I am a fool for ever letting you believe the only thing I wanted from you was this baby. It's you, Angel. It's always been you."

He leaned down, letting his lips finally touch hers. It was the most satisfying thing she'd felt in a long while, but it also stoked a fiery need that seemed to consume her right where she stood.

He broke their kiss, leaving them both struggling to catch their breath. "It's why I was so adamant about fidelity and you wearing my rings. I needed the world to know you were mine because the thought of you turning to anyone else made me want to commit violence."

He pulled her back to him, searing her with a second kiss that left her desperate for more when he tore his mouth from hers. "Please, baby," he pleaded. "Tell me you love me."

She should've made him suffer more. She should've taken the upper hand and cast him aside. It was nothing less than what he deserved. But slowly, she recognized that she needed to focus on what *she* deserved. She deserved the elation of being loved by this man. She deserved the joy of being showered with his love. And once she'd come to the conclusion that what she deserved was happiness and that he was her happiness, her choice became clear.

"I do love you, Lennox."

"Tell me you'll come back to me. That you'll be mine."

"I'll come back," she answered, before initiating a kiss of her own. "I'll be yours." She let her kisses travel to the sharp angle of his jaw and downward until she reached the curve of his neck. "Now, I've got a condition for you."

He wrapped his arms tighter around her, letting her know he'd heard her, even though he didn't verbally respond.

"I need you to go lock my office door so you can come back here and show me just how much you've missed me since I've been gone."

He pulled far enough away from her to look down into her eyes, gifting her with his mischievous smile.

"Just one more reason why I love you so much, Angel."

"Why's that?"

"Because you, my brilliant, beautiful wife, are really good at anticipating what I want even before I recognize what it is."

She wrapped her arms around his neck and nodded. "You're right, Councilman, I do know how to give you what you want. Now hurry up and lock the door so you can give me what I need."

His expression was filled with happiness as he rushed to the door. And for the first time, she realized she didn't feel the need to protect her heart from him. From this moment on, she would never have to hide the love that was bursting through the seams of her soul.

When he returned to her, she pulled him down into a fiery kiss. "You ready to show me just how much you love me today, Councilman Carlisle?"

"Yes, ma'am. Today and every day to come for the rest of our lives."

* * * * *

COMING SOON!

We really hope you enjoyed reading this book. If you're looking for more romance, be sure to head to the shops when new books are available on

Thursday 12th May

To see which titles are coming soon, please visit

millsandboon.co.uk/nextmonth

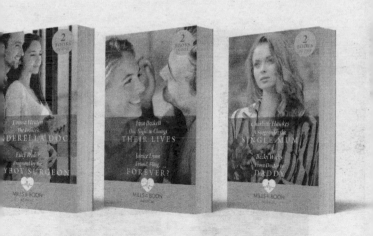